THE STALLION & THE TIGRESS

Destined – Book Two

Michele James

PRAISE FOR THE DESTINED SERIES

The Lion & The Swan

"What an amazing book! Well developed characters, complex and entertaining plot, beautifully described details and settings. Very difficult to put down. It cries for a sequel! Book two, hurry!
~ conniecutie

"The purity of love between Assad and Oona is undeniable and beautiful. I adore Oona's strength and dedication to her sister. Assad was the perfect alpha, sensitive, strong, and passionate. Great, and moving tale." ~ Andrea

"Full of romance and adventure, The Lion & The Swan *is a story of forbidden love between a prince and the exotic Northern slave he vows to help escape from his cruel father, the king."* ~ MCB

"Great love story! Well developed with strong female characters. Thoroughly enjoyed the surprise HEA!" ~ jwrvt

www.BOROUGHSPUBLISHINGGROUP.com

THE STALLION & THE TIGRESS
Copyright © 2020 Michele James

ISBN 978-1-953810-05-2

For Bob and Audrey who courted and sparked for 50 years

ACKNOWLEDGMENTS

To Jim, for everything, always. To Elizabeth Archer for the walks and the talks. To Kathleen Canney Lopez, my web mistress. To Michelle for the encouragement and the edits.

THE STALLION & THE TIGRESS

CHAPTER 1

Autumn's Eve

Aleksi surveyed the field covered with brightly colored tents and the lines of horses staked to the ground around them. It had taken him, Serge, and Pyotr four years of planning, scraping, and saving every piece of silver and gold they had earned working in the king's stables, but they were here. They had made it to the Autumn Festival held in this city on the southern shore of the Great Inland Sea with a string of fine horses to trade, and with enough silver for the fee Aleksi needed to enter the races. Races he meant to win on his stallion, Zolotoy, the last gift his father, King Maksimillian, had ever given him.

He shaded his eyes and turned his gaze to the road leading toward the palace gates as the low hum of men's voices rose to a loud buzzing as the crowd parted to either side of the pathway. Two young, unaccompanied women walked between the lines of tents and horses. In truth, the smaller, finer-boned woman walked. The taller woman strode straight for Aleksi's tent with a sure feline grace, her ocher skirt swinging with purpose around the length of her long legs.

Her hair was covered by a headscarf of green, gold, and red, and she wore her tunic of marigold yellow tucked into her skirt. A belt of plain leather cinched her slim waist where a leather sheath held a small blade. The only adornment she wore was a wrist cuff of etched leather on her left forearm. No earrings dangled from her lobes, no jewels encircled the smooth, tawny skin of her neck, and not one of her long tapered fingers bore a ring.

She stopped no more than a pace from Aleksi, shoulders back and head high, and he knew why she wore no jewelry. No manmade adornment could ever match the crystalline brilliance of her eyes.

Cat-like in shape and heavily fringed with long black lashes, they gleamed like cut emeralds flecked with gold in the sun's light.

"Ladies." Aleksi tore his gaze from the mesmerizing green brilliance and dipped his head to the dainty, brown-haired, gray-eyed woman with a courtly smile. He'd learned enough princely manners in his time at his father's palace to be polite and charming when needs be, and he had discovered the rewards of politeness with women many years ago. "My name is Aleksandr," he said to the dimpling young woman who looked to have some girl in her still, and then he turned his full smile on her companion, who was still young, but all woman. "How may I be of service?"

Piercing cat eyes held his beneath dark, shapely brows, taking his measure. Though no giant, Aleksi was tall and broadly built, and he stood even taller under her scrutiny. He liked women in general, and they liked him, but this one didn't seem outwardly impressed. Perhaps because she was taller than most women and stood eye to chin with him. Or perhaps it was her bearing, lithe and sure, and regal. Yet neither her nor her companion's clothing suggested royalty. Though clean and free of obvious mending, they were made of plain, well-worn linen. There wasn't a scrap of worm weave or embroidery on either of their tunics or skirts, and they were two women—two exceptionally comely young women—wandering through a field full of strange men without guards.

They didn't seem to be pleasure women plying their trade. There was no look of wanton invitation in either their mien or their gazes. Aleksi reminded himself that the people of this city prided themselves on their freedoms of choice and movement.

"I've been told of your golden stallion," the jewel-eyed woman said in a low, smoky voice. "Is he for sale?"

Aleksi pushed a stubborn lock of hair back from his forehead and glanced over his shoulder at Zolotoy who his father had gifted him as an unbroken two-year-old the spring Aleksi had turned twenty and one.

"No," he told her, "he's not. Him I will ride to victory in the races and then pick one of the royal broodmares for him to cover and start my own line of horses that will rival even King Asad's."

Her brows quirked and the corners of her shapely mouth lifted. "Do you have a particular mare in mind?"

"Lasair, I believe she is named. The last filly by the king's stallion Storm Chaser and the queen's mare, Cloud Dancer."

"Impossible," she said.

Impossible was not a word Aleksi cared for, even when spoken in such an entrancing voice. "How so?" he challenged.

"Lasair belongs to Princess Sahar, not her father. Any stallion privileged to breed with Lasair will be chosen by the princess and no other, after they win the races."

Aleksi laughed, quick and short. "You seem to have a good eye for horses. Do you truly believe any mare could beat my stallion in a race?"

She smiled like a cat who had spied a fat, lazy vole. "Lasair is not any mare," she said.

"You've seen her?"

"I have."

"Is she as sleek and swift as they say?"

"She is."

"And her mistress, the princess?"

The dove-eyed girl slid a sidelong glance at her companion whose piercing gaze narrowed on Aleksi.

"What about her?"

"Is she as beautiful and proud as they say?"

Full, lush lips pressed into a thin line. "Do you plan on winning her as well?"

"Now why would I want to win the princess?" Aleksi asked with a derisive snort. "A soft, spoilt, demanding royal pain who's so full of herself that she's turned down every offer of marriage presented to her."

She said nothing, and Aleksi closed the short distance between them, giving her his most charming grin. He had as good an eye for women as he did for horses, and he intended to return to his home with a string of broodmares and a wife to prove to his father and the rest of his royal, full-blooded kin that Aleksi was not some round house dwelling half-breed, but a self-made man, as good as any of them.

"I would rather win you, kitten," he said. He reached up and pushed the scarf back from her head, spilling a mass of thick, wavy curls as black as pitch down to her waist. When she didn't shy away or even twitch, he lifted a heavy tress between his fingers, which shone russet in the sunlight. "I would rather marry a woman of sturdy body and easy temper to bring my sons into this world."

Her spine lengthened and her eyes widened. "Are you proposing marriage to me?"

"I am."

"Why would you propose marriage to a woman you know nothing about?"

"I know you are strong of mind and long-limbed," he told her as he stepped in even closer. He unwound the lock of her hair and pushed it back behind her ear. "I know your hair shines black and russet in the sun's light, and that your eyes flash green fire with sparks of gold when your pelt is ruffled, as it is now, kitten."

He leaned in and whispered into her ear. His senses assailed with the sweet, seductive scent of exotic flowers. "I know you're as intrigued with me as I am with you, and that you wonder what it would be like to breed with me."

Slowly, she turned her head. Her mouth was no more than a breath from his, teasing, tantalizing. "How are you going to sire children with me or any other broodmare, you strutting stallion," she growled, pulling her blade in one swift motion and pressing the point of it into his groin, "if I geld you here and now?"

Aleksi went stock still for a heartbeat, and then he laughed, low and rumbling. "So," he said, stepping back and letting her hair slowly slip through his fingers. "My kitten has claws."

"Claws she will not hesitate to use should you accost her again," she assured him with eyes blazing.

"I am forewarned," he said with a courtly bow and a grin.

"You are foresworn, Aleksandr." She spun on her heels and began to stride away, her black mane swinging in time with her skirts.

"Wait," Aleksi called out.

She stopped mid-stride, her silent companion almost bumping into her as she whirled around to face him.

"What is your answer to my proposal?" She glared at him as if her eyes truly could flash fire and raze him to ash. "At least tell me your name."

"Not 'kitten.'"

Sahar sat at the royal family's long table in the center of the palace courtyard, sipping her spiced wine and picking at the honeyed dates that were the last of the seven courses served for the Feast of Autumn's Eve. As soon as the dates were cleared away the men riding in the festival's races would be introduced to the king, and two things would happen. The arrogant ass Aleksandr who, by his accent and fair looks, hailed from the Northern Steppes, would find out who she was, and she'd be the first and only woman to stand and join the line of riders.

Her parents, King Asad and Queen Oona, wouldn't argue or humiliate her by trying to dissuade her from riding in the races in front of an entire courtyard filled with visiting royalty and the merchants and traders of their city. Once announced publicly, they would have to stand by her. After all, it was they who had told her all her life that she rode as well as any man. Now she would have the chance to prove it.

Halah, her cousin and companion earlier today when they had gone to look over horses for trade, had been the only other person to know of Sahar's intention to enter the races, and she had kept her cousin's secret well. Better than Sahar had. She'd let it slip while challenging the braggart Aleksandr, who had the gall to think his stallion capable of beating Lasair in a race and worthy of breeding with her. He'd obviously assumed Sahar was some simple maid who'd fall at his big feet and weep with joy and gratitude that he considered her worthy of becoming his wife and broodmare, not the proud, spoilt princess he had spoken of with such disdain.

She drank down the last of her wine and felt its easing warmth spread through her veins. Certainly, she had faults enough. Her father, while proud of her swiftness of both mind and body, had often lectured her on her rashness, while her mother, herself a woman who had gone against the traditions of her own clan as well as those of the desert tribes, had often stressed the importance of choices and manners. No, her parents had never spoiled her or her twin brother, Asim, other than with their love. They'd raised their children to be truthful and honorable and to consider others before themselves. Sahar had never demanded any more from others than she did from herself.

So why did this Aleksandr ruffle her fur the wrong way, as he had so smugly put it? Part of what he'd said about her was true. She'd been proposed to many times, and she had refused every proposal. But they had been from men of rank and wealth who knew what she was, men looking to increase their own purses and standing by marrying a princess. Not a single one cared about who she was as a person. What her worth was. At least this Aleksandr, for all his strutting and boasting, had asked her because of his skewed sense of her as a strong woman with an easy temper. She chuffed into her empty cup. Surely her quickness with her blade today had disavowed him of her having an "easy" temper.

Sahar was not against marriage exactly. She had grown up the child of parents famous for their love and long marriage. Her brother, Asim, had already married Rima, the eldest daughter of the Oryx and the Willow, and proudly awaited the birth of their first child.

Halah, two years younger than Sahar, was being courted by Munir, the newest and youngest member of the king's personal guard. At twenty and one, Sahar was more than old enough to marry, but she was quite happy with her life as it was. She certainly had no need for a husband. She had wealth and position of her own, and family everywhere she turned. While she and her brother were her parents' only children, her Aunt Lyrra and Uncle Nasim had four living children, all of whom had grown up together in the palace built by their parents when they had settled here some twenty and two years ago.

They had been happy years, but for the spring of Sahar's tenth year. The shadow of a memory passed through her, and she shivered and smoothed the skirts of her one shouldered gown of emerald worm weave.

Servants began to clear the empty platters and refill goblets of wine and beer as men got up from their seats and started to form a line in front of the king's table. Other men, who hadn't been part of the royal feast, joined the line from outside the palace courtyard. Her father had always insisted that the races be open to all challengers, no matter their station in life.

Soon enough, she caught sight of Aleksandr walking in. He was not hard to find. He stood head and shoulders above every man lining up, but for Prince Taweel the Tall. Aleksandr's hair shone, its color lighter than most, a mixture of brown and gold and every shade between, like finely sanded cedar, cut to below his ears, with a thick shock falling onto his high, wide forehead as it had earlier today. He wore a robe of moss green linen with hems of umber worm weave and leather boots, not sandals, and his waist belt, though loosely cinched, emphasized the breadth of his shoulders compared to the trimness of his waist, and was embedded with stones of amber, as was the sheath of a bone-hilted blade.

He was cleanshaven this evening, which exaggerated the strong line of his jaw and the ridiculously deep cleft of his chin that she had seen only a hint of earlier today beneath several days' worth of dark stubble. Though she could not see the color of his eyes from where she sat, she knew they were the deep brown of loamy earth and that they lit up when he laughed and darkened when he grew serious, as he did now, spying her sitting at the king's table beside her mother, the queen.

He dipped his head in acknowledgement, his gaze never leaving hers, and Sahar lowered her chin a notch in return, a small smile playing at the corners of her mouth. The line of men turned to face the royal table, and Aleksandr, standing dead center and not more than six paces from her, grinned, showing strong, straight white teeth, eliciting girlish sighs and twitters all around the courtyard. His grin widened and Sahar pressed her lips tight.

Her father, King Asad, stood, and the courtyard quieted. At forty and five years of age, the Black Mane still commanded attention. His shoulders were broad and well-muscled, his spine erect, and his mane, though more silver now than his namesake black, was thick and glossy enough to make men twenty years younger envious. He held his hand out to her mother, Queen Oona, who rose from her seat with a calm grace that was as natural to the Swan as breathing. Dressed in her favorite one-shouldered gown of lavender linen overlaid with a sheer sheath of golden worm weave intricately embroidered with delicate blooms of lavender and heather, a fortieth birthday present from her husband, she took his hand and stood beside him, as she had their entire life together.

"Welcome all," he said, his rich voice carrying out across the night. "Welcome to the Feast of Autumn's Eve."

Applause and cheers rang out and Sahar's chest filled with pride. Pride for her parents, her family, for the tribe and the city they had built and ruled over fairly.

"Three days hence the races will begin," her father announced. "The first will be one league for a purse of three gold pieces, the second will be three leagues for a purse of thirty gold pieces, and the third and last will be one hundred leagues for a purse of one hundred gold pieces and breeding rights to any stallion or broodmare in my stables, with the exception of Storm Chaser and Cloud Dancer."

The gathering clapped, the twenty and one men lined up to ride in the races puffed out their chests and jostled their neighbors, and Aleksandr glared accusingly at Sahar. She glared right back. If he truly thought he ever had a chance of breeding rights to Lasair, then that was his mistake.

"And now," her father said, "the riders' introductions."

Her parents took their seats and the first rider stepped forward, a swarthy desert tribesman dressed in a robe of black linen and leather sandals, his waist blade's hilt embedded with rubies and onyx.

"I am Saqr, the Falcon, second son of the Grebe, King of the Marsh Lands." He bowed to the king, and then to Sahar. "I will win these races in your name and honor, Princess Sahar."

She nodded her acknowledgment and the Falcon stepped back as the next man stepped forward and bowed.

"I am Feroz, eldest son of the merchant Gaspar. I will win these races in your name and glory, Princess Sahar."

And on it went, at least every third man declaring their intent to win for her glory until a man dressed in a fine robe of red linen, its hems of black worm weave richly embroidered with threads of red, gold, and green, stepped forward. Tall, though not as tall as Aleksandr, who stood to his right, he was a man built straight up and down with a neatly cropped beard as black as his hair, which he wore tied back, accentuating his high cheekbones and hooked nose, keeping his face on the masculine side of pretty. His skin was not as swarthy as a southern tribesman's or as fair as a Northerner's, and his eyes shone dark and bright as they beaded in on the king.

"I am Yago the Wolf, third son of the Ox, King of the Eastern Grasslands, and eldest son of the Fox, eldest daughter of the Jackal."

A collective gasp filled the courtyard, and Sahar's mother calmly placed her hand over her father's, which was fisted on the table.

The tale of the Lion and the Swan, Sahar's parents, was known far and wide. Her father, Asad, the Black Mane, was eldest son and heir to the Panther's throne, and her mother, Oona, the Swan, a slave when they first met. In truth, the night they met, the Swan and her sister, Lyrra, the Dove, were to be given as dowry for the Fox's betrothal to the Black Mane. The Swan, desperate to keep her sister from becoming a Pleasure Woman in the Panther's palace, had publicly proposed marriage to the Black Mane. Though he could not accept then without starting a war between the tribes, he secretly vowed to help the sisters escape his father and a life of slavery. The Fox, jealous of the Swan, had attempted to have her killed, twice, and the Ox had been her accomplice. His face still bore the scar of the Black Mane's blade for his actions. And now their son stood before her parents.

"Why are you here?" her father asked.

"I am here to win the races," Yago answered. "For I am but a third son and so must make my own way and fortune."

"The Leopard is a third son," King Asad said of his younger half-brother, who had become heir to the Panther's throne after his two older brothers married and went into exile. "Yet, he has become king of the Great Valley. You are still a prince, eldest son of the Ox and Fox, and I have not heard of any discord between you and your parents."

"There is no discord, though they were neither of them pleased that I chose to come and compete in the races."

"And so I ask again, why are you here?"

Yago the Wolf smiled and held his hands out, palms up. "I am here to see for myself this city you have built, King Black Mane. To see how a city raised on the idea of freedom and self-merit works. To be judged only on my own worth, not my family's, something I thought you of all men would understand. I have been told that you once said a son should not be held accountable for his father's actions."

The king chuffed. "I have also said that a man should and will be judged on his own words and deeds."

"Just so, King Black Mane," Yago the Wolf said, dipping his head and stepping back into line. "Just so."

His dark gaze flicked over Sahar, and beside her, her mother stiffened.

Aleksi rarely disliked a person on sight, but he was going to make an exception for this Prince Yago. The man's stated intentions were as real as the kohled black of his hair, and as oily. Who did he think he was ogling Princess Sahar? Why were her beautiful green eyes not blazing back at him as they had at Aleksi earlier today, but coolly taking in this Prince Yago?

An elbow jabbed him in his right side, and Aleksi stopped glaring at the prince to his left long enough to realize he was next in line and that the entire gathering was waiting for his introduction.

He stepped forward and winked at Sahar, whose eyes blazed instantly. "I am Aleksandr—"

"Bastard son of King Maksimillian," a high, feminine voice shrilled out, "and a lowly whore of a kitchen maid."

Aleksi grit his teeth. He would recognize that shrewish voice anywhere. It had plagued his ears his entire life. The firstborn son of King Maksimillian, he had been raised as a prince in his youth, though he was a bastard and his mother a kitchen maid. Proud of his son's size and prowess, his father had provided Aleksi with the best tutors and sword masters coin could buy. His last tutor, a kindly old grey beard who had often despaired over Aleksi's preference for riding and fighting over the studying of figures and governing, had grudgingly admitted that the boy's mind was as strong and fit as his body, if only he would apply it.

Aleksi had been a boy without a care in the world, except for his father's first wife, Queen Theodesia, and her two daughters, Gertruda and Anastasia. Older than Aleksi by several years, they were jealous of their father's favorite, and had been encouraged in their hate and spite by their mother, who had been unable to give her husband a male heir. Aleksi had never known his own mother, for she had abandoned him only a day after his birth, but he had known his father's love and protection up until the summer he had turned ten and two, the summer his father's new, young, second wife gave him a son and legitimate heir. The summer Aleksi had gone from prince to stable boy.

A sea of heads turned toward a still handsome woman of thirty years, her fair hair piled high and glittering with jeweled combs, sitting at a table two rings behind the royal families. Widowed three years ago by her elderly husband, and childless, there could only be one reason she was here.

"Anastasia." Aleksandr dipped his head to her. "Sister," he added to anger her.

"Half-sister," she spat, "and full and rightful daughter to our father, King Maksimillian, and Queen Theodesia."

"Is this to be your introduction to the marriage market, sister, or is it mine as a competitor in the races?"

She wisely, and unusually for her, said nothing. But then she never had been able to beat him in a battle of wits, and she could not bully him here where the long arm and quick slap of her mother could not reach.

Standing tall, Aleksandr squared his shoulders and met the king's watching gaze head on. "I am, as my half-sister said, the eldest and bastard son of King Maksimillian." He locked eyes with Princess Sahar. "I do not pretend to be anything other than what I am, a horseman of the Northern Steppes here to win these races and any prizes I might claim on the merit of my stallion's strength and my riding abilities. I am, if nothing else, honest and straightforward"—he glanced pointedly at the Wolf, whose black gaze coolly assessed Aleksi from head to toe and back again before Aleksi turned back to Sahar—"in my intentions and my proposals."

Beside him, the Wolf snarled low, and before him, green eyes flashed fire. Aleksi stepped back into line with a deliberate low bow to the princess, who placed both hands on the table, hesitated a moment, and then stood and walked around the table and up to the line of riders amidst a grassfire of gasps and whispers.

She eyed each man in turn, and not one, not even one of the many who had pledged to win the races in her honor, would meet her gaze for more than a fleeting moment before looking out into the courtyard of buzzing bees or up into the night sky. Until Yago the Wolf, who met and held her gaze with a smug leer Aleksi longed to swipe off his pretty face.

It was obvious that the prince had no idea why Sahar was standing there, but Aleksi did. He remembered her words earlier in the day when speaking of the princess and her mare winning the races. He jostled the man to his right, making a place for her to stand in the line of riders, and as he did, the Wolf, catching on more quickly than Aleksi cared to give him credit for, swept his arm to indicate the open space. With a gracious nod of her head and a smile that lit her entire face, the princess took a place amongst the riders.

She stood there beaming for a moment before she stepped forward, trailing her intriguing, intoxicating scent. "I am Princess Sahar," she said, her low, smoky voice filling the now quiet courtyard. "Eldest and only daughter of King Asad and Queen Oona. I will win these races on my mare Lasair, the last foal out of Storm Chaser and Cloud Dancer, for the honor of my family and every woman here."

CHAPTER 2

Dance of Blades

The riders' introductions complete, they were seated at three tables facing the makeshift stage of sanded stone where servants brought them trays of sweet meats, and pitchers of spiced wine and yeasty beer. Sahar returned to the royal table, where she sat staring straight ahead at the stage the servants were preparing, studiously avoiding meeting her parent's questioning gazes. After what seemed an eternity, her father stood and the gathering quieted. Again, he held his hand out to his queen, and again she took it and stood beside him.

"My queen and her sister will sing and dance and play for us," the King announced.

He smiled at his wife with pure adoration before loosening his hold of her hand, and the queen returned his smile as she slowly slid her hand from his. Sahar glanced at her brother, Asim, and they exchanged quick smiles.

Their parents had been holding hands their children's entire lives, and always seemed loath to let go. While it had been wonderful growing up amidst and aware of their parent's love for each other, it had also sometimes made them feel like outsiders, though they had neither of them ever felt any lack of love from their mother or father.

Since the night they had first met as the Black Mane and the Swan, her parents had lived in a world of their own, a world that others could be a part of, but never fully inhabit.

Sahar's auntie, Lyrra, gave her husband, Nasim, a tender kiss on his cheek and took her place on the stool in the middle of the stage and began to run her fingers over her harp's strings, slowly at first, then faster and faster, until she had the harp, Nightingale, singing a series of scales. Satisfied, she nodded to her sister, the queen.

"We will sing 'The Sailor's Tale,'" the queen announced, smoothing her skirts.

It had been Grandfather Aaron's favorite. Dead and gone these ten years past, he had been the only grandfather Sahar had ever known, and the man who had taught her how to navigate by the stars. A seafaring Northman trader, it was he that her mother and Aunt Lyrra had sailed across the Mid-Earth Sea with some twenty and three years ago, setting into motion the events that had brought them all here.

"The Sailor's Tale" was a song about a man who had left his family to sail the open seas in quest of treasure and adventure, and his twenty-year journey home. It was a song Sahar knew by heart, and she sang along, her voice barely above a whisper as her mother swayed her hips and rolled her arms and shoulders in rhythm to the sea's swells, her gaze a thousand leagues away. Her father never took his eyes off of his wife, as if he could keep her from sailing away from him with sheer will. And in a way, he had.

He had gone against the Panther, his own father and king, to win her mother and sister their freedom. As part of a bargain struck with the Panther, the Black Mane had sent the Swan and the Dove away, but the Panther went against his word and ordered his guards to go after the sisters and kill them. The Black Mane and his brother, the Cheetah, discovered their father's betrayal and rode after the sisters, saving them from the king's guards. They took refuge in the palace of the Oryx, where the Black Mane and the Swan were married. When they had returned to the Panther's palace, they were husband and wife, but the Panther had refused to accept their marriage, and so they left the City of the Great Valley and never returned.

Sahar glanced over at Yago the Wolf, whose parents had been part of that tale as well, for it was Yago's mother, the Fox, who the prince Black Mane had been betrothed to, and his father, the Ox, who bore a scar across his cheek from the Black Mane's blade in defense of the Swan. Their son, the Wolf had been born only seven moons after his parents' quiet, hasty marriage.

Sahar and Asim, twins who were as far apart in looks as in temper, were the Black Mane's and the Swan's only children, born ten and eight moons after their parent's marriage.

Where Sahar was dark-haired and green-eyed with a temper that flared quickly and burned hot and fast, Asim was light-haired and golden-eyed with a temper that could cook at a low simmer for days before coming to a full boil, if ever. They were a strange mix of their parents, both the good and the bad, as Sahar supposed all children were. But being twins and the progeny of such well-known parents made them all the more noticeable, and notable. It seemed every person who ever met or even heard of them had an idea of them, whether true or not, including that bastard son of a Northern king, Aleksandr—who had called her soft and proud and spoilt—and now watched Sahar almost as much as he did her mother and aunt as they played and sang.

Yago the Wolf watched Sahar as well, though not so boldly. His manners were more courtly, his actions more princely, and it had been he who had stepped aside and opened a space in the line of riders for her. When her mother and aunt finished their song and took their bows, it was he who clapped first.

"We will sing 'The Tale of the Spring Maiden,' 'The Lord of Winter,' and 'The Sun God,'" her Auntie Lyrra said, smiling as shyly as a newlywed bride at Nasim, her husband of over twenty years.

Halah came and sat down beside Sahar in the queen's empty seat as their mothers got into character. The oldest of Nasim's and Lyrra's four living children, she was more like a sister to Sahar than a cousin. Daughters of sisters married to brothers, they had grown up together in the palace along with Asim and their cousin's younger brothers and sisters. Sahar's heart dropped as the laughing face of Ommar, Halah's deceased older brother and Asim's childhood friend, came to her unbidden, and she took several slow, calming breaths until her heart resumed its normal rhythm.

"Munir has asked to speak with my father after the feast this evening," Halah whispered excitedly into Sahar's ear. "Our Auntie Mouse told my mother that she saw Munir at the gem bazaar yesterday."

"Oh, Halah," Sahar said, pushing the memory of Ommar back into the deep, dark recesses of her soul in which it dwelt, hidden and obscured but never fully buried. "I am so happy for you. Munir is a good man and he loves you so."

"As I love him."

Halah was glowing, and Sahar truly was happy for her, if perhaps a little jealous, but if anyone deserved to be happy it was Halah, whose heart was good and pure.

"Come to my chambers after things are settled between you," Sahar said, standing. "Tell me everything then. Now I must go prepare for the knife fight."

The fight was actually a dance she and her brother, Asim, performed. Though well-honed, it was not without some risk, for they had discarded their wooden blades the year they turned ten and six, and now danced with metal blades. They had teased and argued plenty over the years about who would win if they actually fought. Sahar was quicker and likely more cunning, but Asim was stronger and had a longer reach. Still, Sahar was glad they would never have to find out. They had shared a womb for nine moons and a bedchamber until they were seven years of age, and they would gladly sever a limb before they would willingly harm the other.

Plus, Asim was going to be a father soon. Sahar gave Rima, Asim's pregnant wife, a reassuring smile, and then watched as Asim gave his beloved a tender, lingering kiss before standing to join his sister. Sahar turned wistful. Her brother and his wife had found their true loves, as had her parents, her Aunt Lyrra and Uncle Nasim, and, it seemed, Halah and Munir. She sighed and looked up and across the courtyard to find Aleksandr watching her, his head cocked to one side. He grinned and cocked his head to the other side, and with a flick of her skirts, she turned on her heels and headed for the changing room where her maid servant, Safa, waited with Sahar's clothes and blades. The last thing she meant to do was encourage the man, no matter how charming and boyish he looked with that cursed shock of sun-kissed hair falling onto his forehead.

Aleksi's grin widened at the sassy sway of Sahar's skirts as she sashayed from the courtyard. Did the woman never simply walk? A young man who had been sitting next to the king and who was no doubt her twin brother, Prince Asim, stood and followed her. Tall, broad shouldered and lean hipped, his hair a lighter brown than Aleksi's, Asim had the same tawny skin, sharply angled face and round eyes as his sister, though Aleksi could not tell their color from where he sat. The prince was married to Rima, the eldest daughter of the Oryx, King of the City of Hills, and his one and only wife, the Willow. By the sweet kiss Asim had given Rima, she was likely to be his one and only wife as well.

For now.

Aleksi knew only too well how quickly circumstances could change. She might give her husband nothing but daughters and he could marry another, or others, to assure a male heir to the throne. Then what would become of their love and their marriage? It was better to marry for practical purposes. A strong body for bearing children and life's hardships, and an easy temper to bear it all with a smile, that was what Aleksi was looking for.

The sound of clapping brought his attention back to the stage where the queen and her sister were taking their bows. It was obvious where the princess got her looks from. She was a perfect blend of her father's dark features and her mother's graceful build. Her family's physical beauty had not been exaggerated, nor likely their pride. Aleksi had pricked Sahar's this afternoon. He grinned, recalling the fire in her eyes and the heat of her voice as she had threatened to geld him for his brazen boldness, and his grin widened as she strode back into the courtyard dressed in a sleeveless short tunic and leather leggings the color of plum wine, causing a surge of heat to pulse in his groin where she had pointedly menaced him with her blade.

Her tight-fitting tunic clung to breasts as round and firm as autumn apples and nipped down to a slim waist encircled with a leather belt embedded with gems of emerald and ruby and amber and onyx, from which hung not one but three jeweled sheaths, a bone-hilted blade strapped into each. Her leggings hugged every league of her long, lissome legs, which moved in time with her sleekly muscled arms. She wore boots the same tawny hue of her skin, and her mass of dark hair was plaited into one thick braid that hung down her shapely back to the womanly swell of her hips. An armband of gold graced her left upper arm, and etched leather cuffs protected both of her wrists.

She stood in the middle of the stage, chin up, shoulders back, and eyes blazing as her brother, who was dressed as she was, walked up to stand beside her. The pulse in Aleksi's cock hammered. By the stifled groans coming from the table of men, his was not the only one.

Two men set stools at the edge of the stage and sat, a small drum in each of their laps. Sahar and Asim bowed to their parents and then to each other. The men began to beat the drums, slowly at first, softly, and Sahar and Asim began to circle each other, a blade in each hand. The drums beat faster, harder, and brother and sister crouched and doubled their pace.

Asim lunged forward and jabbed with his right hand and Sahar jumped back with the ease of a cat, landing in a loose crouch, and then she lunged forward and jabbed with her right hand and Asim jumped back. Asim repeated his lunge and jab with his left hand and Sahar jumped back again before lunging and jabbing with her left. They continued in this fashion, moving in a circle around the stage, their blades stopping a hair's width from flesh. The gathering clapped in time with the drum beat, and Aleksi sat forward on his seat. Asim was strong and quick and agile, but Sahar, Sahar moved like smoke. Silent, sinuous, and stealthy, striking with the swift, sure precision of an assassin and then slipping away, a mesmerizing spirit dancing beyond her assailant's reach.

Aleksi could not take his eyes off her.

Their circle complete, Asim and Sahar stood face to face and dipped their heads to each other, sucking in deep breaths and blowing them out slowly. Then Asim turned a half circle to his right as Sahar turned a half circle to her left, their blades clashing before they returned to face each other and repeating the movement to their opposite sides. They repeated the moves three times, their blades meeting with a clang before they whirled around again on one foot, the other barely touching ground before pushing off, and then they twirled completely around and began to circle each other, legs bent and arms outstretched.

The drums beat faster and Asim slashed his blade waist high as Sahar dove over the knife and somersaulted to her feet. Asim swung low and she jumped up and over his blade. He swung high and she dropped to her knees and slid in a full circle, slashing at the back of his hamstrings, a fatal blow in a real fight, before jumping back up to her feet with a feral grin.

They flipped their blades full circle, catching them by the hilts, and then they closed the distance between them, striking their blades against each other's in an intricate pattern that mimicked the rapid beat of the drums. They stepped forward, backward, and sideways, maintaining their rhythmic pattern, and then they each whirled around in a full circle, their blades meeting in the middle, and back around the opposite direction, their blades meeting again. Leaping to opposite sides of the stage, they faced the gathering, their faces glowing with the fine sheen of their exertion. Flipping their blades full circle once more, they caught them by the hilts, sheathed them, and bowed low to the gathering.

Aleksi jumped up from his seat, whistling and clapping half a beat before the courtyard erupted into wild applause. Sahar straightened and turned her smile on him, her cheeks several shades pinker than they had been. Aleksi's chest swelled and he was grinning back at her like the village idiot, but he neither cared nor tried to hide it. Yago the Wolf stepped out from behind his table and walked over to her and bowed low before her. He offered her his arm, which she took, her cheeks pinker still, and hand in arm they walked back to the royal table, where she resumed her seat, smiling shyly at Yago's gallant bow before he returned to his own seat.

Aleksi saw red.

Who did this Yago the Worm think he was, insinuating himself into her performance like that? She was not some frail-bodied, faint-hearted, empty-headed doll who could not find her own way back to her seat without his help. Why had the proud tigress accepted Yago's arm and blushed so prettily at the oily snake?

Why did Aleksi care? She was not his. She never would be. She was a princess and he a bastard. He needed a wife of humbler means and easy temper, a wife willing to work her fingers to the bone if need be, not some pampered princess, no matter how fiery and beautiful. Aleksi shook his head and raked his hand through his hair. She was not for him. He did not need a woman like her.

Trouble was, he wanted her.

He should not, but there was no denying the allure she held. If he closed his eyes, he could still see the emerald green of hers challenging him. He could hear her voice, low and smoky, threatening to geld him. He could breathe in and smell her perfume, a tantalizing mix of musky woman and sweet, exotic flower.

The Wolf returned to the table, and Aleksi turned on his heel and left the courtyard. It was either that or entertain the gathering with a real knife fight.

Sahar and Halah lay shoulder to shoulder on Sahar's bed, bellies down, their feet in the air, legs swaying back and forth in time as they admired the hummingbird brooch Munir had given Halah as a gift of betrothal.

"Oh, Lala." Sahar held the brooch up, its body of verdigris copper and wings of inlaid abalone shining iridescent in the rooms candle light. "It's beautiful, like you."

Halah blushed. "That is what Munir said."

"He was only speaking the truth." Sahar touched the side of her head to Halah's. "I am so happy for you both." She caught her breath as a stabbing pain seared her through. "If only Ommar could see you so happy." Shame filled her. "I am so sorry he is not here for you."

"Hush, Sasa," Halah insisted. "You were only a little girl. It was not your fault that you were not strong enough to hold on."

Sahar clamped her hand into a fist as Ommar's ghostly fingers slipped from hers. *Not your fault. Not strong enough. Only a girl.* Those were the words her entire family had spoken over and over, meant to assuage her pain, her guilt. The words she had sworn to prove wrong by not only competing in the races, but winning them.

She handed the brooch back to Halah and gave her a smacking kiss on the cheek. "Munir is a lucky man," she said. "I am glad you will still be living in the palace, though I will miss having you in the room next door at my spoilt brat princess beck and call," she added in her best haughty tone.

"That Aleksandr should not have called you spoilt," Halah said, rising, as always, to her cousin's defense.

"No," Sahar agreed. "That was not politic." She rolled over onto her back and stared up at the draperies of golden worm weave, the image of Aleksandr standing in defiance of his half-sister's denouncement, shoulders squared and jaw jutting forward filling her mind's eye. "But then I do not think he is overly concerned with being so. Lucky bastard," she said under her breath.

But of course, Halah heard her. Like her mother, she could hear a pin drop a hundred paces away as clearly as she could a false note sung or spoken. She eyed Sahar under raised brows.

"I do try," Sahar said. Unlike Halah, all Sahar had inherited from her mother besides her green eyes and the ability to dance was a spine that would only bend so far. "Sometimes more successfully than others."

Halah rolled on to her side and faced Sahar. "Your father was politic in his response to your surprise announcement tonight."

"Indeed," Sahar agreed. He had not said one word about her riding in the races, not yet, but he would, as would her mother the next time they had her alone.

"He was not quite so polite with Yago the Wolf though," Halah said. "Especially when Yago escorted you back to the royal table. I thought your father's glare would burn the Wolf to cinders." She shook her head. "What could the Wolf have meant by doing that? He practically declared his intention to court you in front of not only your parents but every royal from a hundred leagues away."

"I do not think that was his intention."

"Oh yes it was. Your father was not the only man glaring pointed barbs at him for it. Your Aleksandr looked as if he would gladly tear the Wolf apart limb by limb."

Sahar blushed for the second time this day, and she seldom blushed. "He is not *my* Aleksandr," she said.

"You forget, I was there the first time he met you. I saw his face. I heard his proposal."

"Aye, when he thought me some simple-minded, easy-tempered servant girl."

Halah flashed one of her impish grins, another trait she shared with her mother. "Who would you choose?" she asked. "If you had to choose, right here, right now, between the bastard Aleksandr and the prince Yago?"

"To what?" Sahar knew perfectly well what Halah meant.

"To marry. Quit stalling. "

Aleksandr's square jaw, full lips and cocky grin came instantly to mind, and Sahar smiled despite herself as she imagined that cursed shock of hair falling onto his forehead and over his big brown eyes. She breathed in and inhaled the earthy scent of man and horse, sweat and leather that had assailed her nostrils when he had leaned close and whispered in her ear, sending a shiver down her unbending spine.

She thought of Yago the Wolf, of his handsome face and manners. Of how smoothly he had made room for her in the line of riders. She had been caught off guard when he offered her his arm and escorted her back to her family's table, and more than a little embarrassed. That must be why she could not recall any physical reaction to his nearness as she did with Aleksandr, for he was surely as good looking in his way, and, as a prince, much more suitable. Except for the fact that he was the son of her parents' hated enemies.

But Sahar had no desire to marry anyone. Not yet. Not now.

"Neither," she said. "I intend to make my own way. To be the first woman ever to ride in, and win, the races, to fill my own stables with the offspring of Lasair, and to be a doting auntie to all ten of your and Munir's children. What use have I for a husband?"

Aleksi breathed in the fresh morning air mixed with the earthy smell of horse and hitched a foot up onto the lower rail of the fence to the racing kraal. Resting both elbows on the top rail, he and about twenty other men lined the railing to watch the princess training Lasair, a deep-chested, long-legged beauty of a blood bay mare with a mane and stockings as black as pitch. Dressed in a plain brown version of the wine-colored tunic and leggings she performed the Dance of Blades in last night, Sahar hunched over the mare's flexing withers, knees high and head low, the mare's black mane billowing out around her face as they sailed across the earthen track.

"By the gods," he swore half under his breath. "It's as if they can fly."

Beside him an old man with a bald pate and bowed legs chuckled. "An' what else would you 'spect from the firstborn of the Black Mane an' Swan an' last born of Storm Chaser an' Cloud Dancer, eh? They was born and bred for each other, they was."

"You speak as if you know them well, old man," Aleksi said, and was rewarded with a beady-eyed stare.

"An' 'aven't I known the princess since she was a gleam in 'er father's eye," he chided. "An' wasn't it me who pulled Lasair from 'er dam's womb an wiped the snot from 'er nostrils so's she could breathe 'er first breath?"

"I do beg your pardon, sire," Aleksi said. "I am Aleksandr—"

"I know who you be, Maksimillian's young bastard." The man grinned and touched the side of his stubbed nose. "I know everthin' what goes on around my master's palace." His grin widened, showing as many gaps as teeth. "I be the king's stable master. You kin call me Ratter."

Aleksi dipped his head to the old stable master. "The mare's name, Lasair," he said. "I am not familiar with its meaning."

"An' why would ye be?" Ratter answered. "It be the word for flame in the queen's Northern tongue."

"Flame," Aleksi repeated and nodded as mare and mistress raced past, legs stretched and mane and tail flying. "It fits her, and the princess."

"Aye, she's a ball o' fire, our Sahar, always 'as been, ever since the day she came into this 'ere world, squallin' at the top o' 'er lungs 'til 'er brother was laid in the cradle alongside 'er." He grinned and rubbed his bald pate. "She was ever a beauty too, all rosy cheeked an' bright eyed an' curious as a kitten since the day she were born."

"Kitten?" Aleksi eyed the old stable master, looking for claw marks on his leathered face.

Ratter chortled. "Don't ever be callin' 'er that," he said. "She 'ates bein' called that by anyone, but 'er ole uncle Ratter that is."

Aleksi gave a soft snort. "Of course she does."

"Yer gold stallion…"

"Zolotoy."

"I was watchin' you ride 'im earlier. 'E's fast an' strong."

"With the stamina of his Steppe ancestors."

"You plan on ridin' 'im in all three races?"

"I do. And I intend to win all three." Aleksi glanced across the track as Sahar took Lasair over a belly-high jump of stacked logs at a full gallop, never breaking pace. "Other than Lasair and her mistress, which horses and riders should I be concerned about?"

Ratter puffed up and out. "Well now, I 'aven't seen 'em all run yet." He pursed his lips and rubbed his jaw. "But without prince Asim racin', asides from Lasair an' Prince Saqir's stallion, much as it pains me to say it, it's the Wolf's black stallion, Tor, you need be watchin' out fer, as well as 'is master."

Aleksi had watched Yago training with his stallion earlier that morning, and he did not disagree with Ratter's assessment of horse or rider.

"Betwixt you an' me," Ratter said in a low voice, "'is mother's brother, the Falcon, tried to poison Storm Chaser once afore a race. The Black Mane caught 'im red 'anded, 'e did. Shoulda beat 'im bloody, but 'e was still tryin' to protect 'is lady Swan an' keep the peace atween the tribes back then. At's why the Black Mane invites every rider to stable 'is mount in the royal stables, under royal guard, as well as to make sure they's all fed well and kept out o' any weather. 'E don't want any rider 'aving unfair advantage. 'E's a fair king, the Black Mane is, in all ways."

"So I've heard."

"An' you'll be stabling yer stallion in the royal stables?"

"I will." Aleksi had been surprised at the invitation, and impressed. In his experience, most men, kings included, would do anything to ensure their own victory in a contest, any contest, from a friendly game of chance to all-out war, which was why several of the riders had been suspicious of his motives and refused the king's generous invitation. With Serge and Pyotr at their tent to watch over their string of two geldings and four broodmares and tending to the trading of the horses, Aleksi would be able to stay in the royal stables with Zolotoy, where he could concentrate on training the stallion for the races, and winning them.

"'At's smart o' you, young Aleksandr. You know, ever horse 'ats won the races as stabled there. They gets the best care under my watch, they do."

"I am sure they do. Will the princess be moving Lasair to the racing stables?"

"O' course."

"What about Prince Yago?" Aleksi jerked his head toward the track's gate, where the prince stood and bowed low to Sahar as she dismounted from Lasair. He reached for Lasair's reins, and Aleksi snorted as Lasair reared her head back and away from the Wolf, who slunk aside as Sahar calmed the mare.

"You don't like 'im much, do you?" Ratter asked.

"No," Aleksi said as the prince walked beside Sahar and Lasair. "I don't like the preening worm any more than he likes me."

Ratter chortled. "I knew it. I knew it last night at the feast, when you was glaring daggers at 'im in the line o' riders fer takin credit fer letting the princess in."

"You saw that?"

Ratter touched the side of his nose. "I see everthin'," he said. "I see that Lasair, smart mare that she is, she don't like the Wolf none neither. I see 'at it'd be wrong o' me to situate 'er stall next to the Wolf's an' 'is stallion, as he demanded o' me this mornin'. An' seein' as 'ow I'm in charge o' makin' sure everone is comfortable as can be, I'm thinkin' Lasair would be appreciatin' yer golden stallion next to 'er, an' the Wolf clear on the other end."

"Why would you do that?"

"Cos yer good with horses, anyone kin see 'at," Ratter said. He started walking off toward the stables. "An' anyone brave enow to call Sahar 'kitten' an' come away unscathed's all right by me," he chortled over his shoulder.

Sahar was in the palace kitchens rummaging through the basket of bruised apples set aside for pressing into sauce when Anya, the head cook, approached her.

"Yes, Anya?" Sahar said as she stuffed three of the least-bruised apples into her sack, which also held a tub of easing balm Ratter had requested from the palace physician.

Anya stood with her lips pressed together for a long moment, as if trying to form her words, which was unusual, for though she was not native to these parts, she had lived here long enough to speak the language with ease.

"Is there a message you wish me to give my mother?" Sahar asked.

"No, it's you I wish to ask a question of."

Sahar waited for Anya to continue, curious, for Sahar had little to nothing to do with the running of the kitchens. These were the queen's and the head cook's domain. Before Anya said anything more, the king walked in.

"Daughter, I would have a word with you." He wore his robes, which meant he had spent the morning cloistered with the other visiting kings and their counsels discussing the business of running their cities and trade routes. He nodded at her sack. "Heading back to the stables?"

"Yes, Father. I want to make sure Lasair is comfortable in her new stall."

He smiled. "I am certain Ratter will make sure she has every comfort."

"I know. But she's my horse, my responsibility."

"As you are mine and your mother's."

Here it came. Sahar had been expecting it since last night, her parents' loving, rational reasonings against her riding in the races. She stood, ready to listen, and to argue her well-rehearsed defense.

"I, we, wish to warn you against—"

"I can ride as well as any man, Father, you yourself—"

"Yago the Wolf."

"Oh, I, oh."

"I do not trust him, daughter."

"Why not?" Sahar said, not giving her father a chance to answer. "Because of his parentage? As he pointed out last night, you yourself have said that you do not think a man should be blamed for his father's actions."

"That is true enough," he answered in his calm, sensible voice. The voice he had lectured her with too many times to count through the years. "But wiser men than I have also said that an apple does not fall far from the tree, and his parents, how he must have been raised…" He shook his head.

"What of your father, of how the Panther raised you?"

"I had my mother, who was as reasonable and as goodhearted as my father was not."

"Well," Sahar huffed, not quite certain why she was defending Yago to her father. "I prefer to give him the benefit of the doubt."

Her father gave her a rueful smile. "As did your mother his father. She almost died for it, twice."

Chastised, Sahar said nothing.

"Keep your guard up, my daughter," her father said. "And not only toward the Wolf. Our city will be teeming with strangers for the next moon."

"I will, Father," she promised.

He nodded and tugged at the neckline of his robes. "I need to get out of these and into some sensible clothes," he said, and then grinned like a lad let off from his chores to go play in the fields. "Your mother and I are riding over to the Swan's Pond this afternoon."

Sahar grabbed a handful of walnuts and made her own escape out of the kitchens. She tried hard not to imagine what it was that made the Swan's Pond, a league outside of the city's walls and tucked away to the side of the river by a natural enclosure of willows and reeds, so special for her parents. Or why they both would smile for days after their sojourns there.

She had not made it more than halfway across the inner courtyard when Asim came striding toward her. A serious look darkened her usually lighthearted brother's face.

"Is it Rima?" she said.

"No."

Sahar let out the breath she was holding. It was still a moon too early for the babe's birth.

"I must speak with you, sister."

"About the races?"

"About the Wolf."

"What about him?"

"You should stay away from him."

Sahar bristled. "Why?"

"I do not trust him."

"Do you trust me? My judgment?"

Asim shook his head. "Not when it comes to men."

Sahar was speechless.

"You do not know men—"

"I do not know men?" she seethed. "I have lived my entire life amongst a palace full of men. I spent nine moons sharing my mother's womb with you, a man. How can you stand there and tell me I do not know men?"

"Not like him."

"What do you mean, not like him?"

"He is an actor playing a part. To what end, I can't say. But an actor he is, and a bad one. I see it."

Much as Halah had inherited her mother's keen hearing, Asim had inherited their mother's gift of sight. He had the ability with most people to see what was in their hearts, but not with all people. He'd been prejudiced against Yago the Wolf since Asim first heard the story of his parents, the Lion and the Swan.

Still, he was her brother, and he truly cared for her.

"I will promise you what I promised our father," she told him. "I will keep my guard up against Yago the Wolf, and any other man bold or foolish enough to brave the men in my family and show any interest in me."

"Sasa."

She waved him off. "Go see to your wife, brother," she said, walking around him and heading once more for the stables. "May she give you ten daughters," she called back over her shoulder. "All exactly like their Auntie Sasa."

She found Ratter in the tack room of the stables set aside for those horses competing in the races, figuring out who would be situated where. The stables were built to house thirty horses, each with their own stall, and each stall with a small antechamber attached to it, large enough to contain a cot, a wash basin, and a chest or two, along with space to store a saddle and riding tack. The wealthier riders brought their own help with them, but for those who had not, the palace provided well-trained stable hands, if they chose to use them.

"Who is Lasair getting?" Sahar asked as she handed Ratter the tub of liniment from her sack.

"Me."

"Why would you live in a cramped little room for a fortnight?" Ratter had his own roomy, comfortable living chambers in the main stables, built for him where he ruled his own little kingdom. "There must be others willing to take care of her."

Or were they all too embarrassed to watch over a mare ridden by a woman?

"All my top 'ands wanted Lasair as their charge," he said, twisting open the tub and sniffing the stringent balm. He wrinkled his nose and set the tub aside. "But I'm not trustin' anyone sides meself to watch over 'er." He beaded his gaze on Sahar. "I'm not takin' any chances with a certain someone roamin' round all free an important like, an' neither should you. I'll niver forget how yer poor mother looked after 'at bastard Ox got ahold o' 'er, her eyes all bloodshot an' her throat all bruised."

Sahar had heard the story, of course. She had seen the rage still simmering in her father's eyes whenever he spoke of it, and the pain in her mother's, not only at the memory of her physical wounds, but at the knowledge that someone had hated her enough to try to put her in an early grave. Twice. But still. It was bad enough that her father and brother had thought it necessary to warn her about the Wolf. Now Ratter too.

"Yago the Wolf is not his father," she said.

"No, 'e's not. But I don't trust 'im just the same."

"Fine." Sahar was not going to argue the point with him. Ratter had helped foal Lasair. She knew him and was comfortable with him. If he wanted to sleep on a cot in a cramped little room beside her, let him. "Who will be in the stables next to her?"

"Munir an' 'is gelding'll be on 'er right, and Maksimillian's young bastard an' 'is stallion'll be on 'er left."

"Aleksandr?"

"Aye, 'at's 'is name."

"Why would you do that?"

"I likes 'is gold stallion."

Sahar growled low. Ratter had unwittingly put the one man she had no desire to lay eyes on ever again, despite his rugged good looks, right next to Lasair's stall, where she was bound to run into him.

"When did Munir decide to race?" Sahar said, rubbing her temples. "He did not stand in the line of riders last night."

"When yer father the king asked 'im to last night after the feast."

"To watch over me." A girl who could not be trusted to take care of herself.

CHAPTER 3

Kiska

"Well now." Aleksi picked up the scraggly ball of gray-striped fur that had wandered into Zolotoy's stall and held it up for inspection.

"Who are you, little one?" The kitten fit into the palm of his hand and was no more than two moons of age, its gray-green eyes and white-tipped ears too big for its face. Flipping the kitten onto its back, he saw that it was girl. He ran a finger over its protruding rib cage and sunken belly and rubbed its fur back, exposing fleas that weighed more than the kitten. "Have you lost your mama, little *kiska*?"

The kitten let out a pathetic mew and snuggled deeper into Aleksi's warmth. Having spent the past ten and three years living and working in his father's stables, he was as familiar with stable cats as with horses, and next to horses, cats were his favorite animals.

Glancing around the cramped antechamber, he thought out loud. "First thing we need to do is feed you, and I have some jerky in my pack." He tucked the kitten into the crook of his arm and pulled the jerky out with the other and bit a small piece off. Chewing it until it softened, he offered it to the kitten, who practically took the tip of his finger off along with the proffered jerky. "Easy my little *kiska*, your teeth are like needles."

Once he was satisfied that that the kitten had eaten enough, but not too much, he pulled a bar of soap from his pack and tested the water in his wash basin.

"It is not so warm," he told the kitten, "but neither is it too cold, and I need to drown those fleas off of you before they take what little blood you have left." He took a drying cloth off a peg on the wall. "I promise you will like being rubbed dry." He imagined washing and rubbing another black haired, green-eyed kitten. "She would bleed me dry if I so much as suggested it," he chuckled. "And burn me to ash for good measure."

The moment Aleksi set the kitten in the basin it let out a yowl that echoed through the entire stables, and kept up a pitiful mewling as he soaped and lathered its flea-ridden fur, turning the water in his wash basin a filthy brown. He carried the kitten into Zolotoy's stall and dunked it neck-deep into the stallion's water bucket for another rinse. The kitten let out a deafening howl that sent the horse pressing against the wall.

"Such a big brave stallion you are," Aleksi chided as he fingered water over the wailing kitten's head. "Afraid of a tiny little kitten."

"What do you think you are doing?" a low, smoky familiar voice accused from over the stall gate. "Are you trying to drown that poor kitten?"

Aleksi straightened and stood eye to blazing green eyes with Sahar as the kitten dripped and squirmed and wailed even louder in his hands. She had changed from her riding leathers to the marigold tunic and ocher skirt she had worn the first time he had seen her, and strands of her thick black hair had escaped her colorful headscarf and curled around her long, tawny neck.

"I am trying to drown its fleas and save its life," he told her. He pulled the drying cloth from around his neck and bundled the kitten up in it. "If that is all right with you."

"Oh. Of course it is. I thought..."

"It is common for kittens to be drowned in your royal stables?"

"No, of course not."

Aleksi grinned as gold sparks flashed in her eyes. "Then it's me that you would suspect of such cruelty."

"No. I..."

He had her flustered, and found that he enjoyed seeing her so. He held the kitten up and nuzzled its nose, which was all that was visible from under the cloth. "Princess Sahar thinks I would drown you, my little *kiska*. What do you say to that?"

He turned the kitten's face to Sahar, its big eyes and pink nose peeking out at her. The kitten meowed, subdued now that it was safe and warm, and Sahar smiled and reached out to touch its nose. The kitten bit down.

"Ow." Sahar jerked her hand back, blood welling on her finger's tip. She stuck the tip into her mouth and sucked it, and Aleksi's blood heated instantly.

He coughed and shifted the kitten to his chest, holding his injured finger up to Sahar. "I should have warned you, Kiska is a bloodthirsty little girl." He grinned wide purposely. "But as you know, I like kittens that are not afraid to use their sharp points."

Sahar opened her mouth and then snapped it shut, spun on her heels, and stomped the three paces to her horse's stall, throwing open the gate and slamming it shut. Aleksi chuckled as he tucked Kiska into the crook of his arm and left Z's stall to stand at the gate to Lasair's, watching Sahar brush the mare's long flowing mane and waiting for her to acknowledge his presence, which she stubbornly refused to do until at last Lasair whinnied and stepped up to sniff at the bundle of cloth and kitten in Aleksi's hold.

"So," Aleksi said. "It seems we are neighbors."

Sahar glared at Aleksi. "You knew we were," she said. "I would not put it past you to have bribed Ratter into situating it so."

"Actually, it was the Wolf who tried to bribe Ratter into situating him next to you, but I get the impression that Ratter cannot be bribed if he does not wish to be so."

She shrugged and said nothing.

"Do you know why Ratter would not agree to the Wolf's demands?"

Again, she shrugged and said nothing.

"Because he does not trust him. Nor should you."

"That. Is. It." Sahar threw the brush at Aleksi, who managed to dodge it as it flew past his head. "First my father, then my brother, then Ratter, and now you." She stood nose to chin with him, breathing fire. "I have had it with you men thinking you must warn me off of Yago, thinking you must protect me, as if I, a mere woman, am incapable of taking care of myself."

Aleksi's first instinct was to pull her headscarf off, bury his fingers into her thick mass of dark curls and pull her to him, to kiss those full lips and breathe in her fire. She might scorch him to bare earth, but it would be worth it. Still, reason and those men she railed against were enough to rein him in.

"Perhaps you should heed them," he said.

"Perhaps you should mind your own business."

"Perhaps I will."

"Good."

"Good." Aleksi took half a step back, and then stepped right back up. "Listen," he said. "I am no inbred idiot. I know a princess used to life in a grand palace would never lower herself to marry a poor bastard like me. I have no illusions there, now that I know who you are. But this Yago the Wolf, he may be a prince by title, with a pretty face and even prettier manners, but he is a snake in the grass. Do not fall for his flattery."

"Flattery? You think me so spoiled and shallow that I would fall for false flattery?"

It was Aleksi's turn to shrug and say nothing.

"Why do you even care?" she said. "You are not in competition with him for me since you have apparently taken your proposal back." She glowered at him. "I will say you gave up easily. It must be all those other broodmares out there waiting for a stallion such as yourself to pick and choose from."

Aleksi glowered right back. Did she think it was nothing to him to be refused? Did she expect him to prostrate himself at her feet and beg her to marry him so that she could refuse him again? She was angry, he could see that. But was she angry because he had proposed, or because she thought he had taken his proposal back? Had he taken it back? He raked a hand through his hair and saw the quick uptick of her gaze as his stubborn shock of hair fell back down onto his forehead. He was not conceited, but neither was he blind. He had seen that look of feminine approval enough times to recognize it, even in a fire-spitting tigress. By the gods, she was the most maddening woman he had ever met. "Do as you wish," he said.

"I will," she snarled, fangs showing and eyes blazing.

Aleksi laughed, quick and short. "Remember though," he said over his shoulder as he walked away, "even a tigress has need of protection when there is a trap being set for her."

At supper that night, Sahar made a point of sitting at one of the tables set aside for the riders. Yago was the first man to offer her a seat beside him, though this time at least three others shifted and made a place for her as well. Aleksandr had not yet arrived, and she told herself it was merely curiosity that made her look for him—that and the ridiculously appealing image of him nuzzling and sweet-talking the kitten in the stables.

Where he had called her a tigress.

Of course, it was after warning her off of Yago the Wolf, like the other men in her life thought necessary to do. As if she could not take care of herself. She huffed as she took the seat beside Yago. She would show all of them when she and Lasair won the races, and though she had no real need for the winning purses, it would be the first coin she had earned from her own toil and talents. Coin she would use to build her own stables.

"Princess Sahar?"

She turned her attention to Yago and caught a glimpse of her father's glare over his shoulder.

"May I call you Sahar?"

"Just do not call her kitten," a low, resonant voice said from behind her.

"Ah, Maksimillian's bastard," Yago said as Aleksandr stepped up and stood between them, towering over them on their stools, an affable grin on his face.

"Ah, Yago the Worm, er, I mean, Wolf. You know, my desert words, they do not always come out right." He leaned down to Sahar, blocking Yago. "How's your finger?"

"I'll live, thank you. Yours?"

He waggled it in front of her face. "In working order, as you see."

The corners of her mouth twitched up despite herself, and his grin grew cocky. He dipped his head to her and that cursed shock of hair fell onto his forehead. When she pulled her gaze from his forehead, he grinned and then straightened to walk around the table, taking a seat directly across from her, his grin even cockier. She took a long, slow drink of her wine.

"Peasant boor," Yago muttered, his lips thinning into a derisive sneer.

Aleksandr raised his cup to Yago. "Royal prig."

Sahar choked, coughed, and sputtered into her cup, as did several others at the table. The serving maid's tray rattled and Feroz, the merchant's son, laughed out loud and clapped Aleksandr on the shoulder. Yago's black eyes narrowed to slits and his knuckles were white around the stem of his goblet. Aleksandr sat there with a lazy grin on his face, baiting the Wolf.

Yago was neither small nor softly muscled, but given Aleksandr's height and breadth, Sahar thought it prudent that Yago resist the taunt. She raised her cup to Yago with an encouraging smile and took a sip before glaring over the rim at Aleksandr, whose grin faded as his jaw tightened.

Thankfully, the servants entered the salon with trays laden with roasted lamb and savory carrots, onions, and turnips. The table of hungry men filled their trenchers to overflowing and attacked the meat and vegetables, silent but for their chewing, and stopping only to lade their plates fuller from the bowls of seasoned rice and kamut. By the time the trays of cheeses and honeyed dates and pears were brought out, conversation resumed, at least amongst everyone at the table except for Sahar and Yago. Sahar because she was a woman and not invited to participate, and Yago because he sat silent and sullen and drinking more wine than was wise. Not that she blamed him. True, he had insulted Aleksandr first, but it was obvious that the others had sided with Aleksandr, and Yago, alone and far from his home, had to feel the slight.

Yago left the table as soon as was polite, and the mood there instantly lightened. Sahar glared her displeasure at Aleksandr, who shrugged and then picked over his trencher, packing bits of juicy lamb and rice and soft cheese into a square of linen. He folded it up and stuffed it into the pocket of his tunic, ignoring the curious glances of the other riders and giving Sahar a quick grin.

"Once a stable boy scavenging for scraps," Anastasia said from her position standing beyond the table wearing a snide smile on her deceptively fair face, "always a stable boy scrapping for royal leftovers."

"Sister," Aleksandr said through gritted teeth. "How kind of you to watch over your brother so attentively."

"Half-brother," she spat.

Sahar waited for Aleksandr to explain that the scraps were for the poor, starved kitten he had found, but he picked up his goblet and drained it, pointedly ignoring Anastasia's presence as he set the empty goblet down on the table with a satisfied, "Ahh."

Anastasia tossed her flaxen hair and flounced away, settling at a table occupied by two older wealthy princes. Sahar excused herself to visit at her parents' table, while two of the Scorpion's daughters not so discreetly made their way over to the riders' table and held a lively conversation with Aleksandr and Feroz. The girlish giggles assailed Sahar's ears. Pleading her self-imposed training regimen, she said her goodnights to her family and left the salon, but instead of going to her chambers, she took the long way around to the kitchens, where she asked Anya for a small bowl of goat's milk.

"Certainly, young miss," Anya said as she went to the cupboards for a bowl. She poured a ladleful into it and handed it to Sahar. "May I ask you something?"

"Of course."

"This Aleksandr and his sister, Anastasia. What are they like?"

"Why do you ask?"

"My husband and I, we came from the Northern Steppes to settle here with our young son. I was curious. It's been a long time since I have met anyone from our homeland."

"I didn't know that," Sahar said. "Though now I can hear the similarities in your accent to Aleks…them."

Anya smiled sadly.

"You miss your homeland?" Sahar asked.

"I do," Anya said. Then hastened to add, "But King Asad and Queen Oona, this city, have been good to us. We had, I have, a good life here, but yes, I do miss some parts of my homeland."

Sahar nodded, remembering that Anya had been widowed a few years ago now. "Would you like me to ask if you could speak with them?" she said.

"Oh yes, please," Anya answered. "But, perhaps you could ask only the king's son, Aleksandr. I think he would be more agreeable."

Sahar laughed, not at all surprised that Anya realized the chance of Anastasia conversing with a servant for the servant's pleasure was slim to none. Her parents always said if you wanted to know what was truly happening in a household, ask the servants, a piece of wisdom learned from her grandmother, Queen Noor.

"I will ask Aleksandr the next time I see him."

Which would likely be sometime late tomorrow, after he slept off the night's festivities with the Scorpion's daughters.

"Come now, my little Kiska," Aleksi coaxed. "You must try to eat a bit more of this rice." The kitten had eaten what meat and cheese he had allowed her for the night with enthusiasm, but he had to keep a little set aside for the morning before he could bring her some egg and milk from his breakfast. "If only we had some milk now, eh, to soak this rice in and make it more to your liking."

"Ahem."

Aleksi snapped his head up. Sahar was standing at the open half door that separated his antechamber to Zolotoy's stall. She looked as surprised to see him as he was to see her, though it was his room.

"How did you get in here?" he asked. "I did not hear a sound. Not even a single blade of straw shift."

"We cats can be quiet when we wish to." She thrust a small bowl at him, "I brought you, the kitten, milk from the kitchens."

He stood, tucking Kiska into the crook of his arm. "Thank you," he said, taking the proffered bowl in his other hand. He set it down on the chest at the foot of his cot. "Would you like to come in?"

Sahar took in the cramped room with only the cot and a stool to sit on. "No. I wanted to bring the milk. Oh, I promised Anya, our head cook, that I would ask if you would take the time to meet with her. She is from the steppe lands too, and is hoping to speak with you of your homeland."

"Of course." Aleksi stepped up to the door and Sahar took half a step back. He grinned and her cheeks pinked. "Perhaps tomorrow after training I can meet her at the kitchens, maybe sweet talk her into some more milk and meat to fill Kiska's little larder."

"That would keep your half-sister from calling you a scavenger." There was pity in her expression and her voice, something Aleksi didn't want from her or anyone. "You could've explained your actions, then she would have looked the fool, not you."

"What do I care what she calls me, or why," he said so gruffly that Kiska mewled. He tucked the kitten closer and ran a soothing hand down her back. "I know the truth," he said in a harsh whisper. "You know the truth. What do I care what those spoilt, cannot-see-beyond-their-own-royal-noses like Anastasia and Yago think or say about me?"

"What does Yago have to do with what your sister said?" she snapped.

"He's like her, thinking he's above others because of an accident of birth."

Her big green eyes grew larger and she lifted her chin a notch. He had insulted her again. He should be sorry for it, but all he could see was that cursed oily worm fawning over her, and her accepting—no, enjoying it. He set his shoulders and narrowed his gaze on hers. "Why do you defend him?"

"Because," she said, her voice as stiff as her spine, "I prefer to judge a man by his actions, and he was the only man to step aside and offer me a place beside him in the line of riders. He treated me as an equal."

Aleksi snorted. "You are as blind as you are beautiful."

"What do you mean by that?"

"Ask someone who was there, someone who saw, who truly saw."

"Like who, Ratter? Your new best friend, a man who hates the Wolf's parents almost as much as my parents do?"

Aleksi shifted Kiska, who had fallen asleep and was purring in his arm. "They have good reason to hate them," he said. "Surely you have been told the stories. Talk about judging a person by their actions."

"Yago is not his parents."

"And you are not yours, and I am not mine."

"Why do I even try to talk to you?"

Aleksi smiled, slow and sure. He reached out and twined his fingers into the thick, black length of her hair. This he knew the answer to. "Because," he murmured, "you are drawn to me as I am you to. Because you could scorch me to bare earth with those blazing eyes of yours and I would rise back up and take it all again and again and again."

She swallowed hard, and the fire in her eyes melted into swirling pools of emerald. "Why did you call me tigress?" she whispered.

He wrapped his hand around the back of her neck and pulled her closer. "Because," he said, his voice coming from somewhere deep in his chest, "you are a tigress." He closed the hair's breadth between them with his lips. "You are *my* tigress," he breathed into her parted lips and grinned as the breath she had caught and held came out in a sigh. He touched his lips to hers, nibbling lightly, tasting her salty sweetness, and when she neither bit nor pulled away, he covered her mouth with his, devouring her lips, her breath, a starving man granted a sumptuous feast. She moaned in surrender, the most sensuous sound he had ever heard, and he pressed closer. An ear-splitting shriek broke them apart.

Aleksi glanced down at Kiska, who had been squished between them and was giving him her most indignant glare. "So sorry, little one," he cooed, shifting her on his arm. He looked back up at Sahar, grinning from ear to ear. She slapped him across the cheek. Hard.

Sahar slept little and fitfully. The low, resonant sound of Aleksandr's voice vowing to rise again and again, the warm strength of his hand on her neck, pulling her inexorably to him, to his mouth, soft and tender as a whisper one moment and then hard and unyielding the next, swirling round and round her sleep-starved mind with the dizzying heat of a fever dream.

Finally, exhausted, she slipped into a semblance of deep slumber as the sun began its ascent in the eastern sky, and did not rise from her bed until almost noon. Most of the household were already busy with the day's duties, so she grabbed a piece of flatbread and a ripe pear in the kitchens and made her way to the stables, slinking past Zolotoy's stall, which was empty.

"'E's out workin' 'is gold stallion," Ratter said from where he stood grooming Lasair. "As should you be."

"I overslept," she said, stating the obvious.

Ratter stopped combing Lasair's mane and his gaze darted to Sahar. Unlike most young women of royal households, she did not normally sleep in late. She liked to be up and outside with the sun and the horses. "'Is kiss that good, eh?"

"What? Who? Why would you say that?"

Ratter grinned and touched the side of his nose. "I be roomin' wit Lasair these days an' nights," he said. "I was right next door. I 'eard the whole thing. Includin' the slap."

Sahar said nothing, though the flush of her traitorous cheeks told Ratter all he thought he needed to know. Unfortunately, what Ratter knew, he seldom kept to himself.

"Then you heard me walk away from the arrogant ass right after I slapped him."

"I did, an' I 'eard im chucklin' to hisself after as well."

Sahar refused to say more. What would she have said anyway? Yes, his kiss was that good. Yes, he had reason to be pleased with himself because she had fallen into his arms and responded to his kiss despite herself. That the low, husky whisper of his voice calling her his tigress still sent shivers down her spine. She shook herself and adjusted her head scarf. "Is Lasair ready?"

Ratter handed her the mare's reins.

Her thoughts scattered between the race, Lasair's training, Aleksandr's kiss, and Ratter's gossipy tendencies. Sahar led Lasair from the cool dimness of the stables into the blinding sunlight streaming in through the main door, and walked right into the one man she did not wish to see, not yet, not today. Not ever.

"Ooof." Aleksandr rubbed his nose where Sahar's forehead had banged into it. "By the gods, woman, first you put a blade to my stones, then you slap my cheek, now you try to break my nose." He raked a hand through his hair and that cursed shank of golden brown fell right back over his forehead. He grinned. "Are you so concerned that Zolotoy and I will beat you that you must resort to injuring me?"

Sahar tore her gaze from his smiling brown eyes and gathered her wits. "For a man who claims he can be scorched to bare earth and still rise again, you complain overmuch of such trifling inconveniences," she said in her haughtiest voice. She waved him away. "Now, if you would be so mannerly as to move out of my way, Lasair and I have some training to do. After all," she threw over her shoulder as he stepped aside and she sauntered by, "I do not wish to make it look too easily done when we beat you and every other man and their steeds."

He laughed. "There goes my tigress," he said. "Fur ruffled and chin up."

Sahar whirled around. "I am not your tigress," she growled. "I am not your, or any other man's anything."

He cocked his head. "No?" he said. "You are not your father's daughter, your brother's sister?"

She leveled him with her glare. "You know what I mean."

"I do?"

"I am my own woman. I do not need, nor do I want, a husband."

"Who said anything about a husband?"

"You did, the first time you proposed."

"The first time? Does this mean you expect me to propose again?" He stepped up to her and reached for a tendril of hair that had escaped her head scarf. "And again?" His voice was low and teasing. "And again?"

"No," she said, flustered. "Of course not."

"Your words say one thing, but your eyes, your lips, they say another." He smiled, slow and cocksure. "It's the kiss."

She reared her head back. "Do not be so arrogant as to think that kiss—"

"Kept you awake half the night, as it did me."

His confession startled her.

"Was it your first kiss?" he asked.

"No." But it was the first kiss she had felt all the way to her toes. The first kiss she had dreamed about. The first that made her entire body flush while thinking about it. Still, it wouldn't do to have the arrogant ass knowing this. "I am twenty and one years of age," she told him. "I have had marriage proposed to me by at least thirty men since the spring I turned ten and four, and I have been kissed at least that many times."

Aleksandr frowned and the muscle on the side of his clamped jaw ticked.

"What?" she asked, indignant now. True, she'd only kissed three men, including him, not the thirty she had claimed. That wasn't the issue. "You can kiss thirty women but I can't kiss thirty men?"

"It is unseemly," he said.

"It is none of your concern."

After checking on Pyotr and Serge and their string of horses, of which two mares had already been sold at their asking price, Aleksandr slept a good deal of the afternoon away on the cot with Kiska tucked close to his chest, figuring the extra rest would likely do both him and Z some good after the long journey here. He gave the stallion an extra bucket of oats and asked Ratter to watch over Kiska while he supped at the palace, where he arrived as the first course of meat and vegetables were being served. He took the seat held for him by Feroz, glad to see that Yago sat at another table with a hawk-nosed prince called Taweel the Tall, and a few others, gladder still to see that Sahar sat at her family's royal table. He did not like the idea of her sitting beside the Wolf any more than he did of her kissing thirty other men, or even one.

The meal passed uneventfully, and no one said a word when he wrapped up choice bits of meat and rice and cheese in his linen square and tucked it into his pocket. Once the sumptuous meal was finished, he rose and approached the king's table.

"My compliments and thanks for your generous hospitality, King Asad," he said with a dip of his head.

"You are most welcome, Aleksandr." The king's uncanny gaze held Aleksi's for a long moment, and Aleksi was beginning to wonder how much the king knew of his and Sahar's short history together when the king continued. "I hear from my stable master that your golden stallion is the horse to watch these races. I look forward to seeing him run."

Aleksi stood tall and proud, unsure of why it mattered that the king approved of him, but it did. "Thank you, sire. I do believe we will be the horse and rider to beat." He glanced at Sahar, who glared daggers at him. "Though your daughter assures me otherwise."

The king chuckled and smiled fondly at her. "Do not take her assurances too lightly, Aleksandr," he said. "Lasair has both the speed and endurance of her dam and sire, as does our daughter."

"I can assure you, your majesty, I do not take anything about the princess lightly, which is why I have intruded on your family table."

Aleksi dipped his head to Sahar. He could display manners as princely as Yago when he wished to. "Will this evening do to meet with your head cook? Ratter is minding Zolotoy and Kiska, so our conversation will not be rushed, if you do not already have other plans."

He had her, he knew it, and so did she. She smiled and stood. Honey could have dripped from her lips, or venom. "Follow me," she said, sweeping past him.

With a quick dip of his head to her father and mother, Aleksi walked behind Sahar, admiring the twitch of her skirts as she led him out of the salon, a hundred pair of eyes boring into the back of his head.

The kitchen was easily twice as large as the kitchens in his father's palace, with not one, but four long work tables. One for fruits and vegetables, one for grains, one for eggs and cheeses, and another for meat that was closest to the door to the outside ovens and roasting pits. There were six women working at the grain table rolling out flatbreads to be baked for the morning meal, and another four going through baskets of pears and apples, while three of the younger serving maids were busy scrubbing the meat table clean. A tall, slim woman in a plain tunic and skirt covered by a crisp work apron, her gray hair pinned up in a tight bun, turned around from inspecting the cheese larder as the women's lively chatter slowed and quieted. Spying Sahar and Aleksi, she stopped and stood still for a long moment before greeting them. "Princess Sahar," she said with a dip of her head. "This is Maksimillian's son, Aleksandr?" the woman asked.

"Yes, it is. He's come to speak with you, if you have the time."

"I do." She stepped from the side of the table and held her hand out to Aleksi. "It is a pleasure to meet you, Aleksandr," she said with an open smile. "I'm Anya, and I thank you for taking the time and trouble to speak with an old woman about her homeland."

"It is no trouble, mistress. I wish to thank you for the goat milk you have spared for my little Kiska."

"A kitten?" she said, glancing from Aleksi to Sahar. "That's who the milk was for?"

"I have a soft spot for kittens," Aleksi said, winking at Sahar, whose tawny cheeks flushed instantly pink.

"Do you?" Anya asked as a fat, orange tabby wandered over and wrapped itself around her ankles. She shuffled the cat aside and then indicated a small table with four chairs, the closest thing to a quiet corner in the kitchen. "Let's sit and talk. Can I get you anything to eat or drink?"

"Oh no, thank you." Aleksi rubbed his belly. "I ate too much supper as it is. Compliments to you and your staff on the delicious meals you serve."

Anya took the seat beside Sahar's. "I'll be sure to tell them. It's always good to hear that our efforts are appreciated." She glanced at Sahar with a quick smile. "Something the queen is generous and gracious about."

Aleksi sat and straightened his legs to better to help his overfed belly digest. "The princess tells me you and your family came here from the Northern Steppes some twenty years ago?"

Anya nodded. "Yes, my husband Yuri and I, along with our son, Arman, who was but a babe at the time, though it is closer to twenty and five years now since we left."

"What part of the Steppes are you from?"

"We both worked at Maksimillian's palace, which was how we met. I was a maid servant and Yuri a smithy."

"You knew my father then?"

She nodded. "We did, and the queen and her daughters."

"Did you know my mother?"

The question seemed to surprise her, almost as much as it surprised Aleksi that he had asked it.

"No, not that I remember," she said. "Why do you ask?"

Aleksi glanced at Sahar, who was listening intently. "I never knew her either," he said with a voice of practiced indifference. "She left when I was but a day old and was never spoken of again, at least not to me. I never even knew her name."

He'd never asked. Growing up in the palace, he'd never really felt the lack of a mother he had never known. When he was a stable boy, what good would knowing her name have done him?

Anya laid a work-roughened hand on his forearm. "Did they treat you well?" she asked. "The king and his wives?"

"I was raised as a prince until I was ten and two," he told her. "Then my father's second wife gave him a legitimate princeling and heir. I was made a stable boy, and worked with Serge and Pyotr, who travelled here with me."

As a boy, Aleksi had never considered why his father had arranged for Serge and Pyotr to become stable boys alongside his bastard son. For them, coming from families of poor field workers, the positions had been a step up, while he had been brought low. But now, as a man, Aleksi understood that his father had given him the gift of camaraderie and friendship. What he did not and never would understand was how his father could have deprived Aleksi of his mother's love, and then his own.

"That must have been hard for you," Anya said.

Aleksi shrugged. "It kept me out of the queen's sight and reach."

"She always was a right bitch, that Theodesia," Anya said, and then clapped her hand over her mouth, her eyes wide with horror.

"Ha." Aleksi burst into laughter while Sahar watched them both, saying nothing. "Her daughters are no better. Nothing and nobody can please them. I swear the heavens could rain nectar down on them and they would complain it was too sweet." He eyed Anya, a still handsome woman with sad grey-blue eyes whose youthful good looks would have no doubt raised Theodesia's ire. "Was she why you left?"

Anya nodded, slowly, thoughtfully, her serious gaze on his. "She was one of many reasons," she said. Then she glanced at Sahar and her expression brightened. "It was for a better life that we came here to this city, and here it was we found it and lived it until my Yuri passed from this life three years ago last winter."

"I am sorry," Aleksi said. "He was a good man?"

"He was, and his son, our son, Arman, is much like him."

CHAPTER 4

Winners and Losers

Zolotoy was not in his stall when Sahar arrived to ready Lasair for her morning training session. It was the day before the first race, and she and Ratter had decided to give Lasair an easy run this morning and let her rest this afternoon. Yesterday, when Sahar had shown for Lasair's afternoon session, she had been surprised to find Zolotoy in his stall, as Aleksandr usually trained him then. She had crept into the stallion's stall and peeked into the antechamber, where she had spied a sight that still made her grin. Aleksandr, sound asleep on the cot, that shock of hair fallen over his forehead, those full lips she could still taste slightly open, little Kiska snuggled under his chin. He had looked so young and boyish and carefree, something she had learned he had not been for many years.

Though she probably should have left Aleksandr and Anya to their conversation last night, Sahar had stayed and listened intently to every word spoken between them in the kitchens. In doing so, she had learned more about Aleksandr in one night than she had in the three days previous. He had been born and raised as a prince, his father's pride and joy, and then had it all taken from him through no fault of his own. A son and legitimate heir had been born, and the golden boy made a stable boy. A motherless stable boy who had taken refuge with horses and cats, who was fiercely loyal to his two friends, Pyotr and Serge, for whom he had accepted a sack of food from Anya, and who was determined to return home a self-made man with a string of fast, leggy, desert broodmares and a wife.

When Anya had teasingly asked him if he had a wife picked out yet, he had answered that he had his eye on a certain young woman and then had winked at Sahar, a wink that Anya had not missed. He had boasted about winning all three races with their purses of one hundred and thirty- three gold pieces, as well as breeding rights for Zolotoy, in order to further his plans. When Anya commented on how sure he sounded about winning, he told her that was because he was the best rider in their land, and then he had added, with another wink at Sahar, that the best steppe rider would always beat the best desert rider, man or woman.

Sahar had openly scoffed, but secretly she was not so sure he was wrong. She had watched him training Zolotoy—every rider had at one point or another—and she hated to admit it, but he rode as well as any man she had ever seen, and she had grown up amongst the best riders in the known world. He rode with a strength and skill and sureness matched only by the golden stallion beneath him, moving as one as they churned up earth with powerful, league-eating strides and soared over jumps with ease. And whether holding Zolotoy to a tight rein or giving him his head, the Northern Steppes man rode with a combination of complete control and wild abandon that both thrilled and irritated Sahar. In truth, the more she saw of Zolotoy, the more she was inclined to consider the stallion as a breeding partner for Lasair. A foal with her speed and his strength would be near impossible to beat in any race.

Sahar simply had to win the races. That way it would be her choice, not Aleksandr's.

Shaking her head as if she could shake both stallion and man out of her thoughts, she peeked into the empty stall's antechamber and found Kiska sleeping in a box Aleksandr had fashioned for her, curled up in the middle of one of his tunics. The warm, musky male scent of the tunic's owner came to her unbidden, and she turned heel and hurried over to Lasair's stall.

"I was checking on the kitten," she said to a curious-eyed Ratter, who handed Lasair's reins to her.

The mare was already saddled and tossing her head, anxious to get out on the racing track. Born and bred to run, she was one of those rare horses who truly loved it, and riding her at a full gallop, the wind whipping through both their manes, was one of Sahar's greatest joys.

"Come, my beauty," she laughed as she led Lasair out of the stables. "Let us go stretch your lovely legs."

It seemed every man entered in the race tomorrow stood along the fence rails watching them train, and she caught the worried expressions of more than one rider, as well as a few disdainful frowns or ogling leers, as she walked Lasair past them cooling off the mare. Sahar pressed her lips tight and sat straighter in her saddle. They should be worried. She had every intention of beating each and every one of them, especially Aleksandr, who doffed his nonexistent cap to her as she reached the gate and dismounted.

As Sahar led Lasair to the stables, Yago stopped her. He wore a spotless tunic and had not one oiled hair out of place, despite the brisk, autumn breeze.

"Princess," he said with a courtly dip of his black head. "Would you do me the honor of sitting beside me as we sup this evening?"

"I had not thought to..." She glanced over his shoulder and caught sight of Aleksandr's steady stare. "Thank you, Prince Yago," she said. "I accept your kind invitation."

He lifted her hand and placed his cool, dry lips on the back of her fingers. "I await this evening with eager anticipation," he said, smoothly returning her hand.

Sahar glanced over at Aleksandr, whose glare emitted more heat from ten paces than the Wolf's courtly lips on her skin. With a shrug of her shoulders and a saucy tilt of her head, she turned on her heels and gave him her back.

"Easy, Z." Aleksi patted the dancing stallion's straining neck as the horse pranced and pawed at the starting line. "Soon I will give you your head and we will show these desert horses and their riders a lesson they will not forget."

He held Zolotoy's reins in a tight grip, watching the flag flap in the brisk autumn air. It depicted a black stallion and a snow-white mare against a green field under a blue sky. A horse's high whinny and the shouts of men turned his attention to where Yago's black stallion, Tor, reared and pawed at the air, while the gelding next to him broke from the line, a bloody gash on his ear. The gelding's rider brought the frightened horse under control and inspected the bleeding ear, loudly cursing Yago and his "black demon of a mule" for biting his horse. Aleksi shook his head. Horses were not inherently mean-tempered creatures, yet he had seen more than one made so by their masters.

The gelding's rider declared him fit to race and resumed a place in the starting line away from Yago and Tor, as did the other riders, keeping their horses at a safe distance from Tor's teeth and hooves. Aleksi glanced over at Sahar, who was speaking softly into Lasair's ear. She had not spoken one word to Aleksi since the evening before last, when they had been in the kitchens with Anya, though he had found her contributions of a boiled egg and pieces of unseasoned fish to Kiska's growing larder yesterday morning and evening.

Probably for the best they hadn't spoken. The sight of her sitting beside Yago at supper last evening, at her laughing and blushing at his slavish attentions still had Aleksi seeing red. Her father had not seemed amused either. He'd worn a furrowed brow through most of the meal. Aleksi understood the necessity of maintaining politeness and royal manners well enough, but what he did not understand was Sahar's inability to see what a worm the Wolf was. Her mind was as quick and sharp as her blade hand, yet she not only tolerated, but encouraged the man's fawning behavior.

The horses back in line and at the ready, the king held the flag high, and then slashed it down.

Aleksi gave Zolotoy a quick squeeze with his knees and hugged the stallion's barrel sides as the horse surged forward. He leaned over the stallion's bunching withers as they thundered past the other horses, glancing behind them to see the bulk of the racers dropping further behind. That morning, they had all been given the opportunity to walk the course with their mounts, which ran in a looping circle from the palace gates down into the city and along the waterfront and back up to the palace gates where the starting line became the finish line. The city's wide, main road had been cleared and laid every hundred paces or so with jumps of varying heights that the riders were required to take, and spotters were set at each jump to disqualify those who thought to cheat. Aleksi grinned. Zolotoy hated to lose a race almost as much as Aleksi did, and needed no tricks or crops to overtake any horse running ahead of him, which, as they neared the city, was only one long-legged blood bay mare whose rider's shapely seat Aleksi would recognize anywhere.

They turned into the city to the roar of the crowd watching along the roadside, and Aleksi glanced back over his shoulder and growled low in his throat. Yago's black charger was no more than four strides behind them. Zolotoy picked up speed as the road straightened out along the waterfront, eager to close the three strides between them and Lasair, and Aleksi gave Zolotoy his full head. They closed the distance to two strides. The first jump was coming up, and Aleksi slowed Zolotoy's breakneck speed and crouched higher and tighter in preparation for the jump of stacked logs. Lasair sailed over the jump without even breaking stride, and Zolotoy followed, though the big horse did not land as smoothly as Lasair had, and they lost the stride they had gained on the straightaway.

And so it went, Aleksi and Zolotoy nipping at Lasair's hooves along the straightaways and falling behind again each jump. When they made the road leading back up to the palace, Zolotoy was only two strides behind Lasair, and Tor was only two to three strides behind Zolotoy. Aleksi urged Zolotoy on, but Lasair held on to her slim lead. The mare truly could fly, and Sahar was as good and fearless a rider as Aleksi had ever seen. He swerved to miss a rock in the road and heard Yago's muttered curses behind him. Gritting his teeth, he willed his strength into Zolotoy and felt the horse's burst of energy, but it was too little too late. Sahar and Lasair won the race by a head, and Yago and Tor finished third by a stride.

The crowd erupted into cheers as they slowed their horses down to a cooling trot and the other racers trickled in. Sahar walked Lasair to where her father, the king, held the winning purse of three gold pieces, her face split in two with a grin for which Aleksi felt no rancor. The king handed Sahar her winnings with a grin to match his daughter's as chants of "Princess, princess" and "Lasair, Lasair" filled the air.

Next the king motioned to Aleksi and Zolotoy, and handed Aleksi a purse containing two gold pieces. "A well-run race, Aleksandr," he said. "And a close one."

Aleksi glanced at Sahar and Lasair, both rider and horse aglow with the fine sheen of victory and exertion. "Thank you, King Asad," he said. "It was a race well run, and our second place hard earned."

The king nodded, his face suffused with paternal pride. Sahar beamed at them, her smile doing much to assuage Aleksi's disappointment.

Yago the Wolf drew Tor up in front of the king and held his hand out with a scowl on his face. The king handed him the purse of one gold piece with a terse, "Congratulations," to which Yago answered with a wordless dip of his head.

Leaving the princess to enjoy her victory, Aleksi rode Zolotoy back to the stables, where he rubbed the stallion down, with Kiska supervising from her perch atop an overturned bucket. A chorus of congratulations announced Sahar's and Lasair's return to the stables, and Aleksi offered his as they passed Zolotoy's stall.

"Congratulations," he said as she handed Lasair over to a chuckling Ratter. He stepped out of Zolotoy's stall and Kiska jumped down from her bucket and yowled at him. Picking up the kitten, he tucked her into his hold. "Kiska too says well done."

Sahar reached out and scratched the kitten under the chin. "Tell Kiska thank you for the congratulations, and for not biting my finger."

Aleksi chuckled. "We are both of us working on our manners," he said. "Truly, you and Lasair ran a good race today. You beat every last man."

She smiled, and suddenly Aleksi did not mind losing all that much. Besides, he was still two gold pieces richer than he had been. He reached out and pushed a loose strand of her hair behind her ear. "While I admit I generally do not like getting beaten," he said with a knot in his throat, "somehow I do not mind so much getting beaten by you."

"Well that much was obvious," a sneering voice said from behind them.

Aleksi turned and faced Yago. "What do you mean by that?"

Yago flicked his gaze from Aleksi to Sahar with a condescending smirk. "You should thank this Steppe bastard for your, victory," he said. "He was more interested in stopping me from winning than he was in beating you."

Sahar eyed Aleksi. "Is this true?"

"No," Aleksi snorted. "You know it is not." He glared at Yago. "Why would you say such a thing?"

Yago smiled, slowly, smugly. "Why did you swerve your horse in front of mine, blocking me from making my break for the finish line?"

Aleksi laughed, short and harsh. "I swerved to avoid a rock, you sniveling worm. You know you had no chance of overtaking either of us. Admit it and accept your defeat."

"Like you have?" Yago said. "You are little more than a whipped cur after a bitch in heat—"

Aleksi swung without thinking, fast, hard and sure, the smacking, sucking sound of his fist landing square on Yago's cheek giving him some small satisfaction, the sight of him slumping to the ground even more. Kiska and Sahar screeched in unison, and Kiska leapt from his arm as Sahar dropped to her knees and felt Yago's neck for his pulse.

"Yago was right," she hissed. "Your manners are those of a street cur."

"You're defending him?" Aleksi bellowed. "After he insulted you?"

"It was you he insulted."

Aleksi raked a hand through his hair. Did she not hear what the worm said? Or was she as deaf as she was blind to the man's faults? He glowered at her as she cradled Yago's head in her lap.

"Don't stand there admiring your handiwork," she said. "Help me bring him to."

"You are the most maddening woman I have ever had the misfortune of meeting," he grumbled as he stomped into Zolotoy's stall and grabbed the bucket of water. He stood over them, debating with himself over whether he should pour the entire bucket over the both of them or hand her a dipping cloth when Ratter started cackling from Lasair's stall.

"Like father like son," he said. "They's both of 'em got jaws brittle as dry kindle, they do." He rubbed the side of his nose. "Now if I only had a fresh pile o' manure."

"Quit your jawing, Ratter," Sahar commanded. "Help me get him up."

Before Ratter could even open the stall gate, Aleksi emptied the bucket over her head, grinning as her curses mingled with the sputtering Yago's.

Sahar took her seat of honor in the middle of the long table as Aleksandr took his seat to her right and Yago to her left. The other riders were able to sit where they chose, with seven of the riders choosing to sit on Yago's side of the table and the other ten and two, including Munir, sitting on Aleksandr's. Sahar eyed her empty seat beside her mother at the royal family's table with a mixture of pride and regret, for though she was proud of her victor's seat, she would have much preferred to be amongst her loving family than between two men who could not look at each other without baring their teeth and fisting their hands.

"So, Prince Yago," Feroz, the merchant's son said loudly. "What happened to your face?"

Yago sneered, though whether it was intentional or a one-sided grimace due to the swollen mass of bruising that was his left cheek, Sahar could not tell. "I had an argument with a spilled bucket of water," he said.

"And lost," Aleksandr added to raucous laughter. "For the second time today."

Sahar glared at Aleksandr before giving Yago a quick grin of sympathy. She and Ratter had not been the only witnesses to what had happened in the stables, and she was sure every person at the table, if not the palace, knew the story by now, which Yago had to be aware of as well. He did not return her grin, but turned away, the good side of his face impassive. She didn't blame him. His pride had taken a beating today.

But then so had hers.

Yago's accusation that Aleksandr had thrown the race in order to assure her the win had left her, and likely everyone else, doubting her victory. She was not insensitive to the fact that in denying it, Aleksandr had stood up for her, but she could not find it in herself to be grateful for his reaction, which was more likely due to Yago calling him a whipped cur. The man really was an ill-mannered ass, who rode like the wind and whose kiss still gave her fever dreams.

"And now a toast."

At the sound of her father's voice, Sahar yanked her gaze from Aleksandr's mouth, flushing a little as the corners of his full lips twitched up.

"To Princess Sahar," her father said, standing and raising his goblet, "and her mare, Lasair, victors of the one league race."

Sahar flushed even more as cheers of "To the princess and Lasair" filled the courtyard. She stood and raised her golden goblet to her father and then to the rest of the gathering and took a long draught of wine, feeling the warmth spread from her belly to her shaking legs. Fortified with liquid courage, she cleared her throat and held her half-empty cup up.

"To my father and mother," she said, relieved that her voice did not crack. "Who raised me to always do my best. To Storm Chaser and Cloud Dancer, who bred the love of racing into their daughter, Lasair, the last and fleetest of their offspring."

She finished the last of her wine to more cheers and whistles and sat down, grateful to be done with the required toast, and that her backside found her seat the first try. She wiped a fine sheen of sweat from her nose and forehead as a servant quickly filled her goblet and the king held his up again.

"To Aleksandr and Zolotoy," he said. "Who ran a good race and placed a close second."

Aleksandr stood, grinning broadly as he held his silver goblet up to the king. "To King Asad and Queen Oona, for hosting these events." He held his goblet up to the gathering. "To my father, King Maksimillian, for gifting me with my stallion, Zolotoy, the fastest and strongest of a long line of Steppe horses." He turned and held his cup up to Sahar. "To the victor, Princess Sahar, who made my second-place finish truly hard earned." He grinned as she dipped her head in acknowledgement and he dipped his in return. That damned shock of boyish hair fell over his forehead. "Who I plan to beat soundly the next race."

Laughter mixed with applause as he took his seat and she grinned at him despite herself. He was a natural showman. He had spoken with a strong, sure voice, winning the crowd over with his easy charm and wit, and all without raising so much as a single bead of sweat on his handsome face, whereas she could dance and fight and ride in front of thousands without hesitation, but speaking in public made her go clammy from head to toes.

When the laughter and ribbing died down, the king held his cup up to Yago. "To the Wolf," he said in a voice as formal as his use of the Wolf's name. "Congratulations on placing third."

Yago stood stiffly to polite clapping. He held his goblet of copper up to the king with a slight dip of his head and then to the gathering, the unbruised side of his face a mask of princely propriety. "To my father, King Ox, and my mother, Princess Fox," he said, "who taught me to persevere." He turned to Sahar, and the thin smile on his face did not reach his black eyes. "And to Princess Sahar on a well-run race."

He resumed his seat as stiffly as he had stood while those riders on his side of the table clapped a little too loudly and grumbled under their breath about cheaters and tainted victories. Instinctively, Sahar leaned away from Yago's icy bitterness and toward Aleksandr's earthy warmth.

"Princess?" Aleksandr said. "Is there something I can do for you?"

"No, I..." Sahar shook her head and clamped her jaw tight. He was laughing at her, the cocky bastard.

"What is it?" he continued. "Have you figured out that your prince is a whiney worm not worthy of you?"

"How dare you," she hissed.

"How dare I what?" Aleksandr said in a low whisper. "How dare I tell a princess the truth?"

"Why you—"

"Princess Sahar?"

She glanced up at the maid servant holding a platter of cheeses and fruits, the first of what was likely to be a long seven courses.

"Thank you, Ursula," she said. "You may start serving." She rounded back on Aleksandr. "You," she growled, "can go to your ancestors in a shroud of dung."

He laughed before leaning in close, too close. "There's my tigress," he said in a low, intimate tone that brought the heat of his too-familiar gesture to her cheeks and made her itch to claw his.

"Do not speak to me again," she said.

"For the remainder of the meal or for all eternity?"

"Whichever lasts longer."

The next day, two of the riders dropped out of the remaining races due to their horses' injuries, which left ten and nine men and one woman following Brawn, the captain of the king's guard. A swarthy desert man, he wore two blades on his belt and two short swords strapped to his back. Brawn, who looked familiar, led them over the three-league course for the next race three days hence. As victor and placers in the first race, Sahar, Aleksi, and Yago rode alongside the captain, with the rest of the field spread out behind them in no particular order.

The course started at the palace gate and followed the trade road along the river's southern banks, crossing the river at its widest, shallowest point a league east of the city. All Aleksi had to do was turn Zolotoy's head toward the river and the stallion splashed into the water while other riders had to circle several times before their horses jumped in. Lasair hesitated at the shoreline and Brawn drew his roan gelding up beside her, talking quietly to Sahar until she urged Lasair into the water. He kept his horse shoulder to shoulder on the downriver side of Lasair, who didn't act at all skittish as they waded across the swift moving waters while Sahar kept her gaze steadfastly on the approaching shore.

Once across and back on dry land, she exhaled slowly and gave Brawn a shaky grin before he circled around, waiting for the last of the riders to cross. Curious, Aleksi nudged Zolotoy closer to Lasair and cocked his head at the fine sheen of sweat across Sahar's cheeks and the whiteness of her knuckles.

"What?" she snapped at him.

Aleksi shook his head and said nothing, and then chuckled low as she chuffed at him. "You told me not to speak to you again," he said. "I am obeying your command."

"You are insufferable," she hissed, and urged Lasair into a trot.

Aleksi held Zolotoy back, admiring the view of Sahar's well-formed seat as the mare trotted ahead. Yago, his swollen left cheek a satisfying shade of purple, cantered Tor to catch up with Sahar, who took Lasair firmly in rein as the mare tossed her head and gave the black stallion a wary eye and sidled away. The mare had enough sense to keep the Wolf and his stallion at a distance even if the princess didn't.

The group rode south and east across the lush river delta at a slow gallop for another league and then turned north to a wooded foothill. They climbed the narrow path two horses abreast and then the path widened as they rode across the hill's flat top for a good league, affording them a scenic view of the verdant valley and seaside city below.

"So, Brawn," the man called Jibalde the Jackal called out, so named after his grandfather, the king who, legend had it, had gifted Sahar's mother to Asad's father. "How many times has the princess ridden this same course?"

"None," Brawn said over his shoulder. "This course was set yesterday."

"But the princess must know this area well," the Jackal said. "I am sure she has ridden over it many times." He smirked at Sahar as Brawn pulled his horse up with a scowl. "It stands to reason," he continued, "since no one knew she would enter the races, no one would suspect her of preparing for such."

"Are you accusing the princess of cheating even before the race is run?" Brawn asked, fingering the hilt of one of his waist blades. Aleksi remembered where he had seen the man before. It was the first time he and Sahar had met, when he had thought her and Halah unaccompanied. He had noticed Brawn's scarred face and multiple blades as the man gave him the once-over after Sahar had walked away.

"No, no, of course not," the Jackal backtracked. He glanced at Taweel the Tall, his cousin and a prince in his own right, who nodded his encouragement. "I am suggesting that she has an advantage over the rest of us, living here, knowing the area."

"I live here too," Munir said. "As do Feroz and Darius." He pointed to the merchant's son and another of the king's guard. "Why are you not questioning our advantage as well?"

"Because," Aleksi threw in, "none of you won the race yesterday. A race honestly won by Princess Sahar without any help or interference from me, anyone or anything else. Anybody who suggests otherwise," he said with a scowl at the Jackal and the Wolf, "I will break their face. Again."

He glanced at Sahar, who sat erect and still as a statue, her eyes glinting like green shards of glass with golden flares.

"I do not need you or anyone else defending me," she said, her voice as brittle as her crystalline glare. "I can take care of myself."

"Of course you can," Yago said smoothly. "The bastard is attempting to win you over, to claim both you and your lovely mare."

Aleksi snorted. "I'm no fool, Prince Worm. I know a bastard has no claim to a princess."

"In any other royal family perhaps," the Jackal said. "But remember, her father married a slave."

Sahar drew a sharp breath in and her eyes blazed. "Who I marry, if I marry, is my concern, and my concern only." She razed the entire field of men with her fiery glare. "I do not need, nor at this point do I want, a husband."

Aleksi grinned, reveling in the fierceness of her gaze, remembering the soft, surrendering heat of her kiss. "What about a man?" he whispered hotly as he rode past her.

"Princess Sahar." Yago caught her elbow as she left the dining salon after supper. "If I may, I would ask you to walk with me in the palace gardens."

"Now?"

Between the three-league ride and the constant pressure of the other riders' scrutiny, the day had been long and tiring. Sahar had been looking forward to a hot bath and her soft bed.

"If now is inconvenient for you," he said, letting go his hold of her arm with a slight bow, "then I will gladly wait until a time of your choosing."

She started to say that perhaps another time would be better, when she saw Aleksandr scowling at them from the salon's doorway. "Now would be fine," she said instead, placing her hand on Yago's proffered forearm and giving Aleksandr her back, missing neither his deepening scowl nor the Wolf's smug grin.

They walked hand in arm down the hall and out into the garden, garnering curious glances along the way, glances that would soon enough turn to conjecture and gossip. Sahar sighed, for it was the way of life in a palace, whether one was a servant or a royal. She peeked sideways at Yago's patrician profile and wondered what life had been like for him growing up in his father's palace, a man her father had hated for over twenty years, and who had tried to kill her mother. Twice.

She let go of Yago's arm and took a seat on the bench by the lily pond.

"Is there something you wish to speak with me about privately?" she asked as he sat beside her.

He laid his hand over hers. His palm and fingertips were smooth and his skin cool, unlike Aleksandr's larger, calloused hands, which brought heat to her skin merely thinking about them. Mistaking her sudden flush, Yago twined his fingers through hers. She waited to feel the heat spread through her as it had when Aleksandr touched her, but all she felt was awkward. Slowly, she pulled her hand from underneath his and folded it in her lap with her other hand, giving Yago her best impression of an ingenuous smile.

He stood and faced her, his smile preening as he clasped his slender hands behind his back. "I know our family histories should make us enemies," he said, "but I cannot feel anything but awe and admiration for you, my lovely Sahar."

"I, ah, thank you."

"I am sorry that my words regarding your victory yesterday were twisted to make you think I was insulting you, or that I was casting doubt as to the veracity of your win. In truth, I was only challenging that Steppe bastard over his dirty tricks, for once he realized that neither of us were going to beat you, he only sought to ensure that I would not beat him."

"But you told me I had him to thank for my victory," she said. She remembered his exact words since they made her doubt her victory. Despite her angry denial to Aleksandr, they had made her doubt herself.

Yago splayed his hands, palms out. "A poor choice of words, spoken in the heat of the moment by a competitive man." He sat down beside her once more. "Will you forgive me them? If you do not, I shall throw myself into the river and drown my sorrow."

She went rigid.

"Oh, oh no." Yago sat back, a stricken look on his face. "I have done it again. I have caused you pain when I have only meant to assure you of my heartfelt affections." He placed a hand over hers and patted it. "I am sorry to have reminded you of your cousin and his tragic death."

She pulled her hand out from under his. "Do not worry yourself over it."

"From what I understand, it was not your fault. You were only a young girl. You couldn't've possibly been expected to save him."

She stood. "So everyone tells me," she said. She smiled stiffly. "Rest assured, Prince Yago, you are forgiven for your earlier statement. I do not consider you my enemy. Now, if you will excuse me, it's been a long day, and tomorrow promises to be the same."

CHAPTER 5

Accusations

Brawn led the ride over the course as he had done the day before. Also, like the day before, Sahar kept close to Brawn and ignored Aleksi. But, unlike the day before, the Wolf and the Jackal kept their comments to themselves, though not their slanting side glances, which were trained on Sahar. Aleksi told himself over and over again that the princess was not his problem, and he did not care who ogled and leered at her, or who she went strolling with through the gardens. If she insisted she could take care of herself, then by the gods, he would let her, the ungrateful chit.

After another sumptuous supper, he stopped by the kitchens to beg another sack of food from Anya for Serge and Pyotr. Taking the seat proffered him at the small table in the corner, he stretched his legs out with a contented sigh as the kitchen maids scurried about, sorting what little had not been consumed during the evening meal and starting preparations for the next morning's. It was impressive how efficiently the kitchen ran under Anya's stern but fair hand, for it was no small feat feeding all of the riders and the hundred or so visitors and royal household two meals a day, as well as keeping a good stock of food and drink available for the noon repast for those so inclined.

"Thank you, Anya," Aleksi said as she placed a sack of leftovers on the table for him. "Serge and Pyotr wish me to tell you how grateful they are for the extra food. They want to be sure you will not be in any trouble for it."

"None at all," she assured him. "The queen has always shared the palace's bounty." She nodded at two kitchen maids packing sacks with scraps of meat and uneaten loaves of flatbread. "We set our daily leftovers out every evening at the palace gates for whoever needs them."

"Why am I not surprised?" Aleksi shook his head. "Queen Theodesia would never support, much less allow, such a thing. She claimed it was the poor's duty to pull themselves up, not royalty's duty to give them a hand up."

Anya tsked. "That sounds like her."

"As you said, she was a right bitch." He chuckled low, for Anya had summed up his father's first wife quite well. He met Anya's kind gaze, so unlike Theodesia, who had never looked on him with anything but hate and derision. "It was she who demanded my mother leave."

Anya laid a hand on his shoulder and gave it a gentle squeeze. "Since you have come," she said, "I have remembered a little of your mother."

"You have?"

She sat down at the table, her soft gaze holding his. "I remember that she liked to sing as she cooked, that she always had a kitchen cat at her feet, and that she prayed to the gods you would be born a girl so that she would not have to give you over to the king."

"Why did she not leave before I was born?"

It was a question Aleksi had asked himself a thousand times, but one he had never asked of another. Maybe it was because of Anya's kind eyes, or the fact that she was the only person who had known his mother and was willing to speak of her to him. His father never had, and all the queen had ever said of her was that she had been a harlot who had enticed the king into her bed.

Anya spread her hands flat on the table. "As I remember it, your mother was alone in the world, having no family to go to, and there was no one in the palace allowed to help her. As a young, pregnant woman on her own, she had little chance of giving you the life you deserved."

"The life of a stable boy?"

"The king promised her you would be raised a prince."

"A promise he kept only until he had a legitimate heir."

Anya nodded sadly, and then she smiled. "But look at the man you have become," she said. "A fine, strapping young man with loyal friends and a string of his own horses."

"Who will return to his home having won the next two races, with enough coin to build his own stables and the breeding rights to improve his line of horses 'til they rival even the legendary Black Mane's."

"And what of a wife and children to share this dream with?" Anya teased.

Aleksi made a show of taking in the maid servants bustling about. "Is there an especially pleasing, easy tempered, hard-working maid servant you care to recommend?"

Anya laughed. "I am no matchmaker. Besides, I would have sworn you already had your eye on a certain princess."

"I am done with princesses," Aleksi scoffed. "Spoilt, selfish creatures, every last one of them who care not what a man truly is, only that he be a prince."

"Be careful of your words, Aleksandr, for you and I both know that is not true and speaks somewhat of soured hopes."

Aleksi shrugged.

"However," Anya lowered her voice, "the palace gossip says that Yago the Wolf has not only been keeping company with Princess Sahar, but with your half-sister, Princess Anastasia, as well. I would be careful if I were you."

"Don't worry about me," he said, making light of the matter, though Anastasia was easily as vindictive as her mother, Queen Theodesia. "I sleep with one eye open."

"Princess Sahar says you sleep with Kiska tucked under your chin."

"Does she now?" Aleksi spied Sahar hovering at the door to the kitchens.

He grinned and winked at a pretty serving maid who had been trying to catch his attention since he sat down with Anya. The maid's plump cheeks reddened as her high-pitched giggle filled the kitchen. Sahar's glare could have frozen ice as she stiffened and spun on her heels, giving him her back yet again, a not altogether unwelcome view.

"Easy Lasair, easy." Sahar patted the mare's arched neck. "We'll be off and running soon enough."

The riders were lined up and waiting for the signal to start the race, the horses dancing and shaking their heads against their tight reins, eager to be given their heads. Yesterday had been a day of rest for both the horses and their riders in preparation for today, though for Sahar it had been a day of poor rest and a restless night.

After breaking her fast and tending to Lasair, she had spent the better part of yesterday morning pacing her bed chambers trying to contain her thoughts and put them to some kind of order. She should have been concentrating on the race's course, but her mind kept wandering to Aleksandr and Yago, to all of the words spoken between herself and them, from Aleksandr's bold marriage proposal and his heated kiss to Yago's cool, dry lips on her hand after his apology, which had only served to revive the awful memory of Ommar.

She wanted to believe Yago sincere almost as much as she wanted to believe Aleksandr a brutish oaf who had kissed her with as little forethought as he had knocked out Yago. But try as she might, she couldn't rid herself of a niggling feeling in her gut that told her there was more to both of them than either was letting on. It angered her to no end that they had taken over her thoughts. She had meant what she said about neither wanting nor needing a husband, or a man.

Unable to rest in the confines of her bedchambers, she had strolled through the palace garden and then returned to the stables, where she had brushed Lasair 'til the mare's coat shone like polished rubies, then she combed and braided Lasair's mane in an intricate pattern laced with gardenia buds and flowers in full, fragrant bloom. After, she'd lain down on Ratter's cot and had fallen asleep only to wake with Kiska snuggled under her chin, and the sun setting. She'd a vague memory of warm lips on her forehead and a low, deep voice whispering soothing endearments into her ear. When she returned Kiska to her box, Aleksandr wasn't there.

Now, she glanced down the line at Aleksandr, his corded forearm holding his dancing stallion's reins close, his sun-bleached hair falling over his forehead as he leaned into the horse's neck and whispered into the golden stallion's ear, which twitched back and forth as the steed snorted and pawed at the ground. He turned his head and caught her watching him and gave her that cocksure grin that made her grind her teeth and her belly flop like a fish caught on dry land.

On the far side of the line, Yago yanked on Tor's reins as the black stallion reared and struck out at the horse beside him.

"Control your mounts," Brawn called out loudly. Yago brought Tor to earth, and then pulled a riding whip from the side of his saddle.

Her father, whose own father had been renowned for the cruelness of his whip hand, glowered at the whip in Yago's, and then he raised his banner and held it high for a long, interminable moment before swinging it down with a great swoosh. Sahar gave Lasair a quick squeeze of her knees and the mare leapt forward.

Though tall and leggy and deep chested, Lasair was not as large as most stallions, but she was faster, especially for the first ten paces when speed mattered more than power. She was a good three paces ahead of the others and holding her lead as first Zolotoy, then Tor, and then Munir's sorrel gelding, Kedar, charged out from the cloud of dust that was the mob of horses and riders behind them.

Sahar kept Lasair to an easy gallop, staying ahead of the crowd as they raced past a field of drying sunflowers. She knew her mare, and she knew Lasair could keep the same pace for the entire three leagues, the only thing she did not know was how hard and fast a pace the others could keep up. She would soon find out.

They approached the river crossing and Sahar slowed Lasair to a trot, eyeing the swift moving water with trepidation. She had crossed it without incident in the two practice runs, but she had had Brawn by her side then. Now...

"Hold on."

She heard Aleksandr's warning at the same time she heard the slap on Lasair's rump and the mare jumped forward into the river. She hugged Lasair's sides tight and gripped her mane as they splashed into water that instantly rose up to the mare's belly. When she could take a full breath again, she realized that Aleksandr was keeping Zolotoy at Lasair's downriver side at her pace. The cursed stallion could swim almost as well as he ran and could easily have taken the lead.

"Nice day for a swim." Aleksandr was grinning from ear to ear.

"If you like swimming," Sahar grit out, her teeth as clenched as her fists.

"What is there to not like about a swim in a cool, refreshing river on a hot, autumn day?"

"Soggy boots and chafed thighs."

Aleksandr's laugh turned into a scowl, and she followed his glare over her shoulder to see Yago and the Jackal making headway and passing them. She fully expected Aleksandr to leave her and surge ahead, but he stayed by her side, teasing her about how poorly tigresses swam until they reached the far shore.

Once on dry land again, Lasair and Zolotoy shook the river water off their sodden coats while Sahar unclenched her fists and took in several deep, calming breaths. She turned to Aleksandr, nodding her unspoken thanks, and he grabbed her by the tunic and pulled her to him, giving her a smacking kiss on the lips.

"You're welcome," he called out over his shoulder as he sent Zolotoy into a gallop.

Sahar had fallen five riders behind, but soon overtook the fifth and then the fourth as she and Lasair climbed their way up the hillside. Once on the flat hilltop, there were three riders to catch up to: Aleksandr, the Jackal, and Yago. Munir and four others were coming up over the hill's crest behind her. Sahar kept Lasair at a steady pace, maintaining her position between the two clusters of riders and giving the mare a bit of a breather.

Aleksandr made his move before the downhill run, his golden stallion passing the Jackal's roan in a burst of strength and speed that Sahar took advantage of, urging Lasair into a full gallop and edging past the Jackal, who had resorted to using his riding whip on his poor mount. Glancing back over her shoulder, she saw Munir and Feroz overtake the Jackal, who had pushed his horse too hard too soon.

Sahar's legs gripped Lasair's sides as they started downhill. The path was rocky and overgrown with thick brush on either side, leaving only enough space for two horses abreast in the widest, clearest sections and a single horse in others. Lighter and fleeter-footed than Zolotoy and Tor, Lasair soon closed the distance between them, but she could see no way to get past either of them without injury, so she held Lasair back. They were only halfway into the race and she would have plenty of time to take the lead once they made it to the wider path through the river delta.

The verdant delta was no more than fifty paces ahead of them when behind her there came loud shouting and cursing amid a cloud of dust that could only mean that a rider and his horse, or several, had taken a fall, and she gave a silent prayer of thanks to the gods as Lasair's hooves hit flat ground. She glanced back to see Munir and Feroz still riding, and gave Lasair her head.

Twenty paces ahead, Zolotoy and Tor were racing neck and neck, their powerful haunches bunching and springing, their hooves churning up earth and sending clods flying. She hunched up higher on her saddle and leaned closer to Lasair's withers, hoping to take advantage of Aleksandr's and Yago's preoccupation with each other to edge past them. She'd closed the gap to ten paces when Yago's arm shot out and the sound of a whip cracked through the air. Aleksandr swerved to the side so suddenly that he almost fell out of his saddle and then righted himself with a curse. Yago's arm flicked out again and she heard the snap and saw the snaking tip of the whip strike Zolotoy's flank.

"You spineless worm," Aleksandr yelled. "You whip my horse again and I will kill you, the race be damned."

Yago sneered and plied the whip to Tor's rump with three quick smacks as Aleksandr slowed enough to twist in his saddle and run his hand over Zolotoy's flank where the whip had struck. He glared at her as if she had somehow aided or condoned Yago's actions, and then he swung back around and hunkered over Zolotoy's withers, closing the ground they had lost between them and Yago with pure determination.

The crowd of people gathered at the city's edge where the delta path met the road burst into loud cheers as Zolotoy passed Tor, and then cheered again as Sahar and Lasair turned onto the road, followed by Munir and Feroz. They were on the last half league of the race, the last of the flat road before it turned up the hill to the palace gates and the finish line. If she was going to make her move, she needed to make it now.

"Come on, Lasair," she whispered fiercely into the mare's ear. "Come on, girl, show them what you got."

Lasair responded with a surge of speed and Sahar kept up her whispering as they gained ground on Yago and Tor. They pulled up even with them and she was glad of the crowds. Without them, Yago might've used his whip on Lasair as he had Zolotoy, as he now used it on Tor, who had nothing left to give by his labored breathing and the sweat lathering on his black coat. With a disgusted shake of her head, she rode past them and concentrated on Aleksandr and Zolotoy, who were still running hard and steady a good ten paces ahead. She glanced back and saw that Munir had now passed Yago, but was still five paces behind Lasair, whose breaths were growing shorter along with her gait as they started up the hill to the palace.

"Come on, Lasair," she urged, willing her breath into the mare's straining lungs, her strength into Lasair's tired legs. "We can do this."

We can do this, we can do this, we can do this. The thought pounded through her head with the beat of Lasair's hooves, but though the mare gave it her all, it was not enough to overtake Zolotoy. The golden stallion crossed the finish line to wild cheers six strides ahead of Lasair.

Aleksi's belly filled with the sumptuous feast held in the palace courtyard, he leaned forward in his victor's seat and inhaled the sweet and instantly familiar fragrance of the exotic white flowers floating in a bowl of water on the table.

He turned to Sahar, who sat at his right side, nursing the wine in her silver goblet. "What are these flowers called?" he asked.

"Gardenias."

"It is the oil of these petals that you wear on your skin."

It was more statement than question, and he answered with a dip of her head and a flush to her cheeks. She lifted her mass of curls from her neck as if she'd suddenly become heated, which Aleksi did immediately from the intoxicating scent of gardenia and warm skin assailing him. He half lowered his head with the sudden urge to nuzzle the soft underside of her jaw and then jerked his head back as cups clanked on the table to a boisterous chorus of "Speech, speech."

He stood on unsteady legs and raised his golden victor's cup high. "To King Asad and Queen Oona," he said, grateful that his voice did not waver. "I thank you once again for your hospitality and for the generous victor's purse now hanging from my waist belt." He jangled his leather purse, heavy with the thirty pieces of gold added to the two from the previous race as the gathering laughed and clapped. "To Princess Sahar," he said, "and her mare, Lasair. They both ran a good, close race once again." He lifted his cup to Sahar, and her smile lit up her face and his. He gave her a purposely cocky grin. "I intend to beat them two out of three races."

"You will try," she said, lifting her cup of silver to him and taking a drink, her green eyes glinting with the challenge.

Chuckling, Aleksi turned to Munir at his left. "To Munir, stalwart king's guard and newly betrothed to the lovely Halah, and my new friend, congratulations on a race well run."

Munir held his copper cup up to Aleksi and took a good, honest draught.

"Goes to prove the advantage of a home course," a voice said loudly over the huzzahs.

The voice and accusation were familiar. Aleksi had heard them two days before on the practice run, and he did not like it any better now than he had then. He looked down the long table of riders, past the Wolf's sneering face to the Jackal's.

"What it proves," Aleksi said, "is the relationship between a horse and its rider, which is why you, Jackal, and you, Wolf, lost the moment you used your whips."

Aleksi sat down and looked to the king, for he had not intended to insult him or his hospitality in any way, but neither was he going to stand there and let Sahar and Munir be slandered. The king, rather than insulted by Aleksi's response, was glaring at the Wolf and the Jackal.

"What it proves," a feminine voice shrilled out over the grassfire of whispers sweeping across the courtyard, "is that breeding will show every time."

"How so, sister?" Aleksi said.

Anastasia pushed one of the jeweled combs holding her blonde coif deeper into her hair, her ring-laden fingers sparkling in the torch light. "Your horse, Zolotoy, was a gift from our father, King Maksimillian, bred from the royal stable's bloodline. Anyone could have ridden him and won."

Sahar stood in one sinuous movement, impaling Anastasia with her glare. "I did not see you out there riding your horse, Princess

Anastasia," she said. "Though they are presumably from the same royal stables."

Anastasia sniffed and pushed at another of her combs. "I was bred and raised to be a lady, not only a princess," she said. "Certainly not to act like a man."

"What do you mean by that?" Sahar demanded.

"That by your own words, you have no need of a husband, no need of a man." Anastasia pouted prettily, drawing attention to her thin, red-stained lips. "What true woman has no need of a man?"

Sahar stiffened, her full, lush lips pressed tight at the not-so-subtle insinuation. Aleksi rose instantly to stand beside her.

"Princess Sahar is more of a woman than you will ever be, sister," he said.

"How would you know, my father's bastard?"

"I know because I have kissed her." Beside him, Sahar sucked in her breath. "And she kissed me back."

The grassfire of whispers burst into flames of gasps and conjectures that died to a low sizzle as the queen stood and slowly turned her level gaze on Anastasia.

"If I were you, Princess Anastasia," she said, her voice as frosty as her glare, "I would remember whose hospitality you are here enjoying, and learn to use those royal manners I am sure your mother, the queen, has taught you."

Anastasia's jaw dropped open, and then she snapped it shut. She stood and stared down her nose at the entire assemblage before dipping a dainty knee to the queen, and then left the courtyard with a haughty poise learned at her mother's breast. The king stood beside his wife and queen, and taking her hand in the crook of his arm, announced to the gathering that the feast was over. He gave his daughter, who remained stiff and silent as a statue beside Aleksi, a gentle smile of fatherly concern before leading his wife away. Aleksi turned to Sahar as stools were scraped back from the tables and muted mumblings filled the night air.

"Sahar..."

"I did not ask you to defend me," she hissed, her green eyes flashing fire. "I do not need you to defend me. I certainly did not need you announcing to the entire palace that you kissed me."

"What truly angers you," he said with a grin, "is that I announced that you kissed me back."

"Mother?" Sahar knocked softly on the door to her mother's private chambers.

"Come in, my daughter."

Sahar followed her mother through the sitting salon into the queen's bed chamber and plopped down onto the bed, a bed used more often by her children when they had been sick or in need of their mother than by herself. Though few people knew of it, there was a bedchamber that connected the queen's and the king's private chambers, and it was that bed that the king and queen slept in together nightly for both safety and intimacy's sake.

Her mother sat down beside her and waited patiently for her to collect her thoughts and words, as she had done Sahar's entire life.

"You do not care for Yago the Wolf much, do you?"

"No," her mother said without hesitation. "I must admit that I cannot look at him without seeing his parents."

"As does Father."

"You must understand, Sasa, Yago's parents, the Ox and the Fox, they are horrible people. They are stupid and selfish, petty and mean spirited. It is difficult for me and your father to believe that a child bred and born of them, raised by them, could be anything different."

"But what of Father and his father, the Panther?"

"Your father had his mother, Queen Noor. She was as good and kind and reasonable as the Panther was bad tempered and cruel. Your father had his aunties and his brother, Nasim, as well."

"Could not Yago have had someone kind in his life to teach him right from wrong?"

"It is possible," her mother said, though her tone and her expression said otherwise. "Does he treat you kindly and with respect?"

"He has never been unkind to me," she said. "As for treating me with respect," she started to say yes, but he had not treated her with respect when he had claimed that she only won the first race because of Aleksandr's interference, or when he had suggested that it was not her fault Ommar had died, because she was, after all, only a girl. He had been the one to make room for her, the first woman ever to stand in the line of riders, though. Or had he? Ask someone who saw, Aleksandr had told her, who truly saw, and her mother saw everything. "The night of the Autumn's Eve feast," she said, "when I went to stand in the line of riders. Did you see who it was that made a place for me?"

"It was Aleksandr who moved first, shoving his elbow into his neighbor's side to make room for you."

Sahar grimaced.

"As it was Aleksandr who stood up for you tonight and you him."

Sahar shrugged.

"As it is Aleksandr who cannot take his eyes off of you or you him."

Sahar opened her mouth to deny it, but then said nothing.

"As it was Aleksandr who kissed you and who you kissed back, apparently."

Sahar flushed from head to toes.

"You like him," her mother said. "Don't you?"

Sahar bristled. "He is a strutting stallion who thinks women are nothing but broodmares. Who flirts with anything and everything female, from kitchen maids to kittens. He is so cocksure of himself that he kisses me as offhandedly as he punches any man he thinks has insulted me. He thinks I need his protection when I have told him repeatedly that I neither want nor need it. He proposed marriage to me. He calls me his…"

Her mother quirked a finely arched brow.

"Never mind what he calls me," Sahar said.

"I shall," her mother said. "Same as I will not ask you more of this kiss. Though I will ask, he proposed marriage?"

"He did, the first time we met, before he even knew I was a princess." Sahar chuffed. "I meant what I said, what I have been saying for years now. I am fine as I am. I do not need or want a husband. Even if I did, it would not be the likes of him. We cannot speak without arguing. We would kill each other within a moon's passing."

Her mother smiled, as if Sahar's words were amusing.

"You and Father never fight," Sahar said. "You have the perfect marriage. How can you ever understand?"

Her mother laughed. "Oh, my darling daughter." She wrapped an arm around Sahar's shoulder and hugged her close. "Your father and I fight plenty. But we make sure to fight fairly, and never in front of others. That is more because we are king and queen, not Asad and Oona." She kissed Sahar's cheek. "However, you are correct. You have family and wealth enough that you do not need a husband, so promise me, my daughter, if and when you do choose one, choose him because you love him and he loves you, for that is where a marriage like mine and your father's begins. What you do with that love is up to you. You can treasure it and nurture it and help it grow strong and true, or you can neglect it and watch it grow unkempt and thorny as a weed patch, or it can die out altogether."

CHAPTER 6

Betrayals

Sahar led Lasair to the large, grassy paddock where she discovered that Aleksandr had already let Zolotoy loose to graze and laze the afternoon away. It was the day after the second race, a day of rest for horses and riders alike, the day after her talk with her mother and the sleepless night that had followed.

The stallion pricked his ears forward at sight of Lasair, and Aleksandr waved them in. Sahar untied the lead rope from Lasair's bridle and smiled as the mare kicked up her heels and trotted over to Zolotoy. Sahar followed at a slower, more deliberate pace, stopping altogether as she realized that Aleksandr was bare-chested.

She swallowed hard, and resumed her pace, her cheeks flaming.

"Good afternoon," he said, grinning that cursed cocksure grin of his.

She'd seen plenty of bare-chested men. She'd grown up in a palace full of family and servants, and every summer the city and the outlying fields were full of men working without their tunics under the heat of the sun. But this was autumn and she had never seen a man like Aleksandr before. His tawny chest seemed twice as broad and his arms even more thickly corded without the thin veneer of clothing. Then there were the ridges of muscle spanning across his abdomen and narrowing down to his waist belt, which held up a pair of leather riding breeches that hugged the solid length of his thighs. But it was the patch of curly, gold-brown hair in the middle of his chest she couldn't stop staring at.

She watched, mesmerized, as a slight breeze ruffled the hairs, and his nipples, a darker shade of brown, grew tight and taut.

Aleksandr chuckled and lightly scratched the golden patch. "Grass does not grow so well on rock," he said.

Sahar snapped her gaze up from his chest to his laughing eyes, which she had the sudden urge to scratch, and not lightly.

"Is there something in particular you came to say to me?"

"No," she answered, and then recanted. "Well, yes." How did he do that? How did he manage to read her so well? Most people seemed to find her mysterious and incomprehensible. "I, ah, I wanted to thank you for defending me against your half-sister's accusations last night, and for acknowledging me and making a place for me in the line of riders the night of Autumn's Eve."

He said nothing at first, and looked at her with a quizzical half smile. "That was hard for you, wasn't it?"

"You have no idea."

Aleksandr laughed, his laugh deep and rich. "Is it thanking me that's so hard," he asked, "or is it thanking anybody?"

She laughed a little despite herself. "Both," she admitted. "I don't like asking for help, or so I have been told."

"Why is that?"

She tilted her head and met his earnest gaze. No man, other than family, had ever asked her that before, certainly none of the many who had professed their admiration and proceeded to propose marriage. She considered giving him some vague, commonly held belief about her as an answer, but he had asked, and so she was going to tell him.

"Perhaps a lifetime of big, strong men thinking me too frail to hold my head up with my girlish, princess neck, rubs me the wrong way," she said. "Or perhaps it is because I detest those who think me too stupid to complete some inane task without their manly knowledge and guidance."

"I see," Aleksandr said, and he looked neither amused nor insulted.

"Why did you defend me against Anastasia last night?"

"I hate her," he said. "And I like you." He closed the short distance between them, his expression open and warm. "I liked kissing you." He reached out and cupped her face in his big, warm hands. "I think you liked kissing me."

"So, what if I did?"

"So, I'm going to kiss you again."

"It won't change anything," she declared, even as she grasped onto his arms to keep the earth from shifting beneath her. "I still won't marry you."

"I know," he said, his low, rough voice turning her bones to liquid. "I'm not asking you to marry me, and I won't ask again." He held his lips no more than a breath from hers. "Next time it'll be you asking me." He brushed his lips over hers, feather-light and teasing. "Better hurry though, before I find another bride."

She smiled against his lips. "Why would I ever ask you?"

"Because," he whispered as he nipped her lower lip, "this. This heat between us." He nibbled his way along her jawline and suckled her earlobe. "Even you, my hard-headed, hot-blooded tigress," he whispered in her ear. "Even you can't deny this."

She actually growled, low and guttural, and Aleksandr wove his hand through her hair and pulled her head back, exposing her throat, tasting the skin where her pulse pounded. His lips seared a path up her neck, and she gasped as those lips found hers. His mouth covered hers, devouring as she opened to his probing tongue and tasted the salty heat of him. His hands roamed down her back, one settling between her shoulders and the other cupping her backside and pressing her body to his, branding her everywhere they touched. She slid her hand between them and felt his breath catch and his heart hammer beneath her palm. She grinned into his kiss and nipped at his lower lip, her entire body reverberating with his groan as she curled her fingers into the light matting of hair on his chest.

Aleksandr deepened his kiss, holding her so close that her hand was pinned between them. An ache began to grow between her legs, as did something hard that was pressing against her belly.

Her eyes flew open.

"See what you do to me," Aleksandr chuckled hoarsely as she pushed away.

She dipped her head to see the bulge in his breeches, and she swiped at the burning heat sweeping across her cheeks. She pulled her gaze from Aleksandr's arousal to his grinning face, and swung.

Aleksandr caught her hand mid-strike.

"Easy there, tigress," he said, holding her wrist in his vise-like grip. He shook his head and blew his breath out in a strangled laugh. "Surely you cannot blame a man for responding to you. For wanting you."

She wrested her wrist from his loosened grip with an unladylike huff. "I thought you wanted an easy-tempered broodmare for a wife," she said.

"So did I," he responded with a shrug. "I'm beginning to rethink my requirements. What about you?"

"Me?"

"Still think you have no need of a husband, or a man?"

"Need?" She shook her head. "No." But wanting, she was beginning to learn, was something else entirely.

"Beer or wine, my lord?"

Aleksi glanced up into the broad face of a buxom blonde serving girl holding a tray with two pitchers on it.

"I will have beer tonight," he said, holding his cup out as she sat the tray down. "Thank you...?"

"Ursula, my lord."

"Thank you, Ursula," he said as she poured the beer into his cup. "But I am no lord. I am only Aleksandr."

"I do not think you are *only* anything, Aleksandr," she said with a blush and a giggle.

"Why thank you again, Ursula," Aleksi said, glancing over at Sahar, who studiously ignored him. "There are those who would disagree with you."

"Oh, but certainly not Mistress Anya, Aleksandr. She near dotes on you as much as she does her own son."

"Anya is happy to have someone from her homeland to talk to."

"I have worked under cook for five years now, and I never heard her speak of anyone but her own or the king's and queen's family with such praise."

"That is kind of you," he said, outwardly passing off the servant's words of Anya's praise as inconsequential, when in truth they filled a tiny corner of the hole his own father's abandonment had ruptured in his soul with a healing warmth. He eyed the friendly Ursula until her cheeks were as round and pink as grapefruits. "I detect a bit of my homeland in your accent and fair looks as well," he said. "Where are you from?"

"From a village even farther north along the Mother River than your city. My *dedushka i babushka*, my grandparents, moved here with me after my parents were killed."

"I'm sorry."

"It was many years ago," she said. "I was no more than three or four years of age. This is the only home I remember."

"And your grandparents?"

"They are both gone now, but they passed contented with our life here, and were pleased that I have such good work here in the palace kitchens."

"I am sure they were proud of you," Aleksi said.

She dipped a knee, and Aleksi watched the sway of her wide hips as she moved on to another table. Strong of body and easy tempered, she would make a man a fine wife and bear him many sons. So why did he glance over at Sahar, who sat glaring back at him, rather than go after Ursula and ask her to walk with him when she was done with her work for the evening?

Supper over and his appetite sated, Aleksi left the salon through the kitchens, where Anya gave him a small sack of choice bits of meat and cheese for Kiska, and escaped out the door with no more than a quick nod at Ursula, whose open expression and flirty smile told him she would have packed up and followed him back to their home country to tend his house and bear his sons without complaint. All he had to do was ask. He told himself he would keep her in mind, and that he need not be hasty. There were more women in this city to choose from than those in the palace. Besides, his one hasty proposal had gotten him nothing but green eyes blazing fire and a blade in his groin.

Since, there were the constant arguments and a few rare smiles, which had warmed Aleksi with the heat of the sun. And those two kisses. Three, if he counted the quick kiss at the river crossing, which he did.

Aleksi rubbed his chest where Sahar's fingers had played, her touch shooting a bolt of desire directly to his cock. She had been soft and passionate in his arms, until his body's response had scared her, and then his words had angered her, something Aleksi seemed unusually adept at when it came to her.

She had practically run away from him, and she had stayed away the past four days, barely acknowledging him as they passed in the stables or out in the training kraal. He felt her absence. Her smell, her kisses, her lithe body pressed against his. Whenever he considered going down into the city to find the kind of female companionship that would help sate his hunger, the idea tasted as sour to him as Kiska's day-old goat milk.

Maybe he would settle for getting sodding drunk.

"What is the matter with you?" he said as he stopped at the gate to Zolotoy's stall. The stallion was pressed close to the wall farthest from the door to Aleksi's antechamber, pawing at the ground and snorting at the closed door. A mound of straw in a back corner rustled and moved and Kiska poked her head out, ears twitching and meowing at Aleksi. "Why are you out here, Kiska?" he whispered as the kitten burrowed back under the straw.

Slowly opening the gate, Aleksi pulled his waist blade and crept up to the door. He flung it open, blade poised to strike, and stood dumbfounded at the unmistakable figure of a woman sprawled out on his cot.

"Who are you?" Aleksi demanded. "And what are you doing in my bed?"

The woman rose up onto one elbow and ran a seductive hand over the rounded swell of her hip.

"I am Roxanna."

She swung her legs over the side of the cot and stood in one sensuous movement, her gown of sheer worm weave shimmering in the candlelight and clinging to her every curve. She was dark haired, dark eyed, and voluptuous. Her smile was knowing and inviting, her bee-stung lips stained a deep red.

She did not say what she was doing there. She did not need to.

"How did you come to be here?" Aleksi asked. "I did not send for you."

"A friend of yours did."

"Is this friend how you got past the guards?"

"Yes."

"Who is this friend of mine?" he said, stepping the rest of the way into the small antechamber. He stood no more than two feet from her, and could smell the heavy, cloying scent of her perfume.

Roxanna smiled seductively. "I do not know his name, or the name of his servant who sought me out and brought me here."

Whoever it was, they had enough wealth to have a manservant and to pay for an expensive harlot. Roxanna was no tavern wench or street walker. She was clean and well fleshed and had all of her teeth.

"Why would a friend buy your services for me?"

She reached out and lightly raked a long, sharpened nail down his forearm. "I was told it was to honor you for your victory in the last race. I am yours for the night."

Aleksi stepped to the foot of the cot, out of her reach. She was a good-looking woman, though easily over thirty years of age, and her sly eyes, seductive smile, and undulating body all told him she was experienced in the ways of carnal pleasure.

"The thing of it is, Roxanna," he told her, "I have never paid for sex before, and I do not wish to now."

She smiled again, swaying her body from head to toe as she cornered him. "I can easily believe that," she said. "I would gladly pleasure you for free, but I am already paid for, and not by you. So, you see," she purred, rubbing her generous chest against his, "you still will have never paid for sex."

The tactile memory of Sahar's smaller, firmer breasts pressed against his chest, their nipples pebbling as they kissed, came unbidden to him. He clenched his hands, remembering the feel of her taut backside, her sleekly muscled back, and groaned in frustration. Seeming to sense that she was losing his interest, Roxanna pressed closer, moving her pelvis against his surprisingly disinclined cock.

Pushing her away, Aleksi laughed, as much at himself as at the confused expression on the harlot's face. "Do not ask me to explain," he said as he took her by the arm and began to lead her from the cramped little room.

"It is a woman then," she said, grabbing her cloak from the cot. "A woman you wish to be faithful to?"

Aleksi stopped and let her fasten the cloak.

"Is it not?" Roxanna asked again.

"No," Aleksi said. How could a man be faithful to a woman who was not his? Who swore she would never be his, even if her kiss spoke of a heat and passion between them that neither could deny.

"A man then?"

Aleksi laughed. "No, it's definitely not a man."

It was a tigress who had sunk her claws into him, a green-eyed tigress who had glared at him for merely flirting with Ursula. It would not do to have her find him here with Roxanna, though why he should care, he could not say, only that he did.

Taking Roxanna by the hand, he led her from his room and peered over the stall gate. There was nobody about, but that could change in a moment. Opening the gate, he ushered Roxanna out of the stall and caught her amused half smile as she leaned indolently against the wall. He grinned back and latched the gate. He was acting like some lovesick fool, worried that a woman who had refused him would catch him with another. What if she did? She had no claim on him, and had refused his offer of marriage.

He eyed Roxanna, and saw the invitation in her dark, kohled eyes. He reached out and pulled a curled strand of her hair from behind her ear. But her hair was slick with oil and smelled of the same cloying perfume as her body. He itched to run his fingers through thick, wavy tresses that smelled of clean soap and sweet gardenia. Leaning back against the wall, he dropped the curl with an apologetic shrug, and heard voices approaching.

"I am sorry for this," Roxanna said. Dropping to her knees, she yanked his breeches down and shoved her face into his crotch.

"What the—?" Aleksi grabbed her by the hair.

"You rutting bastard!"

Slowly, inexorably, he turned to see Sahar standing no more than ten paces from him. "It is not what you think," Aleksi said, letting go of Roxanna's hair. "I swear to you." Sahar's pointed glare took in the harlot's sheer gown and painted face as Roxanna stood, and then blazed at Aleksi as he quickly pulled his breeches up. Then, not only did Yago the Worm and Taweel the Tall come around the corner, but his cursed half-sister, Anastasia, strolled up between them, followed by Munir and Brawn.

"Oh my," Anastasia trilled. "Is that a woman of ill repute?"

"I would say so," Yago affirmed with a smug leer at Roxanna. Then his leer dropped to Aleksi's groin, where it lingered despite the fact that his breeches were up.

"I am shocked." Anastasia tsked and grabbed Yago's arm as if in need of support, "Shocked, I must say, though not surprised that you would consort with a harlot, Aleksandr."

"Funny," Aleksi said. "You do not look shocked or surprised." He jerked his head at Yago and Taweel. "Nor do either of you." He glanced at Roxanna, who quickly looked away from Yago. "At least now I know who sent her to me." He looked to Sahar, whose blazing eyes had gone white hot. "And why." He stepped forward and reached a hand out to her.

"Do not touch me," she growled and slapped his hand away. "You do not get to touch me ever again."

"You do not mean that," he cajoled, though by the green ice in her glare and the hard set of her jaw, she meant exactly that. After the way she had responded in his arms, to his kisses, after he had refused the willing and able Roxanna's services to keep some mad semblance of faithfulness to her, Sahar would not even listen to what he had to say. "Why am I even trying to explain myself to you?" he said. "You have no claim over me, we are not betrothed, we are not even courting. We are nothing to each other."

We are nothing to each other.

Sahar could still feel the sting of Aleksandr's words as she stormed to the palace. How could he say that to her after he had defended her and she him against others' accusations, after proposing marriage to her, after kissing her? Had their kisses truly meant nothing to him, when she still dreamt of them day and night? He had told her that she could burn him down to scorched earth, and he would rise again for her. She scoffed. Apparently, he only meant until another woman came along, one more practiced in the art of carnal pleasures.

That he had been set up was obvious. Why else would Anastasia have been so adamant that Sahar accompany her to the stables? Anastasia may have claimed it was because Sahar would require another respectable woman to be her escort, completely ignoring the fact that she was in and out of the stables unescorted all the time, but she'd known something was up, and had been glad when Brawn and Munir announced that they would accompany them as well. Then she'd turned the corner and found Aleksi with his back against the wall and that painted harlot on her knees, her face buried in his groin, his hands in her hair.

Sahar may still have been a virgin, but she was no idiot. She knew full well what that whore had been doing. Set up or not, Aleksandr had been letting her, and to make Sahar's humiliation complete, all the others had seen it too. As if that wasn't bad enough, they heard Aleksandr tell Sahar that she was nothing to him.

She'd run out of the stables , not knowing or caring what happened after, though it was a sure bet that the story of the princess happening upon Aleksandr being serviced by a whore would be known far and wide by morning. Brawn and Munir would tell her father, of course, and the three of them would remain circumspect about the whole matter. The others though, Yago and Taweel and Anastasia, they would spread the tale throughout the palace every chance they got. As for the painted harlot, who had been quite pretty actually, Sahar could only guess who and what she would tell.

"Arghh." Sahar gnashed her teeth and fisted her hands so tightly she dug her nails into her palms. Unclenching her fists, she rubbed the tender indents and then glanced up and around. She was standing no more than fifty paces from the entrance to the royal family's private chambers, not where she wanted to be right now. Where she wanted to be was some place she could scream loud and long without being heard, a place where she could rage and rail, and even weep if she wanted to, which she felt ridiculously close to doing now. She paced in a tight circle, trying to figure out such a place she could go to, alone, in the dark of night, when she heard her name being called.

"Sasa. Sasa." Halah was standing in the open doorway, waving Sahar in. "Rima wishes for some female company tonight while Asim is going over the race's course with our fathers. Our mothers are already with her, they sent me to find you."

Sahar stood there for a long moment, unable to think of an excuse for not joining them. The last place she wanted to be was in a room full of happily married and betrothed women whose men adored them and where pregnancy and childbirth would be the topics of conversation.

"What is the matter with you?" Halah asked, closing the door behind them. "What happened in the stables?"

"It was a set up," Sahar said, her voice sounding oddly distant. "Yago, Taweel, Anastasia, they wanted me to go with them so that I would discover Aleksandr in a compromising position with a harlot."

"No."

Sahar nodded numbly. "Oh yes."

"What did Aleksandr do? What did he say when you discovered them?"

"He swore it was not what it seemed." Sahar closed her eyes against the image of the harlot kneeling before Aleksandr and took a shaky breath. "He said he did not know why he was bothering to explain himself to me, that we were nothing to each other."

She stepped away from Halah, refusing to meet her eyes. If she did and saw pity in them, she would surely burst into tears. That she would not do.

"He was lying, Sahar."

"No." Sahar shook her head. "He was set up. I am certain of it."

"I am sure he was too. I am saying that he lied about you two meaning nothing to each other."

Sahar chuffed. "Aleksandr may be arrogant, bold, and beyond cocky," she said, "but above all else he's honest. Brutally at times."

"Perhaps about most things," Halah insisted, "but not about his feelings for you."

"Munir was there, he heard Aleksandr. Ask him."

"Oh, I am sure that's what Aleksandr said, caught with a harlot, by you, in front of all those others."

"Adding to my humiliation."

"And his."

"True enough," Sahar admitted.

The gossip would be as cruel to him as to her, of that she was certain. Still, it was a humiliation they would both survive, yet another distraction to what they both wanted. Sahar wanted to win the coming race, to prove a woman as good and capable as any man, and to show the world that a woman did not need any man. Aleksandr wanted a wife, and not any wife, but an easy-tempered broodmare, something Sahar would never be.

"You are right, Halah," she said. "As was Aleksandr. We may be drawn to each other, but we are nothing more to each other than a passing distraction. When the race is over and done with, he will go back to his home with his winnings and I will stay here with mine."

CHAPTER 7

Wounds

Aleksi slowed Zolotoy to an easy trot for the cool-down lap around the track, pleased with how well the stallion had run. It was the last day of training before the third and longest race, and Zolotoy was well fed, well rested, and well trained for the hundred-league course. Which was more than Aleksi could say for himself.

He was well fed and well trained enough, but he had not gotten much rest the past two nights, not with the memory of Sahar's face blanched white with shock at finding him with Roxanna. When he'd told Sahar that he and she were nothing to each other, her crystalline eyes looked shattered and dulled with his betrayal.

Yago and his pack of Taweel and Anastasia had wasted no time in spreading the story with their own twists and embellishments. By the next morning the palace was abuzz with the tale of how the princess had cried and pleaded with Aleksandr to denounce his favorite whore and come back to her, and how he had rejected her, telling her she was nothing compared to the harlot.

If the tables had been turned and Anastasia had been the princess left publicly humiliated by a man beneath her in station, much less her supposed lover, heads would have rolled, but Sahar had held her spine erect and her head high through it all, refusing to acknowledge the side glances and palm whispering around her. When Aleksi had passed her at the training track yesterday, she had answered his greeting with a stubborn silence, her chin lifted and her eyes glinting green shards of ice.

He had considered eating his supper in the stables last night to avoid any further arguments or fistfights with Yago the Worm, but he had not wanted to abandon Sahar again. Though the meal had been quieter and more subdued than most, everyone had been on their best behavior. Even Yago was not foolish enough to taunt Sahar in front of her father, who at forty and five years of age, still looked more than capable of tearing the Wolf apart limb by limb if incited to do so. By the simmering anger in his golden eyes every time he looked the Wolf's way, it would not have taken much.

Aleksi seemed to have been spared the king's ire, and he figured it was due to Munir and Brawn, who had no doubt informed their king of what they had witnessed in the stables, and of how it differed from the wolf pack's account. If Aleksi could only convince Sahar of their duplicity and his innocence—but first he would have to get her to even acknowledge him.

As he walked Zolotoy out of the training kraal, Sahar rode Lasair in through the gate on the far side and urged the mare into a slow trot to start their training session. Tethering Zolotoy to the fence, Aleksi hitched a foot up on the rail and admired horse and rider as they broke into an easy gallop. It wasn't only that Lasair was a gorgeous animal, or that she ran like the wind, or that Sahar was an excellent rider—one of the best Aleksi had ever seen actually, man or woman—it was the rapport between horse and rider that mesmerized him. How they moved as one, intuitively, instinctually, effortlessly, something few riders were able to attain.

Sahar was not only a good rider, but a good trainer as well. She understood her horse's needs, working the mare hard enough to keep up her endurance, but not so much that she wore her down. Of course, the princess had been raised in a royal household known for its stable of fine horses, and her father was renowned for having won the Great Race of the Seven Tribes four times in a row on his stallion, Storm Chaser. He'd chosen the yearling filly Cloud Dancer as his prize for winning that race. Sahar's mare, Lasair, was the last foal out of the pair and worth her weight in gold in breeding rights.

"Well, Z," he told the stallion as Yago and Taweel arrived for their training session, "you may still have a chance to win the right to breed with that leggy mare, but I would wager all my winnings so far that I have lost my chance with the tigress."

He untied Zolotoy's reins and led him back to the stables.

"At least I still have my Kiska," he said, removing Z's saddle. "Until I leave here to return home, when Ratter will take her in and keep her."

Speaking of, where was Kiska? She hadn't come running out of his antechamber or emerged from a burrow of straw to greet them as she usually did.

"Kiska?" he called. No answer. "Where are you my little Kiska?" She wasn't bundled in the bed linens on his cot, or in his pile of clothing, her two favorite napping spots. "Here, Kiska," he called. "Here, kitty, kitty."

She was nowhere in his chambers, and a knot formed in the pit of his belly as he searched the stall, unraveling only a little when he didn't find her crumpled little body buried in the straw.

He went to Ratter's antechamber, but he was not there, and neither was Kiska.

"Here, Kiska," he called, walking several stalls' distance. She had been growing bolder in her explorations the past few days. "Here my little Kiska, here kitty, kitty, come to me, my Kiska."

He doubled back, calling out and looking into every bucket and every pile of blankets and clump of straw.

"You have lost Kiska?"

Aleksi looked up from the empty bucket he had overturned to find Sahar approaching with Lasair.

"I cannot find her anywhere," he said, the knot coiling tighter in his gut.

"Let me stable Lasair, and I'll help you look for her."

Aleksi resumed his search and Sahar joined him, the both of them calling out for the missing kitten as they checked the stalls to the west. They had finished with the sixth stall down when Sahar held her hand up.

"There," she said, tilting her head. "Do you hear that?"

Aleksi cocked his head and listened. There it was, a faint mewling, high pitched and insistent. They followed the cry to a stall ten gates down from Aleksi's, where they found Kiska huddled between two buckets of oats lined up against the wall.

"Come to me, my little Kiska," he crooned, scooping up the terrified kitten. He tucked her into the crook of his arm and took a good look around. They were only two gates away from the stall where Yago's stallion, Tor, was housed. He walked over to Tor's empty stall and saw nothing amiss, but for a linen rag with a few drops of blood on it. He held Kiska up and saw no blood or open wounds on her, but he did not like the way she was holding one of her hind legs.

They took her back to his room and he set her down on his cot. The knot in his belly twisted as Kiska hobbled across the cot to him, her left hind leg dangling from the knee down.

"I am sorry, little one," he said, kneeling down beside the cot. "I need to find out what your injury is so that I might fix it." He looked up at Sahar. "Can you hold her while I examine her leg?" he said. "She is not going to like this."

Sahar kneeled down on the opposite side of the cot and gently held the scruff of the kitten's neck with one hand while holding her front legs with the other.

"I am sorry too, little Kiska," she said, nodding to Aleksi as she tightened her grip. "Be brave, little Kiska," she crooned as Aleksi manipulated her hip joint. And though Kiska growled and spit as he did, the joint was still in its proper place. "Such a brave little girl you are," Sahar continued her sing-song patter as Aleksi moved his fingers down Kiska's leg. "So brave and strong."

Kiska's femur bone felt intact, but when Aleksi touched her tibia she screamed like she was being skinned alive, and would have jumped off the cot if Sahar had not had such a good hold on her.

"I have her," she said, switching her hold so that one hand still scruffed the kitten while the other held her good hind leg, stretching her out and giving Aleksi better access to her injured leg.

As slowly and gently as he could, Aleksi prodded the length of the bone, grimacing as he felt the broken ends grind against each other mid-tibia. Kiska had stopped screaming and just lay there, trembling, as Sahar's gaze met Aleksi's.

"Is it fixable?" she asked, her expression full of concern.

"It should be," he said. "It feels like a clean break mid-bone. A splint for a moon or two should do the trick."

Sahar let out a long, slow breath as she released her grip on Kiska and cuddled the kitten to her chest, and Kiska seemed content to snuggle. Aleksi went about gathering the materials to make a splint. The handle of his wooden spoon would do, and after whittling it down to size, he tore a clean linen rag into strips and shaved a thin layer of felt from the edge of Zolotoy's saddle blanket for padding. Kneeling across the cot from Sahar as she positioned Kiska, he met and held her gaze. "I'm sorry I hurt you, Kitten," he said.

Raw pain flashed over her face and ripped open his gut, shredding the coiled knot there into tatters. Then she blinked and lifted her chin. "You didn't hurt me," she told him. "As you said, we are nothing to each other."

Sahar took her seat at the table of honor for the winning riders between Aleksandr and Yago, the last place she wanted to be, and the one place she seemed to end up over and over again. She gave each of them a wordless nod of greeting and took a long drink of her wine, and then another. It would not do for her to become drunk at the feast tonight, nor did she want to be starting the race tomorrow with a drunkard's aching head and thickened tongue, but she was not going to be able to make it through this night sober.

Draining her first cup, she motioned for the serving maid to refill it, and caught her mother's furrowed brow as she lifted the cup to her lips and took only a quick sip. She set the cup down and let the warmth of the spirits spread from her belly to her toes. Her mother's attention now focused on the uncomfortably pregnant Rima. Sahar turned to Aleksandr. "How is Kiska?" she asked.

"Better," he answered, his warm brown eyes tender in the same manner he had shown splinting the kitten's leg. That tenderness confused Sahar, for it made it harder to hate him, and she really and truly wanted to hate him. Contrary to what she had told him in the stables, his betrayal had hurt her deeply. A hurt that been assuaged only a little by his apology. "Ratter gave her a drop of Dream Flower and she was sleeping like a kitten when I left for supper."

Sahar laughed despite herself. "You are impossible."

He grinned and gave her a roguish wink. "So I have been told."

"Ahh," Yago said with a voice as smooth and oily as his smile. "It is good to see you two lovers have put the embarrassing incident with the harlot behind you."

"You mean the harlot you hired to set up me and the princess?" Aleksandr said, glaring at Yago. He sat back and his glare softened as he spoke to Sahar. "I was sending her away when you 'happened' by."

"It did not look like you were sending her anywhere," Yago said with a sneer. "It looked like she was sending you—"

"You lie," Aleksandr grit out, keeping his voice low.

Yago's sneer turned into a snarl. "I would be careful about calling me, Prince Yago, a liar, bastard. Wars have been started for lesser insults."

Sahar laid a hand on each of their forearms, and could not help but compare the bunched muscles of Aleksandr's tanned, corded arm with the slimmer, smoother feel of Yago's.

"There will be no war started here at my father's table," she scolded both of them. She narrowed her glare on Yago. "Especially for so trivial a reason."

Yago slid his arm out from under her hand. "You consider calling me a liar trivial?"

Aleksandr's muscles tensed beneath her fingers, and she gave his arm a warning squeeze.

"When you are in truth lying, yes," she told Yago. "I do."

Yago's eyes glinted as cold and treacherous as thin ice over a pit of pitch, and Sahar held onto the solid warmth of Aleksandr's arm. She glanced from Aleksandr's broad, square-tipped fingers to Yago's longer, more slender fingers. She saw him curl the middle finger of his right hand in, but not before she noticed the red, swollen tip, and the piercing wound that looked suspiciously like a cat bite on the pad.

She opened her mouth to ask him about his injured finger, and then clamped it shut. She did not wish to start another fight between Aleksandr and Yago, not here in her family's palace, and not now at a feast celebrating the race tomorrow. There would be time to confront Yago later.

The king stood and the salon went quiet. He raised his goblet to his wife and then to the table of riders. "A toast," he said. "To the brave riders of the third and last race, a course of one hundred leagues that has claimed the life of more than one rider through the years." He met Sahar's gaze, and there was true concern in his, and pride. "To my daughter, Princess Sahar, the first woman to not only enter these races, but to win the first and place second in the next.

Let us see if she and her mare, Lasair, can beat their sires' record of five days in the hundred-league race."

"To Princess Sahar," Aleksandr seconded, holding his cup high and grinning at her. "A most worthy competitor."

Her cheeks flushed, and she nodded her thanks to Aleksandr, whose cocky grin brought even more heat to her skin.

"To all the riders and their steeds," she said, raising her cup. "May the gods watch over us, and may the best man, or woman, win."

It was a feast meant to sate the gathering and fuel the riders for the grueling race ahead, and Sahar ate more than she normally would, filling up on roast goat, soft cheese, and late summer squash before the next several days of salted jerky, flatbread, and dried fruit, which would be her racing diet. Her belly full to bursting, she pushed back from the table with a groan that was echoed by every other rider there. She eyed Yago's swollen fingertip as he drank the last of his wine. He had grown more careless of hiding it with each cup he emptied, and Sahar was grateful that Aleksandr had not noticed or had chosen to ignore the telltale injury. As the meal was at an end, so was Yago's reprieve.

She waited until he stood to leave the salon.

"Prince Yago," she said, standing also. "Will you be so kind as to accompany myself, Aleksandr, and Munir to the stables? There is something I wish you all to see."

Yago glanced at Aleksandr and then Munir, who stood ready to do Sahar's bidding without explanation. "Of course," Yago said with a quick, deferential bow of his head, though his expression oozed suspicion.

He indicated that she should lead the way, and Aleksandr quickly stepped up to walk beside her, leaving Yago to trail behind with Munir.

"What are you up to, my tigress?" he whispered.

"You will see soon enough," she told him. "And I am not *your* tigress."

"Still angry with me then?"

She gave him a glare that would have withered a lesser man, but he chuckled and ran a hand back through his hair, grinning as she watched that cursed sun-kissed lock fall over his forehead.

"Good," he said. "I am glad."

"Glad?"

"It tells me you care."

"I care about many things," she hissed. "But you, you conceited, arrogant, ass, are not one of them."

"Uh huh."

He was still grinning, and Sahar could not decide if she wanted to slap him or kiss him, neither of which would be a smart thing to do, so she ignored him, picking up her pace and giving him her back as she strode the rest of the way to the stables.

She stopped at Zolotoy's stall and called out for Ratter, who came out of the little antechamber holding Kiska, her splinted leg sticking out over his forearm.

"This is what was so important to show us?" Yago asked. "a mangy stable cat with a splinted leg?"

"Not only the cat." Sahar grabbed Yago's hand, but was only able to hold it up for a quick moment before he yanked it out of her grasp and stuffed it into the pocket of his tunic. "Show them your finger," she demanded. "Show them where Kiska bit you when you hurt her."

He laughed and started to back up, but was stopped when Munir blocked Yago's escape.

"Show us," Aleksandr ordered.

Reluctantly, Yago pulled his hand out and held his finger up, the piercing hole of a bite wound in the middle of the red, swollen pad glaringly obvious.

"Why?" Sahar said. "Why would you purposely injure an innocent kitten?"

"For the same reason he set me up with the harlot, and for you to find me in a compromising position with her," Aleksandr answered when Yago did not. "To throw me, and you, off our race. He knows he cannot beat us otherwise."

Yago shrugged. Kiska hissed at him, Aleksandr fisted his hands at his sides, and Sahar threw all her weight and strength into her punch, which landed squarely on Yago's left cheek, which still bore the faintest streaks of yellow from Aleksi's punch days ago.

"You bitch!"

Yago swung at Sahar, who side-stepped his fist as Aleksandr's connected with Yago's belly, doubling him over and leaving him gasping for breath.

"Get this piece of refuse away from me before I kill him," Aleksandr said, and Munir grabbed the still wheezing Yago by the tunic and stood him up.

"You have not heard the last of this," Yago threatened between wheezes. "There will be consequences for your actions tonight, you bastard. My father—"

"Will be so proud to hear that his prince of a son likes to torture helpless kittens and take swings at girls," Aleksandr finished for him. He glanced at Sahar, who still had her fur ruffled, ready to finish this fight, and he laughed, quick and short. "Who not only got beat up by the same girl, but got beat by her in the races, twice."

"Which makes 'im just like is father, it does," Ratter added. He squinted at Yago. "Don't you fergit," he said, "I was there. I saw the queen, who was the Swan then, I saw 'er face all beat up an 'er eyes all red an' swoll shut after yer father tried to rape an' kill 'er. He would 'ave too, ifn not fer the Black Mane." He shook his bald head at the memory, and then he cackled. "It was me that drug yer father out o' the pile o' horse dung the Black Mane dumped 'im in." He took another gander at Yago's swelling cheek and blackening eye, and then winked at Sahar. "I always said you was yer father's daughter."

Aleksi lay on the cot with Kiska curled up on his belly, staring up at the thatched roof of the stables. It was late, close to midnight, but he was nowhere close to sleeping. His mind kept racing, going over everything that had happened from the moment he had first laid eyes on Sahar to Yago's humiliation tonight. Aleksi recalled every word spoken between him and Sahar, and considered all the words left unspoken. He relived the heat and passion of their kisses over and over again, and he dreamed of kissing her senseless while lying on a blanket under a starry sky, of her tautly muscled body beneath his, his hands roaming over every soft mound and round, womanly curve, his mouth tasting hers, covering hers as she cried out with pleasure.

He reminded his wayward body that she had forbidden him from ever touching her again, that she was a proud, royal princess who would never stoop to marrying a bastard, even if he was the bastard son of a king. He forced himself to concentrate on the race ahead and on the road home after, and yet as he imagined himself arriving at his father's palace with a string of broodmares, a purse full of gold pieces and a bride at his side, that bride was a tigress with a mane of thick, black curls that shone auburn in the sun's light and eyes of green fire with sparks of gold.

"Perhaps I will not look for a bride here after all," he told Kiska, who let out a soft kitten snore. "Perhaps I will wait until I return home, until after I have bought my land and have sold my first yearling foals. I will be more settled then, better prepared for marriage and family."

Perhaps by then he will have forgotten his tigress and learned to settle for a woman with the sturdy frame and easy temper he claimed he wanted in a wife.

He shifted slightly, trying not to disturb Kiska, and then went still as Zolotoy snorted and shuffled in his stall. Lifting Kiska from his belly, he set her back down on the cot and pulled his blade from beneath his pillow. He stood and stepped to the side of the door's open top half, his blade hand at the ready as the stall gate clicked shut. The straw rustled beneath Z's hooves and Aleksi flung the bottom half of the door open, knocking it into somebody's legs with a thud and a loud *oomph.*

"Who are you?" Aleksi demanded as he held the point of his blade to the intruder's throat. He had had his fill of uninvited visitors to his private chambers, and was in no mood for any more surprises, although at least this visitor was a man by the height and breadth of his hooded and robed figure. "What are you doing here?"

A large hand reached up and pushed the hood back, revealing a shoulder-length mane of thick, silvered hair and a pair of piercing amber eyes.

"King Asad." Aleksi dipped his head in deference and sheathed his blade.

The king indicated the open door to Aleksi's cramped quarters. "May I?"

Aleksi stood aside to let the king enter. He scooped up Kiska from the cot as the king took in the small but tidy room, and pulled out the stool to sit on. Aleksi sat back down on the cot with the disgruntled Kiska on his lap and waited for the king to speak.

"I have come about my daughter," the king said.

Aleksi's tongue went instantly dry in his mouth.

"I have come to ask you to watch over her during the race."

Aleksi swallowed and nodded. "Of course," he said. "I give you my word, King Asad, no harm will come to her that I can prevent."

"Thank you, Aleksandr. I knew I could depend on you for this."

"You did? Why?"

A keen, piercing gaze held his. "You have made your dislike of the Wolf clear," he stated plainly, "and your interest in my daughter even more so."

"In truth, I despise the lying, conniving worm of a prince," Aleksi told him. "I proposed marriage to your daughter. She turned me down."

"Yes." The corners of the king's mouth twitched up. "I know."

Aleksi cocked his head, unaware that his proposal was common knowledge.

"Sahar told her mother, who told me."

"Does the princess know you are asking me to do this?"

"No," the king answered, confirming Aleksi's suspicion. "I would prefer she never find out, for my sake as well as yours. I love my daughter, and I have great pride and assurance in her ability to ride in this race, to win it even, if it remains a race fairly run."

"But you do not trust the Wolf to keep it fair?"

The king shook his head. "I was willing to give him the chance to prove himself otherwise, but my history with his family and the prince's own actions have shown him to be his parents' son in all ways. I do not trust him, plain and simple, and especially not where it concerns my daughter."

"Especially not after tonight," Aleksi said.

"What happened tonight?"

"Princess Sahar punched the Wolf in the face after it was proven he injured my kitten." Aleksi pointed to the sleeping, splinted Kiska. "In front of Munir, Ratter, and myself."

The king chuckled. "That sounds like my daughter."

"After it happened, Ratter said the Wolf's father tried to rape and kill the queen, and that you stopped him and beat him to a bloody pulp."

"I would have killed the pollution of a man," the king said with a still seething rage, "if not for Oona. It was she who stopped me, for fear of starting a war between the tribes."

"The Wolf truly is like his father then," Aleksi said. "He gave us all a thinly veiled threat, saying that wars had started over lesser insults to a prince such as his exalted self."

The king growled low. "You can be sure the Wolf will never let such an insult go unanswered." He fixed a serious gaze on Aleksi. "If I could prevent my daughter from competing in this last race, I would, but I cannot, not without crushing her fiery spirit." He gave Aleksi a wry grin. "Then she would no longer be Sahar."

"No," Aleksi agreed. "She would be a caged tigress, and I for one would never wish that for her."

The king cocked his head and the briefest of smiles crossed his face. "So, you will do it?" You will watch over Sahar during the race?"

"I will." For as long as she needs me.

"Good. I am glad. Munir will be watching out for her as well, but if I am right, you and your golden stallion will be more likely to keep up with her and Lasair than Munir. If, in keeping Sahar safe, you are caused to lose the race, I will compensate you the winning purse of one hundred gold pieces."

Aleksi's first inclination was to turn down the king's offer of payment, for the truth was he would protect Sahar against Yago no matter what. But Aleksi's practical side asked why he shouldn't accept payment for his services. Wasn't that why he'd come here, to earn enough coin to start a new and better life, and to show his father and his royal relatives that he was a self- made man?

"Throw in my choice of a broodmare from your stables, at a fair price of course," he said, "and you have a bargain."

"I tell you what," the king said. "When the race is over, I will trade you almost any broodmare from my stables for one of yours."

Aleksi clasped the king's forearm. "I have a sturdy little dun steppe mare named Zenya that is yours," he told the king. "What she lacks in stature she makes up for in stamina."

The king shook Aleksi's forearm once. "Deal," he said. He let go of Aleksi's forearm and laid a hand on his shoulder. "I met your father, King Maksimillian, about nine years ago, at the Autumn Festival here," he said. "He bragged to me then about you, about how strong and true you were in mind and body. I'm glad to find he was not exaggerating."

"Nine years ago?" Nine years ago, Aleksi had already been relegated to a stable boy. "Are you sure he was not speaking of Vladimir, his legitimate son and heir?"

The king squeezed his shoulder. "I'm quite sure. I was sorry to hear of your father's illness."

Illness?

"I'm sure, as your sister says, he will recover fully."

"I'm sure he will."

CHAPTER 8

The Race

Aleksi woke with a jolt, his heart hammering in his chest and his bed linens tangled around his legs. He unwrapped the twisted linens and sat up, swiping the sweat from his face as he called for Kiska, his heart kicking back into a somewhat normal beat as she poked her nose out of the pile of his clothes under which she had taken cover.

"Were you hiding from my thrashings, little one?" he cooed as he picked her up and buried his nose into her soft fur, the rhythm of her contented purring slowing his racing pulse.

He had dreamt of the kitten dragging her mangled leg behind her as she crawled into a bucket filled with maggoty oats hidden in the dark, dank corner of a strange stall that reeked of old, moldy straw and horse piss. When Aleksi reached into the bucket for the kitten, it was Zolotoy he pulled out, the stallion unfolding one disjointed leg at a time until he stood on all four legs and shook a grave's worth of dirt off his coat. Aleksi had jumped onto the stallion's bare back and ridden in a frenzied gallop, chasing a blood bay mare and its rider across scorched plains and swollen rivers, up snowy mountain passes and down crowded city streets, their glossy black manes streaming wildly in the wind. Chasing, always chasing, and never gaining any ground until the figures vanished in a cloud of smoke. When the smoke cleared, Aleksi, barely able to breathe for the grief crushing his chest, was left kneeling before his father's body laid out for burial, his withered skin stretched over his bones like dried parchment.

"By the gods," he rasped as a convulsion of shivers wracked his body. He gave the squirming Kiska a smacking kiss on her head and set her down to scramble off as best she could on three legs as he stood and shook the night's terrors from him and then splashed cold water from the wash basin over his face and chest. "It would not take a seer to explain that dream," he laughed hoarsely, rubbing a drying towel over himself, quick and rough, as much to dry his body as to chase the chill from it. "Every fear I currently have made itself known in that one dream." He stepped into his leather riding breeches. "At least now I'm awake, I can confront them," he pulled on his boots, "and do something about them." He stood and donned his soft linen undertunic and leather outer tunic. "For a nightmare surely loses its power in the light of day."

He intended to bring one fear in particular out into broad daylight.

After giving Zolotoy a bucket of fresh, clean oats, Aleksi double checked his saddle bags. One was packed with a change of undertunics, his otter-skin cloak, and a tub of sandalwood soap, and the other with six days' worth of flatbread, jerky, nuts and dates, and a fist-sized packet of rendered goat fat. He tied his bedroll up tight and laid it beside the saddle bags and two full skins, one with water and the other with wine.

The race's course would be crossing many rivers and streams. The water-skin could be refilled easily enough, but the wine would need to be rationed out. He pulled his short sword and tested its freshly honed edge by shaving the fine hairs from his forearm. Satisfied with its sharpness, he laid his two waist blades out next, along with the small, narrow boot blade that his father had given him the spring he had turned ten.

There was a knock on the stable wall.

"Aleksandr? It is Arman, Anya's son."

"Arman." Aleksi let Anya's son into the stall and clasped his arm. "It is good to meet you. Anya has spoken much of you."

"And you," Arman said.

Almost as tall and broadly built as Aleksi, with a head of curly brown hair and his mother's grey-blue eyes, Arman followed Aleksi into the antechamber and took a seat on the stool, eyeing Aleksi's arsenal. Any worries Aleksi had concerning Arman staying here to watch over Kiska and Aleksi's extra gear vanished as soon as Kiska jumped into Arman's lap and demanded attention. Arman, who Ratter had recommended for the job, seemed happy to oblige the little pest.

"I see how easily replaceable I am, you disloyal little wench," Aleksi teased, though he was glad the kitten had taken so quickly to Arman. "Try not to let her jump around too much," he told him. "Remember, she is quite good at hiding, much better than she is at coming when called."

"As is every self-respecting cat," Arman said, laughing as the kitten swatted at the frayed end of his waist belt. "Do not worry, Aleksandr, I will take care of Kiska as if she were my own. Win this race. I have placed a moon's wages on you and your golden stallion."

Arman's words stopped Aleksi short, for he had not thought past what his winning or losing would mean other than for him, Pyotr, and Serge. He had not considered that others would stake so much on the outcome of the race as well.

"I will do my best," he told Arman. Aleksi meant it. He always did.

"I know you will, Aleksandr," Arman said. "Now go and break your fast at the palace. I hear my mother has prepared a feast worthy of twenty kings."

The morning repast looked and smelled as sumptuous as promised, and Aleksi reminded himself not to eat too much as he took a seat beside Feroz. The race would start at noon and an overfull belly was not a comfortable thing when bouncing around on a horse for half a day. Sahar sat with her family, talking quietly with her father and brother, both of whom had ridden in the race before. Her father had won it the first two times it was run, and had not ridden in it since, choosing to retire his stallion, Storm Chaser, from racing. Her brother had finished a respectable third in the last race three years ago, the youngest rider ever to place. Now his sister would be the first woman ever to ride in the race.

Across the salon, Yago sat with Taweel and the Jackal, the bruising below his left eye visible even from twenty paces as he glared at Aleksi who shook his head and tucked into his breakfast, the last hot food he would eat for the next several days. As he ate, he kept a wary eye out for Anastasia, who finally showed up as he was folding pieces of egg and fish for Kiska into a square of linen. He stood and made his way over to her table and took the open seat between her and the rich, corpulent, balding prince she had apparently decided would make a desirable second husband.

"Sister," Aleksi said as he spread his shoulders, causing the prince to scoot his seat farther over.

"Bastard half-brother."

"I have been informed by King Asad that our father is ill. Why did you not tell me yourself?"

"I was not required to by my father. In fact, quite the opposite."

"He told you not to tell me? Why?"

"It is a matter for the royal family, of which you are not a member."

"I may not be a royal," Aleksi ground out, "but he is my father. I have a right to know. How ill is he?"

"Not very. It is actually more of a minor inconvenience than an illness," she said. "Certainly nothing you need concern yourself with."

"You had better not be lying to me."

"How dare you call Princess Anastasia a liar," her prospective second husband-to-be defended her, his double chin jiggling like congealed suet.

Aleksandr stood and towered over the prince. "I dare because I know her to be a lying bitch," he growled. He looked to Anastasia. "It is her defining characteristic."

The prince went bug-eyed and apoplectic, but Anastasia simply shrugged.

"What if I am lying to you, my bastard half-brother?" she said. "What can the likes of you do about it?" She laughed, high and shrill. "Nothing."

Sahar sat astride Lasair, the butterflies in her belly flitting about as the riders maneuvered for position in the starting line. She was not surprised when Munir posted his gelding, Kedar, next to Lasair, but she was taken aback by the two short swords strapped across Munir's back and the lacquered vest and arm guards he wore, as well as two waist blades.

"You are dressed more for battle than a horse race, cousin," Sahar said, using the endearment he had earned with a lifetime of friendship and would soon inherit through marriage to Halah. "Are you expecting trouble?"

"Always." Munir adjusted the straps holding the short swords. "It is what I have trained for."

"It will slow you down."

Munir shrugged. "Perhaps."

He rode not to win, but to protect her, and she could rage and rail all she wanted about not needing his protection. It wouldn't change anything. She didn't blame Munir. She was certain her father had requested, if not outright ordered his guardsman to watch over her.

"Princess," a low, resonant voice ran down her spine as Zolotoy's golden head stopped even with Lasair's on her other side. "Munir."

"Aleksi." Munir returned Aleksandr's greeting, raising her brows at the familiar name, something she had only heard his friends Serge or Pyotr address him by. "It seems I am not the only one ready for trouble."

She eyed Aleksandr, who wore a short sword strapped across his back, and two waist blades, his forearms covered by leather guards. She followed the line of his leather riding breeches down long, thickly muscled thighs and calves to his boots, where the hilt of a small dagger poked out of the top of his right boot.

"Better to be found ready than caught unawares," Aleksandr said with his usual cocky grin.

"Wear all the weaponry you like," she said, trying and failing to ignore the cursed shock of hair falling down over his forehead. "Add a stone or two to your saddle bags as well for all I care."

"Are you worried we will not be able to keep up with you and Lasair?" he asked with a mock frown.

"Worried?" she chuffed. "No."

Aleksandr's eyes narrowed to a spot over her shoulder, and she turned to see Yago riding up alongside Taweel and the Jackal, the three of them as heavily armed as Aleksandr and Munir. She fingered the bone hilt of her solitary waist blade, and regretted not listening to her father and arming herself with more.

"Here." Aleksandr pulled the dagger from his boot and held it out to her. "This doesn't mean we're betrothed or any such thing."

She laughed despite herself as she slid the dagger down the inside of her boot. "I suppose you expect me to swear not to use your blade on you," she said.

"I do."

"Then I swear," she said solemnly, and then grinned wickedly. "Remember, I still have my own blade to use at my discretion."

"I well remember your blade, my tigress," he said, cupping his stones and wagging his brows at her, "and your—discretion."

"Ahem."

They both looked to Munir, who lifted his chin toward where the king sat astride Storm Chaser, the flag with his family's crest flapping in the chill autumn wind.

"The rules of the race are simple," the king called out as the crowd went quiet.

"The course is marked by flags and manned by my guards, who will keep a tally of the riders who pass the checkpoints and when. They will provide you with aide if you need it, but then you are out of the race. You may ride from first light to last, but not at night. This is for your horse's safety, not yours. You will follow these rules on your oath and honor." He paused for emphasis. "Any rider found breaking these rules will be disqualified from this and any future race." He glanced out across the line of riders. "Do you so swear to abide by these rules?"

A chorus of male voices, and one lone female, answered. "I so swear."

The king held his flag high. "On your marks," he called out.

She tightened her grip on Lasair's reins.

"Set."

She shifted higher on her saddle.

"Go."

The king slashed the flag down and she gave Lasair a quick squeeze of her knees. Though the race would cover one hundred leagues and taking the lead this early would mean nothing in the end, she knew how much it signified to the spectators now, especially to those who had wagered on certain riders and their horses, and she was determined not to disappoint any and all who had been brave, or mad enough, to wager on her, the only woman in a field of ten and seven male riders.

Lasair leapt forward and within ten paces she was in the lead, with Zolotoy and Kedar flanking her on either side. The crowd lined the road to the city's borders, cheering the riders on and yelling out encouragement and instructions to their favorites until the road turned onto a path and then open field, where the riders let their mounts slow to an easier pace. For the next eighty or so leagues the race would be all about keeping a sure and steady pace and not getting injured. If a horse and rider made it that far, the last twenty leagues would require every last reserve of speed and endurance they had.

Right now, they were coming up on the first of many river crossings.

Sahar slowed her breathing as her mother had taught her to do when confronted by difficult situations, and called on her courage, as her father had taught her. Gripping Lasair's reins and a hunk of her mane in both hands, she urged the mare into the water, her breathing speeding up to match the rapid beat of her heart despite her best efforts.

"You plunged right in this time," Aleksandr said loudly, his voice carrying over the yells of men and the splashing of horses as he maneuvered Zolotoy to Lasair's downriver side. "Well done."

She nodded, unable to unlock her clenched jaw to answer. She glanced over to her other side as Kedar's bobbing head came even to Lasair's and gave Munir a weak grin. Then she concentrated on the far shore, breathing a little easier with each stroke closer. At last, Lasair's feet hit the river bottom and she breathed a heavy sigh of relief as they emerged onto dry ground. Lasair shook the water from her coat and Sahar pried her frozen fingers from the mare's mane, drug a ragged breath in and let it out in a whoosh. Aleksandr and Munir were both watching her closely.

"Are you two going to flank me every water crossing of this race?" she said, welcoming the more familiar warming flash of anger.

"It depends," Aleksandr said.

"On what?"

"On how far the last crossing is from the finish line."

By unspoken agreement, Aleksi laid his bedroll out on one side of Sahar's and Munir laid his out on the other. Aleksi set his short sword between his bedroll and Sahar's as Munir tucked his under each side of his bedroll.

"Are you certain you want your sword where I can reach it?" she asked pointedly as she pulled the saddle bag with her provisions into her cross-legged lap.

Aleksi lowered himself into the same position, groaning a little as his hips popped and the tight muscles of his lower back released. "You should know by now that everything I do is for a reason," he told her.

"What is your reason for acting like my guard-dog this race?"

Aleksi glared out over several small campfires along the creek's shore to where Yago, Taweel, and the Jackal had set up for the night. "You know why."

"I know why Munir is," she said, shooting the king's man a quick look over her shoulder as he stood and strolled over to a copse of trees. "My father ordered him to." The gold specks in her eyes glowed in the fire's light as she pinned Aleksi with her gaze. "Why are you?"

Aleksi had never lied to her—well, except for when he'd told her they were nothing to each other. He didn't want to lie to her now. But he'd sworn to the king that he would not betray their bargain, and he meant to keep that vow as much for the king's sake as his own. He knew in his marrow that she would never forgive him for taking payment from her father to protect her. Though he couldn't say what they actually were to each other, whether they were friendly strangers, two people physically drawn to each other despite their positions in life, or simply well-matched competitors, he knew bone-deep that they weren't nothing to each other.

"I guard you because I do not trust the Wolf," he said, which was true enough. "Also, I know it rubs his oily fur the wrong way."

"That is the only reason, to anger Yago?"

"No. I also keep close to you because you and Lasair are the horse and rider to beat," he said, which was also a version of the truth.

She gave a small smile and sat a little taller.

"Your father and brother have both won and placed in this race. I figure they have shared their wisdom and strategy with you."

Her smile flattened. "How practical of you."

"I came here to win. I've never pretended otherwise."

"To win enough coin to return home with a string of broodmares and an easy-tempered wife. Yes, I remember."

"And you, what do you race for?"

Her smile was slow and purposeful and did not reach her eyes. "I ride to prove that not all of us princesses are soft, spoilt, and useless, and that women are more than broodmares to be bought and used by men. That we have our own worth in this world."

Aleksi felt the sting of his own words thrown back at him, words that had pricked her pride he'd once thought nothing more than royal vanity like he'd seen in his father's wife and half-sisters. With Sahar, he had learned pride could be an honorably inherent trait.

"Still angry at me then?" he asked by way of apology.

"No." She shook her head and shrugged. "Why would I be angry with you, we are—"

"Don't say we're nothing to each other."

"Why not? You did."

Aleksi had already apologized to her for his cruel words. What more could he say?

"You were right," she added.

"What?"

"You were right," she said. "At the end of all this, we will both go back to our lives. Me, to being Princess Sahar, safe, spoilt, and secure in the folds of my royal family, and you"—her voice cracked, and she took a deep breath and blew it out—"you will return to your homeland half a moon's journey away, where you will show your royal kin that a bastard son is a man of his own making whose stables will rival any king's, and whose sturdy, easy-tempered wife will give him many sons." She smiled, and the tips of her luscious lips quivered. "Whatever it is we are now will be nothing but a fleeting memory."

Sahar unfolded the saddle blanket, laid it over Lasair's back, and tied it snugly under her belly to stave off the autumn chill.

"You kept a good pace today, girl," she said, patting the mare's neck. "Second day of the race and you made those boys keep up with you." She mixed a handful of oats from her bag with a glob of goat fat and coaxed the mare into eating it. "I know it is not your favorite meal," she sympathized, "but it will give you energy when we head up into the foothills tomorrow."

The course had been set to ensure plenty of grazing and water for the horses, but any rider worth their salt knew how important it was to supplement their horse's feed on such a long and arduous trek. Sahar glanced over at Aleksandr, who was feeding his stallion a similar concoction, and then quickly looked away when he caught her watching him.

Unfurling her bedroll onto the cold, hard ground, she added her soft, plush bed to the list of comforts she would never take for granted again. That list included the sight of Aleksandr's broad bare chest as he returned from the stream to lay his bedroll next to hers, his damp hair slicked back and his wet torso glistening in the fire's light.

She flopped down onto her bedroll. It was bad enough Aleksandr had invaded her thoughts day and night. Now his voice was embedded in her head as well. Purposely turning her attention away from Aleksandr's hard chest and tight nipples puckering in the cold night air, she rummaged through her sack of food and decided on a piece of cheese and flatbread with a handful of dates for her supper. While she ate in silence, Munir set his bedroll up alongside hers so that he and Aleksandr flanked her, the two of them eating and talking companionably about the leagues they had covered that day, and what they might expect tomorrow as they rode up into the foothills of mountains whose peaks would be dusted with their first snowfall within a moon's time.

Sahar remained quiet, content to listen to them talk as she sipped out a measured cup of wine, her tight muscles relaxing as the drink's warmth spread from her belly to her limbs. Aleksandr and Munir also took long pulls on their wineskins before capping them and setting them aside. Her cup empty, she stood and stretched and began to make her way to a hedge of bushes. The sound of boot fall followed behind her, and she turned and glared at Munir.

"I am perfectly capable of passing water on my own," she told him, to which he shrugged and remained rooted to where he stood. "Fine," she muttered loudly as she rounded the hedge and pulled down her breeches and squatted. "Sure you don't want to hold my hand, so that I, frail woman that I am, do not fall into my own piss?"

Munir did not look in the least chagrined as she strode back past him a few moments later, nor did she wait for him as he disappeared behind the bushes. She glared at Aleksandr for good measure, and was rewarded with a cocked eyebrow as she returned to her bedroll.

"Rider in," someone called out, and all eyes turned to the latecomer, who would be disqualified for riding past night fall.

It was Feroz, the merchant's son, and his horse was limping. Aleksandr and Munir went straight to him and helped lead the poor animal over to where their horses were staked out alongside Lasair. Munir removed the horse's saddle as the gelding drank from the stream while Feroz finished off his water skin and refilled it. When both horse and rider had their fill, Feroz rubbed the beast down while Aleksandr checked the injured leg, running his big hands down the length of it from shoulder to hoof. Lifting the horse's hoof, he squinted in the darkening light, and Sahar held out the small branch she had pulled from the fire, its tip burning hot enough to provide some illumination.

Aleksandr whistled low and touched a dark spot on the sole of the gelding's hoof, cursing softly as the horse tried to jerk it away.

"Is it a stone bruise?" Feroz asked, though they all four of them knew the answer.

Aleksandr nodded. "Afraid so."

"Damnation."

"We can make a soft boot out of your saddle blanket," Aleksandr said. "It will get you to the next aide station."

"Might as well," Feroz grabbed the blanket from the ground and pulled out his blade, "since I will be walking him there."

"I have some twine in my pack," she offered, silently thanking Ratter, who had made sure she was prepared for anything that could befall herself or Lasair.

"Thank you," Feroz said.

She turned to get the twine and stopped. Yago and Taweel were standing between her and the bedrolls, and behind Yago, the Jackal stood over her bedroll with his back to them. She heard something drop with a soft thud and then the Jackal turned around and walked up to the other two princes.

"What were you doing there?" she asked, craning her neck to where she could see the bedrolls. Nothing looked amiss, and her wineskin and saddle bags were right where she had left them.

"What are you doing here?" Yago demanded. He tapped his riding whip against his thigh as Aleksandr stepped up to her on one side and Munir the other.

"We are helping Feroz tend to his horse," Aleksandr answered. "What's it to you?"

"If he asks for aide, he must drop out of the race," Yago insisted.

Beside her, Aleksandr stiffened and his hand fisted, and though his short blade lay tucked under his bedroll, he still wore his waist blades, as did Munir and the three princes standing before them.

"We know the rules, Prince Yago," she said before any of the men could escalate the situation.

"We are more likely to follow them than any of you," Aleksandr added, doing exactly what she'd hoped to avoid.

"Are you insinuating that I, a royal prince, would cheat?" Yago asked, clearly affronted.

Aleksandr's laugh was short and harsh. "I am not insinuating anything, you royal worm, I'm saying it outright."

"Both of you cease your arguing and posturing at once," she snapped. "If you begin a brawl, we'll all be out of the race."

"It would almost be worth it," Aleksandr grumbled, but he stood back half a step and relaxed his fisted hand.

"Good bastard," Yago jeered. "Listen to your mistress."

Sahar placed her hand on Aleksandr's forearm, and felt the corded muscles flex and twitch. "If you know what is good for you, Prince Yago," she said, holding back a scoff. "You will walk away now."

Yago sneered and slapped the whip into the palm of his hand, and beneath her fingers, Aleksandr's arm tensed and hardened.

"There is no need for a fight," Feroz entreated, palms up. "I am dropping out of the race for my horse's sake. I wouldn't do him a further injury." He stared pointedly at the whip in Yago's hand. "Something you would not understand."

Yago's sneer twisted into a snarl as he raised his whip at Feroz, and then his hand stopped mid-strike, grasped in Aleksandr's iron grip.

"Don't you dare," Aleksandr growled into Yago's reddening face. Yanking Yago's arm down, Aleksandr wrenched the whip from his hand and broke it in two over his thigh. He threw the pieces into Yago's belly. "Don't ever dare raise a whip to any person or beast in my presence again."

Sahar shook her head in disgust. "My father was right about you," she told Yago. "You can't be trusted."

"You think *he* can?" Yago jerked his chin at Aleksandr. "Ask him why King Asad went to his room the night before the race. Ask him what your esteemed father promised him to watch over you during this race. To let you win."

She laughed in Yago's face, and then she looked at Aleksandr's.

"Is this true?"

Aleksi glanced around at the quickly growing crowd of riders. "This is neither the time nor the place," he said.

Blazing green eyes with sparks of molten gold burned into his. "Is it true?"

He'd promised her father that Aleksi would keep their bargain a secret, but he wasn't going to lie to Sahar, not again. Besides, she was smart enough to put two and two together, and it would be better to get the truth out into the open rather than let Yago's lies infect and fester.

"Yes," he said as murmurs swept through the camp. "The king asked me to guard your safety during the race. And no," he hastened to add, "he didn't ask me, or any other man, to let you win."

"Ask the bastard what your father promised him as payment," Yago said.

"I would rather ask how many spies you have set about the palace and the city," Aleksi said, for that was the only way he would have known about the king's visit.

"A question I needn't deign answer. Not to you."

"Perhaps not." Aleksi glanced about at the crowd of riders. His point had been made.

"But I am certain that King Asad will insist on an answer from you. When this race is over, you and I are going to have us a serious discussion."

The Wolf stepped back, a bead of sweat trickling down his forehead. "Come after me, bastard, and my father's army will come after you and yours." He jerked his black head at Sahar. "As well as your host and conspirator, the Black Mane."

"You are quick to threaten the force of your father's army over any perceived slight," Aleksi said as the crowd around them grumbled and grew closer. "Is your father aware of your never-ending threats?"

"My father will stand by me against any and all of our enemies," Yago proclaimed. "Unlike yours, who will not even claim you, or the whore that gave birth to you."

Aleksi shrugged off the insult of his parentage. He had heard worse from his father's queen and her two daughters every day he'd lived in the palace. He glanced around at the restive riders, who were throwing pointed glares the Wolf's way.

"I'd be careful of who I threatened next were I you," he told the Wolf. "I see no enemies here, only fellow competitors."

"That's because you're blind to everything but the twitch of a royal bitch in heat's shapely backside," the Jackal twittered.

Behind Aleksi, a tigress hissed. Before him, the Wolf sneered. Aleksi cocked his fist, and held as the blur of a shadow flew past him, straight for the Jackal. The crunch of cartilage was followed by a high-pitched keening.

"You bastard," the Jackal cried, holding his hand to his nose as blood dripped down his mouth and chin. "You broke my nose."

They all turned to Feroz.

"Someone needed to shut the prick up," he said, rubbing the knuckles of his right hand. He shrugged. "I was already out of the race."

The fight over, the riders made their way back to their fires as Yago and Taweel led the bleeding Jackal over to the stream. Feroz and Munir went back to cutting up the saddle blanket to make a soft boot for the gelding, leaving a fuming Sahar alone with Aleksandr.

"What," she demanded, "did my father promise you?"

"One hundred gold pieces, win or lose, as long as you are kept safe."

She nodded slowly and blinked back tears that burned her throat. "So, you will have enough to buy a wife and broodmares after all. Well done," she said with a quick dip of her head, as if she were truly complimenting him, as if it didn't matter that he'd taken payment to protect her. That he'd betrayed her again. "I'm so pleased to be able to assist you in your purchase of a bride."

"I asked you first," he said. "You refused me."

"No." She shook her head. "I didn't." She watched surprise take over his expression. "If you recall, I never answered your proposal."

"What I recall," he said, "was your blade's point pressed to my stones and your threat to geld me then and there."

"Aye, after your ill-bred pawing and arrogant assumption that I would fall to my knees for the chance to breed with you." As soon as she said the words, the vision of the whore on her knees in the stable, her face deep in Aleksandr's groin, came unbidden, fueling Sahar's growing ire. "After which," she added hotly, "you proceeded to flirt with every kitchen and serving maid in the palace, and consorted with that whore—"

"Roxanna."

"What?"

"The whore's name," he said with maddening calm, "is Roxanna. You know I didn't solicit or consort with her."

She snorted with derision.

"Or any other woman since the cursed day I set eyes on you."

Sahar opened her mouth to excoriate him, but all the angry words she'd been holding and harboring against him expelled into the night air in one big whoosh of breath. Her heart stopped and started again with a queer fluttering beat as she dragged in a deep lungful of air. "Why?" she asked with a ragged whisper.

"Why what?"

"Why haven't you consorted with any other woman, when they so obviously want to consort with you?"

He shrugged and then laughed, short and harsh. "Good question."

One he apparently wasn't going to answer, which didn't stop her from asking others. "Why did my father hire you to protect me?"

"You'll have to ask your father."

She gnashed her teeth at him, spun on her heel to walk away, and then spun right back around. "Why do you kiss me like you do, and then tell me we are nothing to each other?"

She hated the pleading whine of her voice, and stood taller and lifted her chin, holding his gaze and refusing to look away, the queer beat of her heart rushing to her ears.

His expression grew dark and serious for several of those beats, and then he shook himself and ran a hand back through that damned shock of hair, which fell, yet again, over his forehead. He grinned, and the cocky stallion with dark stubble accentuating the square cut of his chin, the one who had stood before her the day she'd first set eyes on him, stood before her again.

"I've kissed many women like I do," he said. "It's not my fault the thirty other men you've kissed aren't capable of stirring your passions, Kitten."

CHAPTER 9

The River

Sahar stared down at the muddy hoof prints leading into the rushing waters of the swollen river. A river she would have to cross to continue the race. It was either that or admit defeat and return back to the check point with her tail tucked firmly between her legs. That she would not do. She had too much to prove, for herself, her family, her tribe, and any other woman competing in a man's world.

She unclasped her otter skin cloak and stuffed it into her saddle bag, her teeth chattering as the sleeting rain soaked her tunic through. She glared at Aleksandr, sitting astride Zolotoy beside her, as if he were to blame for the skies opening up and letting loose the torrent of rain that had turned the hard-packed mountain path into a running rivulet of slick, sucking mud that had taken another two horses down, leaving the field of riders down to ten and four men and her.

"What do you want to do?" Aleksandr asked as he pulled his short sword from its sheath on his back, wrapped it up in his cloak and tied them up with his bedroll. "Cross or not, I get my one hundred gold pieces either way."

She sent Lasair plunging into the river and gasped aloud as the bone-chilling water swirled up to her waist. Panic, pure heart-pounding panic, flooded her senses as Lasair swam for the far shore, fighting against the river's swift moving current. She gripped Lasair's mane in both hands and squeezed her legs tight to keep from being swept off the struggling mare's back. She fought to keep from squeezing her eyes shut as the image of Ommar's frightened face came unbidden as he was carried farther and farther away from her outstretched hand.

She heard her words, her oath to Ommar before his hand had been ripped from hers, only they were being spoken to her in a deep, grounding voice.

"I have you. I have you. I won't let you go."

She looked from the bronzed hand holding onto Lasair's bridle to Aleksandr's strong, determined face, and the panic coursing through her veins receded enough that she could take a full breath and nod her head in acknowledgement. He grinned in response, the rain running down from his sodden hair to his flash of even white teeth, and then his eyes widened.

"Munir," he yelled out over the roar of the raging waters. "Look out, upriver."

She whipped her head around in time to see Munir and Kedar no more than ten feet upriver from them, get broadsided by a branch the size of a tree trunk. Kedar let out a high, frenzied whinny that was cut short as horse and rider went under.

"Muunniirr!" Her cry stolen by the wind, she clutched tight to Lasair's mane as Zolotoy surged ahead, pulling them out of the log's careening path. She untangled her fingers from the mare's mane, twisting on the saddle to jump in after Munir, and felt Aleksandr's iron grip on her arm.

"Can you make the shore?" he yelled.

"But, Munir."

He took her hand and wrapped Zolotoy's rein around it. "Hold on," he told her. "Z will guide Lasair to the shore. I'll get Munir."

She glanced wildly from Aleksandr to where Munir had gone under and still hadn't surfaced. "Go," she said. "Save Munir."

He squeezed her hand. "Whatever happens, my tigress, do not let go." Then he pushed off of Zolotoy and was being swept downriver.

Sahar held on tight to Zolotoy's reins with one hand and Lasair's mane with the other, gripping the mare's sides with thighs numb from the cold and chafed from rubbing as the two horses fought their way to the shoreline. She clamped her jaw so tight that no more than a groan escaped her lips as a thick branch tumbling past scraped her lower back. She glanced downriver, and saw Aleksandr's receding head bobbing above water, but she could see no sign of Munir.

At last, Lasair's hooves hit river bottom and she unwound Zolotoy's rein from around her hand as both horses made the shoreline. She slid off of Lasair and fell to her hands and knees in the muck, sobbing and gasping as the horses hung their heads, sucking in and blowing out great breaths of air. She slapped the muddy ground with an anguished howl, once again unable to do more than stand by as another river took the lives of men, good men trying to protect her. How would she ever face Halah after making her cousin a widow before she even became a bride? How would Sahar ever face herself knowing Aleksandr had died for her?

The arrogant bastard had called her a spoilt, proud princess, and he was right, she was. It was her pride that had kept her from admitting the real danger she had put herself and them in. Her stubbornness had sent them headlong into the river. Because she was the spoilt princess, to be protected at all costs, they would pay the price with their lives.

But he had called her a tigress too. *His* tigress.

Throwing her head back with a guttural growl, she stood and wiped her muddy hands on her breeches and then she jumped up onto Lasair's saddle, grabbed Zolotoy's reins and swung both horses to head downriver. She was a tigress, curse it, not some mewling kitten. She was a woman strongly built and fully grown, no longer the little girl who could do no more than watch helplessly as someone she cared for was swept away to their death.

Aleksi let the current take him downriver, keeping his gaze on Sahar until she made the shoreline, and then he turned and stroked hard for the floating object he hoped and prayed was Munir bobbing near the outcropping of rocks downstream.

The object lifted its head and flailed an arm, and Aleksi stroked harder, ignoring the numbing chill of the water. His arms and legs were as heavy as water-sodden logs, and his chest was on fire, but he kept on. He had grown up swimming in the ice-cold rivers of his homeland, and had swam the width of the Mother River when he was ten and eight, a feat more men had drowned attempting than had succeeded. Aleksi was a strong swimmer, always had been. He'd not drowned then, and he was not going to drown now, nor would he let Munir.

Another three strokes and he reached Munir, who was struggling to keep his head above water. Aleksi grabbed him by the leather straps of his sword's harness, rolled him over onto his back and swam them to the rocks rising up in the middle of the churning river. He swallowed several mouthfuls of water before he managed to push Munir into the rocks, wedging him between the two largest and shuffling his own booted feet onto a slippery semblance of a ledge.

"Munir?" His face was ashen and his lips had a bluish tint to them. "Munir," Aleksi yelled. "Munir, wake up. Wake up," he yelled louder. Munir's head slumped down, and Aleksi stuffed his feet deeper into the rocks as he fought to keep Munir's mouth and nose above water. "Munir," Aleksi yelled at the top of his straining lungs. "Halah needs you. Come back to Halah."

"Halah?" It was no more than a whisper above the roar of the river, but to Aleksi it was a call to battle.

"Yes, Halah. Think of Halah. Open your eyes and help me get you to shore and you will see your Halah again."

Munir's eyes fluttered opened and focused on Aleksi as he fought to keep his grip on both Munir's tunic and the slippery rocks beneath his feet. "Aleksi."

"Welcome back, my friend," Aleksi grunted. "Now let us get to shore."

Munir's eyes opened wider as he took in the water surging around them, and then his face paled even more. "Kedar?" he whispered hoarsely.

Aleksi shook his head. "I haven't seen him," he said, shifting his hold and his stance. "Right now, you and I must get off these rocks." He glanced across the span of rushing current they would have to navigate to make the river's bank. "Can you swim?"

Munir lifted his left arm and grimaced. He tried to lift his right arm and cursed through grit teeth. "I cannot move my arm," he said. "My shoulder, my ribs."

"What about your legs?"

Munir flexed and shuffled his legs between Aleksi's and the rocks.

"I'm not certain," he said. "I don't feel any pain, but I don't think there's any strength left in them."

Aleksi's arms and legs were quickly losing strength as well, but he could think of no other way to get Munir safely on land than to swim with him hanging on to his back, which would be difficult enough with two good arms.

"I'm going to turn around so you can wrap your arms and legs around me," he told Munir. "We will have to swim for it, probably drift downriver some before we make good footing."

Munir shook his head. "No," he said. "I can't let Sahar find both of us drowned. You swim to shore. I can hold on until you get help."

Aleksi eyed Munir's pale skin and blue-tinged lips. He wouldn't last long before the chill made it impossible for him to hold on. He didn't have the strength to fight the current, and Aleksi had no idea if any of the other riders were close enough to be of aid.

"I'm not leaving you here," Aleksi told him. "If I did and you perished, Sahar would burn me alive."

Munir laughed, and sputtered, and coughed up bloody spittle.

"Hold on," Aleksi ordered. He turned, scraping his fingers on the rocks as he adjusted his grip while carefully rotating his booted feet on the precarious shelf in slow, excruciating increments. "Take hold of my sword harness," he said, and felt Munir grab on. "Now wrap your legs around my waist." He nodded as Munir's legs wrapped around him. "On the count of three, we push off."

"On three," Munir echoed.

Aleksi took a deep breath and blew it out, if he pushed off too early, or if Munir could not hold on, they were doomed. "One," he said, "two—"

"Wait." Munir pulled back on Aleksi's shoulder. "Look to the shore."

"Hang on," Sahar yelled, as she pulled the horses to a stop.

Aleksandr and Munir were wedged into the rock outcropping, but were being buffeted by the water swirling and raging around them.

"Hurry," Aleksandr yelled. "I can't hold on much longer."

Sahar jumped off of Lasair, the mud sucking at her boots. "Thank you, Ratter," she murmured as she grabbed the rope from her saddle. She glanced up and down the shoreline, searching frantically until she found a rock heavy enough to anchor the rope.

"Thank you, Father," she said as she tied the rope to the rock, recalling his stories of how he would climb trees in his youth by tossing a rock tied to a rope over a high branch, her mother's faint blushes every time he told the story. Planting her feet as firmly as possible in the mud, she started swinging the rock in a circle.

"Thank you, Brother," she said as the rock gained speed and momentum, for the many games they'd thrown rocks, ropes, and sticks as children, honing her arm and her aim.

She swung the rock out and let the rope slide through her palms, but it fell short of Aleksandr and was instantly carried downstream by the river's current. She hauled the rope back, sodden and heavy with rain and river water, blew out her breath, squared her shoulders, and began to swing it around and around until she could hold it no longer and let it fly. The rock splashed into the river right in front of Aleksandr, but the rock sunk before he could reach the rope. Her arms were tiring, but she gritted her teeth and hauled the sodden rope back onto the shore as Munir's head sagged on Aleksandr's shoulder.

"No. Nononono." Her heart was pounding in her ears and her belly was in her throat. "Not again."

"Sahar." She focused on Aleksandr's face. "You can do this," he yelled over the raging river. "You can do this."

Munir came to from the yelling, and she took a deep breath in and blew it out. Then another. She swung the rock until it started to pull away from her with its own force, and then she hurled it with all her might, skipping forward on her tiptoes as the rock hurtled out over the water and the rope uncoiled, taking chunks of her skin with it. She focused on what she was watching. The rock landed and Aleksandr reached out and grabbed it as the current took it right to him.

"Thank you, Mother," she said, "for teaching me never to give up. You as well, Aleksandr," she whispered as he wrapped the rope around his chest and Munir's back, "for having faith in me, for giving me faith in myself."

She held her end of the rope, fighting to keep it out of the water and as taut as they needed it while Aleksandr labored to remove the rock from its knot and tie the rope at his belly. It was slow going, and he slipped and stumbled several times, causing her to bite her lower lip to keep from crying out and distracting him. He managed to keep his footing and after what seemed like a long time, he signaled, and she quickly tied her end of the rope to Lasair's saddle.

"Ready?" she yelled.

"Ready," Aleksandr called.

She started to walk the mare backward and Aleksandr pushed off the rocks. He and Munir both disappeared under the rushing water and Sahar sucked in her breath as she kept Lasair moving. The rope remained taut, and Sahar counted to seven before Aleksandr's and Munir's heads finally popped up, coughing and spitting. They went under and popped up two more times before they reached the river's bank, which was as steep and high as a man was tall. Lasair had run out of room to maneuver, her rump pressing against a hedge of bushes.

"Stay, Lasair," Sahar commanded. "Stay."

She clopped through the sucking mud as fast as she could and wrapped the slackening rope around both of her wrists and braced her feet.

"On three," she said to Aleksandr. "I'll pull and you'll climb."

"On," Aleksandr coughed and gasped, "three."

She looked to Munir, who nodded feebly and unwound his legs from around Aleksandr's waist.

"One." She dug her boots in. "Two." She bent her knees and took a deep breath. "Three." She blew out her breath and tugged with all her might, leaning back against the weight of the men as they climbed the muddy bank until she fell flat on her back. She started to slide toward the bank, and dug her feet in even deeper. The rope was cutting into her wrists, but she didn't let go, even when it felt as if her shoulders would be pulled from their sockets.

Then the rope went slack.

She lifted her head. Aleksandr and Munir were lying in the mud at her feet.

She burst into tears.

Thankfully, her tears blended into the rain running down her cheeks as she rolled onto her hands and knees and crawled over to them. They were both gasping and sucking in air, but they were alive. She helped Aleksandr untie the rope from around them, and tossed it aside before he grabbed her and pulled her down onto his chest. Holding her face in his big hands, he kissed her hard, stealing her breath and warming her blood.

"Thank you, my tigress," he rumbled. Then he let go his hold of her and rolled over onto his hands and knees, hanging his head low as water flowed freely from his nostrils.

Her head was still reeling from Aleksandr's kiss, as she scooted over to Munir, who lay groaning on his back. His eyes flew open as he started coughing up water. She rolled him onto his side, and then helped him to his hands and knees, where he retched up river water and what was left of his morning meal.

"Kedar," he said when he finally stopped retching. "I must find Kedar."

Aleksandr pushed himself back onto his heels. "You rest," he said. "I'll find him."

"Neither of you are in any condition to do anything but sit and regain your strength," she said. "I'll go."

Another coughing spasm overtook Munir.

Aleksandr stood on legs that swayed and shook like river reeds. "You stay here with Munir," he said. "I'll go."

"You can barely stand," she pointed out, then narrowed her eyes. "You cannot tell me what to do."

"Nor you me."

Sahar glanced at Munir, still on his hands and knees, barely able to lift his head. "One of us should stay with Munir."

"I agree," Aleksandr said. "That one of us should be you."

"Why?" She rose and stood nose to chin with him. "Because I'm a woman?"

"Because, you impossible woman, I don't want anything else to happen to you."

A flash of pleasure rushed through her veins until she remembered her father was paying Aleksandr to protect her. "Worried about collecting your one hundred gold pieces?" She picked up the rope and coiled it around her shoulder.

"Princess," Aleksandr warned. "I told you I would go."

"Then go, or stay," she said as she hung the rope over her saddle horn. "Or go to your cursed forefathers in the underworld, it makes no difference to me."

"Go, both of you," Munir insisted as he slowly pushed himself back onto his heels, his cheeks pinking up and his lips no longer blue. "Go find Kedar. I'll be fine."

Sahar didn't speak a word to Aleksi as they searched for Kedar, which was fine. He was in no mood for small talk. His chest still constricted every time he thought of what could have befallen her crossing that cursed river. The fact that only Munir, and likely Kedar, had been seriously injured was a stroke of blind, stupid luck, and Aleksi was as angry at himself for provoking her into it as he was for taking the bait and jumping.

"Asinine, imprudent, ill-considered…"

"Are you grumbling about yourself?" she asked, her voice as stiff as her spine. "Or me?"

"Take a guess."

They glared at each other a long moment before she laughed, short and harsh. "Then you should probably add headstrong, rash, and impetuous," she said, not sounding or looking the least bit contrite.

What Aleksi should've done was yank her off her horse, bend her over his knee, and beat her comely backside until she came to her senses. What he wanted to do was slide her off Lasair down the length of him, sit her on his lap, and kiss her senseless, which was what he was quickly becoming.

"There," she cried, pointing ahead to a bend in the river where a large brown mass lay along the shoreline, which sent Lasair into a heedless trot.

"Sahar, wait," Aleksi yelled. Though the rain had dwindled to a mist, the ground was still slick and fetlock deep in mud.

She didn't slow down.

Gritting his jaw, Aleksi went after them, trusting Zolotoy's strength and sure-footedness as the mud sucked at his hooves, pulling them in deeper than the lighter mare and her mistress. After slipping and almost going down twice, they finally made it to where Sahar stood staring down at Kedar's lifeless body, his head twisted at an unnatural angle. A deep gash went from the side of the gelding's throat to his ear.

"He died quickly," Aleksi said, dismounting and standing beside Sahar, offering what small comfort he could. "That head wound was a death blow. He didn't feel a thing."

She nodded wordlessly and swiped at the tears falling from her cheeks, and then she dropped to her knees and kissed the gelding's forehead. "I'm so sorry, Kedar," she sobbed. "Forgive me, please. I never meant for any of this..."

Aleksi knelt beside her and laid a hand on her shaking shoulder and put the other on Kedar's. "We honor you, Kedar," he said. "A mighty steed who gave your life in service to your master. May the *bog loshadi* welcome and revere you."

"*Bog loshadi?*"

"The horse gods of my land."

Sahar sniffed. "May you be a king among the *bog loshadi*, brave Kedar."

She looked to Aleksi, her eyes glistening pools of grief, and he coughed, stood, and offered her his hand. He closed his fingers over hers and lifted their clasped hands as she rose with the ease and grace of the tigress she was.

"Aleksi," she said. "I..."

"I know," he said quickly. It was the first time she had called him Aleksi, and it warmed his sodden heart. He squeezed her hand before letting it go. "I know." He blew out his breath and jutted his jaw at a bramble of branches washed up on shore. "Bring what you can to cover him," he said. "I'll collect his saddle and gear. We need to get back to Munir."

"And to the race."

"You intend to continue the race then." It was more statement than question. Aleksi knew her well enough to know she wouldn't quit.

"Of course. Why wouldn't I? Are you suggesting I should quit?" she demanded, and didn't wait for an answer. "Now? When so many have sacrificed so much?"

"I didn't say that."

"No, you said I was a soft, spoilt princess."

"That was before I knew you."

"What about all the others who think they know me, who think all women weak and incapable of anything more than looking pretty and birthing babies, which is no simple task by the way. If I quit now, I'd only be proving their baseless opinions had some merit." She stood at her full height and stared him straight in the eyes, the fire back in hers. "I can do this," she said. "I will, with or without your protection."

"I'm not withdrawing. Not from the race, and not from my oath to your father."

"Or from your reward of one hundred gold pieces."

Aleksi bit back his grin. "Which I only collect if you return to your father uninjured and alive."

Sahar sat cross-legged on her bedroll, drinking wine straight from the skin. After leaving Munir at the check point, where it was determined he had a dislocated shoulder and several broken ribs, she and Aleksandr had ridden hard, making the night's camp as the sun sank below the western horizon. Even after changing into dry clothing, she was still half numb with cold, and her belly was only half full after eating her sparse meal of jerky and dates.

Her heart felt wholly and completely empty.

"It's my fault," she told Aleksandr, who'd laid his bedroll down next to hers and was drinking liberally from his wineskin as well. "All of it."

"All of what?" he said.

"Munir, Kedar, all of it."

"Did you cause the river to swell? Did you loosen the log from its mooring and cause it to go tumbling down the river to hit Munir and Kedar?"

"No." She shook her head, and her vision swam as a warm flush of heat spread from her belly to her head.

"Then you didn't cause any of it."

His low, rumbling voice echoed in the cavernous maw of her chest, and she had the sudden urge to crawl into his lap and curl up in the refuge of his embrace, to breathe in the earthy scent of man and sweat, horse and leather that was Aleksandr. To lay her ear against the solid expanse of his chest and listen to the strong, steady beat of his heart. She took another draught of wine instead.

"But I did," she said, recalling the thread of her thoughts, their conversation, with muddled difficulty. "Munir only rode in this race to protect me. He would be back at the palace, fit and uninjured, guarding my family and basking in Halah's adoration if not for me." She sniffed back unwelcome tears, and hiccupped. "Ke...Kedar would still be alive too, sa...safe and co...comfortable in the royal stables, not bu...buried beneath a hasty grave of brush and bramble. His bo...body'll be gnawed upon by scavengers until there is no...nothing left but bl...bleached bo...bones."

Aleksandr's face loomed close, and she swayed and braced herself with her hands to keep from falling back onto her bedroll.

"Don't blame yourself," he said, as she slowly straightened. "People do what they will do, what they feel they must. You felt the need to ride in this race, and so did Munir. You ride to prove yourself to a world that does not value women as you think it should, and Munir rode to prove himself valuable to your father and your family. You couldn't've stopped him anymore than he could've stopped you."

"What about you?" she asked. "Why do you ride?"

"I told you, for the coin, to return to my homeland and build a stable to rival a king's and raise a family."

She stared intently at the stubborn set of his jaw, the firm line of his mouth, the hard glint of his eyes. Her own vision blurred slightly, and yet she had never seen him so clearly, the pain of a young boy set aside by his father. The shame of a favored prince lowered to a common stable hand. The determination of a man to prove himself to a world that considered him nothing more than a bastard.

"No," she said, reaching out and laying her hand on his. "You ride to prove yourself as worthy as any royal, to build a stable to rival not any king's, but your father's. You ride to prove him wrong for casting you, his firstborn son, aside. He was wrong. So very wrong."

The hand beneath hers turned, and twined long, strong fingers through hers.

"You are a son any man would be proud of, Aleksandr, firstborn son of Maksimillian," she whispered fiercely.

Aleksandr lifted their joined hands and lowered his head, brushing his lips against the backs of her knuckles. "You are a woman equal to any man, my tigress."

His gaze held hers for a long moment, intent and serious and a little sad, and then he let go of her hand, and she reeled back at the vivid memory of another hand letting go of hers. A chill as cold as death passed through her. She shuddered, shivered, and her teeth chattered. She may have helped save Aleksandr and Munir, but she hadn't been able to save Ommar.

"You need to stay away from me," she said, scooting to the far side of her bedroll.

"Why would you say that to me now?"

She clamped her eyes tight against the image of Ommar's outstretched hand, of his frightened face as he was pulled from her grasp. She opened them to the night's blackness and took a long draught of her wine, welcoming the wet tartness as it slid down her throat and warmed her from the belly out.

"Sahar." Aleksandr's voice was tinged with anger. "What do you mean, I should stay away from you?"

She focused her blurring gaze on his. "I mean, Alekshki, that you should stay away from me, as far away from me as you can, for your own sake. I am"—she took another swig of wine and wiped her mouth with her sleeve, pursing her lips at the acrid aftertaste—"bad luck."

He grabbed for her wineskin, but she swung it out of his reach.

"This wine tashes funny," she said.

"That's because you're drunk."

"That may be," she said with a flourish of the skin that almost upended her. "But it doeshn't make me wrong."

Aleksandr took a long, slow drink from his wineskin, pursed his kissable mouth, and then fixed her with a lopsided gaze. "How are you bad luck?"

She swayed as she saluted Aleksandr with her wineskin. "Im's not the only one's drunk," she slurred.

"No," Aleksandr saluted her back. "Yer not. However, you still haven't not answered my question," he garbled.

Sahar uncorked her skin and drained it, trying to drown out the vision of Kedar's rotting corpse. The image of Munir's pale, ashen face. The memory of Ommar's last words.

"Run away, Alekshandar. Far, far away. Any man who shtands too close to me ends up hurt, or dead."

CHAPTER 10

Kidnapped

Aleksi woke face down in the dirt, every bone and muscle in his body cold, stiff, and sore. He rolled over onto his back with a body-wracking groan and tried to lick his desiccated lips, but his tongue was twice its normal size and as dry as salted meat. His head pounded against his skull, his neck was cricked sideways, and his belly was roiling. He peered out from beneath swollen lids into a blue sky thick with white clouds and lifted a heavy arm against the glare of the late morning sun. The last thing he remembered of the night before was sitting on his bedroll, talking with Sahar and drinking his wineskin empty.

Sahar.

He rolled over onto his side, the side she should have been to, and saw nothing but an impression in the ground where her bedroll had been. He heaved himself up onto his hands and knees and when his vision finally stopped swimming he sat on his heels and looked around. The entire camp was deserted except for Zolotoy, who grazed near the streams bank, his tie-line dangling loose from his neck.

Aleksi dropped his chin and slowly turned his head from one side to the other as every muscle and sinew from his neck to his hips resisted and pulled. He sat back and rubbed his face with his hands until the blood returned to his cheeks and his brain. He had never in his life been so drunk that he had passed out before, or woken up the next day in this bad of shape. He supposed the combination of three days and nights of hard riding, little sleep, meager food, and the cold, wet, river crossing and its harrowing aftermath could have made the half skin of wine he drank affect him more than usual.

Sahar had drunk as much, and had been slurring her words even more than he had been, and yet it looked as if she had managed to waken and resume the race.

He grabbed his empty wineskin and stood on unsteady legs, surveying the vacant campsite. By the gods, not one person in the entire camp of riders thought to rouse him from his drunken slumber. Would he have woken a fellow competitor, or would he have laughed at their folly and let them sleep it off? He liked to think he would have chosen to be the better man, but he knew otherwise. He surely would never have even considered rousing Yago or Taweel. But he would've woken Sahar. So why hadn't she woken him?

"I am bad luck. Stay away from me, far, far away from me."

Those were the last words he remembered her speaking to him. Apparently, drunk or not, she'd meant them. He hobbled over to the stream and dunked his head in the water, the chill chasing away the dull ache with merciless efficiency. Drinking his fill of the cool, refreshing water, he filled the empty wineskin with river water and packed his saddle bags, keeping out a piece of salted meat to chew on. Now was not the time to brood over last night, or how she'd called him Aleksi, twice. Now was the time to get back on Zolotoy, catch up to that tricky tigress, and win the damned race.

It was high noon before he caught up to the first straggler.

"Prince Saqr," he called, slowing Zolotoy to a walk beside the prince, who led his stallion on foot, both of them limping.

"Aleksandr."

"Is there anything I can do for you or your horse?"

"No, thank you," the prince said. "Our injuries are only serious enough to take us out of the race, but nothing debilitating."

"I'm glad to hear it." Aleksi took a swig of his water skin and capped it. "Did you happen to see Princess Sahar leave camp this morning?"

The prince shook his head. "No," he said. "I didn't. But I wasn't the first out of camp this morn. Several riders had already left by the time I woke."

Aleksi nodded, neither of them mentioning the fact that he'd been left sleeping. It was, after all, every man, or woman, for themselves.

"I will tell the aide post to expect you," he said.

He came upon two more riders leading lame horses, neither of whom recalled seeing Sahar that morning either. A nagging dread took hold in his belly and would not let go. He pushed Zolotoy as hard as he dared, cursing her for riding out early and alone, cursing himself more for letting her.

He passed another rider on his horse, and then one more as he made the aide post. At least he was not the furthest behind. It was mid-afternoon, so he would be able to make the night's camp in time, barring any other mishaps or foolish mistakes on his part.

"When did Princess Sahar ride through?" he asked.

The two guards manning the post looked at each other and shook their heads. "She hasn't," the older one said. "Not yet."

"Are you certain?" The nagging dread in Aleksi's belly began to stir.

"We haven't seen her," the same guard said. "We wouldn't miss *her*."

"Or forget," the younger guard added with a grin.

"She'd never cheat and bypass this post," Aleksi said, more to himself than to the guards. "I was the last to leave camp this morning, and I haven't passed her on the road." The pit in his belly grew. Unless she was hurt or hiding somewhere. He rounded on the guards. "Who else hasn't checked in?"

The guards recited their list. Yago, Taweel, and the Jackal weren't on it.

"One of you needs to ride to the palace," Aleksi ordered. "Now."

"Swallow."

Sahar spit the wine mixed with the oil of dream flower back at Yago, and was rewarded with the sting of his backhand across her cheek. At least he slapped her on the left cheek this time. The sinister Wolf had slapped her on her right cheek so many times throughout the day that the swelling was beginning to hinder her sight out of that eye.

"I said swallow, bitch."

Yago grabbed her by the hank of her braid and yanked her head back, knocking it against the trunk of the tree she was tied to, forcing her mouth open. Sneering down at her with cruel anticipation, he held the skin of tainted wine over her mouth and poured it down her throat until she was forced to swallow, or drown.

She choked down what she could as the rest spilled down her neck, soaking into the growing stain on her wine-soured tunic. She knew it would be a short time before her vision began to blur and her mind to wander, but at least it would numb the tender bruising on her face and the stinging pain where her wrist ties rubbed her bruised and chafed skin raw.

She'd woken a little before dawn, gagged and tied and strapped into her saddle astride Lasair, who was being led by a tie-line to Tor, Yago's black stallion. As her vision and her mind cleared, she saw that Taweel and the Jackal also traveled with Yago, one riding ahead of them and the other behind. Her body ached almost as much as her head, but every time she was beginning to see and think more clearly, Yago would drug her, which made it impossible for her to get her bearings. The day's journey had been a hazy memory of blurring trees, Lasair's bobbing head, and Yago's stinging slaps. It was night now, and she was able to make out the bear constellation rising to the north as she watched her captors make camp, concentrating on anything and everything the three princes said or did.

"Smart," she said, taking advantage of the fact that they had not replaced her mouth gag, and that her words still came to her for now. "No fire for those coming after me to see. Weasels and curs are known for their slyness."

"Who do you think will be coming after you?" Yago said with a sneer worthy of his namesake.

"Aleksandr," she said without hesitation, without doubt. "Aleksandr will come for me."

Yago laughed, low and sinister. "That bastard will not be coming after anybody ever again," he said. "We dosed his wine with enough dream flower to kill a horse."

"No." It was all she could think, all she could say, and if it were not for the tree she was tied to, she would've sunken onto the hard, damp ground in a hollowed, boneless heap. "No."

"Oh yes." Yago was practically preening. "We dosed both of your skins with dream flower, and several of the other riders' as well. They all slept like babes in their cradles while we took you and made it look like you left on your own. Even if the bastard survived, which is unlikely, he would've been chasing after you in the opposite direction, thinking you still in the race. He won't realize anything's amiss until he makes the night's camp. If he makes the night's camp. With Aleksandr and Munir gone, thanks to me—"

"What do you mean, thanks to you?"

"That log did not come loose of its own accord."

"You murderous pollution of a cur," she hissed.

"Save your breath." Yago knelt down and cinched the rope tighter around her, grinning as it bit into her skin. "There is no one left to come after you, not in time to save you. The other riders will not worry themselves over your absence, and it'll be three days at least before they make the palace, and another three days to pick up our trail from last night's camp, if they're able to find it. By then you will be well on your way."

"To where?"

"To my father's palace."

So, she was to be a hostage. "They'll realize that you and your slavish dogs are responsible for my disappearance."

Yago's thin lips pulled back into a slow, smug, self-satisfied smile. "We are counting on it," he said. He leaned in close to her. "By then, it will be too late for you, as it is too late for your Aleksandr."

"You're a liar," she swore. "A worm, exactly as Aleksandr named you. I don't believe he's dead. A worm such as you could never kill a man such as he."

"Yet, here I stand, not him."

"Aleksandr will come." She couldn't let herself think him dead. She wouldn't, or all was lost. She was lost. "If he does not kill you, my father will."

"The Black Mane will try," Yago said, the sharp lines of his face beginning to blur. "Why else do you think we have gone to all this trouble? If you had let me court you and marry you and poison you on our wedding night, my parents' revenge would have been quick and sweet. But since you were not agreeable to my wooing, you've forced us to improvise."

She shook her head and closed her eyes tight as her vision swam. When she opened them again, Yago was watching her, his gaze as black and smooth as pitch over a bottomless well.

"My father, my mother." Her heart dropped at the realization that she might never see them again. "My brother, Ratter, Aleksandr, they all warned me about you."

"You should've heeded their warnings." Yago tapped her on the nose and jerked his finger back as she snapped at it. Then he wagged his finger at her. "As you shouldn't have entered this race." He shook his head and tsked. "Did you truly think that you, a woman, could finish, much less win this race?"

"I beat you the first two races."

The force of his slap slammed her head back into the tree and left a ringing in her ears.

"You watch your mouth," he snarled.

She licked her cracked and swollen lips, the corners raw and bloody from the gag. "Why?" she whispered hoarsely.

"Because I'll gag you again if you don't."

"No." She shook her still spinning head. "Why take me captive? Why take me to your father? Why not kill me now?"

"To exact revenge on your parents by first defiling and then killing you in a public manner." He grinned, pleased with the chilling effect of his words. "When your precious mare, Lasair, the last foal out of Storm Chaser and Cloud Dancer comes into season, we will breed her with an ass."

Sahar swallowed her rising bile. "Killing me will only lead to more killing," she said. "To war between our tribes."

"Precisely."

Aleksi made the previous night's campsite after nightfall. The drier weather had held, and with the light of a hastily made torch, he was able to find the muddy tracks of four horses leading east from the camp. One of the horse's hoof prints were smaller than the others, and had not sunk so far into the dried mud.

"Lasair." Carrying Sahar.

Until now he'd only had suspicions, but these tracks were proof. Yago and his pack of curs had taken his tigress. Why, Aleksi could only guess, but he knew Yago to be a lying, vindictive corruption of a man, perfectly capable of exacting revenge against anyone he perceived had slighted him. Aleksi would put nothing beyond the worm, and had worn a hole in the side of his cheek and in his gut worrying about how that revenge would be exacted. He'd spent the better part of the ride back praying to every god and goddess he could think of that he would get to Sahar before Yago had his way with her. She was a strong woman, the strongest he'd ever known, but everyone had a breaking point, even a tigress.

Or an arrogant ass.

It had been Aleksi's arrogance that had let her come to harm. He had been so cocksure that his presence was enough to ensure her safety that he hadn't taken Yago's threat seriously enough. Not that Aleksi could have foreseen this. Yet, he should've picked up on the signs. He should've been more suspicious when she caught the Jackal standing over their bedrolls. Aleksi should've listened when she said the wine tasted off. Clearly, their wine had been adulterated with dream flower, and it'd happened while they were busy with Feroz. Aleksi should have known something was amiss when he woke up late and disoriented. He hadn't drunk that much wine. What he had done was become so distracted, so besotted, that instead of protecting Sahar, he had left her open to the Wolf's vile, nefarious attack. Then Aleksi had given the worm a full day's head start.

"AARRGGHH."

He smashed the torch against a tree, his rage splintering into a thousand flaming shards. He had to get her back, before Yago hurt her any more than he had already. Not because of the hundred gold pieces, not to be able to look King Asad in the eyes again, but because Aleksi wanted her back. *Because he wants her.* He always had, since the first moment he had laid eyes on her.

The torch out, he glanced up at the face of the moon, a day away from full and spilling light down the trail before him. Yago and his pack may have gained a full day's ride ahead, but four horses traversing muddy terrain should be easy enough to track. With any luck, and the moon's continued assistance, Aleksi would be able to make a good portion of the distance up if he rode all night.

Following their trail turned out to be the easy part. The hard part was keeping his mind from straying to all the atrocities the Wolf could inflict upon Sahar. The man was a scheming, spiteful, malevolent bully who had already proved he was capable of base, vicious behavior. The chance that Aleksi would not find her in time to save her from whatever horrible fate the Wolf had planned for her gnawed at him, goading him into riding Zolotoy harder than was safe, or smart. If he injured himself or Z, and was unable to reach her at all, what then? Even knowing this, he couldn't slow his pursuit. He wouldn't. Not with every hoof beat pounding the image of her beaten, used, and bloody, or worse, deeper into his worried mind.

Sahar knelt on bruised knees at the stream's edge and quickly lapped up the water from her cupped hands. The chill of the water both stung and numbed the scrapes on her palms and wrists, and eased the swelling of her tongue, which she bit as the Jackal jerked the rope tied around her wrists, causing the water to splash in her face. He cackled with glee as the icy water ran down the neck of her tunic, and she closed her eyes and slowed her breath to keep from lashing out at him. It would only make her situation worse.

Yago had handed her leash over to the Jackal that morning, the second morning of her kidnapping, and the Jackal had immediately taken to playing with her, exacting his revenge for his broken nose and laughing with sick pleasure every time he yanked on the rope, causing her to flail and fight to keep her seat or to trip and fall onto her hands and knees at their infrequent stops.

The more distress and humiliation she showed, the greater her captor's amusement, and she'd learned to hide her pain as best she could. The oil of the dream flower that they continued to pour down her throat actually helped numb the physical and the mental pain, as well as taking the edge off the hunger pangs. They fed her only enough to keep her from fainting, but not enough to fill the hole in her belly. It would've been easy to give in and welcome the numbing relief, but she needed to keep what wits she could about her, and had taken to acting more drugged and subdued than she actually was. The tormenting thought that Yago might truly have killed Aleksandr and that she was the cause of his death had wormed its way into her mind and festered there, its poison spreading into her heart, her blood, her marrow, chilling her to the bone.

Then there was the ever-present threat of rape. A threat she expected would be meted out sooner or later, and that she would not, she could not, allow herself to dwell on. Otherwise she would be useless. She had only herself to rely on. The possibility that Aleksandr would find her in time was slim to none. Her willfulness had gotten her into this predicament, and it would be that same stubborn will that got her out of it.

"Get up, bitch," the Jackal commanded as she took one last frantic drink. "To your feet, now."

She grunted and planted her hands in the mud to push up with. The sharp edge of a small stone cut into her palm, and she dug her fingers deeper around the stone, palming it as she stood. The Jackal jerked her rope taut, cackling as she fell onto her hands and knees. She slipped the stone into her boot and slowly rose back up on stiff, shaking legs, stumbling forward as the Jackal dragged her over to a tree. He tied her to the trunk, yanked her head back, and poured a few drops of the oil of dream flower into her mouth. She made the motions of swallowing, and then spit out most of the bitter oil as soon as he turned his back.

Yago had told her he intended to take her back to his father's kingdom. She figured she had another ten and four days of hard riding before she was served up to the Ox, which meant she had only ten and three nights to get herself and Lasair free. The sooner the better her chances of finding help. If Aleksandr was dead, her only other hope was that the guards at the next post had noted her failure to check in and had gone to search for her. Her heart seized as she imagined them finding Aleksandr at the last campsite, his impressive body stiff with rigor, his warm, earth brown eyes dulled and unseeing.

She shook herself mentally. She couldn't let herself think that way. She had to concentrate on staying alive, on getting herself and Lasair free and on their way home.

If she didn't get free, didn't get home, she'd never be with her family again in this world. She'd never see her mother's understanding face, or feel her father's big paws ruffling her hair, or hear her brother's teasing voice again. She'd never know her brother's firstborn, or be a loving auntie to any of his children. She'd be only a sad, whispered tale of family lore. She'd never be witness to Halah's and Munir's wedding, and their marriage would always be shadowed with Sahar's memory. Ommar's face, Sahar's familiar ghostly companion, came to her, and she squeezed her eyes tight to stop the sudden welling of tears.

She'd be damned if she gave Yago and his curs the satisfaction of seeing her cry. Her mother had been captured by pirates and tied to a pole in the slave market for days, held in a hot hole and almost died of heat sickness. The Ox had attacked her, and her arm was sliced open by a sword, yet she had survived it all. So would her daughter.

"I will see you soon enough, Ommar," she sighed, and then straightened her spine and her resolve. "But not yet." She shook her boot and felt the small, jagged stone lodged above her ankle. "Not yet."

She dropped her chin to her chest, stretching the tight muscles along the back of her neck, and let her mouth hang open, feigning a deep, drugged sleep as boot fall approached. A hand grabbed her by the hair and tilted her face up, and she let her tongue loll as she rolled her unfocused eyes back before slowly closing her lids. The hand let go of her hair and she let her head flop forward.

"The oil of dreams has over taken the bitch," the Wolf said, kicking her boot for good measure. "She'll be sleeping it off until morning."

"Which gives us the night to play," Taweel's voice answered.

Perhaps it was the dream flower, or the fact that she'd been watching every move they made and listening to every word they spoke for the past two days and nights, but something in the tenor of Taweel's voice had changed. As did the Wolf's sultry laughter.

"It has been too long, my randy cock," he chuckled.

"Indeed, my prince," Taweel's voice grew closer, lower. "I've missed your mighty sword these past nights."

"If you two are going to be rutting all night," the Jackal said from across the camp, "I'm going to sleep. You have the first two watches, wake me for third watch."

Sahar was a virgin, but she was no innocent. She'd heard of men lying with men, and women with women. A person couldn't reach maturity living among a palace full of people and not be aware of such differences.

In her father's kingdom they were left to their own preferences, but she knew that was not so in many other kingdoms, the Ox's among them. Perhaps that was why the Wolf was so good at hiding his true self, and not only his sexual preferences. He'd fooled her for a time, though never Aleksandr, who had accused her of falling for the Wolf's flattery. Aleksandr had been right about the Wolf's insincere flattery, about his cunning nature, and the need to protect her from him. He'd likely lost his life because of it. Because of her.

Stop it. You're not doing yourself or Aleksandr's memory any good by wallowing in self-pity. Stay awake. Wait for your chance.

It didn't take long for the sound of Yago and Taweel's muffled laughter to move beyond the edge of the camp. Not much longer before she heard the Jackal's soft, steady snore. Now was her chance. Listening to Yago's and Taweel's low murmurs, she bent her mind and body to shaking the stone from her boot one slow, painful movement at a time while trying, and failing, to stop imagining what exactly they were doing, her half-drugged mind filling in the lurid details.

Concentrate on what matters. Focus on getting this cursed stone out of your boot.

Which was no small feat with her upper arms tied to her sides. Years of riding and blade fighting had kept her limbs strong and agile. After much twisting and contorting she finally managed to drop the stone onto the ground between her booted feet as a man cried out as if in pain, or more likely release, followed immediately by another. Laying a booted foot over the stone, she hung her head low and mimicked the Jackal's snores as Yago and Taweel returned.

She heard the flap of bedrolls being unfurled and peeked out from under lowered lashes, watching with a perverse fascination as both men lay together, forming a two-headed lump under the covers. Their voices lowered to intimate whispers and then the quiet snuffles of early sleep mixed with the Jackal's steady snore, who they'd not woken by choice or forgetfulness. She propped the stone between her boots and splayed her knees, scooting the stone closer and closer, until she could reach it with her wrists and began to saw the rope back and forth over the rocks jagged edge, ignoring the fresh blood and the piercing pain as the rope cut into the open sores on her skin.

To keep her mind from the pain, she counted to ten as she sawed, stopped for another count of ten to look and listen for movement, and then repeated the entire process. By the time she had sawed a decent sized niche into the rope, her neck was cramped, her shoulders were screaming, and her wrists were numb, but she had to keep going, her life depended on it.

"What are you doing there?"

Sahar stopped sawing at the sound of the Jackal's voice and hung her head lower, barely breathing.

"Don't think I don't see you, Princess," he warned as his voice grew closer. He stopped and stood toe to toe with her boots, and then reached down and ripped the rock from her hand.

She bit her lip to keep from crying out in pain and frustration.

"Look at me." He threw the rock down, hitting her on the top of her head with it. "I said look at me."

She lifted her gaze, her hatred blazing in her veins.

"Do not give me that haughty glare, you royal cunt." He sneered down at her. "Your Aleksandr is dead. There's no one left to save you. You are at my mercy now, and if you think a few yanks on your rope will satisfy me, you're mistaken."

He unbuckled his waist belt and tossed it to the ground, and then he leaned over and untied her gag.

"Your virginity might be the King Ox's to take before he kills you," he said, still leaning over her and fumbling with the laces of his breeches, "but I'll have my satisfaction, you bitch."

"Whip your tiny worm out," she croaked, "and I'll bite it off."

"I like me a little nip," he said, slapping her across the cheek with such force that the back of her head struck the tree. "But bite me and you'll lose your teeth."

She tasted blood and spat at him, refusing to cower as he raised his hand up and back, readying for another blow. A shadow moved from behind her, and then the Jackal's face slammed into the tree with a bone-crushing crunch, and his body slid to the ground at her feet, his forehead split open above the bloody, mangled pulp that had been his nose. She tried to focus on the grotesque mask that had been his face, but her vison swam and her ears were filled with a distant ringing.

The shadow moved, and spoke in a ghostly whisper. "Sahar?"

She tried to lift her gaze to the spirit looming over her, but all she saw was a thousand blinking lights and then complete darkness.

Aleksi placed his fingers to Sahar's neck and dragged in a deep breath as he felt the weak but steady beat of her pulse. He had been following their trail when he saw the glow of a campfire about a league up the mountain's eastern face and had urged Zolotoy on, thanking the gods for the Wolf's arrogance and conceit.

Tying off Z in a thick glen downwind from the fire's beacon, Aleksi had continued on foot, walking along the tree line of the path they'd taken, and had been no more than a hundred feet away when the distinct, human cries of sexual release had echoed in the quiet of the night. His heart in his throat and terrible gut-wrenching images in his head, he silently prayed to every god and goddess he knew to keep Sahar's body and spirit alive while he slowly snuck up on the camp, and then let his breath out in a ragged sigh.

The gods had answered his prayers. She was alive.

From what he'd heard of the Jackal's vile threats while creeping up on the camp, she hadn't been violated, though as he took in the cuts and scrapes and bruises that were visible all over her, it was obvious that they had beaten her regularly. His tigress had fought back.

He grinned, recalling her threat to bite off the Jackal's cock.

"My fierce, fearless tigress," he whispered as he cut the ties on her wrists and then the rope tying her to the tree.

Her fiery spirit had held, even if her body had finally succumbed.

She slumped into his arms, and Aleksi scooped her up. He glanced down at the Jackal's smashed face, at his bloodless lips and fixed eyes. The corruption of a man was dead, and good riddance. Aleksi kicked the corpse for good measure, and startled as he heard a groan. The groan didn't come from the Jackal, It'd come from the mound of blankets closer to the line of horses. A mound with two heads.

Aleksi slipped behind the tree and peered back over at the mound that had to be Yago and Taweel, torn between slitting their throats as they slept, and getting Sahar safely away. He wasn't one to murder people in their sleep, but if anyone deserved to die that way, it was those two. If they were dead, she would be safe. That settled it. He started to lay her down, when he heard movement and low voices. Yago and Taweel were sitting up and looking around.

"Damn."

He could stay and fight or he could leave and get her to safety. Yago and Taweel were princes, both of them well taught in the art of sword fighting, and it would be two against one. If he was injured, or killed, he'd leave her to their cruelty and certain death. Holding her closer, he did something he never would've thought possible: he turned and ran from a fight.

Sahar was not a small woman, and carrying dead weight was always harder than a person who could hold onto you, especially when silence and stealth were needed. Aleksi had only made a hundred paces or so when he heard the sound of voices and maybe another twenty before the voices grew loud and insistent.

"The bitch is gone."

"The Jackal is dead."

"These boot prints are too large to be the Jackal's."

"Curse the whore and her whore-mongering bastard."

Aleksi moved deeper into the surrounding brush and hunkered down on a fallen log as the snapping of twigs and crunching of leaves grew louder.

"I can't see a thing," Taweel whispered loudly, no more than a stone's throw from where Aleksi hid with Sahar.

"Me neither," Yago said, not bothering to whisper. "You can bet they're long gone. Still, it doesn't matter. We've done enough. My father will have his war."

At the sound of Yago's voice, Sahar's eyes flew open. Aleksi clapped his hand over her mouth, and she bit down, hard. Gritting his teeth, he held her tight as she twisted and turned in his grip, her nails clawing at his hands, as feral as a wild cat caught in a snare. She was strong and sleekly muscled as a cat as well, and it was all Aleksi could do to keep hold of her.

"Shh," he whispered. "Shh. You must be quiet, my tigress."

Her eyes widened and she stopped her thrashing as they focused on his face. He shifted her on his lap and took his hand from her mouth, putting a finger to his lips as he motioned with his head toward the sound of retreating boot fall. She calmed and settled into his hold, nestling her nose into the crook of his neck, and burrowing her way straight to his heart.

Aleksi sat bolt upright at the thought, and gently peeled her arms from around his waist.

"I don't hear them anymore," he said. "We should move." He stood and held her close as her long legs unfolded and her feet found the ground. "Can you walk?" he asked, taking a step back, still holding her by the arms. She nodded and grasped his upper arms and took a step, and then another before letting go. "Good," he said, his hands at the ready to grab her as she swayed, but she stayed upright. "Z is not too far away."

At mention of Zolotoy, she started and made to turn back around. "Lasair," she said over her shoulder. "We must go back for Lasair."

"We will," he said, grabbing her by the arms and holding her still. "We can't tonight. We aren't in any condition for a fight."

She nodded, still and silent and staring at him with her big, unblinking eyes.

"Sahar?"

"They told me you were dead," she said, her voice a mere wisp of smoke, her eyes welling with tears. "Every day, every night, over and over..."

Aleksi pulled her to him and held her tight. "You should know by now that it would take more than a drop or two of dream flower to kill an arrogant ass like me," he murmured into her hair.

I would come back from the grave for you.

CHAPTER 11

Searching

Aleksi shook out his bedroll and laid it on the ground. "Here," he told Sahar. "You should lie down before you fall down."

It was a testament to how tired and worn out she was that she did what he said without argument. He took his otter cloak out of his saddle bag and covered her with it, clenching his fists at the red welts and raw sores on her wrists as she rolled over onto her side and pulled the cloak up under her chin. Gently, he touched his fingers to the black and blue swelling above the hollow of her cheek, and she whimpered and flinched at his touch.

"Shhh, Kitten," he soothed. "I won't hurt you. I'll never hurt you, and I'll never let anyone hurt you again."

He tucked a snarled, unkempt lock of hair behind her ear, and growled low as she shrank from his touch. It was obvious from her physical wounds that they had beaten her, but as bad as they were, they would heal. What worried Aleksi was the damage done to her spirit. He'd heard every vile word the Jackal said before smashing his face into the tree. They'd meant to hand her over to the Ox, to be publicly humiliated and raped and then executed, to be sacrificed for their war, all to settle a twenty-year-old grudge.

"They'll pay for what they have done to you," he vowed. "As well as for what they meant to do."

"They never would've succeeded," she said, her voice a raw whisper.

"No?"

She shook her head, and his cloak fell away from her chin. She turned and met his gaze, her beautiful face mottled with bruises. Aleksi's bile rose.

"I knew if you weren't dead..." Her voice cracked, and her eyes welled, and his heart stuck in his throat. "I knew if you were still alive, that you'd come after me." She smiled as sweetly and tenderly as she had never smiled at him before. "If you were dead, and I was on my own, then I would die by my own hand before I ever gave in to the likes of them."

"I'll kill them," Aleksi swore. "Yago and Taweel are dead men."

"You can't." Her gaze held his, serious. "We must bring them back to my father as proof of their plans."

"Your father will believe us without them."

"My father will, but the other kings may not. If the Ox gets his war..."

"Your father will need the other kings to ally with him."

Sahar gave a rueful grin, then grimaced and licked the cracked and bleeding corner of her mouth.

"If I can't kill the worm and his cur," Aleksi said, pulling a wash rag from his saddle bag and pouring water from his skin onto it, "then at least I demand the right to repay him in kind."

He touched the wet cloth to her lip and dabbed gently. She reached up and placed her hand over his, and then she grinned, fierce and feral. "Only after I have done with him," she said.

"There's my tigress," Aleksi said, relieved her spirit remained fierce.

He wet the rag again and dabbed at the cuts and sores on her wrists, grinning like the village idiot. "Ratter gave me a healing balm," he said, rummaging through his saddlebag and pulling out the tub. He rubbed the pungent salve on her wrists, and then her lips, the soft, plush feel of them pulling at his cock. He coughed and sat back. She needed comfort and healing, not some randy stallion pawing at her. Which made what he was about to say even more difficult. "We do not dare light a fire," he said, "and we only have the one bedroll. I need sleep, or I will be of no use tomorrow, and you need sleep to heal, so..."

"So..."

"So, Z is tethered next to us, he'll warn us if anyone comes near. I'm going to lay down under my cloak with you, and we'll share our bodies' heat."

She rolled a reddened eye at him, but she scooted forward and made room.

"Do not worry," he said as he lay down behind her. "I am too tired to want anything but a good night's sleep."

She huffed as he slid in closer and reached an arm around her, tucking her in tight. He prayed to the gods that his body would not make a liar out of him as his cock nestled into the firm heat of her round backside. If he became aroused, as he had in the kraal, and she felt it, she would bolt.

"Was that Yago and Taweel I saw tucked up in a bedroll together?" he asked, needing to think about anything other than the length of her pressed against him.

"It was."

"Were they huddled together for warmth?"

"No," she said. She shifted even closer, so that Aleksi's heart was hammering against her back. "They're lovers."

"Are they now?" Aleksi chuckled. "Well, that explains the sounds I heard earlier, as well as a few lingering glances from the worm after he arrived."

She giggled, and it was the sweetest sound Aleksi had ever heard.

"It seems he was jealous of me," she said, "not you."

Sahar woke cocooned by the length of Aleksi's body, his arm holding her tight to his broad chest, her backside tucked into the warming heat of his front side and her legs twined with his. His breath tickled the hairs on her neck where his nose was buried into her nape, but true to his word, he'd demanded nothing of her but easy conversation until they had both drifted off to sleep.

She shifted a little, trying to untangle her legs from his. He mumbled something into her shoulder and tightened his arm around her, his legs tucking into the back of hers. She held still for a moment, and then tried to move again, and felt something growing hard against her backside where there had only been soft heat. Curse the man, he truly was a stallion. She flipped around to face him, ready to accuse him of breaking his promise, and was surprised as his eyes opened and took a few moments to focus on her.

"You were still asleep?" she asked.

He yawned and rubbed his nose and stubbled chin. "Apparently I was more tired than I thought."

"Apparently," she nudged his groin with her thigh, "you're not as tired as you claim to be."

"You can't blame a man for his body's natural response," he said. He chuckled at her glare, not at all apologetic. "It's what happens when a man awakens, even if he is not lying next to a woman as desirable as you."

She licked her dry, swollen lips and touched her fingers to her dirty, matted hair. "You think me desirable?" she asked, feeling about as desirable as the wash rag Aleksi had used to tend her wounds, now hanging dry and stiff on the bush Zolotoy was tied to.

He laughed, short and harsh, and his brown eyes bore into hers. "I don't chase after women, or kiss them, or propose marriage to them, unless I find them desirable, you beautiful, maddening creature."

"Oh."

His gaze focused on her mouth and a pained grimace crossed his face before he gently tipped up her chin to close her mouth. He let out a short, ragged breath. "We better get up," he said, flipping his cloak off of them.

He stood, groaning a little as stiff joints popped, and offered her his hand. Blushing at the obvious bulge in his breeches, she reached up, and saw what looked like fresh teeth marks on the meaty edge of his palm.

"What happened to your hand?" she asked as he pulled her up. Her bruised knees creaked as she stood and turned his hand over to see what were obviously human teeth marks. "Who bit you?"

"A tigress."

Sahar's head snapped up and she felt a pull along the side of her neck as she met his steady gaze. She shook her head, working out the kink and her confusion. "I bit you?"

"Last night," he said, "after I cut you loose and you fainted. You woke up frightened and thrashing while we were hiding in the trees." He gave her a cocky grin. "I had to keep you quiet somehow."

She did not know whether to cuff him or kiss him. He'd saved her life. "I'm sorry I bit you."

He shrugged. "A man can expect nothing less when he tangles with a tigress." He coughed and blew on his cupped hands and went to his saddle bags and pulled out a linen square of dried meat. "Here, my tigress," he handed her a strip, "this will have to satisfy your blood lust for now."

She sat down and tore into the meat, her empty belly growling. She chewed the stringy meat then asked, "What's your plan?"

"My plan," Aleksi said, "now that I have gotten you safely away from those curs, is to keep you that way while staying a league behind Yago and Taweel. Close enough to follow, yet far enough to remain unseen until the time comes to steal Lasair and take the men alive, if possible. We're less than half a league from their camp," he told her as she reached up to assess the mass of snarls and curls that had escaped her unkempt braid. "We'll wait here awhile to give them a head start."

Nodding in agreement, Sahar winced, dropped her left arm and rubbed her shoulder.

"Here." Aleksi sunk onto his knees behind her. "Let me." He started at the bottom of her braid, gently untangling the plaiting. "We will forage as we go," he said, working his fingers up until the braid was undone. "Whatever we find will supplement the dry goods I still have. No hunting or fishing, no fire until we have those curs collared and leashed. They got overconfident last night and lit a fire, which was how I found you in the dark. My bet is that they'll do it again in a night or two, thinking we rode straight for your father's palace." He began to lightly rub his fingertips along her temples. Sahar sighed. "We can bathe in the stream this morning, if you like. I have a tub of soap in my saddle bags."

"Mmm-hmm."

His fingertips moved over her scalp in slow, rhythmic circles. "What was that, my tigress?"

"Sounds wonderful."

He continued circling his fingers down her neck to her shoulders, applying a little more pressure, and her head slumped forward with a soft groan.

"Do you want me to stop?" he asked, kneading the spot between her shoulders where the fulcrum of her tight muscles were knotted.

She shook her head. "No. Please, it feels..."

He resumed his kneading, and leaned in closer, whispering into her ear. "Wonderful?"

Sahar shivered, and he lowered his mouth to her nape and nipped her flesh where her neck met her shoulder. "You taste wonderful," he murmured.

She shrugged him off. "I feel like a piece of dried jerky," she said, skittering away.

"Well that explains it then," he said with a chuckle. "I'm famished."

He went to his saddle bags and pulled out the tub of soap and a clean undertunic. "Here," he said, handing her both. "The stream is past that copse of trees. I'll gather some greens upriver while you bathe." He grinned at her raised brows. "I'd feel safer keeping you in my sights. But don't worry, I promise not to look." He wiggled his brows. "Much."

Aleksi kept his back to her as she stripped and stepped into the stream, laughing at her curses as she waded deeper into the cold water heading to a small pool along the opposite shore.

She set the tub of soap on a rock, and he turned to forage for greens. When he turned back, he didn't see her and panicked.

"Sahar?"

She broke the surface, whirled around, and covered her breasts and with her hands. "You promised you wouldn't look," she accused.

"I promised not to look much."

Sahar lengthened her spine and narrowed her eyes. "What do you consider much?"

"Uh."

"Well?"

Aleksi shrugged and grinned and ran a hand through his hair. "Truly, you are a woman no man would ever get his fill of looking at." She didn't rail at him, or drop down into the water. She stood where she was and dropped her hands to her sides with a hard, hungry look on her face. She was beautiful and desirable, even bruised and bedraggled.

She watched, seemingly transfixed, as he pulled his tunic up and over his head, then his breeches landed beside his tunic, and she licked her lips and surveyed his body. Her gaze stayed on his cock rising between his legs.

She let her breath out and swallowed hard.

"Sahar?"

He stared as she raised her gaze and in her glittering eyes he could see everything she was feeling, most of it echoed his uncertainty, desire, and wonder. He stepped into the water and was standing in front of her before she had taken another breath.

He stood far enough from her that his cock waved between them without touching her. She closed the chasm between them with half a step, and he pressed into her belly, branding her as his throbbing need became almost more than he could bear. He wrapped his arms around her and pulled her even closer so they were skin to skin from breasts to knees. She let out a long breath with a low moan as she melted into him.

"My tigress." Aleksi's voice rumbled low in her ear and thrummed down her spine. His hands went into her hair and his lips were on her mouth, hard, hungry, and demanding, taking all that she was eager to give. As he took, he gave, his mouth trailing hot, wet kisses down her neck and across her shoulder while his hands explored the length of her back and the swell of her hips. He kissed her on the mouth again, long, hard, and deep as he cupped her buttocks with both hands, and then he lowered his mouth to her breast, flicking his tongue out and licking her nipple.

Sahar gasped, and the world around them burst into a cacophony of sound.

Aleksi's heart started racing for a different reason and he pushed her into the water and dropped down next to her as a flock of crows flew squawking from a tree, circling and cawing. They hugged the rocks forming the pool and watched silently, surveying the shoreline for any sign of what had disturbed the birds. A stag with a full head of antlers emerged from the tree line to drink from the stream.

Sahar's teeth started chattering so loudly he turned around and glared. Aleksi palmed a mouthful of water and spat it out. Gods. He could've gotten them killed.

"Curse me for an addlepated, weak-willed fool," he swore as he stood, his cock swinging at half-mast above her face. He grabbed the soap and lathered his head, his arm pits and his groin before dunking it in the water and handing the soap to her. "Here," he grumbled. "Wash up quick. We need to be on the move."

Shortly after coming to his senses, Aleksi stared down at the brush covering the Jackal's body and the boot prints around it. He walked behind the tree and looked down at his own, larger boot prints, which he hadn't had time to sweep over when he rescued Sahar.

"You can bet that Yago and Taweel know it was me who killed the Jackal and took you," he said to Sahar's back.

She nodded. She'd said nothing since the stream. Though her angry, accusing expression had spoken plenty.

They had come close, too close, to giving in to their desires and putting themselves in a dangerous and precarious position. Aleksi knew full well the fault was his. All he'd needed to do was look away as she had risen from the water, her sleekly muscled body, firm, high breasts and gently swelling hips glistening wet and naked, but he hadn't. He should've turned around and walked away from her as she stood there, shy and bold, but he hadn't. He'd walked straight to her, drawn by the look in her eyes and the need in his loins. He could still feel the wet warmth of her skin against his, the taut roundness of her backside in his hands, the heat of her kiss. He could still hear her low moan of pleasure as he held her close, her little gasp of surprise as he had flicked his tongue over her pebbled nipple.

Thank the gods for skittish crows and a thirsty stag. Aleksi had been thinking with his cock, not his brain, and had endangered them.

He glanced at her as she bent and picked up the cut rope that had tied her to the tree, and he vowed he would not be so careless again. Even as he swore to remain her chaste bodyguard, his cock was responding to the memory of her body pressed against his.

Concentrate on finding the Wolf, you fool, before he finds you.

"I am going to walk a circle outside the camp," he said to himself as much as to her. "Make sure they didn't double back on us."

The only tracks he found were of four horses heading south and west. Yago and Taweel must have decided that Aleksi and Sahar were heading back to her father. He smiled grimly. Even after all that they'd put her through, they still did not know her at all.

"You should ride Z," he said, holding the stallion's reins out to her. "I will walk the next league. Keep an eye out for any change in the tracks."

She took Z's reins and put her booted foot in Aleksi's cupped hands, letting him boost her up onto the saddle. He gave her ankle a gentle squeeze, and she kicked his hand away.

"Come on then," he said, starting off at an easy lope. "We have leagues of ground to cover."

They'd walked the half a league between their camp and Yago's this morning. He wasn't looking forward to riding pressed against her. Eventually though, they'd have to ride together. Until then, it felt good to stretch his legs and work his muscles while concentrating on following the tracks. It helped to keep his mind from wandering back to the two of them skin to skin in the stream. They'd covered another two leagues by noon and Aleksi was arguing with himself. He was beginning to tire, but was loath to tempt his self-control by riding double with her. He felt something crunch under his boot. He stopped and lifted it and saw that there were hundreds of chestnuts lying where they had fallen from a copse of trees, ripe and ready for picking.

"Chestnuts," he said, waving her over. "We can pack the saddle bags full of them."

She jumped down and packed one saddle bag with the nuts while he packed the other. He boosted her up onto the saddle and then swung up behind her, gritting his teeth as she shifted her backside into him. He took Z's reins and urged the stallion on. They might well go hungry for want of each other, but at least they wouldn't starve for food.

As they rode, the sun travelled in the sky, and Sahar fell asleep to Z's steady gate. Her head pillowed on Aleksi's shoulder. When she stirred, he muttered in her ear, "Welcome back."

She craned her neck and peered out from under heavy lids into a dusky sky. "Did I sleep the afternoon through?" she asked, yawning.

"You did."

He shifted a little, sitting up straighter.

"Where are we?" she asked.

"About five leagues south of where we started this morning," he answered, bringing a flush of heat to her cheeks and to his groin.

Where they had started that morning was naked together in a stream, skin to skin, mouth to mouth, lips to breast.

"Where, ah, where are Yago and Taweel?"

"A league ahead of us by their tracks, which still show two horses with riders and two without," he told her. "My guess is they'll camp on the mountain's peak tonight and start down the southern slope tomorrow."

"When do we go after Lasair?"

"When they've relaxed their guard and least expect it."

"What if they never do?"

He didn't answer.

"The longer we wait," she argued, "the closer they'll be to the Ox's kingdom, and the longer and more dangerous our journey home."

"True enough," he agreed. "But the Ox's kingdom is still a good eight to ten days' ride. We have time."

Which was a blessing and a curse. Time alone with Sahar in the wilds, riding with her, sleeping with her, without a repeat of what had happened in the stream this morning was going to nearly undo him.

Get over it, you ass. She's not for you. Get Lasair back. Get the princess home. Get yourself home with a purse full of coin and a string of broodmares for Zolotoy to cover. If you're lucky, someday you may look at another woman and not see a pair of blazing green eyes staring back at you.

He rubbed his stubbled chin and took a slow survey of the mountain sloping above them, as much to glean any information about where Yago and Taweel might be as to concentrate on anything but the tigress pacing around the camp.

"Look." He pointed up the mountain's side to where a small fire flickered. "Either Yago and Taweel are thinking we're long gone, or they are trying to trick us into showing ourselves."

"Hard to say with those two."

"True enough." He untied the saddlebag full of chestnuts and tossed it to her, grinning as she caught it without even blinking. "Shell those for our supper while I set up some traps around camp."

"The woman prepares the food while the man lays protection, huh?"

Aleksi understood her aversion to being seen as merely a woman, to be thought of as nothing more than a pretty face incapable of any but the most menial of tasks. Surely, she knew him better than that by now.

"Do you know how to set up traps?" he asked.

"I never have," she admitted. "But I can learn."

"I'll make you a bargain." He rubbed his grumbling stomach. "I'll teach you tomorrow, if you shell the chestnuts tonight. I'm starving."

"We're not going after Lasair?"

Aleksi shook his head. "I want them good and complacent with their guard down. Another night should do it."

Sahar eyed him for a long moment, and then held her hand out. "I need a blade," she said, "to shell the nuts."

After they'd eaten their meager supper of chestnuts and dried meat, she sat down on the bedroll and reached for the leather tie at the end of her braid.

"Here," Aleksi said, kneeling behind her. "Let me."

"I can do it myself."

"I know you can," he said, untying the leather strip, "but I like doing it for you. It gives me peace."

For some inexplicable reason—reason seemed to be in short supply when it came to them being together—when Aleksi had his fingers in her hair gently combing out the tangles into a veil of sooty black, he felt peaceful. He supposed it was like the sense of concentrated calm he always felt brushing down a horse, except his tigress was the one woman he wanted above all others. A princess he'd sworn to protect and keep from harm.

"How did you learn so much about surviving in the wild?" she asked as he unraveled the glossy ropes of her braid.

"Hunting trips with my father when I was younger and still a prince. Though even after I became a stable boy, he would still take me hunting with him as his horse master." Aleksi smiled. His best memories of his father were of their hunting trips, away from the palace and the queen where they could be Maksimillian and Aleksandr, father and son, not king and bastard stable boy. "He claimed that I was his best tracker."

"What did the bitch queen have to say about your hunting trips?"

He laughed at her description of Theodesia as he wove his fingers through her hair and gently shook it out, fanning the heavy veil across her shoulders and down her back. "They say the rafters of the palace were raised more than once by the shrillness of her response when told."

He started to comb his fingers through her hair, gently untangling a snarl.

"But she wasn't able to stop your father from continuing your hunting trips."

"She wasn't, though I know for a fact she tried."

"Because your father's love for you was stronger than his care for her."

Aleksi's fingers stilled as twenty and five years of grief, anger, and longing gripped him by the throat. "Then why," he choked out, "did he deprive me of my mother's love and then his own?"

She turned and met his gaze and held it, and thanks be to the gods, there was no pity in her expression. He couldn't have stood to see that. Not from her.

"Did you ever ask him?"

He sat back on his heels and slowly shook his head. "I only ever accused him of choosing the queen over me, his own flesh and blood."

"What did he say?"

"That he hoped I would understand someday."

Sahar turned to face him. "I don't mean to defend him," she said. "I can only imagine how you must have felt, a young boy seemingly abandoned by his father—"

"Seemingly?"

"Have you ever considered that it was his way of protecting you?"

"He was and is the king," Aleksi said, sounding as petulant as the boy of ten and two he had been when his father had exiled him to the stables. "From whom would the king need to protect his son?"

"The queen, or his second wife, mother to his legitimate son and heir to the throne."

Aleksi was fairly certain she hadn't said it to hurt him, but it hurt and he hated that it did.

"In some ways you should be grateful," she said. "It's made you the man you are."

"And who is that?"

"An arrogant ass who despises royal princesses."

Aleksi chuckled. "Not all of them," he admitted. "Not anymore."

She laughed, light and quick. "If you were still a prince, Aleksandr, you would already be married to some soft, spoilt princess who would be pregnant with your fifth daughter."

"Ha. You have a mean streak."

"It's how I keep my claws sharpened." She arched her brows while flexing her fingers.

He grinned. "Glad to see you back, my tigress."

"I'm not your tigress," she chuffed.

"I'm not only an arrogant ass."

"No," she said, her expression serious. "You're not. You're also a man determined to make his own way in the world. I respect that."

CHAPTER 12

The Peak

Sahar lay shivering under the thin blanket on Aleksi's bedroll, missing the heat of his body while watching him move about their camp as he checked his saddle bags and Zolotoy's ties for the tenth time. In between each check, he would look down at her and then turn away, grumbling under his breath as he sorted through his bag or retied Zolotoy's reins to the bush yet again. At last, he lowered himself down with a resigned sigh and lay behind her, stiffening as she scooted her backside up against him.

She snuggled in closer, waiting to feel his arm reach around and tuck her in to him, but he only stiffened more. It was his morning rejection all over again. She buried her face into her hands and stifled her threatening tears.

He sighed again, heavy, irritated, and started to slide his arm over her shoulder. She jabbed him in the belly with her elbow.

"Oomph." His breath hit her neck in a great whoosh. "What was that for?"

"I don't wish to be forced into bodily contact with you any more than you wish to be physically close to me," she huffed.

"Then why do you keep wiggling like that against me?"

"Like what?"

He bumped his pelvis against her buttocks, shooting liquid heat from her core to her chest. "Like that," he said, his breath close and hot on her nape.

"I wasn't wiggling," she insisted, and purposely wiggled her backside against him. "I was cold." She burrowed her buttocks into the curve between his belly and his thighs. "Why does it bother you so much more tonight than last night?"

"I was too tired to do anything about it last night."

"And this morning?"

"I told you, men wake up that way quite often."

"No." She shook her head, and her body flushed from her head to her toes. "I mean this morning in the stream, when you stormed away from me after we—"

"Stood skin to skin and kissed."

She nodded, the bedroll rough and painful against her still bruised cheek, which was nothing compared to the sting of her bruised pride.

His silence had her ready to jump up and spend the night high in a tree as far away from him as she could safely be. Then he placed his arm around her and pulled her in tight.

"What do you think happened this morning?" he whispered in her ear, his voice low and rough.

"I think you didn't want me after all."

He laughed so sharp and quick that he actually barked. "Is that how you think a man who doesn't want a woman responds?" He nipped the tender skin at the back of her neck and nuzzled her nape. "I want you, my tigress. I've wanted you every cursed moment of every cursed day and night since I laid eyes on you." He growled low, nudging her backside with his hardening length. "I want you so badly it hurts."

"Then why did you walk away? Why were you so angry with me?"

"I was angry with myself. I knew better, and I let my wanting you put you in harm's way."

In a long slow sigh, she let out the breath she'd been holding since he had walked away from her in the stream. Aleksi rolled his forehead between her shoulder blades.

"If those crows and that stag hadn't interrupted us, I wouldn't've had the will to stop." His voice grew low and his cock grew rigid. "I would've laid you down on the grass at the river's edge and made love to you until we both were spent, heedless of the dangers all around us."

"And now?" She knew she was being brazen, but she didn't care. All she cared about was the feel of Aleksi's big, warm hand cupping her breast.

His thumb rubbed her nipple, and she gasped with pleasure.

"Now we are still in great danger," he whispered hotly. He kissed her neck where it met her shoulder, his thumb continuing its tantalizing circle around her beaded nipple. "We are in great danger of crossing a line that once crossed cannot be redrawn."

She rolled to face him, the heat in her body reflected in his gaze. "Who would know besides us?" she asked, her voice lower and deeper than usual.

His thumb stopped its delicious circling, and he held her by the shoulders, looking her straight in the eyes. "Your future husband would, whoever the lucky bastard of a prince turns out to be."

Aleksi craned his neck from side to side as they reached the mountain pass in the late afternoon, trying to work out the kinks from sleeping with his back propped up against a tree's trunk. The almost constant ache in his loins was not so easily assuaged.

He rolled his shoulders and felt Sahar's head loll between them, her soft snore telling him she was finally sleeping after sitting rigidly behind him for most of the day. He held her clasped hands at his belly tighter, to keep her from sliding off of Z onto the damp ground. She'd tossed and turned as much as Aleksi had last night, neither of them getting much, if any sleep.

He snorted at his confession of wanting her more than anyone, and at his "noble" restraint. Z spooked and danced, causing Aleksi to pull up on the stallion's reins. Sahar snuffled and pressed closer. He held his body as still as possible as she settled, chuckling quietly. He'd do to the same with Kiska staying in one position until his limbs grew numb lest he disturb the little tyrant. It seemed he was doomed to serve as a fool and lackey for kittens and tigresses in his attempt to protect them from weasels and wolves.

He'd been terrified when he realized she'd been abducted. Then, after he'd rescued her, when he finally had her panting and willing in his arms, he'd stopped them before they went too far.

Mostly—and in spite of what he'd told her—it was because he was scared. Scared that once he had her, he would go from want to need to nothing. A bastard and a princess had no future. He'd lied when he'd told her they were nothing to each other.

She was everything to him.

Which was why he was doing her bidding to reclaim Lasair and take two worthless princes as captives to try to stop a war from starting between the southern tribes. Meanwhile, Serge and Pyotr were in King Asad's city, trading horses, getting started in the new life they'd dreamed and planned for. A life that would always have a Sahar-sized hole in it. Still, there would be some solace in showing up at the gate to his father's palace with a purse full of gold and a string of fine broodmares.

As long as his father was alive to see it.

Aleksi had tried not to think of his father being ill. Unable to do anything to remedy whatever ailed his father from here, he'd pushed that worry to the back of his mind, which had been filled first with running the race, and then with finding Sahar and keeping her safe, and now with saving Lasair and capturing Yago and Taweel. He hoped Anastasia hadn't been lying that their father's illness was trifling. He trusted her about as much as he trusted the Wolf.

Right now, he needed to concentrate on catching the Wolf and getting Sahar home, safe and sound with her virginity intact.

When they made camp, she shaved the end of the last stick into a spike while he dug a hole to prop it into next to six others set in a line along the only path leading into their camp. When they were done, he spread out the empty husks of the chestnuts they'd eaten around the borders of their campsite.

He tied Z to a bush at the path's opening while she strewed the small pile of twigs they'd collected around the outer edges of the glen.

"There," he said approvingly. "If they come, we'll hear the crunches of their boot fall or them screaming."

She handed him his blade. "If they don't come to us tonight, we go after them and Lasair tomorrow night," she confirmed.

"Barring any unforeseen circumstances."

She said nothing.

"Sahar?"

"Don't 'Sahar' me," she snapped. "I'm going after Lasair tomorrow night with or without you."

"What about Yago and Taweel? How do propose to capture them without me?"

She gnashed her teeth and growled low.

"Be reasonable."

"Be reasonable?" she snapped. "I've been kidnapped, beaten, starved, and threatened with rape, public humiliation, and death. You think I'm being unreasonable?"

"I think," he said calmly, "that you are speaking too loud."

"I think," she hissed, "you are being... That you are..." She gnashed her teeth and fisted her hands at her sides. "Confoundedly reasonable."

He fought his twitching lips and then gave in as his chest shook with silent laughter.

"I'm glad I amuse you," she said coldly. "That my frustration is a matter of mirth for you."

"Sahar." He reached his hand out to her face.

She slapped his hand away. "I told you, don't 'Sahar' me. I'm in no humor to be mollified by you or any man." She glared at him as if it was his fault he had been born male. "None of this would've happened if I'd been a man."

"Perhaps," he said. "I, for one, am glad you're not."

"Why?"

He held her gaze for a long moment, wondering if she was baiting him or that naïve. Then he blew his breath out and ran a hand through his hair knowing he'd couldn't tell her his truth. "Because your father wouldn't've paid me a hundred gold pieces to watch over his son."

They ate their meager meal of chestnuts and jerky in stony silence. Then he checked the traps they set and retied Z's reins to a bush for the seventh time, putting off lying next to her on the bedroll.

He stopped distracting himself and slid under the blanket behind her, keeping his body from touching hers. Making sleepy little snuffles, she wriggled her backside against him. He went stiff and grumbled low in his chest, and she snuggled closer until the length of her body pressed against the length of his. Sahar sighed, then turned to face him.

"Sahar?" He cocked his head and his hair fell down over his forehead. She reached out and pushed it back from his eyes, smiling as the stubborn lock fell again.

"Aleksaandrrr," she purred, running her fingers through his hair.

He reached up and grasped her by the wrist, stilling her hand. "Be careful, my tigress," he warned. "You're playing with fire."

"I'm fire, my stallion," she rasped. "I want to burn with you." She slid her hand down his belly and pressed her palm against the flap of his breeches. He sucked his breath in as she rubbed his already rigid cock. "I want to feel you rise again and again."

"You will, my tigress," he rumbled, pushing his pelvis against her hand and rolling her onto her back in one swift motion. "You will."

Leaning on his elbows, he covered her body with his and cupped her face with his hands.

"You realize your father will likely kill me for this," he said, while he still had sense enough to think.

She twined her arms around his neck. "I will kill you if you don't," she growled low.

"Then let us burn together on my funeral pyre," he whispered hoarsely, lowering his mouth to hers, plundering with wet, hot kisses. When she gasped for air, he laid claim with his tongue, dueling and dancing with hers until they were both panting. He nipped her lower lip and trailed kisses along the line of her jaw and down her neck to the hollow of her throat.

Then he stopped and lifted his head.

"No," she pleaded. "Don't stop."

Aleksi sat up, his hips straddling hers. "I'm not stopping, my tigress," he said, his voice thick and low. He reached up and pulled his tunic over his head and tossed it to the ground.

He motioned for her to lift her arms, and then he relieved her of his oversized tunic with one long, slow pull. Her nipples pebbled in the brisk night air, and grew hard under his hungry gaze. He lowered his head and she moaned and arched her back as he licked and suckled first one breast and then the other.

He kissed and nibbled his way from her breasts to her belly, rested his chin on her hipbone as he took the tie to her breeches in his teeth and pulled, grinning when she sucked in her belly and groaned. Slowly, he peeled her breeches down to her legs, his mouth following, kissing and nipping a path from the inside of her thighs to her spreading knees, her twitching calves, and then to her ankles.

She was naked from head to toe, her body exposed to the night and him. He stood and swiftly shucked his breeches.

Sahar's heavy-lidded eyes grew wide as she took in the sight of his cock at full measure before she held her arms out to him. "Come burn with me, my stallion," she growled.

Aleksi lowered himself over her, covering her body with his, skin to skin, heart to beating heart. At first, he kissed her, softly, tenderly, then his kiss grew in need and intensity as he ran his hands up and down her sides, her belly, her legs. She matched him kiss for kiss, her body warm and pliant under his touch, her hands exploring his chest, his back, his belly, and his backside. He tangled his fingers in the black curls between her legs and moaned as she opened to his touch. He cupped her mound and groaned at her wet heat.

"You burn for me, my tigress," he rasped, "as I burn for you."

He kissed her mouth, hard and hungry, her breathless gasps urging him on as he kissed his way down her chest and her belly. He nuzzled his head between her thighs and kissed her burning flesh.

"Oh," she gasped, and then purred, "Ooohhh."

"You like that, my tigress?"

"Oh yes."

"You taste of smoked honey," he said, drawing slow circles with his tongue.

"I do?" she panted.

"Oh, yes," he said, kissing the inside of her thigh. "I knew you would from the moment I laid eyes on you."

"I, oh, ooh, Aleksi…"

Her words melted into incoherent moans and sighs as he licked and suckled her nub and she groaned and spread her legs wider, moving her body in slow, sensuous circles until she went stiff and still, her sweet juices melting on his tongue as she gasped out his name.

Aleksi took her mouth with his, drinking in his name on her lips, his hunger for her all-consuming. He covered her face with kisses, moved to her neck, the hollow of her throat, tasting the salty sweet sweat of her skin as her passions cooled and his inflamed.

He brushed her tangled hair back from her face and kissed her again, long, measured, and slow. He had wanted her so badly for so long, and now that he finally had her, he didn't intend to come undone and spill his seed like some untried lad.

Her breathing slowed, and he gazed into her unfocused heavy-lidded eyes. He kissed her again, touching his lips to hers as he settled his hips between her legs and gently probed her with his cock.

"This may hurt a little at first," he whispered against her lips.

She smiled, slow and languid. "I'm ready."

Aleksi groaned as Sahar lifted her legs. He plundered her mouth with his tongue, and her body with his thrust. She flinched, and he stilled, his cock growing even harder inside the warm, wet heat of her.

"Ahh, my tigress," he murmured. "You feel—"

"Wonderful." She sighed.

"So wonderful," he rasped, his voice as ragged as his slipping control, "that I cannot hold back much longer."

"Then don't," she said, her voice low. "Let yourself go, my stallion." She smiled, slow, sensuous, and knowing. "Burn with me."

"I burn for you," he whispered fiercely as he pulled back slightly. "I burn with you," he groaned, pushing back in, licking his lips at the wet, hot friction of her. "We will burn together, you and I," he swore as the heat and friction increased with their dance. "We will scorch this earth we lay on—"

"And rise again," she panted.

"And again." Aleksi pushed hard and deep as she moaned. "And again," he ground out as she lifted her legs and wrapped them around his back, meeting him thrust for thrust, her inner muscles gripping and caressing his cock until, with one last deep thrust, he shuddered and broke, calling her name to the heavens.

He fell back to earth a boneless, bodiless, raw nerve, collapsing on her, still cradled inside her. When he could think again, he rolled off and wrapped his arm around her, pulling her to his side.

When he could speak again, he nuzzled her ear. "I knew it would be this way between us."

She turned in his arms and pushed the lock of hair from his forehead. "I didn't know it could be this way between a man and a woman," she said, her voice thick with smoke.

He wiped the fine sheen of sweat from her cheeks and kissed the tip of her nose. "Only between a lucky few," he told her.

Yet, he wasn't feeling lucky. She may be his match physically, mentally, and sexually, but she was still a princess and he a bastard. She would never be his, only his, for any longer than tonight. Tomorrow they would try to rescue Lasair, and capture Yago and

Taweel, which likely meant a fight where anything could happen. But tonight she was his, and he was hers, and he would make sure they made the most of it.

He ran his hands through the wild tangle of her thick, curling mane and kissed her long, slow, and tender, tasting her essence of smoke and honey. He kissed and nipped and suckled his way from her delicious mouth to her throat, her luscious breasts, soft and heavy in his palms. He explored her body, worshiping every sleek muscle and round curve with his mouth, his hands, pressing his skin to hers, tangling and untangling limbs, pressing and rubbing, kissing and suckling. He claimed her body as she claimed his, each branding the other, belonging only to each other and this night.

Sahar woke in the graying dawn to the deliciously tantalizing sensation of Aleksi's big, warm hands roaming over her body. Another deeper sensation began to simmer between her legs, and she sighed with eager anticipation as he plied his talented fingers to stoking her fire. In truth, he seemed to know her body better than she did, but she was a quick learner, and had absorbed many things during their night of love-making, a few of which she fully intended to try again this morning.

Rolling over to face him, she placed her hands on his shoulders and pushed him onto his back, straddling his hips and earning a lusty grin in response. She bent over and kissed him, tasting the salty maleness of him. She sucked in her breath as his hands covered her breasts and his thumbs circled her nipples in time with his tongue in her mouth until she was squirming on top of him, rubbing herself up and down his hard heat as he moved beneath her. He broke their kiss and grasped her by the waist and lifted her up and held her poised over the tip of his cock. She moaned, her muscles straining with the need to close the chasm between them. He held her in his vise-like grip until her body begged for more, and then he lowered her down over his rock-hard staff, slowly and deliberately, groaning as she took all of him in.

They both stilled, and she reveled in the fullness of him inside her as her inner muscles tightened and rippled around him. Then he lifted her hips, but kept the head of his cock still inside her, and pulled her down over him again and again, faster, deeper, and harder until she was riding him at a wild, delirious pace, racing with him to the edge and plunging over the cliff together.

Her passions and her sweat cooled in the brisk morning breeze as she climbed off him and snuggled her backside into his encompassing heat, her breath slowing as he wrapped his arms around her and pulled her tighter into his embrace.

"You know," he whispered into her ear, "we could put off confronting Yago and Taweel another night."

He nipped her neck and bumped his pelvis into hers, and she hardened her resolve, if not her still smoldering insides. "No," she said, refusing to turn and look him in the eyes. If she did, she would give into the promise of their unending pleasures. "I cannot leave Lasair to their capricious mercy any longer."

"No," he said, his voice distant, his arms slackening their hold. "I don't suppose you can."

"Would you wait if they had Zolotoy?"

"No, I wouldn't."

She sighed, and turned and held his gaze. "Aleksi, I..." She didn't know what to say. "Thank you."

"Thank you?" His brow quirked and his body stiffened. "Thank you?"

"Yes," she said. "Thank you for riding downriver of Lasair, for saving Munir, for coming after me, saving me from Yago and his curs. Thank you for helping me go after Lasair—"

"For last night."

"Yes," she said, reaching up and pushing that stubborn lock of hair back from his forehead, and smiling as it fell down again. "Especially for last night, and this morning. I will remember them always."

CHAPTER 13

Choices

Sahar lay belly down on the riverbank beside Aleksi under the cover of night, both of them watching the glow of the campfire on the other shore, straining to see movement, shadows, anything.

"Do you think it's a trap?" she asked.

"I think everything the Wolf does is a trap."

"What's the plan?"

"A cross wind blows the smoke of their fire our way, so we needn't worry about their horses smelling us. But…" He met her gaze and held it. "We'll have to swim across the river to get to them."

She looked out over the rushing water, her blood coursing as wild and swift through her veins. "I know."

He laid a hand on her shoulder and gave it a gentle squeeze. "I know you know, and so does the Wolf. We can be certain he is counting on it."

She swallowed and nodded. "He's counting on my fear," she said.

"Because he doesn't know you."

"No?"

Aleksi shook his head. "No." He pushed a loose strand of hair back from her cheek. "I've heard the story of your cousin Ommar's death. Of how you, Ommar, Asim, and Munir were tossed from your makeshift raft into a rain swollen river. That Asim and Munir made it to shore safely, and you made it to the rocks on the other shore, but that Ommar had injured his back and couldn't climb onto the rocks. You held onto him as long as you could, but the river was too strong, and you, a ten-year-old girl, not strong enough."

She hung her head and flexed her fingers, the old shame filling her.

"What the Wolf doesn't know and I do is that you are not the little girl who could not save her cousin," Aleksi said. "You never were."

"Why do you say that when everyone else, my brother, who was there, my parents, Ommar's parents, everyone, says exactly that?"

"Because they don't know you as I do."

She swiped at the sudden rush of heat to her cheeks. "Nobody does," she said, glad the dark of night hid her furious blush.

"True enough," he said with a cocky grin. "But what I meant, my tigress, is that nobody else seems to know that you didn't let go of your cousin. Ommar let go of you."

The heat rushed from Sahar's cheeks to her spinning head, and her ears rang with Ommar's last words. *Let go, cousin. Let me go. You must let me go.*

"How do you know this?" She'd never told anybody what Ommar said, what he'd done. Not even her brother or Munir, who'd been there. She had barely admitted it to herself. "Nobody knows this."

Aleksi reached over and pulled her to him, holding her tight. "I told you, I know you, my fierce tigress," he whispered into her hair. "I know you would die before letting go, and so did Ommar. That is why he let go, to keep you from being pulled in with him."

She buried her face into Aleksi's shoulder. "He died to save me," she whimpered.

"No," he said, leaning back and cupping her chin, holding her gaze. "He was as good as dead already, and he knew it. He wasn't going to let you die needlessly with him. In that moment the boy Ommar chose to die as a man."

Ommar's eyes, wide with fear and panic came to her, as did the way they had calmed, the way he had smiled, perfectly at peace right before he'd let go of her hand. She shuddered, and when she could speak again, her voice was raw with the pain she had lived with for the past ten and two years.

"Ommar may have died a man, but I have carried the guilt of his death since I was a girl. I fear I'll always carry it."

Aleksi rubbed the pad of his thumb along her clenched jaw, easing some of her tension. He smiled, but when he spoke, his voice, his expression, were serious. "My father once told me that courage was not a lack of fear. It's the strength to fight through that fear, to stand up for what you believe is right, to do whatever is needed to make it right. You, my tigress, have this courage. You've shown this courage time and again. I've seen it. I see it now burning deep in your eyes. The Wolf hasn't because he sees only what he wishes to see, which more often than not is nothing more than his own pretty reflection."

Sahar sniffed and nodded and pressed Aleksi's palm to her lips. He may be proud, stubborn, and arrogant, but he was also strong and true. He didn't lie, not to her, even when it would have been easier to, and she believed him and felt the welcome stirrings of her courage rise up from her belly and light a fire in her veins.

"Do we swim with Z?" she asked, "or tie him off on this side of the river?"

Aleksi gave her a smacking kiss and a playful slap on her backside. "We swim with Z," he said, and then all his playfulness was gone. "Swear to me that if anything happens to me, you will jump on his back and swim right back across this river and ride away as if your life depends on it, because it will." When she didn't answer, he insisted, "Swear you will."

She held up her hand. "I swear I will," she said, and then dropped her hand and muttered under her breath, "*not*."

Aleksi cocked his head as if trying to figure out what, if anything, she'd said after swearing to ride off on Z. Not that it would matter. Nothing he said or did would sway her from going after Lasair tonight.

"So be it," he said with a resigned shrug. He crept back to the copse of trees where Z was tied and kicked off his boots, and then untied his belt and his breeches, letting them drop to his bare feet.

She rolled her eyes. "This is not the time or the place for any of that," she said, waving at his half hard cock.

"No?" he asked with a low chuckle as he pulled his tunic up and over his head. "It's time to strip, unless you wish to try to sneak up on the Worm and the Tall with dripping wet, sloshing clothes, and then fight them wearing damp, chafing leathers."

He rolled up his clothes and pulled his otter skin cloak out, grinning from ear to ear as she doffed boots, tunic, and breeches, her nipples pebbling in the cold night air. She handed her clothes over, and he wrapped them with his. Then he tied the bundle of clothes and both pairs of boots on top of Z's saddle.

He strapped his sword to his bare back and held the belt with his waist blade out to her. "Just in case," he said, tying the belt around her waist, his hands lingering on her bare skin a moment.

She leaned into him and gave him a long, searing kiss on the lips. "Just in case," she said. She walked to the edge of the river and stood, naked and unafraid.

"Hold onto Z's stirrup and let him do all the work," Aleksi told her as they stepped into the water. "All you have to do is kick your legs and not let go."

Sahar clamped her jaw tight and nodded. Aleksi led Zolotoy into the water and swam ahead of him, holding the stallion's reins. Sahar held on to the stirrup strap on Z's upriver side and kicked as she floated out and across the river, keeping her gaze on the back of Aleksi's head.

They made the far shore a good hundred paces upstream from the Wolf's camp, sopping wet and freezing. Aleksi rubbed her icy skin with a drying cloth and then did the same to himself as she dressed. Clothed and armed, he tied off Z to a tree, pulled the sturdy walking stick with the tip he had whittled to a sharp point from the saddle straps, and turned to her as she was tying off her braid.

"If this is to be my last night in this world," he said, "I regret nothing."

"Nor do I," she said. She took a deep breath in and blew it out. "I don't fear the fight to come," she vowed. "A wolf and his pack of one is no match for a stallion and a tigress."

Aleksi held her chin and gave her a fierce kiss. "No," he said, handing her the sharpened stick. "They're not."

Step by slow, cautious step, they walked toward the camp, Sahar following in Aleksi's footsteps, careful not to make any sudden noise. They hunkered down behind the tree line at the edge of the little clearing. From there they could see what looked like two heads poking out of the one bedroll, and heard the low, sonorous snore of a man. They crept a little closer, trying to see the rest of the camp, but the fire had burned to embers and the waning moon had disappeared behind a bank of clouds.

The horses looked to be sleeping where they stood tied to a line, and Sahar breathed a sigh of relief that Lasair was at least upright on all fours. She looked to Aleksi, and raised her brows and jutted her chin forward, but he shook his head and pointed toward a pile of something big and dark that was most likely saddles and gear by the horses, though something seemed odd about the shape and mass of the pile.

They watched it closely for a while, but the pile didn't move or worry the horses, and after giving the camp one more look over, Aleksi nodded to Sahar.

"First we secure the Wolf and the Tall," he whispered. "Then we free Lasair."

"Of course."

He rose to a crouch, indicating that she should stay behind him, and began to enter the clearing. They had taken no more than three steps in when Lasair snorted and threw up her head with a loud whinny. Aleksi cursed and leapt the remaining distance to the bedroll, which was now rolling away from him. The dark pile by the horses rose into the shape of a man throwing off a blanket and closing the distance between them, short sword in one hand and blade in the other. It was Yago who advanced on Aleksi, forcing him to fight, leaving Sahar to deal with the longer reach of Taweel the Tall, the exact opposite of what they'd planned.

"I have Yago," Aleksi yelled over the stomping and snorting of the horses. There was a rending tear and Taweel emerged from the rent bedroll, his blade glinting in the light of the emerging moon. "Sahar," Aleksi yelled.

"I have him."

The Tall was armed with a short sword and a waist blade, and easily had half an arm's reach on her. He had the advantage and he knew it, sneering smugly as he swung his sword with a turn of his wrist. She sheathed her waist blade and gripped her stick with both hands. While it was no match for a sword, it was six feet of sturdy oak honed to a deadly point in the hands of a woman who had plenty of practice stick fighting with her brother.

She bent her knees and glared at Taweel as the sound of metal clanging on metal rang out over curses and grunts from Aleksi and Yago.

"Lay down your puny stick," Taweel said, "and I'll make your death swift and merciful."

"Lay down your sword," she countered, shifting her weight onto her toes, "and I won't cut your stones off and gift them to your father on a golden plate."

Her words had their desired effect as Taweel sputtered and choked on his sneer, and she sprang straight for him, swinging the stick hard and whacking him on the outside of his knee. He bellowed and stumbled. She turned full circle and whacked him on the outside of his other knee. His knees buckled and he stumbled forward, but he saved himself from falling by stabbing his sword into the ground and bracing himself with it. She considered trying to sweep the sword out from under him but didn't want to chance embedding the stick into it and giving Taweel a chance to wrest her weapon from her.

She swung the stick high and brought it down, aiming for the side of his head, but he dipped and rolled and pushed himself up onto his feet as the stick hit the ground, the force of it shooting waves of pain up her arms and into her shoulders. Taweel brought his sword down onto the stick, numbing her fingers and wrists, but she didn't let go. He raised his sword high, readying for another blow. She gripped the stick with all her might and heaved it away as Taweel's sword came crashing down and hit earth. Putting all her weight behind the stick, she swung for Taweel's sword arm, grunting with the effort. It struck the meat of his upper arm with a satisfying thunk, and she stepped back and positioned the stick to jab, jumping away as Taweel pivoted and slashed out with his other arm, the cold gleam of his waist blade shining in the light of the dwindling campfire.

He straightened and shook himself as she set her feet and shoulders.

"I am going to kill you, bitch," he barked, charging her with teeth bared.

"Sahar?" Aleksi yelled.

She dipped one way and leapt the other, dodging Taweel's clumsy charge and ducked behind a tree, glancing over to where Aleksi was raining blows down on Yago, who looked to be struggling to keep his sword up in a defensive posture. Aleksi could kill Yago at any time, but he was keeping his word and working on beating the Wolf down and capturing him alive.

"I'm fine," she yelled back, grinning and taunting Taweel as she danced from one side of the tree to the other.

The heel of her boot caught on a root, and she tripped and fell, landing flat on her back, knocking the breath from her. She gasped trying to suck in air, but her throat had closed and her chest had seized, and Taweel was standing over her, the point of his sword at her heart and a sickening smile on his face.

"I told you I would kill you," he said, planting a booted foot on her throat. "I'm going to enjoy doing it."

Her vision narrowed to a pinprick as she grabbed at the Tall's boot on her neck, but without air in her lungs the strength was quickly leaving her body. Somewhere far away a wolf yelped, a stallion bellowed, and the earth beneath her thundered. As the world was going black, the weight of Taweel was lifted from her, and she sucked in great, gasping gulps of air as she rolled over onto her hands and knees. A cursing, grunting mass of flailing arms and kicking legs rolled and tumbled across the camp as she slowly pushed herself up onto her feet, finally able to take in a complete breath. She felt for her waist blade, her fingers wrapping around the hilt when a pair of hands grabbed her from behind and threw her face-first into the tree's trunk.

When she came to, it was to the sound of clanging metal and the hazy sight of Aleksi's sturdy legs and broad back standing between her Yago and Taweel, holding them off and trading them blow for blow. Leaning against the tree, she slowly rose to her feet and braced herself until her vision stopped swimming and her legs stopped shaking.

"Ride, Sahar," Aleksi yelled over his shoulder. "Ride away now."

She shook her swirling head. Aleksi was a strong man and a good fighter, but it was two against one, and although he was more than holding his own against both princes, she couldn't trust he would come out victorious, much less alive.

"Ride, Sahar," he yelled again when she hadn't moved.

"I will," she yelled back, wincing at the instant throb in her head. She drew her waist blade. "But not without you and Lasair."

"By the gods, woman," Aleksi cursed as Sahar stepped up beside him. "You are as stubborn as—"

"You."

He laughed, short and harsh, and would have kissed her then and there, but Yago and Taweel pressed their attack. She was a good fighter, but she was still unsteady on her feet, and her waist blade was no match for a sword. By unspoken agreement, Yago turned all his attention to her, while Taweel faced off with Aleksi.

It was impossible for Aleksi to concentrate on beating Taweel down while watching her and Yago out of the corner of his eye, trying to make sure she was in no immediate danger as she danced around the Wolf's strikes, jumping back and forth and nipping at him with her puny blade. She didn't look to be losing any ground, but she wasn't gaining any either. Though Aleksi had given his oath to capture the princes alive, this fight was past tiresome.

He doubled the speed of his blows, keeping Taweel on the defensive until the Tall was barely able to lift his sword to block Aleksi's. He glanced over at Sahar and saw that she was still staying out of the Wolf's reach. He resumed his attack on Taweel, a jab here, a feint there, waiting for the right moment to strike.

"Yago," the Tall cried out, "slay the bitch and come help me kill the bastard."

Aleksi swung down, and Taweel got his blade up to block the blow, but as soon as Aleksi's blade hit Taweel's, he swung his sword out and up in a slicing arc, laying the Tall's underarm wide open. Taweel screamed and dropped his sword, pressing the gash with his other hand to stanch the flow of blood. Aleksi turned to check on Sahar and saw the blade flying through the air only a breath before it sank into his left shoulder. Switching sword arms, he grabbed the hilt of the dagger and pulled it out as Yago charged him, sword raised high. Aleksi blocked the Wolf's sword with his and stabbed him in the belly with his own dagger. He pulled the blade out to stab again, but his injured arm was pulled back with a vicious yank. The heavy weight of a man landed on his back and an arm snaked around his neck.

He slammed his elbow into Taweel's belly, once, twice, three times, and felt the Tall's grip begin to slacken, but then Yago was standing before him with a sickening sneer on his bloodied face, gripping his sword with both hands.

"Say farewell to your whore princess," Yago said. He slammed the flat side of his sword down on the wrist of Aleksi's injured arm, and his sword dropped from his numbed hand to the ground.

Yago raised his sword for the killing blow and a tigress roared. The Wolf went heels

over ass, his feet swept out from under him, then the loud, resounding thunk of wood on skull reverberated through Aleksi's ears. The Tall's grip slackened and fell away. Aleksi heard the dull thud of a body hitting earth as he sucked in air and watched the Wolf turn tail and run.

Aleksi bent down to pick up his sword, but the ground came up to meet him as everything around him shimmied and swayed. He braced himself on his hands and knees and took in several deep, steadying breaths.

"Curse this dizzying weakness," he grumbled. "The Worm is getting away."

She laid a hand on his good shoulder. "It doesn't matter," she said.

Aleksi glared up at her. "It does matter. Taweel is dead and you don't have a prisoner. You don't have your proof of the Wolf's treachery." He shook his clearing head and sat back on his heels. "Quickly, bind my wound and I'll go after him."

"Do you think Yago will come back at us?"

"No. I gutted him. He will be in no condition to stand and fight. With any luck, the wound will fester and kill him, but not before we get him back to your father."

Sahar stared off in the direction Yago had fled on Tor. "Let him go," she said.

"What?" Aleksi couldn't believe what he was hearing.

"Let Yago go," she said, meeting Aleksi's angry glare. "The Wolf will live or not and the Ox will have his war or not. Either way, we need to warn my father, and get your wound tended to properly. I will cauterize and bind it tonight."

She stood and walked over to the horses, ignoring Aleksi's gaping jaw as she reunited with Lasair, horse and mistress cooing and nickering into each other's necks.

"Do you mean to tell me," Aleksi stood and glowered down at Taweel's lifeless body, "that I could have killed the Tall and the

Wolf at any time? That this"—he tapped his bleeding shoulder—"was for nothing?"

"Of course not," she snapped. "It was for your one hundred gold pieces. You needed me alive to collect it, and I needed you alive to... It was them or you, I chose you."

"Am I supposed to thank you?"

"Why are you so angry?"

"Because," he yelled, "you almost got yourself killed, and me in the bargain."

Sahar reeled back at Aleksi's stinging accusation as if he had struck her, but what he had said was true. She'd almost gotten him killed, again, and herself. Not that that'd been her intention. He knew she needed to save Lasair and to keep anyone else from being killed, especially the thousands who could die if a war broke out between the tribes. It wasn't her fault the conniving vipers had been lying in wait and put up such a fight. Aleksi could've quickly dispatched them both had he not been trying to wear them down and capture them.

True, he'd agreed to her plan when he could have refused. She'd given him fair warning the night after Munir's injury to stay away from her, far away from her. She'd told Aleksi then that she was bad luck, but he hadn't heeded her.

Shooting him an angry glare, she gave him her back and strode over to the pile of gear in which the Wolf had been hiding. Her saddle was on top of the pile and she took quick stock of her bags, pulling out her waist blade wrapped up in her belt and strapping it on above the belt and blade Aleksi had lent her. She took out a tub of healing balm and set it aside. She went through Yago's and Taweel's bags and pulled out several days' worth of dried meat and cheese and dates as well as a wineskin and extra tunics. She took her blade to a clean tunic and started cutting it into strips as Aleksi dragged the Tall's lifeless body across the camp to the river, where he dumped it into the water and watched it float away. He returned to the camp and pulled his flint out, trying to ignite it, but couldn't with only one good arm.

"Here." Sahar stomped over and tossed a wineskin at him. He caught it with his good hand, and almost toppled from his crouch. She knelt down beside him and held out her hand for the flint. "Let me." She snatched the flint from him. "Stubborn ass," she muttered, getting a spark on her third strike.

"Royal pain," he grumbled, uncorking the wineskin with his teeth and taking a long, slow pull, eyeing her as she fed the growing fire.

He offered her the skin, and she took a good, hearty swallow, then untied his belt from her waist, pulled his knife, and shoved the blade into the fire. She stood and motioned for him to lift his good arm and then pulled his tunic over his head and down over his injured shoulder.

Aleksi took another long drink, capped the skin and set it aside. He watched as she pulled his knife from the fire, the blade glowing red hot. "Don't slip and geld me."

"If I geld you, you strutting stallion," she snapped, holding the fired tip over his wound, "it won't be because my hand slipped."

Aleksi blew out his breath. Sahar pushed the tip of the blade half a finger deep into his wound. His chest and arm muscles bunched and twitched, and he clenched his jaw as sweat beaded on his nose and forehead.

She swiped the sweat from her nose and cheeks as she eyed him. She scooped three fingers full of the healing balm and gently smeared it over and around the cauterized wound, her nose wrinkling at the stench. One by one, she laid out the strips of shredded tunic and began to wrap them snuggly around his shoulder, tying them off with shaky fingers.

"It is not an easy thing to kill a man," he told her, his voice steadier than her hands as she wrapped the last strip around his solid shoulder.

"No," she agreed, her whole body starting to shake now. "It's not." She tied off the strip and lifted her gaze to his. "You've killed a man before?"

"I have," he said. "In battle beside my father." He rolled his shoulder, testing the bandage, and grinned. "You have skills."

"You seem surprised."

"Nobody has ever surprised me more."

She sat back and licked her lips with the same wet, hot little tongue she had trailed along his inner thighs and cock this morning. A groan of pure need and pain escaped his clenched jaw. He was injured, angry, and exhausted, but he wanted her, here, now, even though the both of them were beaten, bloody, and bruised.

He'd once thought if and when they had sex, he'd be able to go his way and she'd be nothing more than a memory, an exciting, maddening, once-in-a-lifetime memory. But the more he discovered about her, the more she gave herself to him, the more he wanted. More than wanted—he craved her fire, her passion. Which was a problem.

Their time together had been limited since the moment she refused his proposal of marriage, sooner actually. Any chance of them being together for more than a passing affair had been decided the days of their births. Their short, sexual idyll was about to end. They'd be returning to her father's palace soon, and then Aleksi would return to his with enough gold pieces and broodmares to start his life as his own man and find a wife he no longer wanted. Not unless she had a thick, curly mane as black as night that shone russet in the sunlight, eyes of green fire, and purred like a cat at his touch.

He reached out his good hand and gently prodded the growing knot on her forehead, willfully ignoring the hardening in his breeches.

"I figure we'll meet up with your rescue party in two to three days if we start back tomorrow," he said, reminding them that their time alone together was coming to an end.

She said nothing.

"I hope your father won't think I'm responsible for your injuries and kill me on sight."

"My father would wait for an explanation first," she said. Then she grinned, slow and teasing. "It is Brawn's quick temper and even quicker blade that you should worry about."

Aleksi chuckled, glad to see her fiery spirit returning. "Thank you for the warning." He dipped his head, and then he too grew serious. "What will you tell your father about us?"

"The truth."

"All of it?"

"Yes," she said without hesitation, and a surge of pride welled up in him. "He'll understand."

"Will he?" In Aleksi's experience, fathers, and especially kings, were not as understanding of such things where their daughters were concerned.

"You've heard the tale of the Lion and the Swan." She quirked her brow. "My father and my mother are known far and wide for their story of forbidden passion."

"Which ended in a respectable marriage."

Her brow leveled, but she said nothing.

"Would he force you to marry me?" he asked, not sure what he hoped her answer would be.

"No." She shook her head. "Not unless..." she hesitated.

"There's a child."

She pressed her lips together and nodded.

"If you do bear my babe, we will be married," Aleksi told her. "No child of mine will be born a bastard."

CHAPTER 14

The Road Back

Sahar woke to the heat of Aleksi's thick erection pressed against her back and his fingers combing through the thatch of hair between her legs. She groaned as he parted her curls and ran a fingertip along the folds of her flesh, and she opened her legs to him with a sigh.

They had slept together on a makeshift bedroll combining Aleksi's and hers after she'd kicked the Wolf's and the Tall's into the camp's fire last night. The thought of lying on any of their bedding had made her belly retch and her skin crawl.

Now, her skin was on fire with mounting desire as Aleksi stroked her lower lips. Dipping his fingertip into her wetness, he drew slow, lazy circles around and around her flesh until she was moving with him, pressing her backside into his groin and her mound into his hand, gasping as he cupped her and began to tap a finger inside her. Her undulations grew quicker and shorter as he slid two fingers deep inside her and pressed her flesh to his palm. She slid her hand over his and clamped her legs tight, riding their joined hands until the pressure inside her erupted in waves.

Her body still rippling with sensation, she moaned with spent pleasure as he pushed his hard, pulsing cock where his fingers had been, and she caressed him with her inner muscles, squeezing and releasing as he moved in and out of her, filling her with his pumping, throbbing heat one moment, and dragging his glorious cock back over her tender flesh the next, until they were both moving at a frenzied pace.

She placed her hand between their bodies, her fingers grasping his flesh and increasing the friction for both of them. Her inner muscles contracted and convulsed, and released in tiny little shudders. Then Aleksi pulled his cock completely out of her and pushed it between her fingers, spilling his seed onto her thighs.

Her first thought was *He doesn't want to have a child with me.* Not thank the gods he had enough sense to spill his seed on her, not in her, but instead, he doesn't want me to be the mother of his strapping sons with golden hair and earth-brown eyes.

It could still be too little too late. She could already be pregnant. Her moon flow had always been as regular as the lunar phases, and was not yet late in coming, but she knew that many things besides pregnancy could cause a woman's flow to arrive late or even dry up completely, including near starvation and extreme stress. All of which she had dealt with since being taken captive half a fortnight ago.

She knew she should be grateful for him showing restraint. She didn't wish to be forced to marry him, or anyone else, any more than he apparently wished to be forced to marry her, despite his proposal in what felt like a lifetime ago. She didn't want to become a mother, not yet. She was alive, free of the cruel captors who had repeatedly beaten her and threatened her with rape and death. She was safe in Aleksi's embrace, the man she had chosen to give her virginity to, about to be reunited with her loving family and resume her life. Why then did she want to sob with bitter regret rather than sigh with relief?

Aleksi nuzzled the nape of her neck, his lips warm and tender, and she pulled away from his solid heat and stood on sticky, shaky legs and walked straight into the river, where she stopped waist deep in the freezing water and dropped, submerging her entire body. She held her breath, welcoming the numbing cold on her aching body parts, not the least of which was her heart, and then pushed up with all her might, bursting out of the water with a scream of pure frustration.

He bolted upright and ran to the river's edge, where he stopped short. "Sahar?" He spoke softly, calmly, as one would to a hissing cat with laid back ears and a twitching tail. "Tell me, my tigress."

"I can't," she said, her voice a raw whisper.

"You can tell me anything. Surely you know that by now."

She stared at him a long while and then pressed her lips together and shook her head.

He stepped into the water and started walking to her, one slow, steady step at a time.

"Are you worried you might be carrying my babe?"

She laughed, short and harsh. "Of course I am," she said, slapping a handful of water at him.

He stopped as the icy droplets splashed his chest. "Because you don't wish to bear my child and marry me?"

"Because I wish to bear a child when I choose, and to marry whom I choose."

"Which is not now and not me."

"Yes," she cried. "No," she keened.

"What is it you want from me?" Aleksi asked. "What? Sex? I can do that. I can have sex with you ten times a day every day from now until the day I ride away if that is what you want. Patience? You want me to wait around, mooning over you like some lovesick pup until you decide whether a bastard son of a king is good enough for you? Or do you want another proposal of marriage, perhaps on bended knee this time? What?"

She narrowed her gaze on his, her anger as cold and sharp as the blade she had once threatened to geld him with. "I want you to go *fuck* yourself."

Sahar dismounted from Lasair and stretched her legs and back as the sun dipped low in the sky turning it a dusky gray. They'd made good time despite their late start that morning, after she'd told Aleksi to go fuck himself. It was a Northern seaman's swear word that she'd heard her grandfather use when he was spitting mad, which was what she'd been this morning. It was also a swear word her mother would cuff her for using if she ever got wind of it, but the release Sahar felt when hurling it at that cocksure ass would still have been worth her mother's censure.

Aleksi hadn't known the exact meaning of the word, but he knew exactly what she'd meant by it. He hadn't cursed or shouted back at her, but had gone as stiff and silent as stone, and had remained that way throughout the day's journey.

For the best, really. As she led Lasair to the stream, she couldn't think of what they'd have to say to each other that had not already been said. That they were drawn to each other physically had been apparent from the start. Equally apparent was their penchant for needling and challenging each other to the point of constantly arguing.

That she had been the one to push them to have sex was on her. She could easily try to blame it on his constant, not-so-subtle pressure, or on the trauma the Wolf and his curs had put her through, but she knew it was her doing. As much of a strutting stallion as he was, he would've never forced himself on her. He would've continued to behave in a princely manner. She had acted more like a wanton harlot than a virginal princess, a reckless, foolish strumpet who hadn't taken any precautions against becoming pregnant until this morning, and even then, it had been Aleksi who had shown common sense and restraint, not her.

Which made her what?

One of a world full of women trapped by the laws of nature and the social mores of men.

Not that she disagreed with the tradition of marriage when children were involved. From what she had seen, children always did better with a mother and a father raising them, as long as both parents were good, decent people. As angry as she was with him, she couldn't deny he was good and decent. Or that his experience growing up the bastard son of a king had given him a unique perspective.

The first day they met, he'd told her he wanted a wife of sturdy body and easy temper who could bear him sons, and she understood his unwillingness to knowingly bring a bastard into this world. She may never have been a woman of easy temper, and her bruised, half-starved body was far from sturdy these days, but she didn't understand why it hurt so much knowing he no longer wanted her to be his wife and the mother of his children. Especially when she swore she didn't wish to be either.

Lasair nosed Sahar's shoulder, nudging her back to the here and now, and she walked her horse over to where Aleksi had strung a rope and tied off the mare between Zolotoy and the two geldings that had belonged to the Jackal and the Tall. She left them to graze as she started to pull supplies from the saddle bags for the night.

"We need to build a lean-to."

Those were the first words Aleksi had spoken to her since that morning. "What?"

"Rain is coming." He pointed up to the gathering clouds in the darkening sky. "We need to build a lean-to for shelter."

He looked around and walked over to a spot under two trees with thick canopies that wove together overhead. "We'll build it here." He handed her his short sword. "Cut at least ten and two leafy branches yea by yea big"—he indicated with his arms out—"for the roof, while I find some base poles."

Whacking small branches from trees and piling them next to the frame he was building turned out to be exactly the release she needed. By the time the lean-to was complete and he'd moved the horses and tied them off under the tree's canopy, her muscles were warm and her head clear of the thoughts that had been swirling round and round without end.

She laid out their bedrolls inside the snug den, one on top of the other. There was no room to lay them side by side. She tossed the dried meat and dates from the Wolf's store that would pass as their supper onto the middle of the makeshift bed, trying not to think about what would happen when they lay down together for the night.

It would likely be their last night alone before the search party her father would have sent found them. Their last night to be free of the princess and the bastard, to be only Aleksi and Sahar, stallion and tigress. Despite everything that'd happened, everything they'd said and done, everything they were and weren't to each other, all she wanted this night was to burn with him, to raze him to scorched earth and have him rise again.

Aleksi sat cross legged on the bedrolls and picked at the pile of dates and dried meat, resigned to a cold supper and a cold bed as the first fat drops of rain splatted on the ground beyond the trees' shelter. If it had not been for the threatening rain, he would've gladly slept in his own bedroll on the opposite side of the camp.

He finished his meager, tasteless supper and stepped behind the lean-to and relieved himself. The trees' canopy still held off the rain for now, and as long as the rain didn't become a deluge, their little lean-to should keep them dry. He checked on the horses one more time, delaying his return to the close confines of the lean-to and whatever creature resided there at the moment: the cool, aloof she-cat, or the hissing, spitting tigress.

Sahar's quicksilver moods usually intrigued and excited him, but tonight he wanted the quiet comfort of a good sleep. With a resigned shrug he stooped and peeked inside. She was already under the covers, her tunic and breeches tucked under her head like a pillow, her big, round, luminous cat eyes watching him, her luscious lips curled up in an inviting smile.

No.

He shook his head. If she thought he was going to forget how angry he was and make love to her, she had another thing coming. He sat by her feet and pulled off his boots, and then his breeches, ignoring her throaty purr. Then he doffed his leather outer tunic and his linen undertunic and folded them, and then set them down as a pillow.

He slid in behind her, skin to warm skin, and bit off a groan. Instead of reaching over and tucking her closer, he scooted back until there was nothing but air between them. He laid his head down, willfully keeping his nose from the warm, sweet spot at her nape, though he could not keep from inhaling the womanly scent of her.

No.

He flopped over to his other side so his back was to her, still not touching her. If she didn't want to bear his babe, then he would make certain she wouldn't, and the only way to do that was to abstain from sex, no matter how much he craved her. Oh, he did. So much so that his hands twitched to reach out and touch her smooth skin, to roam the taut muscles of her legs and the swells of her breasts and hips. He bit off another groan, his cursed cock hard with the memory of nestling in her warm, wet folds.

No.

He clamped his jaw tight and gritted his teeth and fisted his hands. He thought of her fisted hands as she stood in the river claiming she didn't want to marry him or to bear his child, and he jerked the covers up over his shoulders. It wasn't the first or only time since he'd known her that she'd said she did not wish to wed, and not only him but any man. Then why had her refusal this morning hit him like a punch to the gut?

From the moment he had seen her sitting at the royal table he'd known she wasn't for him. A princess and a bastard, even a king's bastard, could have no future together. It wasn't either of their faults, it was the way of the world. Aleksi had told himself from the start that it didn't matter. After the races he would leave with his winnings and never see her again.

He didn't want to care, but he did. She was like no other woman he had ever been with. Not only beautiful and intelligent, but tactile and sensual, and as sure of her body as her mind. As fiery and adventurous in bed as out. Unlike the other women he'd known, he would never forget a single thing about her. Not her spicy, exotic gardenia mixed with earthy, musky womanly scent, or the feel of her skin against his, the pulse of her life's blood coursing through her veins, her heart beating in time to his.

All he had to do was close his eyes to see the flashing green brilliance of hers, or lick his lips to taste her salty sweetness. Then there was her voice, as deep and smooth as smoked honey. A voice that would tease and haunt his straining ears for the rest of his natural life, and likely beyond. He had come to care for her more than he had ever cared for any woman, and that had been his mistake. The more you cared about someone, the more it hurt when they were taken away. This he knew from hard experience.

No.

He huffed and tucked the covers tighter around his shoulders. Better to start getting used to keeping his distance again. By tomorrow night they would likely be with her father's guard and their time together would be over, unless she was already pregnant. Then Aleksi would have himself one trapped, angry wife. The last thing he wanted was to be saddled with a caged tigress who did not want his cub.

No.

Better they stop their reckless foolishness now.

Sahar stirred under the covers and closed the distance between them. Her soft, round breasts pressed into his back and her pelvis cupped his backside. She tucked the long, lean, length of her legs under his and wrapped her arm around him, her hand resting on his belly, her fingers playing in his fur, slowly working their way lower, lower, until…

"Yes."

The word tore its way out of his throat and reverberated down to his cock as she rubbed the flat of her fingers down the length of him, from root to tip to root, and then cupped his stones and rolled them along her palm, her touch firm yet gentle. She ran her fingertips up and down his erection, sending ripples of pleasure out to every point of his body from his toes to his knees, to his nipples to his ears, and what was left of his mind between them. She circled the tender head of his cock with the pad of her thumb, spreading the small drop of fluid that had escaped, and he rolled over and flipped her onto her back, kneeling over her and pinning her arms above her head.

"What do you want? Tell me."

"I want you to *fuck* me."

He laughed, short and harsh. "It'll by my pleasure." Before she could respond, he covered her mouth with his bruising kiss.

He held her hands to the ground as he kissed and nipped his way from her mouth to her neck to her breasts, licking and sucking each nipple until she was squirming beneath him. He lowered her hands to her sides, but did not let go his hold of her wrists as he tasted his way down her belly, nuzzling his nose in her thick, curly thatch. He touched the tip of his tongue to her hardened bud, and her sigh turned into a low moan. Aleksi swirled his tongue around her fleshy lips, and then he licked her and suckled her, and drank in the sweet, hot wetness of her as she bucked her hips and clenched her hands. He kept his tight grip on her wrists and his tongue's assault on her flesh until she was writhing at the edge. Then he pulled back.

"What do you want, my tigress?"

"I want you, inside me."

He let go of her wrists, cupped her buttocks, and lifted her hips high. With one thrust he buried his cock stones deep into her, groaning at the hot, welcoming grip. Then he pulled back and thrust deep again and again, and again, pounding into her with the growing storm inside and outside their little lean-to, taking her as she took all of him, laying his claim to her here in this wilderness, a claim that would count for nothing back in the civilized world.

Right here, right now, she was his, the storm between them building in strength and intensity, carrying them both to the precipice. He gave one last, deep, pulsating thrust, sending her careening over the edge, and when he was sure she had landed back on soft earth, he pulled out and spilled his seed on the damp, barren ground.

Sahar glanced up at the noon sun, a dim yellow orb in the misty gray sky, and shifted on her saddle, trying to find a comfortable position. Between the last ten days of hard riding, the beatings she had taken, and the sex play she and Aleksi had been engaging in, there didn't seem to be a spot on her backside that wasn't sore or tender. Though she could've done without the kidnapping and the beatings, she'd learned much in these past days and nights.

She'd learned she truly was as good as any man on a horse, and she was tough, physically and mentally. A fighter and a survivor. She'd learned to trust a man other than her father with her life, and had saved Aleski's, as he had saved hers.

She'd learned that there were as many different ways to have sex with that same man as there were feelings between them. There was new, exciting, figuring-each-other-out sex, and there was comfortable, I-know-what-you-like sex. There was hurried, raw, purely physical sex, and slow, reverent, body-worshipping, soul-searching sex. There was talking dirty sex and murmuring sweet nothings sex. There was the sex they had had last night: hard, rough, angry sex. Fucking. And the sex they had had shortly after, soft, gentle, make-up sex. Then there was the sex they had this morning, the sex that brought stinging tears to her eyes thinking about it. Unhurried, tender, and soulful, full of soft murmurings and bittersweet goodbyes.

It'd likely been the last sex they would ever have with each other, unless she was pregnant and they were forced to marry, in which case she foresaw a lot more angry sex.

Not that a lifetime of sex with Aleksi, angry or otherwise, would be a bad thing. Sahar wasn't so naïve as to think that good sex between a husband and wife was a given. She wasn't ignorant of the fact that sex with him had been exceptionally good. She'd grown up listening to the women in the palace talk about their husbands and lovers. She knew it was not every man, or woman, who was as considerate of their partner's needs as he was. He'd always made sure she was as satisfied as he. He was neither a stripling lad nor a gnarled old greybeard, but a big, strong, virile man, who knew and enjoyed her body as well as his own. He had helped her discover the power of her body and her passion, and she had reveled in that power, had felt his equal, even though he had been the more experienced partner.

In truth, sharing a marriage bed with him would be no hardship, and the thought that any other woman could have that privilege was like a sharp, penetrating wound to Sahar's chest. She tried to imagine the man she would eventually fall in love with and marry, but her gaze only returned to the man riding beside her. To his straight spine, the solid line of his jaw, and the warmth of his earth-brown eyes, eyes that would light up with teasing laughter and darken with passion.

If she wasn't pregnant and they didn't marry, if he left her and returned to his homeland, she'd miss his teasing and his cocky grin, his solid steadfastness and his will of granite. She would even miss his strutting about, and she'd definitely miss his strutting about naked.

She would miss him.

It seemed her only choices were to marry him or miss him. If she married him and bore his child, where would they live? She was a princess with rank, wealth, and a family who loved her as she loved them, and who would surely accept Aleksi into their fold. He and her father had apparently already formed a friendship of sorts, and her mother would understand his position as a person of lower rank and no wealth marrying into royalty better than anyone. Sahar didn't think her parents would hold her and Aleksi's premarital sex against him. It had been no secret that her mother and father had been lovers before they wed.

No, she did not think her family would be a problem. Aleksi, on the other hand, might.

She couldn't see his pride allowing him to be consort to a princess in her father's court any more than her own would revel in being the wife of a horse trader.

Which left them where?

"There they are," he said.

"Who?"

"Your search party." Aleksi pointed to the far side of the open meadow. "They're here."

Sahar sent Lasair flying across the meadow toward her father, whose black stallion broke away from the group of riders. They met in the middle of the open meadow, where she flung herself onto her father's lap and hugged him with every fiber of her being. She was still hugging him when Aleksi rode up on Zolotoy leading the two geldings who'd belonged to Yago and Taweel.

"Thank you, Aleksandr," her father said. "You brought my daughter back to me."

"You are most welcome, your majesty," Aleksi answered with a dip of his head. "Though it was not all my doing. Princess Sahar kept herself alive while captive to the Wolf and his curs until I could help free her. It was she who killed Taweel the Tall while saving my skin."

"Of course she did," the king chuckled. He ruffled Sahar's hair, hair that Aleksi had been running his fingers through this morning. Then the king cupped her chin and held her gaze. "Are you... Did they?"

"No," Sahar shook her head and gave her father a reassuring smile. "They didn't."

"Not for lack of trying, it seems." The king reached up and touched the purple and yellow swelling on her forehead.

"They starved me, beat me, and threatened me daily with rape," she said, and Aleksi's chest was not the only one rumbling. "They were saving me for the Ox, so he could publicly rape me and whip me before killing me, all to get his war against you."

The king growled. "I should have killed that cowardly pollution of a man twenty years ago." He hugged her close. "I am so sorry you had to suffer because I didn't."

"I survived, Father. My wounds will heal, though the Wolf's may not."

Her father cocked his head.

"Aleksi knifed Yago in the belly," she said. "Yago fled like the coward he is and left Taweel to his fate. The Wolf may be dead or dying along the road somewhere."

"If he is," Brawn spoke up, "I'll find him. Odds are, he'll make for the nearest city two days' ride south and west of here."

"Which is ruled by the Crow, allied to the Ox," her father said. He looked to Sahar. "Was the Wolf expecting to meet up with anyone else?"

She shook her head. "I never heard them speak of it. They only talked of taking me straight to the Ox."

Her father and Brawn exchanged glances. "If he makes it to the Crow," her father said, "they'll be watching everyone coming and going from the city."

"I expect they will." Brawn's brown eyes glinted with the challenge. "Farid, Matin," he singled out two of the six guards, both of them of medium height and unremarkable looks, as long as a person didn't look too closely, much like her uncle Brawn. "You'll be coming with me. We leave at dawn."

Later, Sahar sat beside her father and sorted out clean strips of linen to bind Aleksi's shoulder wound as Brawn and the two guards going after Yago made their preparations. They were to bring him or his body back if found, and if not, to go into the Crow's city and ferret out what information they could before returning home. Another of the guards stoked the camp's fire where a pot of water was set to boil as the fourth laid out a quick meal of cheese and dates and dried meat. The other two guards sat watch away from the camp.

Her father peeled away the blood-stained bandages Sahar had wrapped around Aleksi's wound two days ago as the guard set the pot of boiling water down alongside them. The king, a learned healer, dipped a wash rag into the water and rubbed a dab of soap into it. He began to gently wash the reddened skin around the wound, working his way to the blood-crusted hole, and did not speak until everyone else was out of earshot.

"You tended to Aleksi's wound, my daughter?"

"I did."

"You have done well. I see no infection and the skin is already knitting together."

"I did as you taught me, Father."

He nodded as he rinsed the rag and rubbed more soap onto it. "It helps to have such a fine, strong young man as a patient, does it not?"

She flicked a quick glance at Aleksi, and saw the muscle in his clamped jaw tick. "Yes," she said. "It does." Before her father could say more, she added rashly, "I would say his wound is worth one hundred gold pieces, wouldn't you?"

Her father's hand stilled mid-air. Aleksi met and held the king's accusatory glare without flinching.

"So much for your word of honor," the king said, resuming bathing Aleksi's wound a little less gently than before.

Aleksi said nothing.

"It was the Wolf who gave your secret away," she told her father, not even trying to hide the disappointment she felt that he had not trusted her to be able to take care of herself and shrugging off the fact that he'd proved to be right. Even a grown man such as himself would have been at the cur's mercy under the same circumstances. "One of Yago's spies saw you coming out of Aleksi's room the night before the race."

"His spy would not have known what was spoken between me and Aleksandr," the king said, still eyeing Aleksi. "Nobody but he and I could know that."

"The Wolf is, was, many things," she added stubbornly, "but stupid is not one of them. He knew enough to put two and two together."

Still, her father eyed Aleksi.

"Sahar asked me directly," Aleksi said after a long, terse moment. "I told her the truth."

"Which was?" the king said.

"That we made a bargain, you and I. I would watch over her and make sure she returned home safely, and you would pay me one hundred gold pieces whether I won the race or not." Aleksi turned to Sahar, his expression somber. "I would've done it without the promise of your father's coin. Nothing short of death would've stopped me from going after you."

"I know," she murmured. And she did.

"I knew this also," her father said. "That's why I asked you, Aleksandr. As king and father, I am neither deaf nor blind to what goes on in my household. Ratter was not the only person to notice you two 'courtin 'n sparkin' as he put it. The promise of coin was to repay you if you lost the race due to circumstances exactly like these."

Sahar and Aleksi both sat silent, neither looking at the other. Her father slowly looked from one to the other, his gaze settling on Aleksi.

"My only question now is, could my daughter be pregnant?"

Sahar's mouth went dry and her mind went empty. She'd thought she was prepared for her father asking, but now that he had, she couldn't speak or think.

"I have sworn to stay until we know for certain, one way or another," Aleksi said, and his voice was amazingly steady and sure under her father's heated stare. "I have offered marriage if there is a babe."

Her father looked to Sahar.

"I have accepted, if there is a babe."

Aleksi rolled his bandaged shoulder and donned one of the king's clean tunics. They were of a similar size and the tunic fit well, its fine weave a testament to the rank of its owner who sat nearby watching his daughter as she tucked into the supper set out for them by the campfire. Aleksi's empty stomach rumbled and growled, but he didn't join Sahar. Though her father hadn't said a word otherwise, Aleksi knew that his audience with the king was not over yet. Not by a long shot.

"How is Munir?" Aleksi asked, eager to get the coming interrogation done and over with.

"His ribs and his shoulder will heal," the king answered as he turned around to face him. "He told me you jumped into the river and saved his life."

"He would've done the same for me."

"Yes," the king said. "He would have. I sent word to your father, informing him of what I knew of the situation."

"What? Why?"

"Because he's your father."

"I doubt he will worry himself overmuch about it." *About me.*

The king studied Aleksi for a long moment, but said nothing further. Aleksi recalled hearing that there had been no love lost between the Black Mane and his father, the Panther, even before the Swan. He recalled too what Sahar had said about how his father could've been protecting Aleksi from Theodesia, and the little seed of hope her insight had planted deep in his soul stirred in light of her father's words.

Because he is your father.

Sahar's father still watched him with those uncanny cat eyes that his daughter had inherited, along with a backbone of forged iron.

"Do you love her?"

Aleksi did not need to ask who the king meant any more than the king needed to name her.

"I admire her, and desire her, both her mind and her body," he answered honestly. He had seen the way the king looked at his wife and queen of twenty plus years, the man understood desire. "I believe she feels the same about me, but the word love has never been spoken between us."

"I see."

"You do? Because truly, I don't."

The king gave him a sympathetic chuckle, which was much better than an irate punch. "You two will have some time to work it out," he said, and then he narrowed his gaze on Aleksi. "There will be no more chances at making babies. Do we understand each other?"

"We do." Aleksi was alive and in one piece, and he intended to stay that way, which should not prove to be too difficult. There was little chance of Sahar taking him into her bed as things stood between them now.

Aleksi woke in the dark before dawn, reaching his arm out for the soft, familiar warmth of Sahar and finding only hard ground. He pushed his cold, kinked body up to sitting and gazed over the sleeping figure of the king, whose bedroll was planted firmly between Aleksi's and Sahar's to see her still sleeping, peaceful and safe. He ran a hand through his hair, scratching his scalp, and then rubbed his face and arms to bring some blood and heat into them. He stood and walked over to a copse of bushes to relieve himself, and met Brawn coming back on the way.

The captain of the king's guard moved with a coiled, sinewy purpose that put Aleksi in mind of a snake waiting to strike, and Aleksi had the impression that Brawn would be as quick and deadly. He recalled Sahar's warning about her uncle Brawn being the man he should watch out for, and though Aleksi stood a head taller and outweighed Brawn by two stone at least, the last thing he wanted to do was take him on. From what Aleksi had observed, the man watched everything and missed nothing, and when he spoke, his words were terse and to the point, traits Aleksi admired. He dipped his head in greeting. "'Morning," he said.

Brawn stopped and sized up Aleksi. "'Morning," Brawn replied. "Thanks for bringing back Sahar, and for wounding the Wolf." He grinned, cold and deadly. "It'll be my honor to finish the cur."

Aleksi avoided Sahar throughout the day's journey and into the night, and the next, chancing no more than a few furtive glances her way when no one else was looking, or speaking a few hasty words to her in passing each time they made or broke camp. With her father or one of the guards always nearby and watching closely, Aleksi didn't dare do more, and she didn't seem inclined to want more. In truth, she acted warier of him than ever, and looked ready to jump out of her skin the night they camped at the same spot by the river where she had first stood proud and naked before him. Where they had embraced skin to skin and kissed with a hunger and a passion that had been only a taste of the carnal feast to come. A feast Aleksi hungered to partake of again.

He sat across the fire from her and tore off a strip of stringy jerky and chewed, all the while his mouth watering for the honeyed taste of her tender flesh. He could still see her standing in the river, her long, lithe limbs glistening under the morning sun, the curve of her breasts and hips calling to everything male in him. The challenge in her eyes, unabashed and unafraid. By the gods, she was still calling to him, and his cursed cock, aching for the wet, caressing heat of her, was answering.

He stood and turned his back to the fire and everyone sitting around it and headed for the stream, which was a mistake. Tactile memories of standing knee deep in the water chest to breast with her washed over him, heating his blood and forging his hard cock into tempered steel. He groaned and shook his head and shoulders, pawing at the shoreline as he debated whether to walk into the river fully clothed or fall face first into the freezing water.

Behind him a quiet rustling of fallen leaves told of someone approaching, someone who moved with the stealthy grace of a cat.

"Go back, Sahar," he said, turning sideways so the tent pole in his breeches was visible to her. "Go back to your father."

"No."

He turned and faced her. "What do you want?" He imbued the words with all the bitterness he had felt, and though she flinched at his vitriol, she stood her ground. He splayed his hands and gentled his voice, his cock pointing straight at the only woman he wanted with every fiber of his being. "What is it you want of me?"

She didn't answer him, not with words, but her expression told him exactly what she wanted. He closed the distance between them and took her mouth with his, backing her up against a tree without breaking stride or their kiss. He ran his hands up under her tunic, cupping her heavy breasts and thumbing her peaked nipples as he plundered her mouth with his tongue. She slid her hands from his shoulders to the front of his breeches, deftly untying his stays and freeing his straining cock as she nipped at his demanding lips.

He untied her breeches and cupped her mound. He slid a finger around her folds, dipping in and out of her hot, wet center, spreading her sweet nectar and rubbing the bud that would bring her to climax as she brought him to his with the rhythmic strokes of her strong, capable hands.

He caught her cry of release with his kiss, as she did his, and when it was over, almost as soon as it'd started, they each tied the other's breeches, still catching their breath and neither saying a word, even when she turned and walked away.

CHAPTER 15

Return

They rode through the palace gates in the middle of the night quietly and without fanfare, the guards giving hushed salutes to the king. Yet, lights shone behind every shuttered window of the second floor of the royal household. Sahar knew they would be waiting for her and her father's return, but she didn't think they were the reason half the household seemed to be awake at midnight.

As they rode up to the palace steps, stable boys still rubbing the sleep from their faces came running up to take their horses, Ratter and Arman right behind them.

"What a night it be, what a night it be," Ratter chortled as Sahar slid down off of Lasair and handed him the reins. "Our princess and king be comin' back, and our new prince or princess comin' into this world."

"Rima is having her baby?"

Ratter touched the side of his nose with a gnarled finger. "The women 'ave been in 'er bed chamber since sunset," he said. "An' yer brother 'as been pacing the halls outside it jest about as long."

Sahar laid a hand over her belly without thought, an action that did not go unnoticed by Ratter. Swiping at her flushed cheeks, she turned and ran up the steps into her home.

Home. But for how long? If she was with child and she married Aleksi she didn't think she was long for this city she'd known her whole life.

She looked down at her belly, concave from ten and eight days of camp rations and scavenging, as if the wee one that might be growing in her womb could give her the answer.

"Come daughter." Sahar practically jumped out of her skin at her father's hand on her shoulder. "Let's find your mother."

She followed him up the stairs to the living quarters, and when they turned the corner into the hall, she broke into a run at the sight of her brother and Munir pacing the floor outside of Asim's and Rima's chambers.

"Sahar." Her brother met her halfway, wrapping her up in his arms and swinging her in a circle. "It's so good to see you."

"It's good to be seen."

He set her back on her feet in time for Munir to give her a hearty, one armed hug, his other still in a sling.

"Welcome home." He stepped back and eyed her from head to toe. "Are you well?"

She knew what he was asking, what every member of her family and half the city would be asking. Had the Wolf or his curs violated her?

"I'm well," she assured him, and her brother blew his breath out in a huge sigh of relief.

"Aleksi?" Munir asked.

"He's well also," she told him. "He found me before they could follow through on their vile threats and got me safely away, though he suffered a knife wound to his shoulder when we fought the bast"—she glanced over her shoulder as her father walked up—"the Wolf and the Tall."

Munir mimed spitting on the floor. "Where are the Wolf and his pack now?" he said.

"Aleksi killed the Jackal the night he rescued me, and I killed the Tall the night we rescued Lasair."

"You did what?" her brother asked, his voice, his expression, showing more pride than surprise. She gloried in it.

"Aleksi and I fought the Wolf and the Tall," she told them. "I beat the Tall to death with a stick and Aleksi pulled the Wolf's blade from his shoulder and stuck the Wolf in the belly with it. The Wolf rode off. How far he got, we don't know." She looked to her father. "Brawn went after him to find out what has become of him."

"We'll have much to prepare for," her father said. "No matter what Brawn discovers. But for now—"

The chamber door burst open and the queen stepped out. Her gaze went directly to her husband, and she sucked in a great breath.

She turned to her daughter, and her breath flew out in a rush. Her tears wet Sahar's cheek as she embraced her.

"You have come home to us," she cried softly. "Oh, my darling girl. My brave, brash, wonderful, headstrong girl. You have come home to us." She kissed Sahar's tear-streaked cheek and stood back, holding her shoulders with both hands. "You are well?"

"I'm well."

Her mother looked over Sahar's head to her husband, and was reassured by whatever she saw. She ran her hands down Sahar's arms and held her wrists.

"Good," she said. "I am glad." She sniffed, smiled and then looked over to Asim. "You have a son, my son," she said, grinning as Asim stood there wide-eyed with his mouth hanging open. "Go, meet your son and thank your wife." She laughed as he leapt past her into his chambers, and then squeezed Sahar's wrists. "You, my daughter, can meet your nephew tomorrow. Tonight you must go bathe, then eat, and then sleep." She wrinkled her nose and whispered, "You smell."

Safe, clean, warm, and dry, laying in her big, soft, comfortable bed alone, Sahar was unable to sleep. She knew Aleksi had moved into one of the guest rooms in the palace at her parents' invitation, and for one brief moment she considered sneaking over to his room and getting into bed with him,. Throwing off her bedcovers, she stuffed her feet into her slippers and padded down the hall to the kitchens. She pushed the door open and stopped. Aleksi was sitting at the table he often sat at with Anya, gnawing the meat off a drumstick of cooked fowl. "What are you doing here?"

"I couldn't sleep," he said. "Not without my tigress snuggled up against me, snoring in my ear."

"I don't snore."

"Shall we call it purring then?" He pushed the plate toward her as she scowled at him and took a seat at the table. "Hungry?" he asked.

"Ravenous."

He licked his lips, never taking his eyes from hers. "Me too."

Sahar laughed. She couldn't help it. "You are—"

"Handsome, charming, irresistible."

"An arrogant ass."

He gave her a cocky grin as he cut off a slice of breast meat. "True," he said. He took a big bite and smacked his lips. "Tasty, but then you know how I like a tender breast."

Sahar gave him her best glare even as her traitorous cheeks flushed hot at the memory of his mouth on her body. He may be an arrogant, conceited ass, but the man had reason to be. He was as good in bed as he was on the back of a horse. Which was saying something. He was grinning at her and licking his lips, and she was actually considering climbing on top of him and riding him here in the kitchens when the door opened and Anya walked in.

"Oh, oh my," she exclaimed, her hands to her cheeks. "I was told you'd returned together and safely. Thank the gods. I didn't expect to see you two up before the sun."

"We didn't mean to raid your kitchen," he said. "We're hungry and have become accustomed of late to rising before the sun."

"No need to apologize." Anya shook her head. "You're always welcome in the palace kitchens." She swiped at welling tears, and then wiped her hands on her work apron. "I'm so glad to see you both alive and well, if not a stone or two lighter by the looks of you." She sniffed and grinned. "Well, we'll take care of that soon enough." She went to the larder and pulled out a sack of ground flour. "What a night, eh? You two and the king returned. A new princeling born. It'll be a day and a night of feasting no doubt."

Aleksi stood. "We should be getting out of your way then."

"No." The vehemence of her answer stopped Sahar as she started to stand. "No need," she said, waving them back down. "You two sit, eat. Can I make you some eggs or porridge? More kitchen maids will be joining me shortly. We have orders to pack enough travel provisions for twenty and four riders off on the king's business at first light, but I can cook you something before they show." She smiled and let out a happy sigh. "Please," she said. "Sit and eat and tell me the real story behind all the tales I'll be hearing come the morrow."

"Meet your nephew," Sahar's mother said, laying the bundle of blanket and pudgy-cheeked infant in her arms. "Ammar, son of Asim, son of Asad, King of the City by the Sea."

The newborn gazed up at her with big, round, serious eyes. The corners of Sahar's mouth tilted up, and she found herself speaking in that strange, high-pitched way adults spoke to babies. "Hello, my nephew Ammar," she cooed. "I am your Auntie Sahar, your father's sister." She tickled his palm with her fingertip and smiled as he wrapped his fingers around it. "Ohh, such a strong grip you have my little man." She looked up at her brother and grinned. "You must take after your Auntie," she said in a conspiratorial whisper meant for her brother to hear.

"Ha, ha," her brother said, though he was grinning too. In truth, he hadn't stopped grinning since Sahar walked into their chambers.

"Truly," Sahar said to Asim and Rima, "he is the most handsome baby I have ever seen."

"He looks like his father," Rima said from her bed with a tired but happy smile while Asim gazed down at her with an adoring expression.

Rima lay propped up with six pillows at least, a tray of her favorite sweet breads on the table beside her and a pitcher of frothy beer to relax her strained body and encourage the flow of her breast milk. Many women of rank or wealth chose to use wet nurses, considering the toll pregnancy and childbirth took on their bodies, but not the women of Sahar's family. They chose to hold their infants close, to nourish them with their bodies and nurture them with their mother's love.

Cradling her nephew in her arms, smelling his new baby smell, she understood why. That understanding brought her close to tears.

She handed the baby back to his mother, kissed Rima on the cheek, gave her brother a quick hug, and practically ran out of their chambers. Her mother found her a short time later, pacing her rooms like a tigress in a cage. A cage of her own lustful making.

Her mother sat on the edge of Sahar's bed and patted the space beside her. She stopped pacing and hung her head low. She had no doubt that her mother knew she might be carrying Aleksi's child, and she could not face her, not yet. She'd entered the races to show that she was as capable as any man. She'd proudly claimed, out loud and often, that she didn't need a man, that if and when she was to marry it would be her choice. Now here she stood, having proved she was as trapped by nature and tradition as every other woman.

She lifted her head and met her mother's unwavering gaze. The love and understanding Sahar saw there burst the dam of her tears. She got on the bed and laid her head in her mother's lap and cried. She cried for the girl who had ridden off determined to win the race, certain that her winning would change the ways of the world and the minds of men. She cried for the woman who had returned, wiser in the ways of the world and men, of the hard truths and venal lies to be learned and dealt with, and of the selfishness and selflessness that warred within each and every person. She cried for the loss of her false pride, for Munir's injuries and Kedar's death. She cried out the days and nights of fear and hunger and depravation suffered under Yago's short but cruel reign. Then she sobbed her heart out for the passion she had discovered with Aleksi, and might never know again.

The only thing she didn't cry over was the child she might be carrying. She held a fierce certainty she would love that child no matter what happened between her and its father.

As her sobs subsided, she became aware of her mother's soft, soothing voice crooning calming words and her fingers tenderly combing Sahar's hair from her wet cheeks. The last of her tears finally spent, she rolled over onto her back and stared up into her mother's concerned face.

"Do you love him?"

There was no need to ask her mother who she meant. "I don't know," she said. "Truly, I don't." She rolled over onto her side and curled into herself. "It doesn't matter. We'll marry if I'm with child, and if not, we'll go our separate ways, as we were always meant to do."

She closed her eyes with a long, weary sigh, and when she woke, her mother was gone and the sun was low in the western sky.

Aleksi entered the great hall lit with torches and candles, the savory scent of the coming feast teasing his still half-starved body. He made his way past the rings of tables and the hearty welcomes mixed with backhanded whispers to the royal family's long table and took his seat of honor to Sahar's right, who sat to the queen's right. Beside the queen sat the king, and to his left were two empty seats for Prince Asim, his wife, Princess Rima, and their newborn son, the princeling Ammar, whose birth they were celebrating along with the safe return of Sahar and Aleksandr.

"Princess," Aleksi dipped his head to Sahar as he slid onto the bench beside her. The knot on her forehead was no more than a raised bump, the bruises on her face no more than a pale mottling barely visible beneath a light dusting of face powder, and the raw welts on her wrists had faded to thin red lines. She was still too thin, but in the seven days since the king had found them and fed them, the hollows of her cheeks had fleshed out some and her skin had resumed its tawny glow. Skin he knew the taste and feel of intimately, and his body craved even more than the sumptuous feast being set out before them. "You look much rested."

"As do you, Aleksandr."

So, he was back to Aleksandr. No breathless, panting *my stallion* moaned into his ear. No conversational, companionable *Aleksi*. Not even a spitting, snarling *arrogant ass* hissed at him. Aleksandr. The formal name of a stranger.

He rubbed his shaven jaw, and caught the faint flicker of gold in her eyes. He gave her a purposely cocky grin, and her eyes flashed green fire. He laughed, short and quick. She was not indifferent to him, no matter how hard she tried to seem so in front of the watchful gazes and wagging tongues of the assembled.

A murmuring of those tongues grew louder as Prince Asim, carrying his newborn son in one arm, his wife holding onto his other, walked slowly to the royal table. Both prince and princess were beaming, their pride and joy in the bundled babe and each other obvious. Aleksi glanced at Sahar, and saw the tears welling in her eyes and her hand over her belly. He started to reach out, to place his hand over hers, and drew back. Aleksi's touch she would've accepted, perhaps even welcomed, but not Aleksandr's.

Prince Asim helped his wife to her seat and tenderly set their son in her cradled arms before sitting. King Asad leaned over and said something that only they could hear, which made his son laugh. The queen swiped a tear from her cheek, and Princess Rima placed a kiss on her son's forehead. Aleksi was mesmerized by the familial intimacy of the moment, something he had never known or seen, and he realized with a start that Sahar was watching him, her gaze dark and fathomless.

"Welcome," King Asad called out as he stood. "Welcome all to this feast celebrating the birth of the Prince Ammar and the safe return of Princess Sahar and Aleksandr to our family."

Loud claps and whistles broke out in the great hall, and though Aleksi knew they were for Sahar and the babe, still he felt a warmth in his chest at the inclusion of his name with the word "family." He tried to imagine how it would feel to become an actual part of this family, to be welcomed and honored as Sahar's husband. A stupid dream of an illicit lover, the bastard son of a king. The only way he'd be accepted into this royal family was if his seed had taken root and was growing in Sahar's womb.

Then his dilemma would be staying to be consort to a princess, always less than his royal wife and her family, and never his own man, or dragging her back to his homeland, bringing her down to his level, wife of a bastard horse trader.

"To the Prince Ammar," someone shouted, and Aleksi realized it was Nasim, the Cheetah, brother and chief counsel to the king, and uncle to Asim.

"To the Prince Ammar," the gathering responded, lifting their goblets high.

"To Princess Sahar," Nasim said, lifting his goblet again. "The first woman to ever ride in the races. Who not only rode, but won the first and placed in the second, and who survived the third, despite the Wolf's treachery."

"To Princess Sahar."

"To Aleksandr." He lifted his goblet and nodded to Aleksi. "Who saved the life of my future son-in law, Munir, and who brought my niece home safe to us."

"To Aleksandr." The chorus of voices was praise Aleksi took pride in.

He glanced at Sahar, and she at him, her cheeks flushed and her eyes flaming. It took every shred of self-will to keep from pulling her up beside him, to fold her in his embrace and claim her in front of her family with a kiss as heated and passionate as her glare.

He stood alone and faced the gathering.

"To friends old," he said, raising his goblet to where Pyotr and Serge sat at a table a few rings back from the titled, "and to friends new." He raised his goblet to Munir, who sat at the end of the royal table with Halah. He raised his goblet to the queen and the king. "To my generous and honorable hosts," he said, and then lifted his goblet to Prince Asim and his wife, "and to the newest and cherished son of this esteemed family." He looked down at Sahar and lifted his goblet high. "To Princess Sahar, who rode as good a race as any man, and who saved my life as surely as I saved hers."

The gathering clapped and whistled as Sahar slowly stood, a fine sheen of sweat beading on her flushed cheeks and forehead. Aleksi started to sit, and stopped when she grabbed his hand and held on tight. She took a sip of her wine and cleared her throat.

"To my family," she said. "For believing in me enough to let me go and loving me enough to bring me back." Her father chuffed and her mother smiled and swiped at her tears. Sahar's voice caught and cracked. "To my—my brother, and his loving wife and their glorious son, born of their love. I am so very happy for you." She sniffed and Aleksi gave her hand a gentle squeeze. "To Aleksandr," she said. "Who could have easily won the last and most prized of the races, but who chose to come after me instead." She raised her goblet to him. "He saved me from evil men intent on evil deeds."

Aleksi lifted her hand in his and placed his lips on the back of her fingers, inhaling her warm, exotic fragrance. The hall filled with a mixture of applause and whispers, rent by a shrill feminine twitter.

"Are you courting the princess now, my bastard half-brother?"

Aleksi lowered his and Sahar's hands, but didn't let go. "If I was, Anastasia," he answered her evenly, "it would be of no concern to anyone but myself and Princess Sahar's family."

"What of your family?" she insisted with such high-handedness that Aleksi bit off a snort of laughter.

"What family is that?" he said. "I'm the bastard son of a king who does not claim me. I have no family."

Wearing nothing but a loose bed tunic, Aleksi went to the door of his chambers that led to a small balcony overlooking the inner courtyard and opened it at the light but insistent knocking.

"Sahar? What are you doing here at this time of night?"

She nodded toward the hundred-year-old cedar that ruled over the courtyard gardens. "Get dressed and meet me in the tree," she said, and then slipped back over the balcony wall and down the trellis she'd climbed to his rooms.

He quickly donned a pair of breeches and went over the balcony wall to the hand and footholds carved into the ancient cedar's trunk. He climbed up, then pushed open the trap door to a platform built amongst its sturdy branches. There he found a small gallery with high rails, two benches and a pile of pillows and blankets strewn about. Sahar was sitting cross-legged on a blanket on the floor, her back against one of the benches. Aleksi sat, crossed his legs and leaned his back against the opposite bench.

"I'm sorry if I woke you," she said.

He shook his head. "I wasn't sleeping. I find I'm not used to such comfort. In truth, I find my bed too soft and too empty."

"I find my bed too empty these past nights as well," she admitted.

He reached out to pull her to him, and she held out a stiffened arm. "That's not the reason I asked you to meet me here."

"No," he said, pulling his hand back and splaying it against his thigh. "I didn't think it was."

"What are we going to do?" she asked.

"What we agreed to with your father," he told her. "I'll stay until we know if there is a babe. If there is, we'll marry. If there's not, we won't. I'll return home with my string of broodmares and purse full of coin, and you'll stay in the bosom of your family, free of me or any other man you do not want."

"You know that's not true."

"Which part?"

"The not wanting you," she chided. "That's what got us into this mess."

He laughed, short and quick. "True enough," he agreed. He met her gaze and held nothing of what he felt for her from his. "For my part, my tigress, I don't regret giving in to your want of me, or mine of you. No matter what comes of it."

Sahar blinked, swallowed and sniffed. Then she sat up straighter and squared her shoulders. "If we do marry, where will we live? Will our child be raised here, a royal with wealth and position in the loving bosom, as you put it, of my family, or do you intend to take us back to your home, where our child would grow up with toil and uncertainty?"

"Nothing in life is certain, my tigress. Mine is the perfect example of that. Our child will not have nothing but toil, not that a little toil is a bad thing. Our child will grow up straight and true and strong. Well-fed and well-loved in a home built by their father's sweat and ambition. Not some soft, selfish royal who knows more of palace gossip and intrigue than the hard work of real life."

"How is palace life not real life?"

"A handful of people who have servants to take care of their every whim versus thousands who do not eat lest they grow, harvest, and cook their own food. Who haul their own water and who shovel their stocks' manure to grow that food. Who empty their own piss pots. You tell me."

"That same handful of royal people make sure there are trade pacts so the thousands can trade that food or craft or other essentials. The royals make sure the people are safe when they haul that water with laws and alliances and pay people a living wage to empty their chamber pots."

Aleksi snorted. "Your father's palace may pay people for their work, but how many other kings do?"

"Your father paid you, Serge, and Pyotr."

"My point is, my child will not be raised a cosseted, spoilt royal."

"Mine will not be raised an uncouth, roundhouse-dwelling, ignoramus."

Aleksi left, slamming the trapdoor over his head, dropped down to the ground, and stomped through the gardens to the lattice that led to his chambers, grumbling under his breath the whole way.

"Royal fucking bitch. I was more than good enough for her when it was the two of us alone in the wild. I was her stallion, and she couldn't get enough of me. I thought she was different than other royals, that my touch meant as much to her as hers did to me, but we get back here to her royal family's palace and she wants nothing to do with me. She swore she had no need or want of a man, until she wanted me, gave herself to me, trusted me."

He stopped and turned around, eyeing the cedar.

"Until she cursed me with wanting her so badly I gave in. I gave in and lay with her and loved her until I not only wanted her, I craved her, needed her, needed her to be mine." He took a few steps back in the direction of the tree and the woman still there. "Is that why I let myself be blinded by our passion? Why I acted like some lovesick lad and did not take precautions against planting my seed in her womb? Was I trying to trap my tigress?"

He took another few steps and leaned against a column.

"Stupid man. If I've managed to trap her and tie myself by the stones to her, do I truly expect her to choose the life of a poor, horse-trading bastard over that of a privileged princess? Would I choose that life for our child, our children, over one of wealth and ease? Could I be the bigger man and accept being consort to a princess, and have my life ruled over by her royal family for the sake of our children?"

Aleksi rolled his forehead against the column as if he could press an answer into his brain.

"I could leave. Take my coin and horses and head south instead of north. Serge and Pyotr would likely join me. We could settle in some new city, set ourselves up, start new lives. Sahar would keep her father from coming after me, her pride would never let him chase me down like the dog I am for even thinking such a thing. No. I would never abandon my child. My children shall know their father's love until the end of their days."

He walked slowly to the cedar.

"Her family may be royal, but they are as different from mine as night from day. They have already taken me into their home, treated me like a hero for doing what was right when they know I've done wrong and lain with their daughter." He stood at the foot of the cedar and gazed up. "Yet it felt so right."

He started to climb up the tree, and stopped at the sound of quiet weeping. He continued and tried to push open the trapdoor, but she had thrown the bolt shut.

"Sahar," he said, and he knew she heard him when her weeping turned to snuffles. "If you are with child, I'll stay. I'll stay and raise my child in your city with your family. I'd hoped you had enough faith in me, in us, to make a good life by our own efforts. That you would be proud to stand by me and work by my side to build that life together."

CHAPTER 16

Alliances

Since her argument with Aleksi in the cedar tree, Sahar was acting more like a chicken than a tigress hiding in her chambers for the past three days. In that time, three things of importance had happened. The first of the messengers her father had sent out had returned, bringing with them oaths of alliance should the Ox start a war. Brawn had come back with the news that the Wolf had made it to the Crow's city alive, barely, and that riders had been sent to the Ox to inform him of his son's condition, purportedly caused by Sahar's and Aleksi's treachery. Sahar's moon flow had arrived with a vengeance that left her curled around a hot brick on her bed with a cool, wet cloth over her forehead.

The first two happenings she knew because her mother and Halah—the only two people she admitted into her chambers other than her maid servant, Safa—had told her.

The third she'd told her mother with the promise that Sahar would be the one to tell Aleksi.

Aleksi.

She'd heard every word he said to her through the bolted door to the treehouse, and the myriad of emotions she'd felt, that she still felt, overwhelmed her. Shame, regret, pity, anger, frustration, and guilt, especially guilt, because he was right. She should've had enough faith in him to know he would take care of her and any babe they made. He was a good, strong, honorable man, who would have given his life for her, and who had proved it many times over. He'd never gone back on his word, and never would. He'd told her from almost the moment they met that he wanted a good, strong-bodied woman with an easy temper to marry and raise his sons.

She'd never been, and would never be that easy-tempered woman whose only dream in life was to marry and have babies, a fact she had made clear from the start. She'd never pledged her love, or made any commitments during their few nights of physical passion. He was a strutting stallion looking for a docile broodmare, and she, by his own words, was a fierce tigress wary of traps. Ah, but while she may not have set her trap, she had fallen for the handsome bait and walked straight into it. Straight into the arms of a man whose cocky grin and hearty laughter made her smile despite herself. Whose easy company and teasing banter soothed and inflamed her. Whose touch turned her bones to liquid fire, and whose strong, steady presence grounded her.

Who had told her she meant nothing to him in anger once, though his body, his eyes, his whispered endearments had told her otherwise since.

He'd never told her he loved her. They had never promised that to each other.

She didn't know if she wanted him to love her with more than his body. The idea of loving him, all of him, body and soul, as her mother and father loved each other seemed impossible. Yes, they shared desire and passion that burned hot and fast, but they'd never had the easy, effortless relationship that her Uncle Nasim and Auntie Lyrra had, or even the sweet adoration that made her brother and Rima glow when gazing at each other and their newborn son.

Sahar rolled her aching head from side to side and laid a hand over her empty womb before pushing herself up and off the bed. None of it mattered now. She was not with child. She and Aleksi wouldn't marry, and he'd be leaving for his home soon with his string of broodmares and one hundred and thirty-two gold pieces in his purse. Enough to start his new life without her.

"Enough," she said as she stood on shaking legs. She drew a deep breath in and blew it out. "Enough." She opened her bedroom door to her outer chambers. "Safa," she called. "I'd like to bathe." As a woman in flux, she wouldn't bathe in the woman's pool, but there was a wooden tub kept for such times. "Please tell my mother I'll be supping with the family this evening."

"It is a formal supper this evening, mistress, held in honor of the emissaries who have come bearing oaths of alliance from their kings."

"Thank you. I'll wear my red worm weave."

Aleksi looked up from the table where he sat with Serge and Pyotr watching Sahar's entrance. This was the first time she'd entered the hall since the feast celebrating upon their return, and the first time he had seen her since their argument in the treehouse that same night. The red, one-shouldered gown she wore with a red shawl draped over her shoulders skimmed curves he knew intimately. Her black mass of curls, set high atop her head with ruby-encrusted combs, showed off the proud, elegant line of her neck. Aleksi's wasn't the only male, or female's, head to turn and watch the regal tigress take her seat, but he'd wager the hundred gold pieces her father had given him that he was the only one to notice the hollows beneath her eyes, or that her tawny skin was a shade paler than usual. Well, he amended as her mother cast a lingering eye over her daughter, perhaps not the only one.

"Your princess is looking rather well for having been ill these past three days," Pyotr said.

"Hmmph."

"What is that supposed to mean?" Serge asked.

"It means that she's not my princess."

"No?" Serge quirked a brow. He glanced from Aleksi to Sahar and back again. "Then why does she watch you as intently as you watch her?"

Because she and I shared a passion that seared us both to the bone. Because she may be carrying my babe in her belly even now. Because she may soon be my wife and does not wish to be.

"Because we have become used to watching out for each other," Aleksi said. "Our lives depended on each other for a time and it's a hard habit to break."

"Uh-huh."

"What," he turned on his friends with a snarl, "is that supposed to mean?"

"Nothing," Serge said, sitting back with both hands up.

"It means," Pyotr puffed his thick chest out and sat forward, "that you have been a morose bastard for the past three days, the same three days the princess took to her chambers. It means neither of us is stupid. We can add one," he eyed Aleksi as he held up an index finger, "and one," he glanced at Sahar and held up his other index finger, "and come up with," he pressed his fingers together to form a single column, "two."

Half expecting Pyotr to say three, Aleksi let out the breath he'd been holding with a snort. "Do you truly think a princess would consort with a bastard?"

Before they could answer, Munir walked over and sat down across from Aleksi. "Serge, Pyotr," he greeted them each with a nod. "Aleksi."

"Munir," they all said at once and laughed. "I have a favor to ask of you," Munir said to Aleksi. "You saved my life. If it were not for you, I would not be getting married, so, I would like for you to stand by my side along with Asim at my wedding a fortnight from tomorrow."

Aleksi liked Munir, and he respected him. He wasn't insensitive to Munir's request. A fortnight was not too long a time away, and if Sahar was pregnant, he would still be here planning his own wedding. Besides, he had already decided he would stay to stand and fight by King Asad's side if the Ox was successful in starting his war. A war Aleksi had had a hand in provoking and intended to have a hand in preventing. If that wasn't possible, then he'd help them win. King Asad had welcomed Aleksi's decision yesterday.

"I'd be honored," Aleksi told Munir.

They stood and shook on it.

"You two are invited as well," Munir told Serge and Pyotr. "I hear Anya is planning a feast to surpass all feasts."

"Then we'll be there," Pyotr said, slapping his barrel of a belly, which had grown a stone or more since Anya's sacks of food had been delivered daily. "Especially since King Asad has generously offered to keep stabling us and our horses until Aleksi finishes his business here, whatever that may entail."

Munir glanced at Aleksi and then quickly looked away. He knew. He knew exactly what it was that Aleksi was still doing here, what he was waiting for. Aleksi glanced over at Halah, as close to

Sahar as a sister, and then back at Munir, who gave a quick, unapologetic shrug.

"Tell me what I need to do and where I need to be when," Aleksi told Munir.

"I will," Munir said. He glanced at Halah, who was watching them. "I should go take my seat beside my betrothed. She'll be pleased you accepted."

Pyotr and Serge were eyeing Aleksi expectantly, waiting, he guessed, for more of an explanation what his business here entailed, but Aleksi ignored them. They may have been his best and oldest of friends, but he wasn't going to tell them about what happened between him and his tigress. Too many people knew already. Not that he was embarrassed or ashamed, but she would be.

The first course of greens and fish soup was being served when Anastasia made her appearance on the arm of the corpulent prince into which she had sunk her royal teeth. Why they were still here Aleksi didn't know. The prince was the second son of a kingdom three days west of this city who should've returned weeks ago, with or without Anastasia, who slid a sideways glance at Aleksi as she flounced by. Aleksi shook his head. He had more important things to worry about than his husband-hunting bitch of a half-sister.

One of those things was the way Sahar was looking at Aleksi with none of her usual humor or fire, but with a solemn expression he had never seen before. It hit him like a punch to the gut. Gods, she wasn't pregnant. Her moon flow had come, that was why she had taken to her chambers the past three days.

He should've felt relief. His life would be his own again. Once Munir's wedding was over, and the Ox and the Wolf dealt with, Aleksi would be free to return to his home and build his stables. Find a strong, easy-tempered wife to work and toil by his side and raise his sons and daughters. He should be elated, ready to celebrate his close escape, but all he wanted to do was rage and howl as he sat there staring at Sahar's beautiful, somber face. In that moment, it came to him. He didn't want a wife and a child by anyone else but her. He wanted their child.

And he'd lost both.

Sahar couldn't sleep, which had nothing to do with staying in her rooms the past three days and everything to do with the look on Aleksi's face at supper. The way his eyes had bored into hers and his jaw had clamped tight. The moment he'd realized what she had yet to tell him.

Tired of pacing and fretting, she slipped out her balcony door, climbed down the trellis into the courtyard and up the hand holds into the cedar's treehouse where Aleksi was sprawled out on a bench, a wineskin in hand.

"Come on up," he said, saluting her with the skin. "What shall we drink to? Our safe return? Our near escape? Our chance to prove the world wrong about bastards and women?"

Sahar reached for the wine and took a swig from the half-empty skin, and then another, and another while Aleksi watched with an amused smile on his half-drunk face. The warm liquid spread to her hands, her toes, and her tongue.

"Munir said you have agreed to stand for him at his wedding."

"I did."

"My father says you have sworn to stay here until the threat of the Ox is dealt with."

"I have."

She took another drink and handed the almost empty skin to him, wishing the spirits had loosened his tongue as much as hers. At the thought of his tongue and all the delicious, tantalizing sensations it had brought her, her nipples hardened, her core melted, and her cheeks flushed. She licked her aching lips, and Aleksi drained the wineskin.

"How did you know?" she asked, her throat almost closing before she got the words out.

His throat worked as if he were swallowing around the same stricture. "By the way you looked at supper tonight."

"Which was...?"

"Pale, somber...sad."

She said nothing. Her throat closing completely.

"That, and you had taken to your chambers the past three days."

She nodded, still unable to say anything. Besides, what could she say? That she wasn't sad she didn't carry his child, she was bereft. Her narrow escape felt more like a trap of regret and grief. As glad as she was to have proven a woman could ride in and win a race, she was tired of showing the world that she was more than a pretty princess in need of a husband. The princess didn't need a husband or a man to complete her, but Sahar the woman wanted Aleksi in her life.

She couldn't tell him this. Not now. Now that the life he wanted and had worked so hard for was about to come to fruition.

She stood on shaking legs and gave him a wan smile. "You're right," she said. "I'm not pregnant. We are free to go our own way. You to return to your home a self-made man, to build your stables and find yourself a wife of easy temper and me to..."

Aleksi stood, his spine as stiff as his jaw. "To what?"

She swallowed her tears and pain to meet and hold his gaze. "To live my royal life."

Aleksi hunkered low over Z's neck, the stallion's hooves churning up earth as they galloped at full speed across the river delta with no destination in mind other than getting away from the palace. Aleksi needed air and open space to think.

In the past ten days, ten and two more emissaries had returned to the palace, all with pledges from their kings to ally with King Asad against the Ox, which left only another two still to return. Word was, the Ox had been doing the same, with much less success. In fact, four of the kings the Ox had sent emissaries to had sent their own to King Asad with oaths of alliance to him. Which left the Ox's armies outnumbered four to one.

The riders Asad had sent to King Maksimillian had returned this morning with the message that Maksimillian was on his way and was expected to arrive at the palace in three days with twenty horsemen.

Aleksi's father was coming here.

To ally with King Asad, Aleksi told himself, though if that were the case, Maksimillian would surely have brought more men. He had an army of five hundred horsemen, and two thousand yeomen and foot soldiers at his command. King Asad had to've sent his missive when Sahar had first gone missing and Aleksi had gone after her, weeks before Asad knew of the Ox's plan.

Aleksi couldn't puzzle why his father was coming now with no more than a traveling guard. To force Anastasia's portly prince to marry her perhaps, but he could've sent a proxy with her dowry, unless Theodesia had insisted their father come himself to ensure his daughter an advantageous match. That didn't seem likely, especially for a second marriage. Anastasia had her prince slavering at her heels, and she could've married him any time she chose. Not for the first time, Aleksi wondered why they hadn't left to complete their nuptials. When, over breakfast, King Asad told Aleksi and Anastasia of their father's missive, it was as much news to her as him.

So why was his father coming? The question reverberated in his brain to the pounding rhythm of Z's hooves as they galloped across open fields and meadows. He slowed Z as they reached the wooded river course and gave the stallion his head, content to let the horse pick their way along the river path as Aleksi laid back on his saddle, his face to the noon sun, soaking up the last of autumn's heat, giving himself up to Z's rolling gait as the sound of birdsong and rushing water filled his racing mind.

Step by rocking step, Aleksi's breathing slowed and his jaw unclamped and his shoulders dropped down from his ears. Zolotoy stopped, and Aleksi sat up and opened his eyes to the vision of Sahar sitting on a boulder with her cheek on her knee, facing downriver, her loose hair falling in black waves down to her waist.

It was the most he had seen of her in the past ten days, other than at supper, where she would sit with her family, as beautiful and untouchable as a statue. The rest of the time she'd been like a ghost, slipping in and out of the stables whenever he was least likely to be there, flying past him in the racing kraal, her face buried in Lasair's mane, or pacing her balcony at night, a haunted spirit in a flowing white nightgown.

Lasair whinnied at sight of them and Sahar whipped her head around, her hands on the boulder, her long legs bunched up beneath her, a tigress ready to spring. He nudged Z forward and dismounted, then tied off his horse next to Lasair under Sahar's guarded gaze.

Aleksi walked over to the boulder, climbed up, and sat beside her, his shoulder barely touching hers. They sat silently, and he hated not hearing her sultry voice.

This, he knew as surely as he was sitting here, was the boulder she'd lain on, belly down, hanging over the edge holding on to Ommar's hand, unable to pull him up out of the swift running current below until Ommar had let go. This was where she'd watched helplessly as her beloved cousin had been swept away to his death, unable to do more than scream his name. This was the place she'd found her outer strength lacking and vowed never to be found lacking again. To prove to the world that she was more than a girl, and to prove to herself that she would hold on, no matter what.

This was where a kitten had become a tigress.

"The palace is abuzz with the news of your father's imminent arrival," she said.

They were the first words she had spoken to him in ten days and nights. "Yes," he answered, his witty conversational skills deserting him. "It is."

She turned her gaze to his, and Aleksi could have happily drowned in the mossy green depths of her eyes. "He comes for you."

Hope, as unsure and shaky as a newborn foal, rose in his chest. "Why do you say that?"

"For him to be only three days away already, he had to leave his palace almost as soon as he received my father's missive." She echoed Aleksi's earlier thoughts. "At which point all anybody knew was that I was likely kidnapped by the Wolf, and you had gone after me, alone, into the wilds. He has come with enough men to fight for you, not enough to go to war with my father. He comes for you, to take you back home with him."

"That may be," he said, unwilling to give his tentative hope. "But I will never go back to being his stable boy."

She smiled, eclipsing the late autumn sun. "If your father knows you at all, he realized that the day you left."

Aleksi chuckled.

"You'll go back with him once all this posturing and war threat is over," she said.

"I have no reason to stay," he replied, and when she did not dispute him, he changed the subject. "You don't think the Ox's threats will come to war?"

"No." She shook her head. "The Ox has been outplayed once again by my father, who has the oaths of ten and six kings to the Ox's four. Even the Ox is not that foolhardy. It's almost certain that he'll back down and try to save face, and the Wolf will live to tell his own twisted tales of our ordeal, making himself the hero, no doubt."

"Too bad," he grumbled. "I was looking forward to meeting the worm on the battlefield."

She gave a rueful laugh. "As if he would ever brave the battlefield, or you, again." She met his gaze and held it. "I should've let you kill him right off and been done with him."

"You had your reasons, and they were good, sound reasons, which is why I went along with the plan to capture him alive."

She nodded, and then fixed her piercing green cat eyes on his. "Plans do change, don't they?"

He wanted to laugh. "They do."

"And yours?"

"Have changed daily since the day I met you." *And asked you to marry me.*

"And what are your plans today?"

"To kiss you until you beg me to take you home with me."

Sahar could have turned away. She could've told him no. She should have, but she missed his kisses and how he could make her beg for more of everything he had to offer. She smiled into his earth-brown eyes and ran her fingers along his clean-shaven jaw, wrapping her hand around the back of his neck, and whispered, "Kiss me then, kiss me until you're begging to stay here with me."

He kissed her softly, tenderly, his lips brushing hers as lightly as his fingertips played over her breasts until he pushed her tunic down over her shoulders, exposing her pebbled nipples to the brisk air and his warm touch. He rose to his knees, bringing her with him, and pressed the fullness of his mouth against hers, slipping the tip of his tongue between her lips as he cupped her breasts in his palms, his thumbs rubbing tantalizing circles around her nipples as she groaned his name and nipped his lower lip.

He deepened his kisses, filling her mouth with his slick, probing tongue as his big, strong hands roamed the length of her back, holding her to him. She could feel the length of him rising against the softness of her belly.

She moaned and pressed her pelvis into his hard heat, rubbing and rolling her aching flesh over him, desperate for the feel of his skin against hers. They both wore leather riding breeches, and she fumbled for his stays and untied them without breaking their kiss. She yanked down on his breeches, freeing his cock, and rubbed her hand up and down the length of his hot, pulsing flesh.

Aleksi groaned into her mouth. "My man-eating tigress."

She smiled into his kiss and nipped his chin. He flipped her onto her back and was untying her stays and pulling her breeches to her knees. He bent over her and placed a kiss on one knee, and then the other, slowly making his way up her inner thighs, kiss by kiss, nip by nip, until his mouth hovered over the center of her desire and her flesh wept for want of him.

With a sure, cocky grin, he gently blew on her mass of curls, his warm breath teasing her, and she tried to open her legs, but her breeches stopped her at her knees. She squirmed and shimmied and pushed them down with her hands until they were down to her ankles, and then he took her by the wrists and pinned her arms over her head, leaving her exposed to his lusty gaze.

She thrilled at the raw hunger in his eyes, and raised her head to meet his mouth, her kiss as fierce and demanding as his. She raised her hips, tapping the tip of his thick erection with her flesh.

"I want you," she growled. "All of you, inside me now."

But instead of burying his cock deep inside of her, he buried his forehead into her shoulder.

"If I plant a baby inside of you now," he said, "your father will cut my cock off."

"But..."

"There are no buts," he said, lifting his head and meeting her frustrated gaze. "Unless you want to become the wife of an uncouth, lowly roundhouse-dwelling bastard, we can do everything but."

He was right, she knew he was. He may not want to marry her, but now, in this moment, he wanted her as much as she wanted him.

She wrapped her hands around his neck and pulled his head down and kissed him, kissed him so that he would want her for the rest of his days. They rolled onto their sides, and she kissed her way down his corded neck, kissed his small, erect nipples, the patch of hair on his broad chest. She turned and kissed her way down the rippled muscles of his belly, down the line of hair leading to his groin, and then she licked and kissed the pulsing length of his cock and wrapped her lips around the tip, her moans reverberating in her mouth as he drew tantalizing circles around her nub with his tongue.

They kissed and licked, nipped and suckled each other until they were both writhing and moaning with mounting pleasure. She peaked first, breaking with a melting heat, and then her mouth filled with Aleksi's warm, yeasty seed. She turned her head and spit it out into the river below, where it was washed away into oblivion. Then she stood, pulled up her breeches, tied her stays, and jumped off the rock and onto Lasair's back.

Once they were out of the woods and in the open meadow, she gave Lasair her head and let the mare run away from Aleksi and all of the things that Sahar had said and done and felt with him. She heard the pounding of hooves and glanced back to see Z bearing down on Lasair, who for some reason had slowed and pranced and nickered as Z came up alongside her.

"Sahar, wait," Aleksi said. "Sahar," he called louder, more insistent as she ignored him. He reached over and grabbed Lasair's reins and slowed both horses to a stop.

Sahar bared her teeth. "What?" she snarled.

"Do you want me to put a baby in you?" he asked. "If you do, I can accommodate you right here, right now."

"You are an insufferable—"

"Arrogant ass, I know, but this arrogant ass can't figure out if you are angrier with me for chancing getting you pregnant before or for refusing to chance it now."

She couldn't admit to being equally confused. "I don't wish for you, or any other man, to put a baby in me," she said. "I'm not a broodmare in need of a stud, or some poor maid in want of a husband."

"No. You're a proud, stubborn woman, determined to prove to the world that you're as callous and capable as any man in anything you choose to do, even in choosing and casting aside your lovers."

"What do you care?" she seethed. "What is it to you if you are the first or the fiftieth man I take to my bed or if I remain childless or have ten children? Since none of those children will be yours, you are free to go charm some easy-tempered serving maid to marry you and bear your brats. As you said yourself, in the end we are nothing to each other. I suggest you take advantage of your narrow escape from marriage to this spoiled princess and start scattering your seed where it will take purchase."

Aleksi ran a hand back through his hair. "You're angry you aren't pregnant."

"How foolish would that be?"

"Marry me."

"What?"

"Marry me. Be by wife. Bear my children. I'll make us a good life."

"Why?"

"Why what?"

"Why should I marry you?"

"Because we're good together. We watched each other's backs, kept each other alive when others would have given up. Because we fight as well for each other as with each other. Because we are both hardheaded and strong-willed enough to complete any task we put ourselves to, and because we desire each other and are cursed amazing in bed together."

"You think those reason enough?"

"They are better reasons than most marry for."

"They are not reason enough for me."

"What would be? Wealth? Rank? A big, shiny crown?"

Sahar ripped Lasair's rein from his hand. "You truly are an ass," she spat before sending Lasair flying.

CHAPTER 17

Wars and Weddings

Aleksi stood on the steps to the palace along with Anastasia, King Asad, and Queen Oona, as well as several other members of the royal family, including Sahar, dressed in the same gown of green worm weave that she had worn the night of Autumn's Eve. Except today she wore a woolen shawl of burnt umber to ward off the late autumn chill. The inner gate to the palace opened, and Aleksi tore his gaze from her to the company riding in. He saw his father's graying head and let out a relieved sigh at sight of his erect, unbent spine after a fortnight's trek, which had left Aleksi bone-weary and saddle-sore.

He hadn't known what to expect since Anastasia's cryptic comments about their father's health. He'd been worried about his father undertaking a long journey. Now that his father was here, Aleksi was truly glad to see him.

The company stopped at the steps as stable hands came running to take their mounts and house servants to unload their pack horses. Aleksi never took his eyes off of his father, whose gaze met and held his a long, searching moment before giving him a quick nod and then turning to King Asad, who was walking down the steps to him.

"Welcome, Maksimillian, my friend," King Asad greeted with a hearty handshake. "It's good to see you again."

"Thank you, Asad." Maksimillian broke the handshake, and though he still spoke to Asad, he was looking at Aleksi. "Praise be to you and the gods for bringing my son and your daughter home safe."

"It was more their own doing than mine or the gods," Asad said. "By the time we found them, they were well on their way back."

Aleksi swallowed past the hard lump in his throat as his father walked straight up to him, ignoring Anastasia's simpering. Aleksi offered his hand. "Father."

Maksimillian took his son's hand and then pulled him into his embrace. "My son. I am more glad than I can say to see you alive and well."

Aleksi breathed in the familiar scent of sandalwood and leather, and buried his nose deeper into his father's neck, the breath he had been holding releasing with a sigh when he didn't smell the faintest trace of death or decay.

"I can say the same," he replied, as they both stepped back and eyed the other closely. "You look good, Father, especially after such a long journey."

"I feel good," he said, and then fixed his gaze on Anastasia. "Daughter." He gave a formal dip of his head.

"Oh, Father." She threw her arms around his neck and hugged him, a hug he didn't return. "I'm so glad you're here. I was so worried about you, traveling such a distance in your condition."

"What condition is that?" he asked, disengaging himself from her stranglehold.

"You were so ill when I left, I feared I would not make it home in time to see you again."

"Yet you still left."

"So did your bastard," she sputtered.

"Which is another part of an interesting tale," their father said, "but one for another, more private telling." He turned and walked over to the queen and dipped his head. "Queen Oona, you grow more beautiful and gracious with every passing year."

"And you more full of charm and flattery." She smiled. "I see where your son gets it from."

"Along with his good looks," Maksimillian said with a grin. "This must be your daughter, Sahar, who, the last time I saw her, was still in side braids." He took Sahar's hand and placed his lips on the back of her fingers. "You have grown to be as beautiful as your mother. And as hard to kill, from what I've been told."

Sahar's big eyes widened, and then she grinned, fierce and feral. "Thank you, King Maksimillian."

"Thank you for helping bring my son home to me."

"Let's get you inside, out of this chill," King Asad said, leading them all into the palace. "Our cook is preparing a feast with enough food to feed a hundred and twenty hungry travelers. My manservant will see you to your chambers where a hot bath awaits. Then we'll sup."

Sahar sat between her brother and Halah at the family's long table, to the left of her mother and father, with King Maksimillian sitting to King Asad's right. To Maksimillian's right sat Aleksi. It was the first evening meal that he'd eaten in the hall since his and Sahar's fight at the river three days ago. He'd been taking his meals in the kitchens after the family ate, and enjoying the attentions of Ursula, no doubt. The kitchen maid had been looking overly pleased with herself of late.

Anastasia sat to Aleksi's right, which would've been decided by Maksimillian, and was a public display of the king ranking his bastard son over his daughter, who was both older and born in wedlock. Sahar couldn't help but smile every time she glanced down the table at them, and caught Aleksi's bemused gaze more than once, as well as Anastasia's spiteful glare.

It was hard to feel any pity for the harpy, especially knowing how miserable she'd made Aleksi's life. He was a victim of his birth, as was anyone, but how they chose to deal with their life's circumstances were as different as night and day. Anastasia, born to privilege and wealth, had chosen to use her elevated rank in selfish, hateful ways. Aleksi, raised in his youth as a prince and then brought low, had chosen to work hard and prove himself a self-made man, helping his friends Pyotr and Serge along the way, as well as any stray, starving kitten he found.

Sahar had chosen to fight and rail against the preconceived notions of a woman in her privileged position. She had proved she could ride as well as any man and better than most, and that she could survive bad men trying to defile and debase her. But she hadn't helped anyone else. Certainly not any of the hundreds of thousands of poor women in the world who survived hardships daily, and had little choice or say in the matter.

She felt ashamed.

Ashamed that she had acted exactly like the proud, spoilt princess Aleksi had accused her of being. If her biggest problem was proving people's ideas about her wrong, at least she had that ability. She could play to or against their prejudices without having to worry about having a place to live or feeding her children, and without being at a man's capricious mercy. She could choose a husband because she wanted to, not because she needed to, though she also knew that not all daughters of royal households had that choice.

She could kill a man who attacked her and not be hung for it.

"Sahar," Halah asked, "are you all right?"

Sweet, good-hearted Halah, who was getting married on the morrow and still aware enough of others to ask after Sahar because she sat frowning at her wine.

"I'm fine," she lied. "You, my dearest of cousins, are getting married tomorrow." She smiled into Halah's beaming face. "This time tomorrow eve will be your wedding feast."

"Then the wedding night," Halah said, biting her lower lip.

"It's a night to look forward to." Sahar had told Halah of the passion she and Aleksi had shared in the wilds, though not in detail. She knew with a woman's newly woken instinct that Munir and Halah would share a happy marriage bed. "Munir loves you. He will be a gentle lover, until you do not want him to be so gentle anymore," she said with a purposely wicked grin.

Halah blushed beet red and Sahar laughed lightly and patted Halah's hand.

"You will be fine, Lala. I'm sure of it."

"Then I'll smile as satisfied as you when you talk about laying with Aleksi."

It was Sahar's turn to blush furiously, and Halah laughed, the two of them catching the rest of the table's attention. They both raised their goblets and sipped their wine until their cheeks cooled and curious gazes found other points of interest.

"Aleksandr looks much like a younger version of his father," Halah said. "Though Aleksandr is a hand taller and broader through the chest."

Sahar's cheeks flushed again, and her nipples hardened at the memory of Aleksi's bare, broad chest skin to skin against hers. "So he is," she agreed, swiping at the bead of sweat on her cheeks, "and so he does. The king couldn't deny his parentage even if he wished to. By their warm greeting this afternoon, he does not."

"Anastasia looks as ill-disposed by it as the king and Aleksandr are pleased."

Sahar chuffed. "She's a cold-stone bitch."

"Sahar."

"Well," she said, ignoring her brother's sideways glance. "She is. She, her sister, and their mother, Queen Theodesia, did nothing but make Aleksi's life miserable. It's because of them that his father took him from the palace and made him a stable boy once Maksimillian's second wife presented him with a legitimate male heir."

"And now?"

"Something's changed, though I don't know what. We live in a palace, and we all know how well secrets are kept in a palace."

"Which means," Halah said, "that we will find out sooner than later."

The next night, the great hall glowed with torchlight as Sahar followed behind Halah, who shone as bright and iridescent as the dragonfly brooch clasping her shawl of sheer worm weave over her gown of pearl white, her lustrous brown hair flowing freely to below her waist. At the end of the tunnel of family and friends stood Munir, his eyes never leaving his beautiful bride-to-be as she walked to him, his grin growing with each step that brought Halah closer.

Standing beside Munir were Asim and Aleksandr, who wore a robe of rich ocher with hems of earth brown embroidered with threads of gold, russet, and green worm weave. He wore sandals rather than his usual boots, and his face was clean shaven, the lights and shadows playing off the square cut of his jawline.

Pick your feet up, Sahar. Do not trip over your tongue drooling over the man, no matter how handsome he looks standing there in the torchlight. He's not yours, not since you drove him into Ursula's waiting arms.

She stepped to the side as Halah took her place beside Munir as the priest began his marriage litany. Sahar tried to listen, but her attention was drawn to Aleksi, whose eyes were fixed on hers. She shifted from foot to foot under his unwavering gaze and pushed at the jeweled comb pinning up her hair. She dropped her gaze to her hands, folded together at her front, pale against the deep red of her gown, and looked up again to find his gaze on her, a quick half smile playing across his face.

She chanced a glance at Asim, but her brother was paying attention to the ceremony, as Sahar and Aleksi should've been. She looked down to Halah's slippered feet and stayed that way as she listened to the priest's solemn words, only lifting her head when Munir and Halah spoke their vows of faith and fidelity.

Aleksi's words through the treehouse door came to Sahar. *I had hoped you had enough faith in me, in us, to build a life together.*

She looked to him staring at her as if he could read her thoughts. She bristled. It wasn't that she didn't have faith in him. She'd put her faith and her life in his hands out in the wilds. Besides, he hadn't exactly been faithful, going from Sahar to Ursula so quickly after their last fight. Sahar had heard the news from her maidservant, Safa, that Ursula was newly betrothed and moving back to her homeland with her future husband when King Maksimillian and his party returned.

Loud claps and shouts and whistles brought Sahar back to the wedding, where Munir and Halah had become husband and wife. She hugged Halah and then Munir, and Asim did the same, and then Aleksi shook Munir's hand and kissed Halah's, bringing a pretty flush to her cheeks.

"Hands off my wife, Aleksi," Munir said, taking Halah's hand and placing it in the crook of his arm. He wagged his brows at Sahar. "Go find your own."

"He need look no further than the kitchens," Sahar said, and realized she was speaking to Munir's back as the newly wedded couple were already walking arm in arm to her parents and his, where they were enveloped by family and well-wishers. Asim followed, joining Rima and the king and queen, leaving Sahar standing alone with Aleksi.

"What do you mean I need look no further than the kitchens?"

Before she could answer, a wave of wedding guests surged, sweeping them toward the dining hall and the feast waiting there.

Munir and Halah took their seat in the center of the long table, their parents on either side of them, and Sahar took her seat among

Halah's brothers and sisters, that thin, ghostly voice in her head whispering that Ommar should be there.

He was, she told herself. He was there in spirit, and she owed it to him, Halah, Munir, and their entire family to celebrate that spirit.

She ate and drank, smiled and laughed, and raised her never-empty goblet to too many toasts to count. After the formal supper, when the last of the toasts were made, the guests milled around, sitting and talking at different tables. She made the rounds of all her relatives while keeping an eye on Aleksi.

She told herself it was habit, even though she knew better, and realized as she watched him that he'd made more friends in the two moons he had been here than she had in one and twenty years. Oh, she had friends, but they were all family or family related, people she had grown up with. She envied him the ease with which he made friends, an ease she never possessed. He seemed to get along with everyone at the wedding except for his half-sister who sat alone at a table with her prince, glaring at her brother.

Aleksi had ushered his father over to the table where Serge and Pyotr sat with Saqr and Feroz when Ursula sashayed up with a full pitcher of beer, smiling and chattering away as she poured. When her pitcher was empty, Aleksi stood and hugged her and kissed her on the cheek, and as the serving wench walked away, every man's eyes were on her full, swinging hips. Aleksi and Pyotr clasped each other's forearms, and Pyotr slapped Aleksi on the back as King Maksimillian beamed at his son.

Every drop of wine in Sahar's belly soured to vinegar.

Aleksi woke to a loud pounding that echoed in his aching head.

"Enter," he bellowed, a mistake he instantly paid for as the pounding in his head threatened to split it in two.

Yacoub, the manservant tending to him, entered, carrying a tray of warm beer, fried eggs and flatbread, which he set down on the small stool by the bed. "I thought you might be needing this," he said.

Aleksi's stomach grumbled. "Thank you, Yacoub. I do."

He wolfed down the eggs and bread, and sipped the yeasty beer as Yacoub poured water into the wash basin and set a fresh cleaning cloth on the side.

"The kings Asad and Maksimillian request your presence in the council chambers at noon," he said.

Aleksi squinted at the shuttered window. "What time of day is it now?"

"Late morning," Yacoub said. "Closer to noon than dawn."

Aleksi rubbed his stubbled face. He had gotten drunk at the celebration last night, and stumbled back to his chambers sometime after midnight. "I overslept," he stated the obvious.

"The entire palace has overslept," Yacoub said with a quick grin. "People are just now stirring." He moved to the hearth and started stacking wood. "I'll get your fire going and leave you to your ministrations."

"Thank you."

His belly settled with food in it. Aleksi took his time washing up and dressing, donning a clean undertunic and breeches and an overtunic of leather lined with felt. Even with the hearth fire going, the autumn chill had seeped into the palace.

He wandered the mostly empty halls for a while, killing time and trying not to worry about why he was being called before his father and King Asad in the council chambers.

When he arrived, Brawn was standing guard outside the door, his face giving nothing away. Aleksi nodded a greeting to the inscrutable captain and entered the chambers where King Asad and Queen Oona sat with Asim at one table, and his father and Anastasia sat at another. Sahar paced along the far wall, a felt vest over the tunic and skirt she'd been wearing the first time he saw her.

The door closed and Brawn threw the inside bolt and sat down at an empty table, indicating that Aleksi should sit with him. Sahar, eyeing the room, took a seat on the other side of Brawn.

King Asad cleared his throat, and the already quiet room went silent.

"King Maksimillian and I have called you all here for several reasons," he said. He glanced at Anastasia, who sat smiling smugly. "There have been accusations made, accusations which we intend to have answers to, and these answers will affect our decisions on some important matters. So, I—we—expect the truth."

Aleksi nodded, and out of the corner of his eye, he saw Sahar do the same.

"Aleksandr, you agreed to a payment of one hundred gold pieces, win or lose, to protect my daughter, Princess Sahar, during the one-hundred-league race."

"I did."

"You accepted that payment upon your return to this palace."

"I did."

"Where are those one hundred gold pieces now?"

"Serge and Pyotr, my partners in our venture here, each have twenty and five, and I kept fifty, as was our deal if I had won the race."

Sahar sat straighter on her chair, and he could feel her eyes boring into the side of his head. King Asad's mouth twitched up, and Aleksi cocked his head, not sure where this line of questioning was going.

"What do you intend to do with your coin?" his father asked.

"To return to our homeland and build a stable to rival any king's," Aleksi told him.

"To become a lowly horse trader, you mean," Anastasia scoffed.

"To be a self-made man, you mean," Sahar said hotly.

Both king's mouths twitched up.

"Did you propose marriage to Princess Sahar?" Maksimillian asked.

"More than once," Aleksi answered.

"She refused you?"

"We are not betrothed."

"Why not?" Maksimillian asked Sahar. "Is my son not a worthy man?"

"Your son, Aleksandr, is a good and honorable man," she said without hesitation. "He has acted more princely than many of those who claim that title."

"So, it's because he is my bastard son and not heir to my kingdom?"

Sahar bristled and said nothing.

"Princess Sahar has told me many times that she neither wants nor needs a husband," Aleksi said, defending her.

"That," Anastasia said with a pouty smirk, "is because she has no want or need of a man at all."

Sahar's breath hissed in and her eyes blazed. Both kings remained expressionless, and Aleksi wondered how much his father knew of his and Sahar's time alone in the wilds.

"Do you have anything to say about Princess Anastasia's accusation?" Maksimillian asked Sahar.

"Princess Anastasia can think or say whatever her walnut brain wants," Sahar answered, her fiery glare razing Anastasia, who sat with her mouth gaping. "I know who and what I am, and so do those who matter to me. Not that it would be a bad thing if I was so inclined to prefer women as she has insinuated. As your son and I are not betrothed, I don't understand why we're even being questioned about this."

Aleksi pressed his lips together to keep from smiling.

"I apologize for the intrusiveness of my questions," his father said. "But I need to know the truth of your current relationship with my son. In time, you will both know why."

Sahar inclined her head in acknowledgement, and Aleksi sat straighter in his chair.

What was his father up to?

Aleksi glanced from king to king to queen, but none of them were giving anything away. Asim looked curious and Anastasia looked confused. Brawn was his usual silent, watchful self.

Maksimillian stood and approached their table. "As you have all no doubt been told," he said, "I have been suffering from a general malaise for several moons now, the cause and severity of which my physicians were unable to agree upon."

"Have you been taking your healing tisane, Father?" Anastasia asked. "You know you need to be taking your tisane daily."

Maksimillian grimaced, though it looked to be more from mental pain than physical. He had not looked or acted ill since his arrival here. In truth, his complexion was more ruddy than pale, and he was only a shade thinner than usual.

"Thank you for your concern, daughter," he said, turning to Anastasia. "You, your mother and sister have all been adamant I take it."

Anastasia smiled prettily.

"My poor health was the argument used by my loving wives, daughters, and physicians against my traveling here," he continued, "but I would not be dissuaded." He turned to Aleksi. "I wanted to be here to do whatever I could for my son."

Aleksi worked to swallow around the lump in his throat.

"So, I left my home amid much pleading and wailing from my wives with the physician they demanded I take to watch over me, and a sack full of the medicinal herbs used to make my healing tisane that I promised to consume three times daily as I had been since the inception of my symptoms."

He turned from their table and strolled around the chambers as he spoke. "But then, only a day or two into our journey, a strange thing happened. I spilled my cup of tisane one night before I drank any and didn't tell anybody or go to the bother of refilling it. The next morning I was breathing easier, my stomach was cramping less and my arms and legs were not so heavy. The next day and night, I poured out my tisanes without anyone knowing, and felt even better the next morn. I did this every day and night for half a fortnight. When my physician realized I was growing stronger rather than weaker by the day, he put it to the tisane he didn't know I was pouring out and recommended that I double my doses, so as to increase its healing power."

He stopped and glanced about the chambers, all ears and eyes on him. Aleksi looked over at King Asad and Queen Oona, who didn't look surprised by Maksimillian's tale.

"Now, I am not a naturally suspicious man, though perhaps I should be," his father continued, "but I'm not a stupid man. Two days before our arrival here, I confronted my physician." He turned and stared at Anastasia for a long moment before standing at her table and setting both hands down flat, facing her. "What do you think he admitted to, the physician handpicked by your mother, my daughter?"

Anastasia shook her head, her eyes grown wide and her complexion pale. "I—I don't know."

"Yes you do," their father said softly.

"No, no, I don't—"

"Yes," he shouted and slammed his hands down on the table. "You do."

"No," Anastasia cried, shaking her head harder. "No, I know nothing."

"You know nothing," he growled, his face only a hair's breadth from hers. "You know nothing about my queen, your mother, slowly poisoning me with help from the physician with whom she is having an affair. You know nothing about the bargain she made with my second wife, that when I died from this poisoning, my second-born son, Vladimir, would inherit the throne, with Theodesia acting as chief counsel to the boy?"

"No, Father."

Aleksi sat at attention as his father straightened and stepped back, standing at the table's edge.

"Then why are you still here?"

"I don't know what you mean."

"I mean that you are still here to send word to your mother if Aleksandr headed home before I died, before Vladimir became king. So she could make certain my firstborn son didn't return home alive to challenge for the throne."

Anastasia shook her head, sobbing wordlessly. Aleksi sat as still and rigid as stone, trying to take in all that his father had said.

"You may as well admit it," their father said to Anastasia. "The physician told me everything, including that your sister, Gertruda, is your mother's right hand in all of this."

Anastasia dropped her head into her hands, moaning and wailing. Their father turned around and looked at Aleksi, his expression asking his son's forgiveness. Aleksi gave his father a nod of his head, acknowledging the request, which his father returned in kind.

Maksimillian rolled his shoulders and turned back to Anastasia. "So, my daughter, for your part in this, I will give you a dowry of two hundred gold pieces, which your prince has already agreed to, with the understanding that you leave the palace of my friend and host, King Asad, by tomorrow dawn, and never set foot in this or my kingdom again."

"But, but, Father—"

"Do not call me father. I'm done with you. You were raised with plentitude and privilege. You had your every need and whim answered, yet it was not enough, it would never be enough, because you have your mother's selfish, greedy heart."

Anastasia started to stand, but their father held up his hand, stopping her.

"Before you leave us," he said, "I want you to know that I will be announcing my successor tomorrow eve at a feast generously hosted by King Asad, so if anything were to happen to me before I return home, there will be no confusion over who inherits my throne."

"Why would there be confusion, Fa—my king?" Anastasia asked. "The throne goes to your legitimate son, Vladimir."

"No," Maksimillian said. He turned to Aleksi. "The throne will go to my firstborn son, Aleksandr."

CHAPTER 18

The Heir

The entire chamber went silent for a breath before Anastasia screamed in indignation. "You can't name your bastard your heir."

"I can, I will, and I have."

"But, he's a bastard," she screeched.

His father smiled at Aleksi, who still was not certain he had heard him right. "Aleksandr is my son, and I may not have been married to his mother, but I loved her, and she loved me."

Aleksi sat back. It was the first time his father had ever even mentioned his mother. Somehow, hearing that he was born of love, not mere lust, mended another small part of the hole in his heart where he had buried his mother.

"And," his father said as he slowly turned back around to face Anastasia, "he is the only person in my immediate family who has acted, as Princess Sahar so succinctly put it, in an honorable and princely manner." He pivoted back to Aleksi, who sat taller with his father's praise. "Even as a stable boy, he always made me proud, and will make me more so as a good and honorable king."

"King Asad," Anastasia whined. "How can you sit there and allow this travesty? Surely you can see that my father has been touched in the head by his illness?"

"I see a man who loves his son, and a son who has earned that love and more," King Asad told her. "I see a king, a good king, whose entire family, but for this son, has conspired against him, have tried to murder him, not for the sake of his kingdom, but for their own vanity and greed." He gave her a withering glare. "In truth, when he asked for my opinion on this, I encouraged him to name Aleksandr successor to his throne."

Aleksi sat speechless, unable to do more than nod his appreciation to King Asad, who dipped his head in acknowledgment.

Anastasia stood, her face the same pomegranate hue of her gown. "I do not have to stand for this," she shrilled. "My mother, your counselors, they will never allow this aberration."

"Your mother and her co-conspirators are already prisoners in my palace," their father told her. "I sent word back to my chief counselor days before I arrived here."

"Well, I, you…"

"You and your mother have lost your palace coup." Queen Oona spoke for the first time, her voice as calm and serene as her face, and no less forbidding because of it. "I suggest you take your father's more than generous offer of exile and pack yourself and your prince off to his city, before his family hears of your disgrace and disallows your marriage."

Aleksi couldn't help but grin as Anastasia huffed out of the chambers, blowing hot air from her cheeks as she waited impatiently for Brawn to slide open the bolt. Once she was gone, Brawn stood sentry at the door and Aleksi's father stood before him.

"Do you accept my offer, my son? Will you return to our home as my heir and successor to be trained in the art and politics of ruling a kingdom?"

Aleksi glanced at Sahar, who sat beaming at him. She'd been right about his father, and equally right about him. He was a stubborn, arrogant ass. But she'd also called him good, honorable, and princely. He vowed then and there to prove her right. To prove his father right in choosing him. His heartache of regret was that Sahar had not chosen him to be her husband. That she would not be his queen.

He stood and clasped his father's forearm. "I accept, Father," he said. "My only condition is that I remain here until the matter of a war is settled between King Asad and King Ox."

His father clasped his arm tighter. "Of course, Aleksandr. A king must hold to his alliances."

Sahar sat in bemusement as everyone in the chambers, including Brawn, stepped up to congratulate Aleksi and Maksimillian. She was glad for Aleksi. Thrilled, actually. Proven right in a way even she hadn't dreamed of. As for herself, she would never be more than a memory to him. She had lost her chance of loving him, of him ever learning to love her. She had chased him away and into the arms of Ursula, who had been smart enough to accept his marriage proposal when he was nothing more than a king's bastard to the world.

Ursula would make him a good wife, the wife he wanted, a wife of strong body and easy temper, but she would never love him as Sahar had, as Sahar did—this she knew down to her marrow. She knew she loved him, and, she realized, she had almost from the moment she'd met him. Her pride and stubbornness had kept her from admitting her love, even to herself.

She'd been so set in her mind that love had to be a certain way that she had been willfully blind when it came to her as an arrogant, strutting stallion who teased her, challenged her, and called her his tigress. She dared not admit it to him now that he would be king. He would think his change in fortune was the reason for her accepting him.

She was too late. He was betrothed to another.

As if reading her thoughts, Aleksi turned to her, his head cocking slightly. She stood and walked across the room to him with a shaky smile. "Congratulations, Aleksandr."

"Thank you, princess."

He dipped his head, and that shock of sun-kissed hair fell over his forehead. She started to reach out and push it up, and then stopped her hand in midair. His brown eyes darkened to earthy loam and he took her hand in his and kissed the backs of her fingers.

"Thank you for what you said to my father," he told her, still holding her hand in his. His big, strong hand that knew her body more intimately than she did.

"I spoke the truth," she said, slowly pulling her hand from his.

He dropped his hand and flexed his fingers. "It gladdens me that you think so." His voice was low and caressing…and confusing.

"Ursula has chosen well for her husband," she said.

He cocked his head. "Yes," he agreed, and managed to say it without gloating. "She has chosen the best of men."

Sahar swallowed past the lump in her throat. "You will both do well, as a king and a wife," she said, her voice cracking.

Aleksi quirked his brows. "We will both do our best, I'm certain." He reached out and tucked a stray curl behind her ear. "Sahar, I..."

She started to lean her cheek into his palm, and then she stepped back, away from his touch. He may not want Ursula the way he wanted Sahar, but she was not going to play the wanton.

"I must go," she told him, though she had nowhere she needed to be other than alone with her tears and regrets. He would marry Ursula. Sahar's own stubborn idiocy had kept her from seeing what was right in front of her, had kept her from deserving his hand in marriage, and what she wanted most in this world, his love.

She took another step back, and that was when she realized that every person there had been watching them and listening to them. She turned on her heels and fled the chambers.

Aleksi's first instinct was to go after Sahar, to chase her down and shake her, or kiss her, until she told him what was going on in that beautiful, maddening head of hers. He ran a hand back through his hair, his throat catching as he recalled how she had started to reach up to push his hair back, and then stopped.

She had started to say and do several things before fleeing the chambers that had him wracking his brain and shaking his head, including her congratulations on Ursula's and Pyotr's betrothal, which had not been officially announced yet, but he wasn't surprised she knew. News traveled fast in a palace.

He wondered how long it would take for news of his change in status to be common knowledge, and figured the odds of it staying a secret until the feast tomorrow eve were slim to none. In fact, he would wager every gold piece in his purse that Anastasia was even now spreading her venomous version of what had transpired in King Asad's council chambers. Another new reality of his changed life was that winning or losing those eighty and two gold pieces would neither make nor break him, not anymore. As a wealthy prince, he was on even footing with Sahar now. Whether that would make a difference to her seemed to be out of his hands, and he wasn't certain he'd want it to.

"Aleksandr."

Aleksi turned from the closed door he had been staring at, the door she had practically run out of, to King Asad.

"Stay," the king said. "Our allies' emissaries will be joining us soon. If you are to learn to be a king, you should stay for the war council."

"Of course." Aleksi took the seat offered by his father's side.

Asad's son, Asim, stayed in his seat as his mother, Queen Oona, stood and kissed her husband on his cheek. Aleksi didn't miss how the king held onto his queen's hand until their fingers slipped apart as she moved away from the table, or the look of pure adoration on his face as he watched the graceful sway of her skirts disappear through the door. The king grinned, unabashed and unapologetic as he leaned back on his seat, and Aleksi felt a stab of jealousy pierce his chest. To be able to love a woman so openly, so freely, so completely.

And to have her love you back.

The door opened, and Brawn escorted ten and six men, all in richly embroidered robes denoting their importance, into the chambers. Aleksi's father introduced him to the group, who, one by one explained who they represented and why they had allied with Asad over the Ox. Each emissary informed the council of any new developments and discussed what was to be done.

"The Ox knows how outnumbered he is by now," the emissary to the Oryx said. "He would be a fool to insist on waging a war he can't win."

"True enough," Asad agreed. "But my experience with the Ox has proved him to be a fool of the greatest order. This war of his is nothing more than a grudge match over twenty years in the making. I don't believe he cares how many others would die, as long as he could cause me and my queen pain."

"What if this grudge match could be settled without a war?" Aleksi offered. "What if the Wolf and I finished our fight, which the Ox is using as an excuse to wage his war, and settled it between us, man to man?"

"No." His father was adamant. "You can't. You're to be my successor. You can't put yourself in such danger."

"I can if my life will save thousands of others."

"No," King Asad said. "As much as I and every other person here appreciates your selfless offer, your father is right. You can't be so reckless with your life. You must start thinking like a king who is responsible for the health and wealth of the people in his kingdom."

Aleksi shifted uneasily under the combined stares of two kings and the emissaries. He may have shown how new he was to the politics of ruling a kingdom, but he still thought his solution a better one than endangering thousands of lives. He may have been a king's successor today, but yesterday he had been a stable hand and a bastard whose life was no more important than any other man's. He was not completely convinced that he was wrong in this, and he really wanted another shot at the Wolf.

"Besides," King Asad added, "I don't believe the Ox and his spawn would ever agree to such an arrangement. We'll do better to wait him out, let him find some way to back out and save face."

Sahar brushed and combed Lasair until her coat shone and her mane flowed tangle free. She'd meant to ride the mare away from the palace, but the rain that had been threatening all morning finally let loose. She played with Kiska for a while, letting the kitten chase a length of leather around the stables until they both tired of the game. She took advantage of a lull in the downpour and made a run for the palace where she considered going to the kitchens to scrape up treats for Kiska, but decided against it on the chance that she might run into Ursula.

The last thing she wanted was to be witness to the kitchen maid's triumph on accepting the betrothal of a stable hand who wound up being a prince. Especially since that prince was Aleksi.

Skirting the kitchens, Sahar decided to bury herself under the blankets of her bed and sulk the remainder of the day away, but as soon as she entered the hall to the family chambers, Halah came floating toward her with a beatific smile on her glowing face. As far as Sahar knew, it was the first time since the wedding Halah had left the new chambers she was now sharing with Munir.

"Oh," she said, a pretty blush on her cheeks. "You weren't wrong about the joys to be found in a marriage bed."

Sahar laughed. "I told you, Lala."

"Yes you did." Halah's grin widened and she let out a sigh of satisfaction. "It truly is a wondrous thing, and to think, I will have a lifetime of such wonder with my husband."

A pang of jealous longing sliced through Sahar's chest, dropping her heart to her feet. "I'm truly happy for both of you," she said, hoping she didn't sound as morose as she felt. She forced her mouth into a smile. "I knew it would be so between the two of you."

Of course, Halah heard the pain and longing in Sahar's voice. "Oh, I did not mean to..."

"It is not your fault, Lala. It's all been my own doing. It's been my pride that kept me from accepting his proposal, if not his passion. My willful stubbornness that chased him away."

Into another woman's arms.

"There's still hope. I saw the way he looked at you at our wedding. I may be a newly wedded woman," she said, blushing again, "but I know desire when I see it in a man's eyes, and Aleksandr desires you."

"Lack of desire has never been our problem," Sahar said. "Other things have come to pass recently, things that I am not at liberty to tell you or anyone else yet, things that have made it impossible for us to be together."

"Impossible?" Halah asked, "or improbable?"

Sahar shrugged. "Either way, Aleksi will not be asking me to marry him again."

"So you ask him."

"No." Sahar shook her head. "I've lost my chance."

My stallion has moved on to greener pastures.

"If that's true, then I'm sorry for you both," Halah said, patting Sahar's shoulder.

"Thank you, Lala." Sahar gave her cousin a sad, rueful smile. "It's good to have someone else know what I've lost. Someone who understands."

"I'm here for you," Halah assured her. "Always."

Sahar nodded, ridiculously close to tears.

"I was on my way to visit Rima and Ammar," Halah said. "You should come with me. Rima will be glad to see you, and a baby can't help but cheer you up."

Two happily married women and a newborn baby would only be reminders of all that Sahar had lost, but her life had to go on without Aleksi.

She rolled her shoulders back and lifted her chin.

She may as well get on with it.

Aleksi pushed back from the table with a groan, glad for once to be wearing robes instead of breeches. Anya had outdone herself with the feast tonight celebrating his ascension as his father's heir.

The announcement had been received with shocked silence at first, but then King Asad had stood and clapped, followed by his queen, and his son and his daughter, until one by one, every person in the hall was standing and clapping. Aleksi's father had beamed and Aleksi had smiled and accepted congratulations. He shook hands with seemingly every person there, but for Sahar, who had sat down without a word, her hands primly in her lap until the first course of the meal was served.

She'd remained quiet, partaking of more wine than food and keeping her gaze on the table or off in the distance somewhere, except for whenever Ursula was in the hall. Then her narrowed gaze followed the maidservant's every move, and would flicker over at Aleksi with a quizzical glare.

Which was one of about a hundred questions Aleksi wanted to ask Sahar, but he hadn't been able to get her alone for days, not since their encounter at the river. About the only question he had no intention of asking her again was to marry him. She had stated repeatedly she had no want or need of a husband, or a man. Especially him. Though Aleksi knew that was not completely true. She may not have needed him, but she had wanted his body and the sensual pleasures it could give her. As he wanted her. The difference between them was, he wanted more than her body—he wanted her mind and her heart too. He wanted her standing by his side as his wife and his queen, the same as she had stood and fought by his side in the wilds. Her, and no other.

Maybe if he'd courted and wooed her rather than competed and argued with her.

Aleksi snorted into his goblet of wine. The tigress he knew would have eaten him or any other man alive who tried. She was not one to fall for false praise and flattery. Well, he amended, remembering the Wolf's oily courting, not for long anyway. Aleksi supposed he and Sahar had courted in their own way. They'd teased, argued, and tangled with each other, eventually becoming allies and lovers who had fought for and saved each other's lives. It hadn't been enough for Aleksi to win his tigress, a woman who refused to be any man's prize. As much as he hated that he'd have to go on without her, he had to respect her for being true to herself.

"Well, Father, would you like to meet the head cook now?"

His father patted his full belly. "I would indeed."

They made their way to the kitchens where Aleksi spied the back of Anya's head at a table she and two other women were working at preparing dough for the next day's flatbread. He led his father over and tapped Anya on the shoulder.

"Father," Aleksi said as she turned around, her wide eyes fixing on his father, "this is—"

"Anya?" his father called. "Anya, is it really you?"

Anya nodded wordlessly, her gaze never leaving his.

"Anya." His father wrapped her in his embrace. "My Anya."

Tears spilled from eyes squeezed tight as she hugged him back, and when she opened them again, they focused on Aleksi, who stood dumbfounded. Anya broke the embrace first, stepping back and gazing at Aleksi with a tremulous smile.

"My son," his father said, his voice quavering for the first time in Aleksi's memory. "Meet your mother."

Sahar left the dining hall not long after Aleksi and Maksimillian had gone to the kitchens. She'd fled straight to her bed where she had tossed and turned most of the night and paced her chambers the rest of it, finally falling asleep close to dawn and not waking until noon when she groggily stumbled out from her bed chambers into her common room.

"Have you heard, mistress?" Safa said as Sahar lay down on a sofa, her head pounding and her tongue thick in her dry mouth. "Princess Anastasia and her prince have packed up and left, the Ox has taken back his threat of a war, and King Maksimillian and Anya, the head cook, are to be married, here, before they leave for their homeland in three days' time. Ursula will be married once they return."

"Married?" Sahar was not sure she had heard Safa right. The woman could speak as fast as a bird twittered. "Anya and Maksimillian?"

Safa grinned and offered Sahar a wet cloth for her forehead. "It turns out that Anya and Maksimillian were lovers when she was a kitchen maid in his palace. She's Aleksandr's mother."

Sahar dropped the wet cloth and her jaw. "Aleksandr's mother?"

Safa picked up the cloth and rinsed it and handed it back to her. "Arman is Aleksandr's half-brother and will be returning with them as well."

Sahar laid the cloth over her face, as much to hide her warring emotions as to cool her aching head. She was happy for Aleksi. Truly. He'd gained a father, a mother, a brother, and a wife in the last three days, as well as a string of prime broodmares for his personal stables, which would not only rival a king's, but be a king's. He had gotten everything he had wanted, and more.

So had she. She had proved herself equal to or better than any man on a horse. She had discovered her own strength and courage. She had proved she had no need for a husband or a man.

But she wanted one.

She wanted Aleksi. She wanted him so badly that she actually ached. She ached so deep inside that she thought surely it must be her soul grieving. She'd lost her chance. He would marry Ursula upon his triumphant return to his home.

"They leave in three days' time?" she whimpered from under her cloth.

"King Maksimillian's wedding is to be day after tomorrow," Safa's disembodied voice came at Sahar. "They will all leave the day after."

Sahar strangled a wail that was starting somewhere in her belly trying to claw its way up and out of her throat. "Will you bring some bread and cheese to my chambers, Safa?" Sahar asked when she could speak again, intending to avoid the kitchens and Ursula for the next three days. If Sahar came face to face with Aleksi's betrothed, there was no telling what she would do: scratch the lucky woman's eyes out, or crumple into a pitiable, mewling heap at her feet. "Wrapped, please, so that I can pack it in my saddle bag."

"You're going riding, mistress? The sky has been threatening rain all morning."

Sahar tossed the cloth and slowly rose to her feet. "I need air." A little rain, or even a sleeting downpour couldn't dampen her spirits any more than they already were.

Throwing her otter cloak over her shoulders and trying not to think of how many nights it covered her and Aleksi on their bedrolls, she snuck out of the palace and to the stables. She stopped outside of Zolotoy's stall when she heard Aleksi's voice coming from the antechamber attached to the stall.

"So, my little Kiska," she heard him say, "you'll be moving to the stable master's quarters today. My newfound brother, Arman, will be returning to my homeland with us." He laughed softly. "Who would've thought that by traveling to this city, I've reconciled with my father, found my mother and brother, become a prince and heir to a throne, and found and lost my tigress."

Sahar stood rooted to the spot.

"Ratter will be coming for you sometime this afternoon," he told the kitten. "I'll be busy with my parents' wedding tomorrow, and packing everything and everybody up for our journey home the day after. This is likely our goodbye, my little Kiska. May you have a long, happy life catching mice and keeping Ratter's feet warm."

Sahar stepped back from the gate as Aleksi came out of the antechamber and laid a blanket over Z's back. "Rest up, Z," he told the stallion. "We have a long trek ahead of us. Come spring, you and my new broodmares will get busy making babies." He patted the stallion's rump. "I would've liked to see a foal out of you and Lasair.

It would've been a beauty with your strength and her speed. I guess it wasn't meant to be."

He shut the stall's gate behind him and Sahar stepped forward. Without a word, she strode straight into his arms, wrapped her hands around his neck and kissed him as if she had never kissed him before, and never would again.

She ended the kiss as abruptly as she'd started it.

"Goodbye, Aleksi."

CHAPTER 19

Everything

Sahar stood on the palace steps alongside her brother as her father and mother said their goodbyes to King Maksimillian and his bride, Anya.

"I am glad for you, my friend," her father said, clasping Maksimillian's arm, "even if you have taken my best cook and stable hand."

"Thank you, Asad, for watching over my son, and my love. If it were not for you, I fear they would've been lost to me forever."

"I wish you and your new family joy and prosperity," Asad said, clapping him on the back and moving on to Anya, whose hand he took and placed a kiss on the back of her fingers. "As for you, Anya, though we will all miss you, I could not be happier that you have found each other again, and wish you every good thing."

"Thank you, my king."

Asad chuckled. "You have a new king now, Queen Anya."

Anya blushed prettily and laughed. "That part will take some getting used to," she said, beaming at her husband. Then she turned to Sahar's mother and dipped a knee. "Queen Oona, I can only strive to be as good and fair a queen as you."

The queen pulled Anya in and hugged her and kissed her on the cheek. "You will be a wonderful queen, Anya," she said. "You have a generous and loyal heart, and you understand the life of the worker. I am certain having you as queen will make the people of your kingdom's lives better."

Arman stepped up to say his goodbyes, and then Pyotr and Serge, followed by Ursula, who Sahar had been watching carefully, wondering why she hung back with Serge and Pyotr rather than stand by Aleksi's side. His father had married a palace cook and made her his queen. Sahar didn't think Ursula hung back because she'd been a serving maid. She was betrothed to a prince now. If Sahar had been betrothed to Aleksi, she would've been right by his side. She'd lost her chance, and now she had to say goodbye forever.

She shook hands with Serge and Pyotr, and then stood face to face with Ursula, whose cheeks were round and rosy with the perpetual smile that had been on her face for days now.

"Congratulations on your betrothal, Ursula," Sahar said, managing not to snarl. "You have chosen the best of men. I'm sure you'll be happy."

"Thank you, princess." Ursula dipped her knee. She glanced over at Serge and Pyotr and her rosy cheeks grew even rosier. "I'm sure we will be."

Sahar tilted her head and raised her brows, but before she could say anything more, Aleksi stepped up to her.

"Princess," he said, lifting her hand in his and kissing the backs of her fingers with his warm lips. "It's been an adventure."

"It has been that, Prince Aleksandr."

They stood there, Aleksi holding her hand, Sahar loath to break his touch when she heard Ursula's hearty giggle.

"Congratulations, Aleksi," Sahar said, pulling her hand from his. "You have accomplished everything you set out to do and more. Not only have you amassed a string of broodmares and a wife of easy temper and strong body, but you have reconciled with your father and mother."

"Wife?" he asked, cocking his head, that cursed shock of hair falling over his forehead. "What wife?"

"Your betrothed then."

He shook his head. "Unless you have changed your mind, I'm not betrothed."

"But—but, what about Ursula?"

"Ursula is betrothed to Pyotr. Why did you think she was betrothed to me?" Sahar didn't know what to say or think, and so she said nothing. "Is that why you have been so distant and angry?" Still she said nothing. Aleksi leaned in and whispered in her ear. "Why didn't you ask me?"

"I couldn't."

"Ask me now,"

"Ask you what?"

"You know."

"Why should I ask you, you strutting stallion?"

"Because, my tigress, you want me as much as I want you. It's now or never, Kitten."

If Aleksi had said anything about love, Sahar would have gladly gotten down on one knee in front of her family and his to propose marriage. But he hadn't. Not ever. As much as she loved him, she wouldn't marry him if he didn't love her. She'd learned that she was worthy of love, and she wouldn't settle for less. Especially not from Aleksi.

She stepped back from him, hot tears welling in her eyes. "Have a safe journey, Prince Aleksandr."

Aleksi turned and looked back over his shoulder at the palace on the hill where he had left Sahar standing on the steps. She had thought him betrothed to Ursula. Only days after having sex with her by the river, only one day after kissing him in the stables with such heat and passion and sadness that he still felt it in his bones. Apparently, she thought so little of his feelings that she believed him capable of becoming betrothed to another in a matter of days, and thought him so dishonorable that he would have sex with her, kiss her like he had, while he was betrothed to another woman. After everything they'd been through she didn't know him better than that.

He ran a hand through his hair and turned back to the road ahead. The road that would take him home. Three hundred leagues away from Sahar. A road he had always planned to take, had told her he would be taking back, with or without her. He should've been pleased to be returning home. He'd accomplished almost everything he had planned, and more. A lot of it, not on his own. He couldn't have done any of it without Serge and Pyotr. They'd watched over the stock and done all of the horse trading while he trained and raced, and chased after his tigress. Surely, he couldn't claim reuniting with his father or finding his mother as anything he'd done.

Although he was not returning with a wife, now that he was a prince and heir to a throne, his field of choices had broadened greatly. He had thought he wanted a wife of strong body and easy temper, a wife to meekly follow his lead and raise his sons.

Then he had met Sahar.

Proud and beautiful, with a royal pedigree he was foresworn to despise, but whose blazing green eyes, stiff spine, and fierce determination he'd come to admire. He had discovered, somewhere out there in the wilds with a bloodthirsty tigress, that she was who he wanted. She was who he needed by his side, not some mealy-mouthed, meek-tempered, weak-willed maid who would blindly do his bidding, but a strong-willed, fiery-tempered woman with a mind of her own who would challenge him when she thought him wrong, and fight beside him when she knew him to be right.

He'd been more right than he knew when he told her they should marry because they were good together. They *were* good together. Not only in bed. They made each other better. So much better together than apart.

He pulled Zolotoy up to a stop.

"Aleksandr?"

He met his father's quizzical gaze. "I have to go back," he said. "I have to tell her."

"Tell her? Who? What?"

"The Princess Sahar," his mother said with a knowing smile. "That he loves her."

Sahar sat on the rock overlooking the river and pulled her cloak tighter around her shoulders, trying to stem the shivers coursing through her body as waves of grief washed over and through her. She planted her hands firmly on the rock where she had lain with Aleksi, seeking to ground herself, to keep herself from drowning in sorrow, a sorrow so deep, so all-encompassing, that she felt as if she would never draw a full breath again.

A sorrow that she'd brought upon herself.

Not only had she let Aleksi leave without her, but she'd sent him away. The only man who'd known her. Who'd teased her, challenged her, and fought with her and by her side. Who'd made her burn and who had burned with her, only to rise again and again. The only man she'd ever loved with a fire and a passion that she'd never know again. She'd let her bruised pride send him away from her.

She would be alone. Forever.

Wasn't that what she wanted? What she had always told anyone who asked, including Aleksi? That she needed no man, wanted no man. That she would make her own way in this world. That she didn't need a partner to hold her hand and stand by her side, to love her as she loved him.

Aleksi had said that they should marry because they were good together, and not only in bed. He was right, they were. They brought out the best in each other, as well as the worst. He'd cheered her on when she beat him and every other man in the race. He'd championed her when his half-sister and the Wolf had made insinuations and outright lies about her. He'd helped her cross river after river until she could cross on her own without fear. He'd been a willing partner as she transitioned from girl to woman. He was a generous teacher and a passionate lover. He'd given her his solid strength to lean on, his broad shoulders to cry on, his pride to bask in, but he had never given her his love. Not in words. But then, she had never told him that she loved him. She hadn't admitted she loved him to herself until she had thought it too late.

She'd been wrong. Wrong about not telling him. Wrong about not putting her heart into words and handing it to Aleksi, palms up. To deserve love, you had to give love freely and without expectation. She hadn't done that.

She stood, hoping she was wrong about it being too late, hoping what she had felt with him, what his body had made hers feel, what his earth-brown eyes and cocky smile had told her, if only she had listened, were true. Hoping.

She turned, ready to jump on Lasair and race to Aleksi, and froze where she stood.

"Aleksi. What are you doing here?"

"I've come for you." Aleksi took a step closer to the wary tigress standing on the rock they'd pleasured each other on only a few days ago. The rock where she had spat out his seed. "I've come to tell you I'm sorry."

"Sorry?" She jumped down from the rock. "For what?"

Aleksi took another step closer. "For lying to you."

She shook her head, her cloak falling back and her black hair spilling down to her waist. "When did you lie to me?"

"When I told you that we were nothing to each other," he said, closing the distance between them. He saw the flash of pain in her expression, an old pain that he had caused her in a moment of frustration and embarrassment. He held her gaze, feeling contrite. "You are not and have never been nothing to me."

"No?"

"No." He reached out and pushed a curling tress back from her cheek. "You are everything to me. Everything."

She smiled and sniffed then laid the apple of her cheek in his palm. The tigress tamed for the moment. "I am?"

"You are." He cupped her chin and lifted it so that she could see the truth. "I love you. I have from almost the first moment I laid eyes on you."

"You mean the first moment you insulted me and I put my blade to your stones?"

He laughed, glad to see the green fire back in her eyes. "I thought I wanted an easy-tempered woman, a broodmare I could ride at will and keep full of babies. Then I met this fierce, fiery tigress, who rightly named me an arrogant ass and proved all my prejudices about royal princesses wrong. A princess I could never hope to have."

"But you could have me." She gave him a wicked, wanton, smile. "You did have me."

"For a short time, a time we both knew would end once we got back to the rest of the world."

Her expression grew serious. "It was never about me being a princess and you being a bastard."

"No," Aleksi agreed. "It wasn't. It was about both of us being too stubborn to admit that we needed someone else. That we need each other." He waited for her to argue with him, to tell him that he was wrong, that she did not need him or anybody else.

"You're right," she said. "About all of it. About us." She took the hand cupping her chin in hers and kissed his open palm. "I love you too."

He grinned like the lovesick fool he was, and took both her hands in his. "Will you marry me, Sahar? Will you do me the honor of taking me as your husband?"

She smiled, and Aleksi basked in the brilliance of her glow.

"At least you knew my name this time," she said.

"I know more than your name, my tigress. I know you. I know you are the only woman I want by my side and in my bed for all the days and nights of my life."

She slanted her green cat eyes at him and smiled.

"Yes, Aleksandr. I'll marry you. I'll gladly take you as my husband and proudly be your wife. I'll stand by your side and love you in bed and out. I'll bear your sons, and your daughters, and we will raise them together. We'll raise them and they'll always know they are loved, and they'll always know they are deserving of love."

Aleksi wrapped her in his embrace and kissed her. He kissed her so that she'd never have to question his need, desire, and love again. So she would know he loved her down to her marrow.

She kissed him back, hot, demanding, and passionate. Her hands clutching his arms as if she would never let him go.

When at last they broke for air, Aleksi led her over to their horses and booted her up onto Lasair.

"Where are we going?" she asked as he mounted Z.

"We're going back to the palace to make love in your soft, clean, warm bed, where I am going to put a baby in you before you can change your mind about marrying me."

She grinned, baring neat, white teeth that he could not wait to have nipping at his flesh.

"Perfect," she said.

EPILOGUE

"Our firstborn foal," Aleksi beamed down at his wife, who swiped a bead of sweat from her flushed cheeks.

"As handsome as his sire," she muttered wearily.

"He'll have his mother's grace and speed."

"And his father's strength and stamina."

Aleksi crouched beside Sahar. "You look worn out, my beautiful wife." He kissed her cheek.

"What I am is hungry. Labor works up an appetite."

"I'll have Ursula cook you up a feast of all your favorites."

"I'd like that. Your mother taught her well. Ursula's running the kitchens here as smoothly as Anya did at my parents' palace."

Aleksi plucked a sweat-plastered strand of hair from her neck and leaned in for a nuzzle as a crowd of voices approached.

"We heard the new arrival is here," his father called out as he entered the stables, flanked by Anya and Vladimir.

Ten and four years of age now, Vladimir had taken to his new family, and had confessed to his father and Aleksi that the boy had dreaded ever becoming king. He was glad Aleksi had been named heir. His mother had been allowed to stay and live in the palace as the king's second wife, and Vladimir had been as happy as the palace servants to bid Theodesia and her waspish daughter, Gertruda, good riddance. They'd gone to live with Anastasia and her new husband.

Aleksi stood and stepped aside so that they could see the new arrival for themselves.

"He is a handsome one, my son," his father said, slapping Aleksi on the back. "Congratulations."

"He looks to be a fine combination of his sire and his dam, does he not?" Aleksi said.

"As is your son, my son," Anya said, handing little Maks to Aleksi.

Born one year to the day he and Sahar had first met, the child was, according to his grandfather, the spitting image of Aleksi as a babe, except for the mass of black-brown curls on his head. That hair was all Sahar. The stubborn streak and willfulness Maks was beginning to show were a matter of continuing discussion.

Juggling his chubby-cheeked son in one arm, Aleksi held out his hand and helped a stiff-legged Sahar stand from where she sat by Lasair's head where she'd petted, soothed, and urged the mare on throughout her labor.

Pyotr and Arman, his stable masters, though perfectly capable of helping the mare give birth, had known better than to try to talk Sahar into leaving the mare's side until the foal was born. They urged the mare to stand, and helped the golden colt with black stockings to his unsure feet, grinning as the colt latched on to his dam and began suckling with vigor.

Aleksi kissed his son's curls and wrapped his arm around Sahar's shoulder, pulling her close, a surge of pride welling up inside of him.

"Thank you," he whispered in her ear. "My tigress, my wife, my love." He ran his hand down her arm and held it over her blade's hilt as he nuzzled her neck. "My kitten."

TURN THE PAGE FOR A SNEAK PEEK AT

THE LION & THE SWAN

THE LION & THE SWAN

"What ails you, Black Mane?" his brother, the Cheetah, asked as Asad pulled harder at his robe.

"My betrothal nears," Asad said with a low growl, "and I can see no way free of it." He glanced back over his shoulder at the women's table and eyed the Fox, his intended, who wore a gown of russet weave that pushed her fleshy breasts up to almost spilling out of the tight, low-cut bodice. The last time he had seen her, she had been a girl of ten and five who had liked her sweets as much as she disliked the word no, and by the way she had indulged in the honeyed dates that were the last of the seven-course feast, she had not changed much in the three years since.

"Duty and honor to family and kingdom," Asad said as much to himself as to his brother, "all require that I sit here like a sacrificial goat and let myself be bound and caged."

"At least the Fox will be your first wife of seven," the Cheetah offered with his cursed calm.

Asad huffed and then cocked his head. There was a rustling beyond the path that led from the stage of polished sandstone into the dark shadows of the garden. The still air moved, and he caught the sweet scent of night-blooming jasmine. He sat forward on his haunches as the Jackal, a thin, balding man with a nervous twitch of a smile, stood from his stool at the king's table and held his cup high. The Jackal had threatened his household with beatings if the secret of his dowry gift was revealed before this evening, but Asad's manservant, the Crab, knew every servant in every palace of the Seven Tribes, and had the entire story before sunset, though they had only arrived that noon.

The gift, the first and most valuable of seven to be given, were two sisters from the far north called the Swan and the Dove, whose pale, otherworldly beauty left the menservants speechless, the maids jealous, and the women of the household sour with envy, especially the Fox of the Swan.

The sisters had tried to escape twice already, and had made it as far as the city's third wall the first time, and the stables the second, after which they had both been thrown into hot holes. They had been sentenced to three days in the deep pits dug into the ground and covered with tightly slatted palm fronds that could sweat the water out of a full-grown man in five days, but the Swan had become ill in two and the Jackal had been forced to pull her out or lose her. Tonight, she would sing and dance for the gathering, and her sister, the Dove, would play the harp and sing. Then they would be given by the Jackal to the Panther as dowry for the Fox's betrothal to the Black Mane: eldest son to eldest daughter, as was tradition.

"Welcome, friends," the Jackal said, his tongue darting out and sweeping across his thin lips. "Welcome to my home on this Summer's Eve." Claps and loud murmurs broke out all around the courtyard and the Jackal raised his cup higher. "I am honored to host this, the hundredth gathering of the tribes. For the next twenty and one days my home is yours." His lips twitched up and he licked them again before nodding to the Panther. "And now, my honored guests, I bring to you the Swan and the Dove."

A bare foot, as white as milk, arched out of the garden's shadows and stepped onto the torch-lit path, the trim ankle turned just so, the calf long and leanly muscled, the knee as well turned as the ankle. Asad sucked in his breath as shimmering panels of white weave parted from a thigh as long and lean as an alabaster column. He let his breath out slow and measured, watching the graceful sway of shapely hips that nipped up to a slim waist draped with a finely wrought gold chain. A sheer bodice gathered beneath breasts as round and firm as pomegranates, and collarbones of chiseled ivory winged out from the one-shouldered gown to arms as long and lean as the legs they swung in time with.

A veil of hair as pale as moonlight framed high, angular cheeks, and finely drawn brows, a darker shade of pale, arched over eyes as big and round as mossy river rocks. Eyes that met his and held, and studied him as keenly as he studied her.

ABOUT THE AUTHOR

Michele James lives in a southern California beach town with her understanding husband, two lazy house cats, and two crazy cattle dogs. She is the proud mother of an adult son and daughter, and is Oma to the world's most adorable grandson.

A mostly retired veterinarian technician, she enjoys reading everything from cereal boxes to serious tomes, watching movies without commercials, cooking, gardening, walks on the beach (especially in winter), and practicing yoga.

CONNECT WITH MICHELE:
website: michelejamesauthor.com
instagram: @michelejamesauthor
facebook: facebook.com/michelejamesauthor

www.BOROUGHSPUBLISHINGGROUP.com

If you enjoyed this book, please write a review. Our authors appreciate the feedback, and it helps future readers find books they love. We welcome your comments and invite you to send them to info@boroughspublishinggroup.com. Follow us on Facebook, Twitter and Instagram, and be sure to sign up for our newsletter for surprises and new releases from your favorite authors.

Are you an aspiring writer? Check out www.boroughspublishinggroup.com/submit and see if we can help you make your dreams come true.

Made in the USA
Columbia, SC
02 October 2020